THE LEMON GARDEN

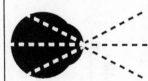

THE LEMON GARDEN

ELIZABETH ROSSITER

Thorndike Press • Thorndike, Maine

Library of Congress Cataloging in Publication Data:

Rossiter, Elizabeth.
   The lemon garden / Elizabeth Rossiter.
       p. cm.
   ISBN 1-56054-261-6 (alk. paper : lg. print)
   I. Title.
[PR6068.O833L4   1991b]   91-30943
823'.914—dc20   CIP

Thorndike Press Large Print edition published in 1991 by arrangement with Carroll & Graf Publishers, Inc.

Cover design by Sean Pringle.

The tree indicium is a trademark of Thorndike Press.

This book is printed on acid-free, high opacity paper. ∞

THE LEMON GARDEN

1

The stranger said, "Hallo, Joanna." He smiled, lighting up the room with his presence, and I, feeling a quickening of interest, even delight, found myself smiling too.

My first visitor. Chosen deliberately to be the first, as someone likely to make the maximum impact?

Impact there certainly was, although, perhaps, not quite the expected kind.

I said with careful politeness, "It's very nice of you to come and see me. Won't you sit down?" And I did catch a sharpening of his attention, the slightest narrowing of the eyes, before he nodded, still with that charming smile, and fetched a chair and set it down beside me.

"How are you?" he asked, and "They're looking after you all right here, are they?" I said that I was getting on fine now, thank you, which was true, in a way, and that the nuns were very kind; and he said that was fine, and he was so glad.

We'd made out quite well up to then with these routine courtesies, but after that I couldn't think of anything else to say, except the one thing I had to say some time and didn't

7

want to. I found it difficult to look at him directly, as the good looks and the powerful masculine appeal were now, perhaps, a bit too close for comfort. I took in details with swift sidelong glances, forays, as it were, into strange territory: the casual, but elegant clothes; no jacket on this warm Italian day in late May; a silk shirt undone down the front, revealing a tanned chest and a lot of silky brown body hair. A gold chain round his neck with a St Christopher medal on it. A gold watch on a lean tanned wrist.

He must have been watching me, too.

"They've cut all your lovely hair off." He spoke tenderly, reaching out to touch a lock of it, just with one finger. "What a shame."

"Oh! Yes . . ." I resisted an impulse to jerk my head away. "That's because of the scalp wound. It had to be stitched, you see. I know it looks a mess . . ."

"You don't look a mess. You look beautiful."

"Oh . . . thank you." This wouldn't do. It wouldn't do at all. I took a deep breath and plunged.

"Look, I'm very sorry about this. But do you mind telling me who you are?"

There was a pause, and then he said simply, "Oh God."

I said gently, "This must be very upsetting

8

and I really am sorry. But surely they told you?"

"Oh yes, they *told* me. I suppose I didn't really believe it, that you wouldn't remember *me*." He added with a disarming grin, "An ego the size of a house, you know me. But of course you don't know me, do you? Oh lord — difficult, isn't it?"

"Yes," I said bleakly. "More than difficult, really. I mean . . . I don't remember you, and that's bad enough. But, you see, I don't remember *me*, either. I just woke up in this place, was told I was in hospital, that I'd had an accident, and that was it. I've no serious injuries . . . just that cut on the head, concussion, fractured ribs and lots of bruises . . . and shock, I suppose. You wouldn't think any of that would make this happen, would you? But it has. I haven't just lost my memory. I've lost myself . . . ."

I tried to keep the distress out of my voice, but he wasn't deceived. He put a hand over mine — a nice hand, dry and cool — and said gently, "Poor love. Poor old love. Never you mind. It's going to work out, you know. It's got to." He had, I noticed, a faint, residual cockney accent. And how did I know what *that* was, I wondered, and was able to give it a name?

I still didn't know what his name was. I

wished he'd say.

"Look," he said. "Brought you these."

He took some papers from his pocket and gave them to me. They were press cuttings, from newspapers and one or two glossy magazines, some English, some Italian. One was a big picture in colour. It showed two people standing on the steps of a house: stone steps, a portico behind them over which hung a huge shaggy mass of bougainvillaea in bloom. One of the people was the man before me, the other was a girl. Her red hair fell carelessly across her forehead, curled under round her neck; she wore blue linen pants and a sleeveless sweater. She looked superbly self-confident and carefree. I looked again more closely. I didn't believe it, but I had to.

"Me?" I said.

He nodded. "You."

The caption said that this was Roddy Marchant, on location in Italy for the filming of *The End of the Day*, and Joanna Fleming, whose first big film role this was. There were rumours of romance, it said. I decided to ignore that, for the moment anyway. I put the cutting down and riffled through the others. There was a long interview with an Italian women's magazine — with me? Was it possible? Two pages plastered with photographs: there I was, in a bikini on a beach somewhere; in a long romantic-looking dress; in jodhpurs, on horseback; at the wheel of a rakish-looking car. At some time I had posed for these pictures, and talked to the interviewer. At some time; at a time now lost, it seemed, for ever.

I sat holding the cuttings, very still, willing the foggy darkness to lift. After a little, Roddy Marchant reached out for the cuttings and took them away from me; and I let him do that, not speaking.

"Hey," he said. "I'm still here."

I backed out of my fog. There was nothing there, anyway. I tried to smile.

"No good?" he asked.

"I'm afraid not. Well, that's not quite true, I suppose . . . It doesn't help me to remember, but in a way it does . . . build up a sort of identikit, of myself. You know?"

He nodded. "In a way. Maybe you'll just have to start again from scratch, Joanna. From here, I mean. Maybe *we* shall have to, too."

"We shall have to what?"

"Start again. You and I. That might be fun, don't you think?" and he grinned again and held my eyes a moment with his own, and very challenging and compelling eyes they were too. But alas, I couldn't meet that challenge, I didn't know what to do, and I heard myself saying, in a small, cold voice,

"Were we lovers, then?" and saw his head go back as if I had slapped his face.

Thank heavens, just then someone came in with a tray of tea for us. He hadn't answered me; he had taken offence and I couldn't blame him.

When we were alone again I said unhappily, "Please don't be offended, I'm probably going to say the wrong thing to everybody all the time for a bit. It's all part of what's wrong with me; I can't help it, honestly."

To my great relief, he grinned. "That's all right, love. Jumped the gun, didn't I? Didn't think, really, just hoped it might work. I don't know much about this sort of thing — I want to help but I don't know how. Shall I pour this tea out?"

"Please."

He poured the tea, gave me mine, and settled back with his own. I don't think either of us knew what to say next. Then he caught my eye, and suddenly we were both laughing. He said with satisfaction, "That's better. That's more like my girl."

My girl. Well, I couldn't, wouldn't, pursue that line.

He became serious suddenly. "Look, Joanna, what's going on? I mean, what sort of help are you getting for this thing?"

"There's this psychiatrist. He comes out from

12

Milan twice a week. Or he did . . . I don't know who arranged it."

"Steffy, I suppose."

"Steffy?"

"Never mind about her for the moment. Tell me about the quack. Wasn't he any good?"

I said reluctantly, "I suppose he'd say *I* wasn't any good." I had not, to be truthful, liked the psychiatrist very much; he was a youngish man with a smooth olive face, an impenetrable expression and a manner to match.

"But what did he *do?*" Roddy asked.

"Nothing very much. But then they don't, I suppose. You're supposed to do it all — the patient, I mean. He used to suggest a subject, and then I had to respond, by saying whatever came into my head first, and take it from there. Free association, it's called, I think. I wasn't much good at it. He said I was resisting. Whatever that meant."

"Is that all that happened?"

"Almost all. He didn't tell me anything much. Except one day when he suddenly said to me — in English — 'Your Italian's very good.' Perhaps he thought it would trigger off something. But it didn't."

"You're bilingual," Roddy said. "You didn't know?"

"No. Well, anyway, the last time he came, he suggested hypnosis. He explained what it meant, and I was absolutely horrified. I mean . . . it made me feel as if my past . . . all my life that I can't remember . . . was a great black hole, and he was going to push me down it, head first . . ." To my annoyance, I heard my voice trembling.

"You didn't let him do it?"

"No. I freaked out, I think . . . there was rather a fuss and he left and he hasn't been since. I must have been a very bad patient, wasting his time. I feel rather ashamed of it, really."

"I don't see why you should. What use is he, if all he does is frighten you? Look, Joanna, I think this way of doing things is a lot of old cobblers, I really do. You don't need a psychiatrist. What you need is to meet people you know or who know you, anyway — and talk, and let them talk, and see if it sets off something. Right?"

"Right," I said, smiling. He was nice, I thought gratefully.

"Well, then. What shall we talk about?"

"Tell me about the accident," I said.

"There isn't much to tell, really. You skidded on a bend and nearly went over the cliff. Not quite, thank God. There'd been a shower earlier on; a sprinkle of rain on top of all that dust made a skiddy surface; and it was dark, of course . . ."

"It happened at night, then?"

"Early hours of the morning. Blame myself," he said suddenly. "Shouldn't have let you go. We had a fight, you see; you were upset. But I was in no mood to . . . well, I was pretty drunk, actually. Went off to bed when the party packed up, went down like a felled tree, and didn't know a thing till next morning when Frank came in to say you were in hospital, and heap accusations on my defenceless and *very* thick head. Not that he was worried about *you*, you understand. Thinking about his budget. He was shouting, 'No thanks to you that all her scenes are in the can.' Very one-track minded, is Frank. Has to be really. If film directors weren't like that no movie would ever get finished. Don't get me wrong — he's human enough when he's not making a picture. Enquired about you a lot. Sent flowers and all that. And he's coming up to see you, I believe . . . None of this means a thing to you, does it?"

I sat there, thinking. A party; a quarrel. What about? I said at last, "You'd better tell me. Did I do a lot of that sort of thing? Getting upset. Rushing off . . . Was I difficult, neurotic?"

"Good lord no, not a bit . . . oh, I see. You think there's some connection? With the amnesia? Look, love, you were in an accident . . ."

"All the same," I said.

"Well, you're a bit temperamental, I suppose, and I'm a mite highly strung myself. So when we fight, we do it in a big way. But there was no crisis. I told you — I was pissed anyway, chatting up the local talent, and you didn't like it so you left, and that's all there is to it. Honest."

"Yes. All right. So when I rushed off, where was I going?"

"Home, I imagine. I mean, where you were staying. With Stephanie . . ."

"Who's Stephanie? Oh, I know, this must all be very trying and I'm sorry. *I'm not doing it on purpose . . .*"

"All right, all *right,* take it easy." He took hold of my hand again and held it. "Look. I think I'd better start at the beginning, don't you?"

"Wherever," I said bleakly, "the beginning *is.*"

"Well, I can't do the background, childhood bit. Stephanie knows all about that, you'll have to ask her. She's a relative — aunt, cousin . . . not sure, aunt, I think; she's getting on a bit. She's an old friend

16

of Frank's . . . they were in pictures together in his acting days, just after World War II I suppose that must have been. Anyway, she lives here, got a rather run-down villa on the lakeside . . . so she sussed out the location for Frank and also found the villa he rented. In return, and maybe for old times' sake, he gave her a bit part in the picture. Poor old Stephanie . . . I don't think she reckoned that much, playing some old peasant crone after romantic leads in her younger days. But I daresay she's glad of the money; don't think she's too flush with that."

"He sounds nice," I said. "Kind . . . Did his kindness extend to me as well? I mean, did *I* get into the picture because of Stephanie?"

"Nepotism, you mean? No, no, nothing like that. That would never work with Frank. Maybe he's a bit sentimental about Stephanie but he wouldn't have let her have a bit part, even, if she wasn't capable of doing it. As for you . . . that was nothing to do with her. He'd seen your work somewhere and liked the look of you; that's all. Kind . . . I wouldn't call him kind. Bit of a ruthless bugger, actually."

Laboriously, we sorted out the rest of it. Roddy and I had met for the first time on the set in Rome. Later we had come north, to the shores of Lake Garda, where the location work was to be done. This meant that I went to stay with Stephanie; Roddy shared the Villa Flora with Frank Harmer though, as he made clear, he wanted to share a place with me. Frank, however, who had, Roddy said bitterly, eyes in the back of his head, knew everything that was going on and put his foot down. He expected his actors to be like athletes in an Olympic village, chastely getting ten hours sleep every night: love, it seemed, would have to wait. No doubt this had had some effect on our relationship, hence the fights, perhaps. As before, I didn't want to go into that.

"Tell me some more about the party," I said.

From this, it appeared Frank Harmer was not quite such a killjoy after all. With the location work completed, and the whole unit getting ready to go back to Rome, Frank decided on the party; meant, it was supposed, to be a sort of "sorry and thank you" gesture to cast and film crew whom he had been harrying and bullying for weeks, not to speak of some of the locals who had been inconvenienced by our presence. But, as Roddy explained, the publicity department in Rome had got wind of the idea and seized on it; so that what had been intended as a private *festa* ended as a full-scale public relations exercise, with an extended guest list, the press invited, and all the rest of the brouhaha which goes with that sort of event. I wondered where, exactly, in the villa Roddy and I had quarrelled: in front of them all? Perhaps I had behaved badly. Perhaps I was drunk. A woman who would behave like that, make a jealous scene in public, rush off in a rage, seemed to have little to do with me. Yet if Roddy were telling the truth, she *was* me. People could tell me anything: you did this, you said that, you loved this person, you hated that person. *You* did those things, *you.* I had no answer to any of it. And I didn't know whom I could trust, either.

There was this woman, of course. Stephanie. I wondered what she was really like.

"What happened," I asked, "to Stephanie that night — she must have been there. How did she get home? If I went off by myself in the car . . ."

"She wasn't there. Had a migraine and was laid low. Went to bed with her pills, she says, got to sleep when the attack wore off. Frank rang her when he got the news and had a job to wake her; her maid only comes in by the day and hadn't arrived."

"She didn't miss me when I didn't come home, then?"

"My love, you're a big girl now. I shouldn't think Stephanie would have sat up for you, even if she hadn't been ill. Anyway . . ." he grinned, "I daresay she didn't expect you to come back."

"Oh," I said flatly. "I see."

If we hadn't quarrelled, I should have spent the night with him. For the first time, or not for the first time? I didn't ask. I could have no idea whether this was a real love affair, or just one of the games that people play. Surely, if I had been in love, there would have been a greater response in me when I saw him?

Roddy peered into my face and said, "Hey. You've gone away again."

"Have I? I'm sorry. I'm afraid we're not getting anywhere much —"

"We will," he said confidently, reassuring himself, I think, as well as me. "You're tired, aren't you? Want me to go?"

"Well . . ."

"You've done enough talking, I think, for one day."

"Perhaps. It was good of you to come," I said. "Thank you."

He leaned over and kissed me lightly. "I'll be around," he said, "take care," and he went away.

I sat there for a long time after he'd gone,

thinking. Roddy had left the press cuttings on the table beside me and I reached for them again and tried to relate to the confident face of the woman in the photographs. It was that confidence that got to me. She looked, above all, secure. The clothes were nice; she, or somebody, knew what suited her. In one of the pictures she was wearing a bracelet which looked both pretty and expensive; where was it now? It occurred to me that everything would be easier if I had some of my own gear round me, the clutter of my unremembered life: clothes, ornaments, jewellery, letters, records. Surely, among all that, would be the key that would unlock the door to the past?

There didn't seem to be much here, in hospital; but there was the locker by the bed. I had never looked into it, never, up to now, felt interested enough or strong enough. I got up and walked, rather gingerly, over to the cupboard and opened it.

The first thing I found was a bundle of letters and cards, addressed to me by a variety of people I didn't know. That would be useful. I must get down to reading them all some time. Then there was an evening hand-bag — with nothing inside but a small amount of Italian money, a mirror, a comb, an unused handkerchief. That seemed to be all there was, but some instinct made me delve further, into the back of the cupboard, just to make sure I'd seen everything. My fingers closed on something small, hard, and smooth; I drew it out, and looked at it.

It was an earring, the stud kind which clips on: a square, large stone with little diamonds round it.

I can't describe the feeling of nameless horror which came over me when I looked at this inoffensive little object. I held it in my hand and waves of terror seemed to radiate from it. My hand was shaking, I was shaking all over; my mouth was dry and my heart beating somewhere up in my throat. People talk about blind panic and that's exactly what mine was, a formless cloud of black fear and revulsion. But that's all. It told me nothing. I remembered nothing. There was only the fear which at that moment seemed to fill the world.

I put the earring into the handbag, and put the bag and the letters back into the locker. I crept back to my chair and lowered myself into it, leaned back and closed my eyes.

It was all I had the strength to do.

Stephanie came the next day. I knew instinctively that it was she. Before she even got to my room I heard her arrival, the clack of her heels in the corridor, the high carrying voice. Evidently she didn't believe in a gingerly approach. She came into the room in a rush, swooped on me, cried "Darling!", threw her arms round me and hugged me. It was so spontaneously done that my natural reaction was to want to hug her back. That would have put us both in a false position so I didn't do it. I patted her shoulder in a friendly way, though, just to show there was no ill feeling.

She let me go then, and sat down beside me, and we looked at each other.

She was a small, slender woman who might have been fifty or sixty or more; you really couldn't tell. Her hair was skilfully tinted, she had kept her figure, and her face had the soft, unlined, slightly fleshy look of the actress who for years has larded her skin daily with theatrical cold cream. Only the darkened skin round her huge expressive eyes, and a fold under her chin, gave her away. But even these signs of age, I thought, would not be noticed much because the face itself was so mobile and vivacious. She was charming, and she would charm me if I let her. I was not sure yet whether I was going to let her.

"No go," she said at last, sadly. "Is it?"

"Not really, I'm afraid. But I think I know

who you are, though. You must be Stephanie."

"Steffy, dear. You've always called me Steffy, ever since you were little." She stumbled over this a bit, and looked as if she might cry.

I said gently, "Well, hallo Steffy. This must be very upsetting for you. I'm so sorry."

"My God," said Stephanie, staring at me, "guts you certainly have. Not that *that* ought to surprise me. But how did you guess? About me?"

"Roddy Marchant told me about you. That man who came yesterday."

"*That man,*" Stephanie repeated under her breath, "*who came yesterday* . . . oh well, never mind. How did you get on with him?"

"All right. It was a bit embarrassing. He was upset, too . . . I can't blame him. But I can't do anything about it, either."

"Poor darling. Of course not. You're not to worry about us. How are you, otherwise, I mean?"

"Oh, fine. Getting stronger every day —"

"That's splendid. I think, you know, you've had this hospital business. You need to be among people and in familiar surroundings. It will all come back to you, then, love. You see."

"I hope so," I said.

24

"Of course it will," said Stephanie, but she looked at me, I thought, doubtfully.

A nun came in with some tea for us. She was young and very pretty. Stephanie began to joke with her mildly in her fluent cackling Italian and the girl dimpled and smiled. When she'd gone Stephanie exclaimed, "Isn't she lovely? What a waste. I don't know why it is, I've lived in this country for years but I never really get used to nuns. I never see them without thinking about them wearing those awful clothes and probably still more awful underclothes, and never having any *fun*, you know, and being so innocent and jolly."

I burst out laughing. "Well, they *are* innocent and jolly."

Stephanie began to laugh too. She patted my hand, and said in a relieved tone, "It's nice to hear you laugh. That's more like my Joanna."

"Is it?" I said.

"Darling, what do you mean, 'is it?' "

"Exactly the same thing," I said slowly, "happened yesterday. Roddy Marchant said something about 'that's more like my girl'. You said 'that's more like my Joanna'. But, you see, I don't know what I'm like. You all know more about me than I know myself. I need your help, Stephanie."

25

"Darling, anything," Stephanie cried emotionally. "I'll do anything to help you. But you must tell me how."

"Just tell me things. I need to know about my background, home, family. I mean . . . he's been to see me. You've come. But my parents haven't."

My voice faded, seeing her expression. "Are they dead?" I asked.

She nodded. "They were killed in an air crash when you were twelve."

"I see." But I saw nothing. I tried to imagine it, the child Joanna, bereft and weeping, being comforted by distracted adults, among them, I supposed, Stephanie herself. A sad story. It moved me not at all.

"I was an only child?" I asked.

"I'm afraid so. I'm really the only relative you have, Jo. Unless you count Angelo, of course. Angelo's my stepson," she explained; "Gianni — my husband's — child by his first marriage."

"So you brought me up, after my parents were killed?"

"Oh no, dear. I was living out here then, and my husband was still alive. No. You lived with your grandfather in London. Of course," she added with a tinge of acerbity in her voice, "it would have been a great deal more suitable if you had come out here to me, but the old boy wouldn't hear of it. Nothing was to be done for you that he didn't do. Anyway he didn't approve of me; I wasn't fit to bring up his beloved Lisa's child. So there you were, rattling round in that damned great house — I mean, who would *have* a London mansion these days except ambassadors and such, and Mario? — with nobody to talk to except the servants and the old boy himself; going to that posh private day school in a chauffeur-driven limousine every day. What sort of life was that for a child? He did let you go to boarding school eventually. Because you wanted it. You soon learned to wind him round your little finger. Only three people in this life have ever done that to Mario: my mother, your mother, and you. He was an old devil, really. A real old Italian patriarch. A sort of Godfather without the criminal bit, if you see what I mean."

I didn't. The allusion escaped me.

"So that's where my home is. With him. In London . . ."

"Well, it was. The house has been shut up since his death."

I was silent, trying to understand it all. A rich old man. My grandfather. A real old Italian patriarch, she said, who had doted on me. And that really did seem sad, since he, like everything else, was totally lost.

I said at last, "You know, Steffy, if you don't mind, I think you'd better start at the beginning. Tell me everything you can think of. Please."

Stephanie was hardly the best raconteuse in the world. Her inconsequence was maddening when she was trying to make a straightforward statement of fact. Disentangled from all the asides and parentheses with which Stephanie embellished it, the story went like this.

Some time in the '20s a young man called Mario Danieli had left his native Cremona and emigrated to Britain, where he settled as many *émigré* Italians had before him, in Scotland. Mario was poor, but he was young, strong, and ambitious. In those early days he sold ice-cream on the streets of Edinburgh, lived in penury, saved every penny he could, and eventually opened a little café. The café prospered and in time he opened another, and these were the small beginnings of the great catering empire which Danieli's was eventually to become. Mario had foresight, flair, and a mountain of luck, and the thing rolled like a snowball. He had no desire to be a smart restaurateur providing an exquisite cuisine for rich gourmets; cheap eating-places for the people was what he was out to provide, eating-places where the turnover was great because the customers were not encouraged to linger. Every development in mass catering over the past fifty years was there in Mario's history, and he initiated many of them: milk bars, coffee bars, pizzerias, steak houses, an enormous network of roadside eating places known as Danny's Diners where motorists could get a quick hot meal and decent coffee in clean and attractive surroundings. "And, of course," said Stephanie, "by that time he was into hotels as well." Through the Depression of the '30s and the Second World War, Mario continued his upward path.

In the meantime, his personal fortunes did not go so well. His English wife, Margaret, whom he adored, died while his children were still young. His only son died in the war, and Lisa, my mother, was killed, leaving only me — and his other daughter, Stephanie. She and Mario didn't get on, and, I suppose, seeing the sort of man he was, that was hardly surprising; he wanted his daughters to be ladies, to be a credit to him, to enjoy the wealth he had accumulated, and marry well. Lisa's only act of defiance had been to marry my father. Stephanie ran away from home, and as far as Mario was concerned only surfaced again when she had got her break and made her first featured appearance in films. Then they were reconciled for a while, but what Stephanie called her "goings-on" — a disastrous marriage, a noisy divorce, and various other scandals which hit the headlines — caused another breach.

Stephanie had had a successful career, but I got the impression that whatever money she had earned, and the alimony from past husbands, had mostly disappeared long ago. Eventually, after an illness, she realized middle age was creeping up on her. She retired, and went back, as she said, to her roots, settling in Italy not far from where she was living now. Within the year she had met Gianni Valente, a widower with a young son, and married him. Even after she was widowed she was never really reconciled with her father. "Of course," Stephanie said gaily, "the old man and I were both as obstinate as mules, but when you think that he was absolutely rolling, I must have wanted my head examined . . ." She caught herself up, and gave me a rather uncertain look. "Still, there you are, that's the way it was. I did try, after Lisa was killed and you were left — I offered to look after you — but he saw that just as an excuse to try to grab a bit of gravy before it was too late. So I came back here and here I've stayed, vegetating and living on past glories. Not that it isn't very pleasant," she added defiantly. "I'm not lonely. Angelo comes up for week-ends as often as he can. And of course for the past few weeks before the accident, I had you staying with me, and that was lovely."

But I was thinking about Mario. "One thing puzzles me," I said. "That's about *my* work. Didn't he object to it? I mean, he didn't approve of you —"

"Oh well. Times have changed. The old man always moved with the times, that was one of his talents. Besides, he would have indulged you in whatever you wanted to do, I think. He really did adore you, you know."

"And now he's dead," I said. "How long ago?"

"Just a few weeks. Since your accident. That's what did it, really. He hadn't been well for some time, and the shock killed him. He had a stroke and didn't last the night."

I was silent. I groped for some feeling. He was old, and I suppose I must have expected him to die fairly soon; but, surely, there should have been some grief? Surely I'd remember that, at least?

"We didn't tell you," said Stephanie, "before. What would have been the point?"

No point at all, either then or now. I would have welcomed grief, a sense of loss, remorse for careless words spoken or for duties unperformed. But there was nothing. My heart was cold.

"Of course, you realize what this means," Stephanie said. "He was a very rich man, you know."

I stared at her. "You mean he . . ."

". . . left it all to you, I believe," she said lightly, her smile, brilliant, looking as if it were painted on her face. "Every penny, darling. Isn't that lovely?"

2

Stephanie came to fetch me when I was discharged from hospital. She brought with her, thoughtfully, a whole suitcase full of my clothes, so that I would have plenty to choose from. I picked out a pair of blue linen pants and a sleeveless top, and put them on. In the mirror I looked quite like the girl in the photographs, except that my hair wasn't long any more and still looked a mess. I said so to Stephanie, who said doubtfully, "Well . . . I did think about that. I brought you this."

It was a wig. A brown wig.

"Tried to get you an auburn one," Stephanie explained. "But of course, there's not much choice in Denzano and the red ones were truly awful. Try it, anyway."

I tried it; it felt hot and heavy, and I took it off, shaking my head. "It's not very comfortable, I'm afraid. But it was sweet of you to think of it. I'll just wear a scarf instead, I think."

There's a trick with scarves which I seemed to know instinctively, and I tied it tightly in the nape of the neck and looped the triangular end inside. I made up my face and turned to Stephanie with a grin. "There. I can face the world now, I think."

Stephanie said delightedly, "Darling you look terrific. Just like your old self."

Well. Whatever . . . whoever . . . my old self might be. I might look like her. Now I had to learn to *be* her.

That task seemed less daunting than before. I felt quite cheerful and hopeful that morning. I was young, I was getting well again, and outside was the world, and life to be lived. The future was open, knowable. It was mine. I thought about it with a quickening of the heart.

We said our good-byes and thank-yous and came out on to the hospital steps. It was quite early in the morning. I looked up into the new-minted brilliance of the Italian sky and felt a sense of joy and release.

"There's the car," said Stephanie. "The Fiat. The white one." There were two Fiats at the kerbside: the other one was blue, rather shabby. Near it a man stood, leaning against the wall. He seemed to be waiting for us.

"Oh Lord," I said, "I hope he's not a reporter."

"No way," said Stephanie confidently. "Nobody knows you're coming home today. Anyway, don't worry. Just get in the car and leave him to me."

But the man didn't approach us. He just stood there, watching us, while Stephanie stowed my stuff away. When we went to get into the car, he walked briskly over to the other car behind us, got in, and continued to wait until we moved off. When we did, so did he. I looked back once, and he was still there, behind us. Well, the road was narrow and twisting; it was hardly safe to pass. However, I forgot him quite soon in the anxieties caused by discovering that Stephanie was a truly terrible driver. As we slithered down the hill, mostly taking the corners on the wrong side, I sat and prayed that we wouldn't meet anything coming up, and I was thankful when we emerged, at the bottom of the hill, into a small square. It was bright with the awnings of market stalls and crowded with shoppers, and we had to slow down to a walking pace. It was a lively and endearing scene, and I looked about me eagerly.

"Denzano," said Stephanie. "Terrible little dump, isn't it?"

She swerved to avoid a dog that was nosing among the cabbage-stalks and nearly hit a fat woman carrying a bulging string bag. When I had recovered my breath, I said, "I think it's rather fun, myself."

"Fun," Stephanie snorted. "Take a look up some of these picturesque side alleys. Very slummy, and smelling to high heaven. Still, if you'd like to hang around for a bit, I promised Maria I'd get a few things. You could have a coffee while you're waiting. The café on the corner there, by the church . . . I'll join you when I've finished. Okay?"

She slammed the car into the only available parking space near the church steps and hopped lithely out, pulling a large basket after her. As I got out of the car too she looked at me doubtfully. "Will you be all right, love? Shall I come with you and order the coffee?"

"Oh, really, Steffy!"

"All right, all right. I just . . . see you in a minute, then."

She went away, and I strolled over to the cafe. I hoped that Stephanie was not going to get into the habit of cosseting me. Above all I needed to recover my confidence, my independence. Yet, as I sat down at one of the tables, it felt strange to be alone there.

The waiter came out: *"Che vuole, signorina?"*

"Cappucino."

A verbal exchange which must have happened hundreds of times in my life before, and I couldn't remember one of them. Never mind, it was pleasant there. The umbrellas had not yet been unfurled above the tables, and the sun was warm on my face. The coffee came. I sat there idly, absorbing the scene before me.

It was not strange to me, that was the comforting thing. It was not that I remembered this particular town; for all I knew, I had never been in it before. But the ambiance was familiar, the sounds, the shapes, the colours, all were as I expected them to be: the cobblestones patched with dazzling sunlight and blocks of violet shadow; walls of ochre and terracotta; the stalls in the centre of the square selling fruit and vegetables, lake fish, tourist trinkets, and cotton dresses swinging on hangers. The smell of coffee and freshly baked bread mingled with the sharper aroma from a pizzeria a few doors down the street. The sun beat down, there was the sound of hooters and revving engines; women clothed from head to foot in black, as if in perpetual mourning, bantered and haggled with the stall-holders. All around me I could hear the tinny cackle of the northern dialect, the consonants ripping off the tongue like machine-gun fire, like cloth being torn. Behind, a backcloth, as it were, to the bright scene before me, were the buildings — old, shabby, the upper storeys still retaining the remnants of an immemorial grace, the ground floors occupied by dark little shops, their doorways hung with bead curtains. Above me in the church tower a bell tolled out the hour.

I sat back in my chair, breathing a deep sigh of content. This was Italy; warm, familiar, and reassuring as a mother.

A shadow fell across the table.

I looked up, thinking momentarily that Stephanie had been very quick.

But it wasn't Stephanie. It was the man who had followed us from the hospital.

He stood there beside me and said softly, *"Buon giorno, signorina."*

I didn't answer. He pulled out the chair opposite me, and added, *"Permette?"*

It was all the same whether I permitted or not. He sat down. I found my voice and said, "I don't know you. Please go away."

He didn't move. The blank, dark surfaces of his sun glasses stared at me like inimical eyes. He had sallow, sharp features and a long thin scar on his left cheek. He showed his teeth in a wolfish grin, and said, still in that soft, insidious voice: "Lost your memory, signorina?"

"I . . ." I caught my breath, and said idiotically, "How did you know that?"

For a moment, he didn't answer. Then

38

his grin broadened.

"You have just told me, signorina. May I say I think you are very wise?"

One of his teeth had a gold filling in the front. His mouth had hardly any lips; it was a cold, mean face altogether.

"Some things," he said, "are best forgotten, are they not?"

"I don't know what you mean," I stammered. All the pleasure had gone out of the bright morning, now full of nameless menace.

"No? Perhaps it is better so." He laughed, a dry chuckle that rasped along my nerves. "A beautiful young lady like you should have only happy memories. And good friends. Yes, good friends," he repeated, and nodded his head, still smiling. "Good friends are loyal, are they not? They keep the secrets? I am such a friend, signorina. Or if that is too presumptuous, a *tifoso* . . . a fan. I wish you well —"

"It doesn't sound like it," I said. "I don't know what you're talking about and I don't want to know." I looked vainly about for the white summer uniform of a policeman. "Stop pestering me, or I'll call the police!"

"Alas," he said, "they are never there when you want them, are they? But I think you do not really want them, signorina. The publicity would be unwelcome, would it not?"

"Look," I said, "I'm not well, I've just come out of hospital. I just want to be left alone . . ."

Heavens, I was beginning to plead with him. Then, thankfully, I saw Stephanie coming towards me across the square. I said quickly, "There's my aunt. If you don't want to explain yourself to her, you'd better go."

Rather to my surprise, he rose lightly to his feet, made me a polite little bow. "We will meet again, signorina."

"I sincerely hope not," I said.

There was mockery, now, in his grin. "Ah," he murmured sadly, "in this wicked world, signorina, one's hopes are not always realized. *Arrivederci*." He turned away, and in a moment he was gone, melting into the crowd like a lizard slithering under a stone.

Stephanie came up. "I popped back to rescue you, love. Saw somebody was bothering you. Sitting here by yourself, you're bound to attract these types. I shouldn't have left you, sorry."

I said, "It wasn't like that."

"What do you mean?" She peered at me, and exclaimed, "Darling, what is it? You look as white as a sheet!"

"He . . . he frightened me."

"Frightened you? They're not usually that objectionable . . ."

40

I said irritably, "I told you, it wasn't like that. It wasn't a sex thing at all. More like . . . like veiled threats. Blackmail. Something like that."

"Blackmail? Threats?" Stephanie burst out laughing. She sat down and threw her arm round my shoulders. "Joanna, love, you're imagining things. Threats about what? Blackmail about what?"

I said dully, "I wouldn't know, would I? I didn't know what he meant."

"Did he ask you for money?"

"No."

"Well, there you are then. You must have misunderstood him. The language . . ."

"Steffy, I speak the language as well as you do. I understood him perfectly."

"But you said you didn't know what he meant."

My exasperation mounted.

"I didn't know what he meant. But I understood the *words* . . . He said I was wise to have lost my memory. He said there were things best forgotten, and then something about keeping secrets. And he kept smiling all the time, as if there were some joke that he knew and I didn't. It was horrible."

"I see," said Stephanie, though it was plain that she didn't see at all. "So what happened then?"

"I saw you coming and said so. And he took off."

"Well, that figures. He wasn't going to tangle with a chaperone, was he?"

"Steffy, I told you. He *wasn't* trying to pick me up."

"No, dear. All right. But he didn't ask you for any money."

"No. I told you —"

I broke off when I saw her expression: the look of wary indulgence, like a mother humouring a fantasizing child. I said, "You don't believe me, do you? You think I'm making it up —"

"Darling, of course I don't think you're making it up. Of course I believe you." Stephanie's voice was studiedly patient. "But if he wasn't trying to proposition you, he must have been a nut case. After all, you've had a good bit of publicity since you came out here; I suppose he recognized you —"

"Oh yes. He seemed to know who I was."

"There you are then. It probably gave him a kick, to frighten and disturb you."

"Yes," I said. "Yes. I suppose so." I thought of the man who had been sitting here opposite me, uttering those terrifying innuendos. He might be vicious, but it seemed to me that he was certainly sane. Yet who was I to judge? With my memory gone, I was as totally without experience as a newborn baby.

Stephanie sighed. "Poor lamb. You have let this get to you, haven't you? You really think there's something in it —"

"Steffy, look. How can I possibly know there isn't? I don't know anything about myself or about the past. *Only what other people tell me.* So if somebody comes along and makes insinuations —"

"Insinuations?" said Stephanie. "What sort of insinuations?"

"I don't know. That I'd done something to be ashamed of that he knows about. Committed a crime, perhaps."

"Oh, darling!" Stephanie began to laugh. "You? A crime? You'd got a marvellous part, a good contract, plenty of money, you were in love and absolutely radiant. Now what could you possibly have done?"

"I don't know." That's all I ever said, I thought drearily, when it comes down to it. *I don't know, I don't remember.*

"I think what you need is a nice rest and a good lunch. It will all seem different when we get home, Joanna. You'll forget all about horrid little men talking a lot of nonsense. You see."

"Yes." I tried to smile, though I felt a lot more like tears. "I'll try. You are good to me, Steffy."

"Darling, you're my only surviving relative and I love you dearly. So why wouldn't I be? Come on."

Before I could enjoy the relaxing programme at home that Stephanie had described, I had to get there, in Stephanie's car with Stephanie driving. We climbed out of Denzano and turned on to a wide straight road flanked by fields of maize.

Stephanie put her foot down. The fields switched by at what seemed an enormous speed; sign posts, billboards urging one to drink Stock or Cinzano flickered past. As we swung out and passed a huge tanker which seemed to be doing its best to race us, I found I had both feet pressed against the floorboards and my hands gripped together till the knuckles showed white. I expect it was all quite ridiculous, the road was wide and I don't suppose, really, we were travelling all that fast: but there it was. Stephanie made me nervous anyway, after her earlier performance, and probably, locked somewhere inside me, was the fear of the accident I couldn't even remember.

So I was profoundly relieved when the maize fields gave place to houses, the road forked, the view opened up, and there for the first time Lake Garda lay spread before me, limpid and sparkling in the morning

44

sun. Below us, by a small jetty, sailing dinghies and skiffs lay motionless on the mirror-smooth water; on the far side of the lake lay the tumbled curves, purple and green and grey, of the mountains. "Oh," I said, "how beautiful . . . ."

"You've always loved the lake," Stephanie said.

From across the water came the sound like a hunting horn. "What on earth is that?" I asked.

"The *aliscafo*. We'll watch it come in if you like."

She found a place to park and we waited until the *aliscafo* appeared, winging its way towards us like a large white bird just skimming the surface of the water, making that merry ridiculous noise announcing its arrival. I suddenly felt better, childishly delighted with the *aliscafo* and the radiant lake and the bright morning, and the terror I had felt in the café receded.

Stephanie's villa was about three miles from the point where we stopped to watch the *aliscafo*. It was perched on a tongue of land which ran out into the lake. A small road led down to the iron gateway flanked with cypresses and a drive beyond. Another car stood in the drive. "Visitors?" I asked nervously.

Stephanie shook her head. "That's Angelo. He's come up for a few days. Here, I'll have that case . . ."

Maria, obviously, had been forewarned. She came out, smiling, tactfully greeted me. There was no sign of Angelo, and for this I was thankful. He was water-skiing, Maria said, and would lunch at the clubhouse.

Inside, the villa was shuttered and cool, the rooms marble-floored, scattered here and there with good but rather shabby rugs, and rather bare. The heat of the day was beginning to gather, the way storms gather, and that bare green coolness was very welcome, at this time of the year. In winter, surely, with the wind howling down from the mountains and lashing the lake into a fury, it must be exceedingly cold. Roddy had said that Stephanie was hard up — whereas I, it seemed, had inherited everything from my grandfather, Stephanie's father, and was now rich. That sent a little cold shiver through me. I was rich, and Stephanie was poor. You're my only surviving relative, she had said, and I love you dearly. Well, perhaps it was true. I dismissed that thought, and came up with another. I can do something for her, if I've really got all this money. Like putting central heating in this place.

But, looking around more closely, I saw

that that, at least, wouldn't be necessary. Radiators were already there, and so was double-glazing on the windows each side of the french door which led on to the terrace, with venetian blinds cunningly disposed between the two layers. The central panel, I guessed was taken out for the summer. Shabby the place might be, but the essential comforts were there; someone else had seen to that.

Stephanie and I lunched alone in a corner of the terrace, where a very old vine, the grapes not yet ripe, screened us from the sun. The vine like so much else in that place, had been badly neglected, and probably the grapes would never come to anything much, but the leaf-shadows cast a dappled pattern across the table, and it was delightful to sit there in an oasis of shade and look out over the garden to where the lake lay shimmering in the noonday sun. We ate cannelloni and lake trout, and there was a jug of white wine. "Our own," Stephanie explained, pouring it out. "We have a little vineyard some kilometres from here. Nothing very wonderful, and there's never enough to sell, but it does mean that we can keep some wine to give our friends."

After the meal she insisted on settling me

in a long chair with cushions and magazines, while she went off into the house, perhaps to help Maria clear up. I could hear their voices in the kitchen. They sounded like two peasant women gossiping together, the occasional cackle of laughter and the rapid rattling speech which so often sounds as if people are quarrelling. Then, I think, Stephanie must have gone to her room, and the house was quiet.

I went on lying on the terrace for a while, idly turning the pages of a magazine. I tried, for a little while, to sleep. But sleep would not come. I felt restless, and presently I got up and went out into the garden to explore.

The garden ran level from the foot of the terrace to where one came to the top of the bluff that overlooked the lake. From there the ground fell away to the water's edge, a little hill in which some stunted olive trees maintained a precarious foothold. I found a path between them, and made my way down it to the lakeside. Here the ground levelled out for a few yards and ended in a reef of rock gleaming goldenly under a few inches of pellucid water. A rather dilapidated jetty reached out, over the reef, to the deep water beyond.

Of course, I realized when I got to the bottom that I should not have come at all.

Even the climb down had tired me, and I was sitting, rather shakily and thankfully, on a rock at the bottom, when I heard the staccato roar of a speed-boat. It came hurtling by, towing a water-skier. As I watched, the helmsman pulled the wheel hard over, and I found myself watching with bated breath — surely, surely the skier would never make it. But he swung out and away in a huge arc, the water fanned into a thousand blue and silver ripples, and then he was back on course again, effortless, confident.

They roared away down the lake, made another perfect turn and came flying back again across my vision. I couldn't forbear to wave as they approached. They both waved back and I felt absurdly pleased. They disappeared round the promontory, the noise of the engine died. I felt suddenly lonely and a bit chilled, deprived abruptly of the sight of all that powerful, vibrant life.

Then I heard the boat returning, more slowly this time. As it came in sight, I saw that the skier was on board. The launch bumped gently against the jetty; the skier jumped out, his friend threw out a towel and a pair of jeans after him, there was a shouted, joking exchange, unintelligible to me because of the engine noise. The boat drew away, the helmsman opened up the throttle and in a moment it was gone, leaving only long streamers of foam on the surface of the water.

The skier wrapped the towel around his neck, and, swinging the jeans by one hand, walked up the jetty towards me.

It had all happened so quickly and unexpectedly that I had a ridiculous urge to get up and run — ridiculous, for there was nowhere to run to. This nervousness with strangers — and who, to me, was not a stranger? — had got to be conquered. Somehow, like some sea-creature vulnerable to a thousand enemies, I must build a shell round my soft and shrinking inner self.

So I didn't move. I waited for him to come to me, with a nonchalance I didn't feel. I looked up, straight into his eyes. When he smiled, I smiled. It was quite easy, really.

He said in English, "Hallo, Joanna."

"Hallo," I said: and then "Angelo?"

I was getting used to the reaction, the faint wince with which people registered my complete non-recognition of them. It didn't happen this time. Angelo didn't bat an eyelid. He said merely, "That's me."

I said, as I had said before, "I'm sorry."

"Forget it," said Angelo. "Not your fault, is it? And it can't be much fun, either." His English, I noted, was not just faultless;

it was the pleasant speech of an educated Englishman, easy on the ear, but casual, occasionally slipshod, only a slight trilling of the 'r's gave away his origins. I noticed all this as I had noticed Roddy's faint cockney intonation.

I said without thinking, "Your English is very good."

That did make him stare, and I followed it up quickly, "That must sound very silly, I expect."

He grinned. "A bit. But then you don't know me, do you, any more? Steffy brought me up. I spent three years at an English university. So English is a second language to me, more or less."

He dropped down to the ground at my feet and began to hunt through the pockets of the jeans for cigarettes and lighter. He seemed so indifferent, so perfectly at ease, that I began in a curious way to feel more at ease too.

He found the cigarettes, waved them at me.

"No, thank you. I don't smoke."

"No more you do," said Angelo. "You've remembered that, anyway."

"So I have," I said, pleased.

I was sitting on a rock a little above him, so I was able to observe him as he took a cigarette from the packet and lit it, squinting

51

into the sun. Raggedy locks of wet black hair fell over his forehead. He had a bony dark face, not handsome, with a long ironical mouth. He looked as if he didn't suffer fools gladly; he looked as if he could be impatient and harsh. A formidable face, revealing, in so far as it revealed anything, a rock-hard, uncompromising personality. My feeling of ease faded and I felt the first flickers of alarm.

"Well," he said, "what now? What are you going to do, now you're out of hospital?"

"I don't know. Stay here, I suppose, till I'm stronger. I feel rather bad about inflicting myself on Steffy. She's been very kind . . ."

"Kind," he repeated.

"Does that sound very odd? My talking about her as if she were a stranger?"

"Not really, I suppose. We're all strangers now, aren't we? Does Steffy know you're down here?"

"No. I never thought . . . she wouldn't worry would she, if she couldn't find me?"

"She might. You're just out of hospital, after all. I don't suppose she'd expect you to get this far. Should you have done, anyway?"

"Probably not. I did feel a bit groggy when I got to the bottom. But I'm all right now. Perhaps I'd better go back."

I scrambled recklessly to my feet, and suddenly the lake and the sky and the olive trees spun giddily round me. I felt myself lurching, stumbling. He sprang up and caught hold of me in a light, firm grip.

"Sit down again." His voice sounded a long way off "Put your head down . . . that's it . . ."

The world stopped spinning. I felt rather sick. Heavens, I thought, don't let me *be* sick. Not in front of this man. That was an indignity I couldn't bear.

I looked up cautiously. He was standing over me, looking more exasperated than concerned.

"Better now?"

"Yes, thank you. Perhaps you'd be very kind," I said with an effort, "and go and tell Steffy I'm all right. I'll come up in my own time."

"You won't. It's steeper than you think. Hold these." He thrust the damp towel and the jeans into my arms.

"What are you going to do?"

"Carry you up."

"You can't do that, I'm much too heavy —"

"Don't be ridiculous. There's nothing of you. Just relax and leave it all to me."

It would be nice to be able to say that he carried me tenderly back to the house, cradled in his arms, but in fact he slung me briskly over his shoulder in a fireman's lift and in this undignified fashion transported me back up the path to the top. There was a big, spreading fig tree in the middle of the lawn, and a stone bench under it. Angelo slid me neatly on to the bench. "There you are. I'll go and tell Steffy you're okay and bring you a drink. All right?"

"All right. It's very kind of you —" but he had already gone, striding away rather impatiently towards the house. He was gone some minutes; the feeling of nausea and faintness faded and I sat there tranquilly in the shade, thinking about the man who had just left me. Abrasive, intimidating, he was all of that, but, in his own brusque way, kind as well. It would be like this all the time now, coming up against new personalities, having to evaluate and judge them, make choices in the fashion in which, I supposed, ordinary people without my disability made choices every day.

Angelo was back, carrying a long glass chinking with ice.

"Here you are. Steffy's asleep, so she didn't know you'd gone. I didn't disturb her."

"Oh . . . good. Thank you." I sipped my drink. He sat down at the end of the bench, watching me. I found this embarrassing, and

I said, to divert his attention, "This is a beautiful place."

He grimaced. "It was once. It began to crumble a long time ago and Steffy didn't have the money to keep it up. I'm in a better position to help her with it now, so at least it's watertight and has some proper heating and so on; it can be very cold here in the winter. The garden is something else again. We have a man in twice a week to keep it from turning to jungle and that's about all we can do at the moment. I'm not here enough, and Steffy, for all she's so active and youthful, can't do much herself."

"I shouldn't worry about the garden," I said. "It's still beautiful. I like it like this — a bit wild."

"Yes. Well . . . wild gardens are the style in England. But at one time this was a garden in the classical Italian manner. Over there — where the columns are — that's the lemon garden. Steffy likes to keep that going because of the scent; the crop isn't anything much nowadays. And on the other side, where you see that low wall — that was an old-fashioned *giardino segreto* — like a little room with no roof. What's the matter?"

"I don't know."

The familiar nightmare misery was upon me again. *The lemon garden. Giardino segreto*

. . . secret garden. Good friends are loyal,
signorina, they keep the secrets . . . lemons . . .
the lemon garden . . . the words were like
little points of light in a fog, like will o'
the wisps, they appeared and disappeared,
beckoning, mocking me; the sweat broke out
on my forehead.

Angelo, watching me, spoke again. "Are
you all right?"

The awful frustration made me explode,
and I shouted, "You know I'm not all right.
Why don't you shut up, and leave me alone."

Silence. If I had been he, I would have
got up and walked away. But he didn't walk
away. He said, grinning, "That's more like
it. Par for the course, I'd say."

This seemed like some sort of joke at my
expense. I said unsteadily, "Look. I was rude,
and I'm sorry —"

"Oh, don't apologize," he said airily. "If
you can't shout at me, whom can you shout
at? An old friend . . . or an old enemy,
whichever you choose to call it."

"An old enemy?"

"We don't get on," said Angelo. "Let's
put it that way. It's not altogether your fault."

"Oh, charming," I said drily. "You do
accept, then, that some of it may be yours?"

"More than likely. I'm not very tolerant,
especially of spoiled brats."

"And how much have you seen of me, anyway, to make that sort of judgement?"

"Ten years ago was the first time. I was in England then — at university — and I made contact with you and the old man: a courtesy visit. Steffy's idea, not mine, I may say." He didn't elaborate. "Well, we'll cast a veil over that one. You were thirteen at the time. A difficult age, of course. Five years later you took a fancy to come out here and visit us. You were eighteen then, and bloody insufferable; the original little rich bitch, arrogant as hell, dripping with money. I don't say you weren't generous with it, money I mean. You came loaded with expensive presents for Steffy and she was childishly delighted with them. In the circumstances I found all that extremely unamusing. So we got across each other a good deal, you and I."

"I see," I said again. I was silent for a moment, trying to absorb the unattractive picture of myself which Angelo had conjured up. I felt no resentment. It all seemed, somehow, to have nothing to do with me. I didn't ask him what he meant by 'in the circumstances'; I knew, perfectly well, what the circumstances were: the money. The contrast between Steffy's situation and my own. I was not going to discuss any of that with Angelo, or tell him of my intention to put things

57

right. That was a matter between Steffy and me, and not his business.

I said with a brisk, dismissing air, "Well, I'm sorry you don't like me, but there's not much I can do about that, is there?"

"Did I say I didn't like you? I said we didn't get on; not quite the same thing. Anyway," he added, "since this happened, you seem to me to be a good deal improved. Remember the story of the fairy godmother in *The Rose and the Ring?* No, of course you don't. There was this infant princess who had a whole gaggle of fairy godmothers at her christening, all bringing gifts, beauty, health, riches and so on. Then the last one came and set the whole court by the ears. Because she waved her wand and said, 'I bring you, my child, a little misfortune.' "

"And do you," I asked after a moment, "call this a little misfortune? The accident, the amnesia?"

"Well, it's hardly a major disaster, is it? You could have been killed in that crash. You could have been crippled or disfigured. You could have come out of that hospital with no money, not knowing who you were, and found nobody else who knew or gave a damn either. As it is, you're nearly fit again already; you've got money, friends. Things could be a lot worse."

I said, with more than a touch of bitterness, "You don't understand at all, do you? Of course I'm thankful I got out of the accident in one piece. But how can you possibly imagine what it's like to be me just now? I've lost one of my major faculties, it's like being blind —"

Angelo said drily, "But you're not blind, are you? And this thing, unlike blindness, isn't final. Look over there."

I looked out over the lake. The afternoon heat was on the wane; there was no haze on the opposite shore which lay bathed in the light of the westering sun and appeared much nearer in the clear air. Red shingled roofs climbed upwards from the water's edge: the light rested gently on old golden stone, on a church spire, the brilliant white rectangle of a new hotel, the dark accents of conifers, and beyond it all the purple and green and umber of the great hills.

"Well, there it is," he said. "It's beautiful, it's real, and short of an earthquake or a nuclear disaster, it's permanent, and you can relate to it. It was there before you forgot and it will still be there after you've got things together again."

"I'm not sure I know what you mean."

"Well," said Angelo briskly, "think about it." He got to his feet and added, "And now I think you've talked enough for one afternoon. Go and get some rest before dinner. And stop being sorry for yourself."

"You think I've no right to be?"

He stood there a moment, looking down at me.

"My dear girl, you're suffering from a temporary aberration which will go away in time, if you don't keep picking at it like a sore spot so that it won't heal. In a world like this your troubles are very small beer. There are plenty of people who'd be glad to be in your shoes, believe me. To be able to forget. To have a curtain drawn over nightmare memories of death, destruction, torture. Just remember that. Even," he added with an ironic, rather cruel smile, "if you don't remember anything else."

3

Roddy Marchant telephoned several times during the next few days. He was still in Rome, he said, where the shooting of the picture was now almost at an end. Frank Harmer, he told me cheerfully, was being bloody impossible, and everyone else was on edge and longing for the whole thing to be sewn up which, with any luck, it would be soon. After that, Roddy said, he hoped to come up again and see me.

These messages from the outside world seemed to emphasize the tranquillity of the Villa Medina, an oasis of sunlight and shade and blue water, in which I did little except eating and sleeping and soaking up the sun.

I never went into the lemon garden.

From time to time I told myself that what I ought to do was to get in there and find out what it was that scared me so much. I never got round to it: in fact I tried, after a while, to put it out of my mind, together with the other things which set off alarm signals. I had locked the earring away, and I was beginning to believe, with Steffy, that the Denzano episode had indeed been merely "a try-on of some kind", unimportant, meaningless.

Apart from Roddy's calls, nothing much happened along then. There were no visitors — perhaps Steffy had arranged to keep them away. Angelo was still there, of course, but he made it clear that whatever he'd come to the lake for, it wasn't on my account. He spent most of his time on his own rather strenuous forms of relaxation, which meant that he swam or skin-dived or water-skied, and was often away for most of the day. In the cool of the night, or in the early morning, I could hear through the thick walls of the old house the woodpecker clacking of a typewriter. I wondered about this, but was determined to show no curiosity, and it was Steffy who explained that Angelo, formerly a staff journalist on a Rome newspaper, now freelanced and also wrote books. Steffy was vague about the books, which, she said, were above her head. The journalism, from her account, seemed to be the investigative kind — "what we'd call muck-raking, I suppose, really, dear. He mixes with the most peculiar people . . . criminals, some of them, I shouldn't wonder. It really worries me sometimes. I mean, in this country, if you get the wrong side of the Mafia . . ."

"Have you told him it worries you?" I asked.

"Oh yes. He only laughs and says I shouldn't.

He says he hasn't an enemy in the world."

If he behaves to other people as he does to me, I thought, I rather doubt that — although, to be honest, I couldn't say that when we did meet he was really unfriendly. Occasionally he would even seek me out and so, one day, found me sitting in the garden going through a packet of correspondence I had found in the hospital locker.

"What have you got there?" he asked idly.

"Letters, cards . . . mostly from people I've never even heard of. You wouldn't care to help me sort them out a bit, would you?"

"I don't necessarily know all your friends. But I'll try."

"There's one here, rather a nice one. An address in Verona and it's signed 'Katie.' She writes as if we've known each other for years."

"Kate Castelani," Angelo said at once. "English, married to an Italian banker called Giorgio. Quite a buddy of yours. Delightful creature. He's a nice chap too. You should get over there and see them; they'd do you good."

I pondered over the letter. I felt the warmth and affection in Kate Castelani's big scrawl, like the hand of a friend.

"She writes about the accident," I said. "But not about the other thing."

"I don't suppose she knows. We haven't spread it abroad much. But if I know Kate at all, she'll react very well and be helpful."

"Yes . . . well, I must answer this, or telephone her, or something. There's a card here from Frank Harmer, the director of the film . . . it must have come with some flowers. He may be coming up to see me. Do you know anything about him?"

Angelo laughed. "Don't look so apprehensive. He's not an ogre. What sort of thing do you want to know? Like, he's one of my stepmamma's old flames?"

"So you know about that," I said curiously.

"It's not a secret, you know. I've known Frank since way back. Not that he ever came here in my father's time. But later he turned up here, at fairly rare intervals. I recall him chiefly as the source of generous tips and as someone who took Steffy's attention away from me; I was an extremely possessive child."

"You're very attached to her, aren't you? To Steffy?"

"Natural enough, don't you think? I don't remember my own mother. I was six when my papa turned up with this pretty lady and said he'd married her. She was warmhearted and kind, and I latched on to her like the proverbial limpet. Fortunately the affection was entirely reciprocal; she never had any kids of her own so I got it all, the affection I mean. She looked after me when I needed it. Now I look after her."

"I see." I spoke thoughtfully. "To go back to Frank Harmer . . . it doesn't sound as if you liked him much."

"In those days, I suppose I didn't. But that was just an insecure kid's reaction. He's a remarkable man, a great film director. He can be very difficult but he's also extremely kind and generous. And he thinks well of you," Angelo grinned, quite kindly. "There's absolutely no need to be scared of him, really."

"Oh well . . . good." I picked up the next letter. "Do you know anything about this one? Someone called Cyrus B. Hoffman?"

"Never heard of him. But he just has to be a Yank, with a name like that."

"Yes, he does, doesn't he? It's a rather formal letter. As if he doesn't know me very well. He says, "My wife and I hope to have the pleasure of meeting you again in happier circumstances." I can't think what that can mean. He writes from Rome . . ." I read the address out.

Angelo, who was lying on the grass, rolled over and stared at me.

"What's the matter?"

"That's the American Embassy."

"Really? It doesn't say so. The address is

just written at the top."

"A modest, unpretentious fellow," said Angelo. "He's got to be a diplomat, just the same."

"Good heavens."

"I don't know why you should say good heavens. In the circles in which you moved before all this happened, diplomats were common currency. Especially the young ones — third secretaries and such. He's probably one of those. Met you at a party, probably."

"A party? I hope it wasn't that party, that's all. The one at the Villa Flora . . ."

"Why?"

"Happier circumstances, he says . . ." I caught myself up. "Oh well. It doesn't matter. You weren't there, were you?"

"Yes, I was."

"Were you! Then you can tell me about it."

"Hasn't Roddy Marchant done that?"

"He told me a bit. I'd like to hear your version."

"Why? Don't you trust him?"

"Trust?" The word fell into the bright air like a swooping insect about to sting. "Why do you say that? Why shouldn't I trust him?"

Angelo shrugged. "Well, do you? Yes, I was at the party. So were a hundred or so other people. Cameras rolled. Champagne flowed. People showed off."

I couldn't help laughing. "It doesn't sound as if you enjoyed it much."

"I've been to too many of these shenanigins, I expect. Anyway, I only went because you would be there. Oh, don't get me wrong. I was just curious to see how you would conduct yourself in that sort of set-up. No need to worry, so far as I know. You behaved beautifully."

"You weren't there when I left?"

"No, I left early. I had an appointment in Rome the following day, so I drove back through the night."

"Oh! So you don't know what happened, later?"

"No. Is something supposed to have happened?"

"I think I must have made a scene —"

"Perhaps you did. What about it? In the milieu in which you live, my child, drama is the stuff of life."

"Oh dear," I said.

"Well, don't make another drama out of it," said Angelo in his usual rather irritating way. If he intended to be bracing, he succeeded. I was determined not to let myself down by showing my worries and fears too openly. I'd get no sympathy in that quarter, I knew that already.

I didn't let myself down. Life, however, did and with a resounding bang, the very next night.

Because it was the very next night that the apparition visited me.

Of course it was human enough, really. I knew that, because it spoke to me.

It happened in the early hours of the morning. I was beginning to sleep quite well now, not needing pills any more. I must have been quite deep in a peaceful slumber.

Then, suddenly, I woke.

It was not quite dark in the room. I had opened the shutters and the window and pulled the curtains right back before getting into bed, to let in as much air as possible on that languorous hot night. Something was silhouetted against the window. First of all, I saw just a dark, immobile figure — and then the light. It flowed from the creature's head, streaming, pale green from the empty eye-sockets of a hideous, snarling mask. From the curled back jaws came more light, flowing red, like blood.

This was the very stuff of nightmare, but I knew, I knew from the first instant of shock and terror that it was no nightmare, this was real.

The apparition began to move towards me,

68

and I opened my mouth to scream.

It was Angelo who reached me first. He burst into the room, flinging the door back with a crash, grabbing at the switches, and flooding the room with light.

"What's going on?" he shouted.

At that moment I was incapable of coherent speech, but I must have made some sort of wild gesture towards the window. Angelo sprang towards it, went out on to the balcony, came back. He sat down on the bed and gathered me into his arms, not tenderly, but with a firm, almost bruising grip. I was shaking with *rigor*, terrifying enough in itself, and gasping and crowing like a child with croup.

"Hey," said Angelo, "steady now. Steady."

I managed at last to croak out something incoherent about the Thing in my room.

"But there's nobody here," said Angelo.

It was true. The room, brightly lit, apparently completely undisturbed, was empty apart from ourselves. It looked as it usually did. The apparition might never have been there. But it had been there. That I knew.

Steffy came in, agitated and exclaiming. Angelo said quickly, "Leave this to me, Steffy. I'll come and see you in a minute," and she went away again. Angelo turned back to me.

"Joanna," he said, "listen. Are you listening? *There's nobody here but you and me.*"

But I was still struggling to control my gasping and shivering. Angelo tried once more, as he thought, to reach me. "Joanna, you've had a nightmare. There's nothing here. *Nobody was ever here.*"

This made me furiously angry, and somehow the anger gave me back some coherence and I shouted, "No, no, you're wrong, there was somebody, there was, I saw him, I tell you, I saw him —" And Angelo reached out for the water carafe on my bedside table and emptied it over my head.

Well, I suppose he was right to do it, in a way . . . The water had been standing for some hours and in that hot night it was not as cold as it might have been, but cold enough. My hair was soaking, and the water dripped off it and ran down on to the bed, the pillow, between my breasts. I had gone to bed on that hot night without a stitch and Angelo had been holding me naked in his arms. The shock of the cold water got me together at lightning speed, hysteria replaced first by indignation and then by embarrassment. I grabbed hold of the sheet and wrapped it round me, saying furiously, "Damn you, what did you do that for?"

"That's better," said Angelo. He offered

neither apology nor explanation. He got up, marched off to find a towel, came back with it and handed it to me. "There. Dry yourself off with that." He reached for a dressing robe I'd left thrown over a chair and tossed it on the bed. "You'd better put that on too, I suppose."

While I was drying myself and putting the robe on, Angelo wandered out to the balcony again. "Can't see properly," he said. "I'll get a torch." Returning with the torch he subjected the whole area around the window to a careful scrutiny. Then he came back to me once more and said quite gently, "All right? Now tell me all about it."

He stood beside me, hands in the pockets of the towelling beachrobe he was wearing. He seemed immensely tall standing there, tall and formidable. He had been kind in his way. But I looked at him both with dislike and a feeling of despair, because he was not, of course, going to believe me.

While I was telling him what happened I knew just how it sounded, totally unconvincing. An apparition, a snarling face, red light, green light . . .

Angelo said carefully, "So when you screamed, he vanished."

"You don't understand. He didn't *vanish*. And that was before —"

"Before what?"

"Before I screamed," I said.

"Joanna," said Angelo, "you're not making much sense."

"I know I'm not," I said angrily. "It's because you're not listening to me properly, you don't believe me. You think I dreamed it, but I didn't. I said he didn't *vanish*. He climbed over the balcony and dropped down to the lawn. It was after that I screamed, I didn't before because I was too frightened and anyway he didn't let me . . ."

"He went over the balcony," Angelo said. "Then you must have heard him running away."

"No . . ."

"There was nobody there when I looked out," said Angelo reasonably. "There's no cover, so he must have taken to his heels, really run for it. What happened before he went over the balcony? You said you didn't scream because he didn't let you —"

"That's right. He put his hand over my mouth, it was soft and rubbery, as if he had gloves on, and he kept whispering . . . whispering . . ."

"What did he whisper?"

"I can't tell you. It was too horrible." Remembering the stream of whispered obscenities, I shuddered. "Then . . . then he showed me a knife and put it up against my throat, it was quite sharp, I could feel the edge . . . and he laughed . . . well, it was an awful sort of soft giggle. And then he went away."

"I see. But he didn't actually attack you?"

"No."

"And nothing's taken?"

"I don't know."

"Let's have a look." Angelo went over to the dressing table. "Gold watch, bracelet, couple of rings . . . money?"

"I haven't any cash. I haven't needed any since I got here."

"And that's all there is?"

"All I know about," I said.

"I see. So he came, woke you up. Stopped you from screaming. Said a lot of unpleasant things. But he didn't try to rape you, he didn't take anything. And the room is just as it was when you went to bed?"

"It seems to be," I said.

"I've looked all round the balcony and the window," Angelo said. "Can't find anything unusual."

I said coldly, "Would you expect to?" Because, of course, he wouldn't; he didn't believe me. I was defeated by the total normality of everything; the apparition had come and gone as if indeed it were just an apparition, leaving no marks on the balcony when it had vaulted over; no footprint; no fingerprints; not a single object disturbed — except, of course, myself. And even me he had not harmed physically, my distress was all in the mind, which, of course, was just where Angelo expected it to be.

I said drearily, "Yes . . . well, I'm sorry I disturbed you. Go back to bed. I'm all right now."

Angelo peered at me and said gently, "You're not all right, are you? And that bed's soaked. You won't feel safe in here anyway. The best thing would be for you to sleep in my room . . . if you don't mind using my sheets . . . and I'll fix this bed up and sleep in here. How would that be? And knowing your invincible Britishness, I'd say a nice cup of tea would be a good idea. You go and make yourself comfortable next door, and I'll just have a word with Steffy. And for the time being, we'll shut this window . . . there, that feels better, doesn't it?"

"Yes. Thank you."

He went away to find Steffy and make the tea. I heard them murmuring together; like anxious parents, it seemed to me, coping with a child crying in the night. To them, no doubt, that's just what I was.

I wrapped the robe round me and went

into Angelo's room. This was unknown territory for me: a large, spare, masculine room, used for work and study as well as sleeping; bookshelves, a desk, a typewriter. The bed was tumbled, as if he had had a restless night. I straightened it out and got into it. The sheets smelled of him, faintly and not unpleasantly. Presently he appeared again, brisk and smiling, with the tea. "I brought a cup for myself," he said. "All right?"

"Of course." The tea was poured out and Angelo began to talk inconsequentially about other things. Taking my mind off my delusion, no doubt. I let him talk, saying yes and no at appropriate moments. I drank the tea and put the cup back on the tray.

"Another cup?" he asked.

"No, thank you."

He put the tray on the desk. "Will you sleep now?" he asked. "Can I get you a pill?"

"No, thank you. I'm off the pills . . . I'll be all right now. I'm sorry to have been such a nuisance."

"That's all right. Don't worry. Look, I'll close the shutters — they can't be opened from the outside. You're quite safe. OK, then?" To my surprise, he bent down and kissed me on the cheek. *"Dormi bene, cara."*

He was at the door before I said, "You don't believe me, do you?"

"Of course," said Angelo nicely, "of course I believe you."

It was late next morning when I woke, the sun already high; slivers of burning light thrust through the chinks of the window shutters like sword blades. I never slept with the shutters closed. That, and the strange room, Angelo's room, had me puzzled for a moment. Then all that had happened the night before came back to me and I was wide awake.

It was stiflingly hot. The sheet, twisted and crumpled, was lying on the floor. I sat up and swung my legs over the side of the bed. I put my elbows on my knees and my head in my hands, and tried to get myself together. I felt perfectly calm, that was the strange thing. I could recall those frightening moments (recollection in the short term seemed no problem, thank God) as if they had happened to somebody else. Perhaps it was shock, I don't know, but what I actually felt was a growing realization that I was absolutely on my own. I could trust nobody, and it was time to take hold of the situation. It was time, in fact, to be brave.

I went back to my own room, which looked

perfectly normal. Somebody, Maria I suppose, had already been at work on it. The bed was freshly made up with clean sheets, the room tidy and dusted, empty now of Angelo's presence. Empty of anyone's presence.

I stepped out on to the balcony, and the radiant day-time world burst upon me. The lake gleamed, mirror-still, under the morning sun. Everything was bright, clean, astonishingly normal, and very quiet. The house was quiet. I might have been alone in it. I stood and stared at the lake without seeing it. I was thinking about the balcony.

This balcony, with its worn old balustrade, its swept stone floor (swept, perhaps, that morning?) gave away no secrets, no clues. There was no sign that anyone had vaulted over it the night before. There would be no finger-prints on the balustrade, he had been wearing gloves. He — and who was he? — had known where to find me. He had climbed up there, to my room . . . *climbed?*

I looked down. The old vine under which we had our meals graced the other side of the house. Here, from this parapet, the wall with its flaking stucco fell sheer away to the ground. So how had he got there? I thought vaguely about rope ladders: how did you fix them? With a grappling iron. Which had to be thrown. Which would make a noise.

The intruder must have come in some other way. He must have been inside the house.

The balcony ran the whole length of the wall that side and another window, further along, also gave on to it, as well as mine. I hadn't thought much, before, about the geography of the house; another window — whose? I walked along the balcony and looked in. How could I have been so stupid? It was the room I had just left; the room I had slept in. Angelo's room.

Angelo . . .

Look at it this way: Angelo, hearing me screaming, had burst into my room with a crash, flinging back the door and shouting . . . giving time, perhaps, for the intruder to make his getaway? Covering the noise he made doing it?

In his irritating, arrogant way Angelo had been kind, then. Kind, yes. Coping with my hysteria in the time-honoured fashion; and then being soothing, as with a frightened child; trying to persuade me that it wasn't real.

So the intruder had had one job to do: to terrorize me. Angelo had had another: to convince me that the whole thing was a figment of my sick and bewildered imagination.

Frightened out of my mind. Persuaded that I was out of my mind. Heads I win, tails you lose. And if anybody heard me propounding this theory aloud they would most certainly think that I *was* crazy. Heads you win, tails I . . .

But why?

Angelo. What did I know about him? Nothing, except what he had told me himself; what Steffy had told me; and what I had seen with my own eyes. What I had seen didn't tell me much. Angelo water-skiing. Angelo diving off the end of the jetty and swimming powerfully far out in the lake. Angelo sitting back after lunch with a glass of wine in his hand, talking idly in his easy joky way, teasing Steffy affectionately; being offhand and casual with me. The surface of a man. But who knew what depths there were beneath that surface? I remembered how, that first time, I had had a sense of what might be there: something hard, reckless, and ruthless.

No sense in any of it really; no motive, no proof. Only intuitive suspicion which might be entirely groundless. Yet, it would not go. My God, I thought, I must get away from this place.

The telephone rang in the hall downstairs and I heard the clack of Maria's heelless slippers on the marble floor, and her voice, answering; the heavy, hesitant voice of an elderly peasant woman who hates the telephone, speaking too loud, as if the caller must be deaf. She called Steffy, then, who came hurrying from somewhere, and began to talk to the caller in English. She sounded gushing and enthusiastic. "My dear! Yes, of course! That would be lovely! What? Oh, much the same . . . well, we . . ." She dropped her voice, then, and I couldn't hear any more.

I suppose, after that, she heard me moving about, and presently came up with a tray.

"I've brought your breakfast."

"Oh . . . that's sweet of you. Thanks, Steffy."

"We thought we'd better let you sleep on . . . how are you this morning?"

I could see, by her nervous look, that she didn't want to get involved in a discussion about what had happened the night before. I smiled, and said pleasantly, "I'm fine, thank you. I slept very well. That coffee smells good." I drank the coffee and buttered a roll and began to eat it hungrily. Steffy lingered, watching me. After a while she said, "That was Roddy Marchant on the telephone."

"Oh yes?"

"He's coming up for a day or two. I hope that's all right with you."

I said quietly, "Steffy, if you wanted to know if it were all right with me, you could have asked me, couldn't you?"

"Don't you want him to come?"

"It isn't that. I'd just like to be . . . well, consulted. To have some say in arranging my own life. That's all."

Steffy stared at me, and burst out suddenly, "It's all so difficult. I don't know what to do. I don't feel I know you any more."

Poor Steffy.

I said gently, "Yes, of course, I can see that, and I'm sorry. You've been wonderfully patient and kind. I don't know how you've put up with me, really. But I hope it won't be for long."

"What do you mean?"

"I think it's time I moved on."

"Where to? You're not well enough —"

"I soon shall be. I haven't decided where to go, yet. To Rome, perhaps. Or back to England."

"You can't do that. You'd be absolutely lost. You don't know anyone there."

"I don't *know* anybody here," I said drily. "Still, I don't suppose I'll leave Italy just yet. This is where the key will be, won't it?"

"The key?" Steffy spoke bewilderedly, out of her depth.

"To my memory," I said. I drank some coffee, and added, "Where's Angelo this morning?"

"He's gone to Milan. He had some business to see to . . . he'll be back tonight," she ended, as if reassuring me.

I wondered why Angelo had gone to Milan. But I was glad he had gone. I felt safer without him.

I was in the garden that evening when I heard Roddy arrive. It seemed that he had not come alone. It sounded like a party of people: Roddy's voice, another, deeper man's voice; and a girl's, soft and rather giggly. Steffy was there, too, out on the drive, greeting them. A cheerful noisy lot, they sounded. I couldn't meet them, not yet. I made my way round the other side of the house to the kitchen.

Maria was there, already starting on the preparations for dinner. The kitchen, large and old-fashioned, smelt of herbs and onions, and of some aromatic concoction already simmering on the stove-top. Maria was mixing something in a large bowl; she worked with rhythmic sweeping movements, drawing up the smooth golden mixture with her hand and turning it over and over. She looked up and smiled as I came in, and I smiled

82

back. She was a skinny, elderly little woman, dressed invariably in black, even to the long apron she wore, now lightly spattered with flour; she had a craggy olive face and sharp black eyes like a bird's. I liked her, and the sight of her now, standing at the big wooden table peacefully performing a traditional task, was immensely reassuring. She alone, I felt, was exactly what she seemed, and nothing more.

"The signorina wants something?"

"I just want to get back to my room, Maria, without meeting all those people who have just come. Is there some way I can sneak upstairs from here?"

Maria hesitated, looked at me oddly, and then rallied. "But of course. The back stair-way . . ." She left her work, came with me to point out the way with hands covered in dough. "Turn to the left at the top of the stairs. At the end of the passage there is a door; through that you will find yourself in the gallery, above the hall . . . you will know your way from there?"

"I think so. This must seem very strange to you, Maria, but I don't know this house, not any more."

"*Capito*," said Maria gently. Understood. She looked rather sad about it.

I went away, up the stairs, and found my

way, as Maria had directed, into the gallery, which I crept along quietly, so as not to draw the attention of the people below.

Steffy was there, and Roddy. A blonde girl, very young and very pretty; hers was the voice I had heard. Who was she, and why had she come? And another man. Not young, this one, far on in his fifties, I guessed, massively tall, with an upright, soldierly stance. He had a handsome leonine head with a mane of silvery hair, and looked distinguished, possibly famous. I heard him say in the deep, warm voice I had heard before, "Now, Steffy, I won't have you worried. If you're overstretched here, Carole and I can easily go to an hotel . . ."

"Don't be absurd," said Steffy, "you know I love having you. Of course we can manage."

"Well, at least let me take you all out to dinner tonight?"

Steffy shook her head. "It's sweet of you, but Maria will have started dinner; she'd take one of her kitchen knives to me if we weren't going to eat it. Besides, I'm not sure . . . dining in public . . ."

"Oh yes, I see. How is she?"

"It's difficult to say. Very moody . . . it's hard to know what she's going to be like, from day to day. More than a bit paranoid. We had a bit of trouble here last night . . .

84

it would take too long to tell you now. Anyway, she's always been a bit scared of you, you know, so watch your step."

"You're wrong about that. A young tigress, that one. Not scared of me, or anyone."

Steffy sighed. "She's scared now," she said, and added, "I'm glad you've come, Frank."

"Well, we must do what we can," said the man called Frank. "One feels responsible, in a way. And I never did get to see her in hospital, so . . . Oh, by the way, I did call Calvoretti and he said . . ."

He turned away as he said this, or dropped his voice, and I could no longer hear clearly. I went away to my room and sat on the bed and thought about them, down there, talking about me. Calvoretti was the therapist. He and this man Frank — Frank Harmer, he must be the film director — had discussed me on the telephone. It made me feel put down, angry and resentful. Yet what was it Frank had said? *A young tigress, that one.* I didn't feel like a tigress. But if that's how he saw me . . . all right, I thought, I'll show them.

I went to have a shower; turned the tap to "cold", and shut my eyes, and stood there meeting the bracing shock of the icy water. Then I scrubbed myself back into warmth and went back into the bedroom to find myself something splendid to wear.

That was quite fun, in a way, rummaging in the wardrobe for a suitable dress. I was amazed at the amount of clothes I had, and wondered where I had bought them all and how much they had cost; a lot, apparently — I found famous names in some of them. And then, as I pushed the dresses along the rail, I saw, on the floor at the back of the wardrobe, a heap of white material.

I picked it up. It was a long white dress, an evening dress, very crumpled, as if it had been screwed up into a ball and flung down there. I stood there holding the dress in my hands, and as I did this I began to tremble. It was not a reaction of fear, as it had been with the earring. It simply triggered off some shapeless response. I tried to relax, to be receptive. The dress was whispering something to me, but I couldn't hear what it was saying.

I smoothed the dress out as well as I could. It was totally unornamented, simply cut in the Grecian style. On impulse I threw the towel aside and stepped into the dress. It flowed over me, some of the creases smoothed out by the shape of my body. I pulled up the zip and stood looking at myself in a cheval glass. Even though it badly needed pressing, it was still a superb dress, one of those rare garments that have something magical about them. If you were not beautiful such a dress made you feel so.

Yet it had been lying, rejected, crumpled, at the back of the wardrobe.

Why?

The answer came from nowhere, a flash of lightning, a clap of thunder: *you were wearing this dress the night of the party.* It had to be. Just so would any woman have acted after a quarrel with a lover, her evening in ruins. Strip off the dress, bundle it up, throw it down. The beautiful dress in which she had set out, full of happy expectation. The hateful dress.

It all fitted perfectly with what Roddy had told me.

But of course, I realized a moment later, it couldn't be. I had crashed the car. I had been injured and taken to hospital. The dress would surely have been ruined . . . and, anyway, I had never come back here at all . . .

Or had I?

The dress. The earring. The lemon garden. The strong vibrations from all three, two of them at least so frightening. What did all that mean? What could it mean, except that something was terribly wrong, that something had happened, some monstrous unknown thing, here, in this house? My imagination was taking me into strange and terrifying places. But there were some things I hadn't imagined. A blackmail attempt. A frightener in my room. For the rest, nothing except the crippled memory mechanism, touching and flinching from the surfaces of fear.

I was standing there, looking at the dress in the mirror and trying to sort out my chaotic thoughts, when there was a tap on the door; it was Steffy again. "I've been looking for you everywhere —" she began.

Then she stared at me and made a smothered exclamation.

"What's the matter?"

"You can't be going to wear that tonight. It's all crushed . . ."

"It can be pressed," I said. "It's a lovely dress really. I found it in the back of the wardrobe, bundled up on the floor. I wonder why? Am I usually so careless with clothes?"

"Sometimes," Steffy said. "Anyway, you aren't going to dress up, are you? I'm sure nobody else will —"

"I bet the little blonde bird will," I said. "Who is she, by the way?"

"Oh," said Steffy, "you've seen them, then?"

"I was in the gallery," I said. "You said Roddy was coming. I didn't know it was going to be a house party."

"I didn't know either. Frank decided to

come at the last minute. The girl's called Carole Something — she's just come along for the ride."

"Oh yes," I said, "Frank. That's Frank Harmer, isn't it? Is Carole riding with him, or with Roddy?"

"With Frank . . . he's usually got someone like that in tow. You know how it is —" She looked at me nervously. "I was afraid you wouldn't like it," she said.

"Oh, I don't mind. Let them all come if they want to. Tell me something, Steffy. What dress was I wearing, the night of the party? What colour was it?"

"I can't tell you — I wasn't there. I had one of my migraines, I didn't go."

"But I must have got dressed here. And at least, surely, I must have come into your room, to say good-bye and, you know, how do I look? Didn't I?"

"Yes, I think you did, but I had this terrible head and the shutters were closed and it was dark . . . yes, it was a light-coloured dress . . ."

"What happened to it, after the accident? You must have collected my things from the hospital —"

"There was nothing to collect, they had to cut it off you and it was ruined anyway. I expect they put it in the incinerator."

"I see." But I didn't see. Two dresses: the white one bundled up in the back of the wardrobe; the other — another white one? — burned in the hospital incinerator.

"So you never saw it again," I said.

"*No*. I *told* you . . ." Steffy stared at me and burst out, "Jo, what is it?"

"Nothing," I said. "You know, I think I'll wear this dress this evening. Do you think Maria would press it for me?"

"Maria's busy cooking. You've masses of clothes. Why does it have to be that dress?"

"I've taken a fancy to it," I said. "Where's the iron? I'll press this myself."

Against Steffy's protests, I did iron the dress. I brushed my too-short hair into some semblance of shape. I made my eyes enormous with glossy eyeshadow and mascara. I painted my nails. I put the dress on again. I had a little trouble with the zip fastener; it didn't move quite smoothly; a tiny thread was caught in it; and once again I experienced that faint flutter along the nerves: a whisper in the ear, a hand on the elbow: *Listen, listen* . . .

Pressed, the dress was even more beautiful than before; I knew I looked good in it. When I was ready, I remembered the earring.

It still made me sick, to look at it or handle it. But after a short struggle with myself I took it out of the jewel-case and fastened it to the lobe of my left ear. If it meant anything at all, perhaps I should soon learn. Stiff with resolution, I started downstairs.

It was like a stage entrance, coming down those stairs, and I made the most of it. I didn't have to be told that I had done this sort of thing before.

They heard my steps on the bare marble treads and they all turned to look at me, a battery of eyes. I smiled, and paused with my hand on the balustrade, letting them look. I had done this before, too. *Hold it there, Miss Fleming . . . one more please . . . head a little more this way.* Yes, I must have done it before. But this time I had another of those moments of pure terror, shapeless and unfocused; just so must an animal feel, scenting danger. Were they then, all my enemies, these people?

It didn't seem like it, really.

There they all were, five of them, three men, two women. Steffy, looking anxious. The girl, Carole, a trifle beady-eyed — she could see competition coming. Roddy — I had forgotten just how attractive he was — staring at me with kindled male awareness. The big man, Frank Harmer, had a look of unfeigned pleasure and astonishment. Then there was Angelo, just returned, I suppose, from Milan. He looked up at me, too. I met his eyes, gleaming dark eyes, cold and hard as agate. Unsmiling, he looked me over. It seemed to me that he saw and noted everything and understood the significance of it all, the dress, the earring, even, perhaps, the gesture of appearing like that, a gesture of defiance and provocation. *Angelo knew*. But I wasn't going to dwell, just now, on what it might be that Angelo knew. I had an audience to face. I said brightly, "Well, hallo, everyone," and moved down the stairs to join them.

Frank Harmer said, "Joanna! My dear!" He came striding across the floor towards me. I had an impression of giant vitality, of charm turned on like a light: brilliant blue eyes, under bushy grizzled eyebrows, gazed down at me with delight and affection. The next moment he had enveloped me in a bear-hug. I found that hard to take, and had to control an instant wish to struggle free. But it didn't last long, thank goodness. Releasing me from the bear-hug, he held me off to look at me again. "Darling child, you look wonderful!" He turned on his heel to face the room, somehow backstepping so that we were side by side — a neat manoeuvre. "There," he said, with an arm round my shoulders, "doesn't she look wonderful, folks?" He might have created me himself; perhaps, in a way, that's how he saw it: all his own work and now he was showing me off. I saw Angelo's long mouth twist lopsidedly into a cynical grin.

"Now," Frank said, "who out of this lot haven't you met? Ah yes. Carole, come over here and meet Joanna."

He was behaving rather as if Carole had to approach me to be presented, as to royalty, which wasn't exactly going to endear me to her. However, she got up obediently, and loped sulkily over to us, waggling her tight little hips, and held out a limp hand ornamented with long, bright green nails.

"Hallo," she said indifferently. She had a small, piping voice.

I smiled and said "hallo" too. To make sure, I added, "We haven't met before?"

"Didn't you hear Frank?" said Carole. "I've never seen you before in my life. As far as I know." The implication clearly was that she wouldn't have recalled it if she had. She looked at me coolly, and then said, in that little voice, with an air of childlike directness, "Don't you remember *anything,* then?"

"*Carole,*" Frank Harmer said in a tone of

sharp rebuke. I saw a cowering look come into her eyes. But I didn't want to be protected, not like that. I said quickly, keeping the smile on my face, "Not a thing."

"How *peculiar*. Not even Frank? Or Roddy?"

"Not even Frank or Roddy." I glanced up at Frank and added, "I'm sorry."

"That's all right, sweetheart," he said.

"So you see," I went on, speaking to Carole, "I'm especially glad to meet *you*."

Her mouth opened slightly but she didn't speak.

"You see," I went on, "we've never met, so I don't have any sense of obligation. I don't have to consider your feelings, or worry about you at all. It's such a *relief*. I'm grateful to you, I really am."

She stared, flushed and was silent. Frank Harmer burst into a yell of laughter.

"That's my girl," he cried. "Quick on the draw as ever, I see. Now then, you lot," he added genially, "you can all get lost for a little bit, while Joanna and I have a chat. Yes, and I mean you too, Carole. You look a mess. Go and change." He let go of me, spun her round, and sent her on her way with a slap on her small behind. "Go on, now. Split."

Carole, trying to reassemble her dignity,

went away. Angelo shrugged his shoulders and went away too. Steffy murmured something about the dinner and departed in the direction of the kitchen. Only Roddy remained, ignoring Frank's edict. He came over to me and said quietly, "Hallo, my love." He didn't touch me or kiss me, but he didn't need to; his look, alone, was an onslaught on the senses. I must, after all, have been feeling very much better, because I found myself responding; I was, as it were, touched, caressed, penetrated, just by that look. Roddy knew it and smiled, with, it seemed, both tenderness and triumph.

"Your hair's growing," he said. He made this simple remark seem extraordinarily intimate. "And you're wearing earrings. I thought you didn't like them." He peered at me and added, "You know, you've lost one of them already."

My heartbeat began to quicken, but I managed to say, "Oh, have I? I must have dropped it on the stairs somewhere . . ."

I waited for him to say something about the dress; but of course he was not interested in the dress, having mentally taken it off already.

Frank made a sort of hurrumping sound behind him. Roddy said, "I'll talk to you later, love," and went away.

Alone with Frank, I couldn't think of anything to say. The brightness of the day was fading into the rosy-golden light of evening. I looked at it, and thought about the night, and was silent.

"Would you like a drink?" Frank Harmer asked. "Is that allowed?"

"Oh yes . . . I'm not on any drugs now. Thank you."

He fixed the drink and brought it over, sat down beside me, taking out a cheroot and lighting it: the pleasant aroma wafted on the evening air. I stole a look at him. Frank Harmer, film director. He was very much as I had expected from what Roddy and Angelo had told me. I could imagine him at work, bullying, cajoling, frightening the daylights out of people, then suddenly bursting into roars of Homeric laughter. Yes, an intimidating man, when he chose. At the moment he simply sat there peacefully smoking, leaving it all to me.

"It's very kind of you to come," I said at last.

"Not at all. I would have come before, if it had been possible. Couldn't make it until we finished shooting."

"No. No, of course not."

He said gently, "We all want to help you, Joanna. We're all on your side, you know.

96

Of course, wanting to help is not the same as being able to do it. Maybe you can tell us how you need help."

"Yes," I said, "I can. You can start by listening to me. Believing me. I may have lost my memory. I haven't lost my mind. I am *not* suffering from delusions, whatever you may have been told."

"My dear Joanna, I am sure nobody —"

I cut in swiftly, "I'd rather you didn't pretend. I was upstairs in the gallery, when Steffy was talking to you. I heard what she told you. Paranoid, she said."

Frank Harmer shifted his huge bulk on his chair and said softly, "Oh dear, oh dear." He paused, and then added gently, "Joanna, I doubt whether Steffy really knows what the word means, clinically speaking. Look. Because of your condition you're very vulnerable, hyper-sensitive. I am sure that's all Steffy meant."

"I know what she meant. She thinks I imagine things. Cook them up."

"What sort of things?" The recognizable note was there in his voice already: indulgent, patient, jollying me along. I said coldly, "I don't suppose it's much use telling you. You won't believe me either."

He twitched his thick eyebrows and said, "Try me."

"All right. There was this man in Denzano . . ."

As I recounted the conversation it sounded thin and absurd, even to my ears. I got to the end of the story somehow and added crossly, "I suppose now you'll say I imagined it."

"Of course not. But you could have misinterpreted it, couldn't you? Because it doesn't make sense —"

"How would I know?"

"My dear child! Are you suggesting that you've committed some crime, that you're being blackmailed? Your life is an open book —"

"That's what Steffy said. I don't believe it. Nobody's life is an open book. Why are you looking at me like that?"

"I was thinking that was a very shrewd observation."

"From someone with my handicap? You mean, how can I possibly know? Of course, I don't know. It's just instinct —"

"Fairly sound instinct, I'd say. It applies to people who have lived a long life, some of it good, some bad . . . like me, for instance. But I am pushing sixty, Joanna, and you are twenty-three." He smiled. I sensed a deep sadness behind the smile, but it was only later, when Steffy told me more about him, that I understood that sadness.

Frank had arrived in England when only in his teens, friendless, stateless, a Displaced Person as the cold official jargon of the time had it; no more than a piece of driftwood washed up after the storms of war. The Harmer story as the public knew it was a success story, but Steffy said that nobody, even she, one of his oldest friends, knew much about Frank's early experiences. He rarely mentioned them; perhaps, being one of those Angelo had spoken of, with memories he would rather do without . . .

Whatever they were, they had made him very understanding. He said, "Don't look so worried, sweetheart. I don't think you've done anything bad. And you *could* have misread the situation, couldn't you?"

"I could. I didn't misread the situation last night."

"What happened last night?"

I told him. He listened carefully, without comment.

"Angelo and Steffy think I had a nightmare. But it wasn't a nightmare. There *was* somebody there. Somebody who wanted to frighten me."

There was a pause. Then Frank said carefully, "Why do you think anyone would want to frighten you?"

"I don't know . . . you don't believe me, do you? You're being tactful, like everybody else, because you don't want to say outright that I'm deluded. Do you think I wouldn't rather believe it was a delusion? Wouldn't that be easier than knowing this horrible thing is real? Someone out there, somewhere . . . has got it in for me. Is thinking about me. Planning his next move . . ."

Frank said thoughtfully, "It could be your kinky friend in Denzano."

My sense of relief was immediate. "Then you do believe me!"

Frank leaned over and took both my hands in his. He held them firmly and looked deep into my eyes. "Now look, sweetheart. It's not a matter of believing or not believing. It's a puzzle, isn't it? All right. I accept everything happened just as you say and it leaves the whole business wide open. We can't make it a police matter because we've no evidence to offer. You weren't physically attacked, and we've nothing to give them as a motive — except that lovely ladies like you who have got into the public eye sometimes attract some very sick people. So we shall just have to take care of you, until we can find out more. And that, I assure you, will be done. In the meantime, you might get your memory back and then it will all get sorted out anyway. Does that make you feel any better?"

"Yes it does." I tried to smile. "You're being very kind."

"Why wouldn't I be?" said Frank. He gave my hands a last reassuring squeeze and stood up. "I must go and have a shower before dinner. Just remember this, Joanna. We're all behind you. We all love you. Try not to worry, eh?"

"I'll try," I said.

When he had left me I sat on alone in the hall, thinking about what he had said. His promises, really, were empty. We all love you, he had said, in that large easy way people in show-business and the movies talk about love. But who loved me? Roddy, perhaps, but the others? Between Steffy and me lay the great inheritance, from which she might benefit if I did not exist. Angelo . . . I didn't want to think about Angelo. Carole didn't count. Frank . . . well, Frank was a famous and distinguished man who had taken a little time off to be kind to a young actress he had employed for the first time in a film. It was nice of him, certainly, he had been really nice. But he would go back to Rome and forget me.

No. Talking to Frank had been comforting while it lasted. But I knew that there was still nobody on whom I could really rely.

4

As usual that evening we dined out of doors on the terrace. The gnarled old vine above us, with its raggedy bunches of immature grapes, had some lights rigged up in it so that we could see to eat. Like that, we sat in a pool of light, as on a stage set; out there, in the shadows of the garden, was where the audience would be if there were one. My memory, copping out at once when it came to anything remotely personal, could still oblige with general recollection, like knowing what a stage set would be like. There was the set, and round the table were the cast. The only thing was, I didn't know what the play was about, or what character I was supposed to be playing; and I didn't, of course, know my lines.

So. If I didn't know my lines, I had to make them up. The determination to assert myself had been growing in me all day. I had, after all, one great advantage of them all — I didn't remember them; and that meant they were nothing to me; it didn't matter what they said, and what was more important, it didn't matter what I said to them.

I drank quite a lot of wine. Roddy never

took his eyes off me; whenever I looked towards him his hungry gaze leapt at me, eating me up. There's nothing that gives a woman more confidence than having a man look at her with desire. And I made the most of it, held the centre of the stage, being very merry, making a joke of my condition and other people's reactions to it. I was rather like an over-excited child at a party, riding an all-time high brought about by my resolution to take command of things, by the wine, by Roddy, and by a reaction from my terrors.

They didn't know how to deal with it, and that suited me fine. Carole sulked, having the attention taken away from her. Steffy, her eyes anxious, laughed at everything I said and tried to go along with it all. Roddy, his mind wonderfully concentrated, wasn't in the mood to analyse my behaviour. Frank . . . well, I was sure that nothing in this world would surprise Frank; he had seen it all before. He sat there smiling, massively at ease, going along with it too. Only Angelo remained unamused. He sat back in the shadows, smoking and not saying anything much, simply watching me. He was the only person in that company who really made me feel afraid. I wanted to resist that. I felt a wave of recklessness coming over me, a desire to challenge him, anybody.

Steffy gave me an opening. "Jo, I thought you never wore earrings."

"That's what Roddy said. I'm wearing this one — only one, I don't know where the other one is — to see if it would remind anyone."

"Remind anyone? What's it supposed to remind us of?" That was Roddy, sounding bewildered, as well he might.

"I don't know. Anything. I found it in my locker at the hospital. Just the one. It gives me a peculiar feeling. Scary . . ."

Angelo stirred. "I've seen ones like it around," he said. "It's a cheap mass-produced thing. Someone left it behind, I expect."

"I told you," said Steffy, "she doesn't wear earrings."

"No? Well, I just thought I'd wear this tonight. To see if it means anything to anyone else except me. It's like this dress. I'm wearing that for the same reason. I found it at the back of the wardrobe, all crumpled up. It fairly shouts something at me, but I don't know what it's saying. I thought maybe somebody else does."

Nobody said anything. I looked round the circle: Carole's sulky expression had turned to something like triumph. I could read her thoughts, Good lord, she's crackers. Roddy

104

104

was still bewildered; Steffy anxious, and as if about to cry. She was the weak link and I pounced on her.

"I think you know, don't you, Steffy? You were really upset when you saw me in this dress. What's wrong? Why don't you tell me?"

Steffy didn't answer. Angelo did that. He got up from his place at the table and came round to where I was sitting.

He said quietly, "Joanna, you've had too much to drink, and you're over-excited and over-tired. I think you'd be better off in bed, don't you?"

"No," I said, "I don't."

Our eyes met; I was looking up, he was looking down, and I couldn't bear that, so I sprang up, to be more on a level with him. I looked into his cold eyes, I stared him out, the battle joined. Beside me, Roddy had sprung up too. He said angrily, "Leave her alone, can't you? Who asked you to stick your oar in?"

Angelo said coldly, "You don't know what you're talking about. Joanna's not well. She needs rest."

I said quite nicely, "I'm sure you mean well, Angelo. All the same, I'll decide, thank you, when I go to bed. And . . ." some devil in me made me add, "with whom." I looked round the table again, and said, still quite pleasantly, "Well, if you can't help me, you can't. It's such a lovely night. I think I'd like a stroll round the garden. Are you coming, Roddy?"

Angelo was standing right in my path, between me and the terrace steps. "Excuse me," I said; and he stood aside to let me pass. Roddy followed and we left them like that.

As soon as we were out of earshot, Roddy chuckled. "Well, you certainly gave him his come-uppance. I can't stand that arrogant bastard."

I didn't answer. I was suddenly totally sober, suffering from a reaction from the scene at the house, and from my own behaviour which had been both insolent and foolish; but I was deeply grateful to Roddy for his defence of me. He was on my side, he was the one I could talk to. He would believe me, help me sort things out . . .

We were well away from the house now.

Roddy reached out an arm and pulled me into the shadow of the big fig tree. The banked-up fires which had been smouldering all the evening burst out and enveloped me; no, there was no talking to Roddy now, he had other things on his mind. His tongue was in my mouth and he was holding me and caressing me and thrusting against me. I had a moment of bewildered resistance and then I, too, took fire, from the power and urgency of it; but not so much that I was not still aware of the party on the terrace, not fifty yards away, the faint sound of voices, and the light from the house filtering through the leaves of the fig tree; so that when he began to thrust me down towards the ground I muttered, "No, Roddy, not here."

"Oh, Joanna darling . . . it's been so long. Christ, it's been so long . . . Did you mean what you said, back there?"

No, I had not meant what I said. It had been an act of defiance, a foolish, childish gesture, designed to outface them all. At that moment I had been using Roddy, which was cruel and unfair . . .

That was five minutes ago. Now the sheer sexual excitement which he generated took away the power of thought. Now there was only the darkness and the man and his passion — beautiful, old-fashioned word that nobody uses any more. Only not here; I managed to keep that idea, at least, before me.

"Yes," I said. "Yes, I did."

He let out a long breath and relaxed his hold on me. He was more gentle now, tender, kissing me, small butterfly kisses, all over my hair and face and throat. "Well," he said at last, "welcome back, love. What are we going to do? Do you want to be discreet, or what?"

"No," I said. "We'll just go back and say good-night. It's nothing to do with them, anyway."

So we went back, walking with our arms round each other, to the terrace where the rest of them were still sitting like a sort of tableau. As we walked, a small, cold thought came into my mind: *well, anyway, you didn't want to spend this night alone.*

We walked up the terrace steps. I nodded at them all, and smiled, and said pleasantly, "Well, good-night, everybody."

I couldn't help looking at Angelo, who was staring at us both with narrowed eyes. He didn't speak. In fact nobody said anything except Frank, who wished us both good-night. As we walked away, still entwined, towards the stairs, I heard him give a snort of laughter.

Well. It was all right. Not world-stopping, though. I should have let Roddy make love to me under the fig tree; after my gross and public announcement of my intentions, some of the spontaneity had gone, perhaps. But it was all right. Roddy, being now sure of me, was more relaxed and became an accomplished and tender lover; and I . . . I no longer doubted whether I had been here before. I had, and with him; so that there was the ease of familiarity, and, in the aftermath of love, comfort. There was companionableness there, a friendly affection, half joking, half tender. At least I would not lie alone this night, staring into the frightening dark.

I had insisted earlier, against his protests, on shutting the windows; the walls of the old house were thick, but I could not help remembering who occupied the room next to my own, that the windows of that room would be open on the balcony we shared. Later that night Roddy got up and opened the windows again and I didn't stop him. If Angelo could hear our whispers, our laughter, so much the worse for him.

I slept late next morning and woke only when Maria brought my breakfast tray. Roddy was no longer there, which I thought tactful of him. I said a drowsy good-morning and thank you to Maria, and, when she had gone, propped myself on my elbow and poured out my coffee. I was thinking, not of Roddy, but of the dream from which I had woken when Maria came in.

I had dreamed often during the past few weeks, and from most of those dreams I had woken crying out in fear. This time it wasn't like that. This was a good dream, a kindly visitation.

I had dreamed of Nonno. He was there, in my dream, with his Vandyke beard and his bald head with the thick tonsure of grey curls. He was sitting in the high-backed carved chair that was his favourite, in the library of the London house; full of treasures, an Aladdin's cave of glowing rugs, priceless paintings and ornaments. It was all quite clear in the dream, Nonno there in his favourite chair with a Shiraz rug at his feet and behind him the creamy shape, lovely and spirited as when it was made hundreds of years ago, of the T'ang horse which was Nonno's most precious possession, and which as a child I was never allowed to touch.

Nonno. He was getting old and frail; I'd known that for some time. There was a shawl over his knees and his shoulders were thin and bent, but there was still that sharp look about him that frightened people, the eagle gleam in his old black eyes. The old devil: difficult, ruthless. But not to me. He had been both father and mother to me, and I loved him dearly.

In the dream, he was smiling and shaking his head at me. I had done something of which he perhaps disapproved. He was saying something to me, but I couldn't hear. I kept saying, "I can't hear, Nonno, speak louder," but still I couldn't hear; and then quite suddenly he wasn't there any more. The room was still there, but it was empty. The chair was empty.

The dream was so vivid that it seemed to have a life of its own. I groped for the coffee cup and began to drink the coffee; and then, quite suddenly, I realized there were tears running down my cheeks, and I found myself saying out loud, "Nonno's dead, Nonno's dead," and I was weeping, with real grief, for Nonno, whom I had loved and now remembered.

I didn't however, remember anything else. There was the room in the dream, seen in recollection as brightly as a picture, but isolated, like a picture. The frame remained. There was nothing else, no memory of the rest of the house, the street, the servants — I supposed there must have been servants — or my life there.

But none of that mattered for the moment. I had remembered something, someone important. Now I felt something other than fear and anxiety. Love. I knew what love was. Now I knew that a cure was at hand. I had remembered Nonno, the rest would come, and I would know everything.

I got up and showered and dressed and went downstairs. Steffy was with Maria in the kitchen. There seemed to be nobody else about. The men were swimming perhaps, with Carole doubtless showing off her exquisite self in the briefest of bikinis. All that suited me very well, as while I was dressing I had made a plan.

I walked out into the brilliant, silent morning to the drive where Steffy's little car was standing. I hoped I would remember how to drive, and that she had left the key in the ignition.

She had. I slipped into the driving seat, started the car and put it in gear; it all came quite naturally to me, as I had hoped it would. I let the clutch in, accelerated smoothly, and was away.

I was going to the Villa Flora. I had asked Roddy the night before where it was, and he had told me, and said he would take me, some time. But I wanted to go alone. Roddy had said that the owners, the people who had let it to Frank, were back, living in the house. Perhaps if I called on them and explained things, they would let me look round.

I found the Villa quite easily. As with Stephanie's house, one turned off the main road for a short distance, and then came to the gateway and a wall which shielded the property from prying eyes. The gates were closed. I parked the car by the roadside and got out, and strolled over to the gateway to look through it, up at the house. That delighted me because I recognized it. There was the portico, with the columns and the canopy, and the bougainvillaea sprawled over it, a great swatch of burning magenta. Yes, I'd seen this before. And then, disappointed, I had to accept that this was not a true memory. It was the portico in the photograph which Roddy had shown me that first time, in the hospital. That was where I had seen it before.

"Che vuole, signorina?"

I jumped. I had been so absorbed in looking at the house that I hadn't noticed an elderly man who had come down to the gates to open them. I started to explain, but he cut me short.

"The signora can see no one. The *padrone* is dead."

I was completely taken aback. I stammered something about being sorry and not wanting to intrude.

"It was sudden," said the old man. "A heart attack. He is to be buried today. The cortège will be leaving almost immediately, so if you will excuse me, signorina . . ."

I mumbled some more apologies and retreated. I could not turn the car now and get away before the funeral procession passed, for it was already approaching. The hearse with its flower-laden coffin went by slowly, followed by long black cars filled with mourners, the women's faces curtained with black veils. Nobody looked at me or noticed me, absorbed as they were either in grief, or at least in its conventional expression.

When the cars had gone the old man clanged the gates shut. He didn't look at me or speak to me again.

I got back into the car and sat there for a few minutes, resting my arms on the steering wheel and my head on my arms; absurdly, inexplicably, shaken by the sight of that coffin containing the body of a man I had never known.

I drove slowly back to Stephanie's, where I found the whole party standing about in the drive. Evidently there had been a hue and cry going on.

Angelo came over to me: he looked furious. I was hardly out of the car when he shouted, "Where the hell have you been? What do you mean by it, disappearing like that without telling anybody?"

Roddy came up. He said, "Don't talk to her like that."

"I'll talk to her as I bloody well please," said Angelo. The two men glared at each other and it almost seemed they might come to blows. Frank intervened, moved smoothly between them, a hand on the shoulder of each, and said soothingly, "Now, now, boys, don't squabble over the lady."

Angelo shook him off. "Personally," he said, "I couldn't care less if she drowns herself. But Steffy's been frantic."

And, indeed, Steffy did look upset, and my conscience smote me. I went over to her. "Steffy, I'm terribly sorry, I really am. I only went out for a little while; I didn't think I'd be missed. But I shouldn't have taken your car without permission; I'm sorry about that too.

"Oh darling . . . it doesn't matter about the car, except that I wasn't sure you were fit to drive . . ."

Carole said suddenly in her little, indifferent voice, "She thought you'd been kidnapped."

"Kidnapped?"

"Now, Carole," said Frank. His attitude to his current lady seemed rather to be that of a father with a tiresome child.

"Well, that's what she *said*. She really panicked."

"Kidnapped," I repeated again. "Why should I be kidnapped? Oh yes, of course . . ." *The money,* I thought, but I didn't say it aloud. "Well, I wasn't kidnapped, as you see. I've been to the Villa Flora to see if it would help me remember. But I couldn't call on them. There's been a death there."

This simple statement fell like lead into a sudden silence. Then someone, I don't remember who, said, *"A death?"*

"Yes," I said, "a death. What's so odd about that? I was going to call, ask them if I could look round. But the owner's died. A heart attack, they said. The funeral's today — I saw it go by while I was there. It upset me rather. All the same, I've had one bit of luck today. I've remembered Nonno."

"Nonno?"

Frank was doing it now; they all seemed to keep repeating what I had said.

"My grandfather. I've remembered him. I dreamed about him last night. When I woke up I knew it was Nonno in the dream."

Stephanie said gently, "What was he like, Joanna?"

"Well, an old man, of course. Beaky nose, black eyes . . . and he was bald, with a lot of thick, curly, grey hair round the back of the bald patch. He was sitting in a room . . . a library, would it be? . . . with a lot of lovely things in it. There was a Chinese horse on the table behind him."

116

"The T'ang horse," Stephanie nodded. "Yes. That's the place. And that's my father all right. Darling, that's wonderful!"

And she really did seem pleased. They all seemed pleased, except Angelo who said nothing at all. Of course, he was still angry with me for having upset Steffy. That was a simple explanation, too simple. I had no way of telling what went on behind that dark, bony, shuttered face, whether he was enemy or friend, whether, two nights ago, it had been his hand that enmeshed me in a trap of terror. It couldn't go on like this, I had an urge to challenge him, to plunge into the heart of the matter, to clear it up once and for all . . .

The chance to do that came, unexpectedly, just before dinner that evening when I came down to find him alone on the terrace; and at once my urge to confront him seemed like a piece of foolish bravado. I stopped short, muttered some excuse, and turned on my heel.

He said quietly, "Don't go away, Joanna. I want to talk to you."

"What about?" As usual, he had taken the initiative. Then, to my astonishment, he said quite gently, "Are you angry with me?"

"Not in the least," I said smartly. "To use your own delightful phrase, I don't

117

care if you drown yourself."

He grinned ruefully; it was a good act, if it was an act.

"I asked for that, didn't I? I lost my temper I'm afraid. What more can I say than just that I really am sorry about this morning: it was simply that I was concerned for Steffy . . ."

I listened to all this with total distrust. The diffident smile, the apologies, the show of humility was all so totally out of character that it couldn't be real. So why was he doing it?

He was saying, "She really was very upset, you know."

"Yes," I said. "I know, and I'm sorry, and I've told her so. And perhaps, too, I owe you all an apology. About last night. Getting high and cooking up little dramas out of nothing; it all seems very silly in the light of day. Well . . . now we've both apologized, perhaps we could leave the subject, could we?"

"Are we friends again?" he asked.

I looked at him. "From what you've told me, Angelo, I don't think we have ever been that, exactly, have we?"

I don't know what he might have said to that, because I heard steps on the terrace behind me, and there was Frank, genial as ever, interrupting us. Angelo muttered an excuse and went away.

Frank looked at me rather hard and said, "Has that young man been saying something to upset you?"

I opened my mouth to burst out with it all, and stopped. *A bit paranoid,* Steffy had said. If I came out now with another set of possibly baseless suspicions, Frank really would begin to think that an exact description. If he didn't already. I said lightly, "Actually, he was apologizing for shouting at me this morning. Which makes a nice change, really. Angelo and I always have got across each other, or so they say."

"Yes . . . well, that figures. As you probably know, I've known him since he was a youngster. A bit of a difficult customer, in some ways. And I daresay there's a little stockpile of resentment there."

"You mean on account of my grandfather? And the money?"

"Well . . . of course it's none of my business. But Steffy did say something about it, her father's will, I mean."

"But it isn't anything to do with Angelo, you know. Steffy's the one who's affected."

"Of course. But I daresay he figures that at least a bit of a fortune like that would rub off on him, if it were hers. And anyway she's absolutely devoted to him, and she'd have it to leave."

"Yes. But Steffy's been awfully sweet about it all. And of course I'm going to do something about it. Make a settlement, or whatever one does. The way Nonno left things is really quite unjust."

Frank smiled. "A generous child, aren't you? But be careful. Whatever you settle on Steffy would be best tied up in some way. She has no idea of money at all. She made a good deal in movies at one time, and it all trickled through her fingers. She was a sucker for every con man and hard luck story that came her way, and of course plenty did." He spoke with a reminiscent, indulgent affection.

"Yes, I know," I said. "That was the problem, with Nonno of course. He looked on money as a sort of sacred trust, and thought people who didn't know how to look after it shouldn't have any more because they'd only waste it. Not my attitude, I may say, which makes it all the more odd . . . what is it?" For the substance of what I was saying didn't seem to warrant the absolutely riveted attention he was giving me.

"What is it?" I said again. "What did I say?"

He laughed and patted my shoulder. "Don't look so bothered. I was just struck by it —

not about your grandfather's attitudes, I don't mean that. But you were speaking so spontaneously about him — don't you see?"

"Oh, yes, I do. As if I've remembered him, you mean?"

"Well, of course," said Frank, "you did say you had, this morning."

"Not really. I saw him in the dream. But that was just a flash in the pan, a single image. I don't remember anything else, really I don't. What I said just now . . . that's just surmise, from what I've been told; something Steffy said, I expect. It's like seeing the Villa Flora, thinking I remembered it, when all I remembered was the picture Roddy had shown me. The whole thing is a bit like that . . . Separating fact from imagination." I looked very directly at him and added firmly, "And I do know the difference, in spite of what anyone may think."

Frank smiled. "Don't look so fierce. I wouldn't worry too much what anybody thinks. What about Roddy?"

"What about him?" I countered warily.

"Well, you could say, and maybe you will, that this isn't any of my business. But it did seem to me that you were coming to terms with that situation. And that could be a great comfort to you."

"Yes, well . . ." I smiled, faintly embarrassed. "He did suggest that we ought to . . . well, start again. And that's what we've done, I suppose."

"You're not in love with him?"

"Oh, Frank, don't ask me questions like that. How do I know?"

"Then you're not. But that question may resolve itself, one way or another, if you're together for a while. I'm not going to snatch him away, you know. I have to get back tomorrow but he'll be staying on, for a few days at least. You're well enough now to get around a bit, have some fun . . ."

I could not help smiling inwardly at his easy way of directing our plans for us: just Frank's way, from what I had heard about him — dominating every situation, playing God, as usual. So all I said was, "That does sound a nice idea. But I'm sorry you're going so soon."

"Needs must," Frank said. "And, naturally, Carole goes with me, so you won't have to be bothered with her either. So just have a good time, my dear, and don't be bothered by anything — not even those little mysteries that worry you so much. I'm sure they will all turn out to have the most commonplace explanations."

I said again that I was grateful to him for

having come to see me.

He said that was all right, and a pleasure, and added with a twinkle, "Anyway, I have an ulterior motive. You're a valuable property, my child, and we all have to do what we can to get you well and back to work. We — and you — just have to give it time, that's all."

The others began to gather then, and we couldn't talk any more. I was rather silent for a while, among the pre-dinner drinks and chatter; thinking. Give it time, Frank had said. He was right, of course. But how long, I thought, was time?

Angelo left early next day, without saying good-bye to me. I heard his voice and Steffy's outside the house, while I was having my breakfast, and the sound of the car dwindling into the distance as he drove away. Later that morning Frank and Carole also took their departure, not without a lot of fuss and flurry and last-minute hunts for things Carole thought she had left behind. This seemed to be Carole's line: the pretty blonde scatterbrain, helplessly feminine in the old-fashioned manner, lovably absurd. I was not in the least deceived by this, sensing that behind these goings-on was a quite other, shrewd and calculating, lady;

and I wondered whether Frank was deceived, as even very astute men can be deceived in that situation. No fool like an old fool, they say, and I hoped, for Frank's sake, that he didn't seriously care for her.

Frank's leave-taking of me was as warm and affectionate as ever but I wasn't entirely convinced by that either. I must be, I thought, becoming a bit of a bore to Frank. He had made the kindly gestures and promised me help, and would now go away and forget me, for the time being anyway. Carole, if she could, would certainly see to it that he did just that.

Roddy drove them in to Milan where they were going to catch a plane back to Rome, promising he'd be back before lunch. That morning I sat on the terrace in peace and silence, looking at the lake and the mountains wrapped in their milky haze, and awaited his return with a feeling I recognized almost incredulously, as happiness. He was winning me back, as he had said he would. We were beginning again, falling in love again, and for me that was all new and joyful and re-assuring. The stresses of the past few days, even the episode of the Frightener, began to fade into the background, with Roddy filling the front of the picture.

He got back, as he said he would, to a

rather belated lunch, and later, in the drowsy afternoon, when Maria had gone home as she did each day, and Steffy was asleep, we found ourselves alone.

"Nice," said Roddy idly, "to get rid of them all, isn't it?"

"It was kind of Frank to come," I said.

"Yeah . . . but I can't say I wanted him to. I find it a mite oppressive having him around on a social level — as if he's trying to direct what I do, like he does on the set."

I laughed. "Well, he is a very dominating character. It makes me wonder . . . a man like that . . . what he's doing with a girl like Carole."

Roddy shrugged. "She's pretty, sexy, and above all young. Everybody has an Achilles heel of some sort, I suppose, and that's Frank's — pretty, sexy, young ladies. They make him feel young again."

"M'm . . . it's rather sad, really, isn't it?"

"Sad?" Roddy stared at me and grinned. "I wouldn't call it sad. He's got her taped, as he has everything else, you bet. Well, my love, what are we going to do with our little holiday? You're here, and I'm here, and we've got time to ourselves, and we ought to get out and about. Have some fun. You've spent quite enough time mooning around this place —"

I could not help smiling inwardly: what he said was so much an echo of what Frank had said. Did he but know it, Roddy was still being directed, even though Frank had gone. But it didn't matter whose idea it was; they were both right. I was beginning to find the villa and the garden more than a little restrictive. A thought struck me. "Do you know anybody called Kate Castelani?" I asked.

"Sure. Friend of yours. You've remembered her?"

"No, not that. She wrote to me while I was in hospital. I haven't replied, or done anything about her yet. What's she like?"

"Well, I'd have to describe her on two levels. She's both an extremely glamorous bird, and a very nice lady. She lives in Verona, doesn't she? Want me to take you over there?"

"If it can be arranged. There's just one thing . . ." I hesitated. "I don't think she knows anything about — about my trouble. I'd rather leave that till I see her. It might be better that way, don't you think?"

"It's up to you, love. Whatever you think best. You go and give her a ring, eh, and fix something."

"What, now?"

He smiled. "Now's as good a time as any, sweetheart."

I knew he was right about this too. I went into the house and found Kate's number and dialled it.

It was quite easy after all. Directly I heard Kate's voice at the other end of the line, a warm, rounded voice, the kind which never seems far off bursting into a bubbling chuckle, I felt reassured.

I only had to say "Kate?" and she knew my voice, exclaiming instantly, "Joanna! Darling, how lovely to hear from you! How are you? You're really better? That's marvellous. Where are you ringing from? Oh, Steffy's, of course. Well, look, I'd love to see you, shall I drive over one afternoon?"

"Well, actually, Kate, I'd rather like a change of scene. I wondered if I might come and see you. Roddy's here, he could drive me, if you don't mind entertaining him as well . . ."

"Roddy Marchant? That lovely feller? *Do* I mind entertaining him! If I hadn't got Giorgio, and given half a chance, my love, I'd swipe him off you any time. Now when shall we make it? Hang on, I've just had a super idea. You know they're doing opera at the amphitheatre just now? Well, we've got tickets, four tickets actually, for *Il*

Trovatore on Thursday and Luciano Pavarotti's singing . . . we were taking some friends, and one of them's ill and they've cried off. So we could all go. But look, love, if it would be too much for you, just say. Only seeing you're a bit of an opera buff . . ."

Was I? I had no idea. This was something else I was learning about myself.

I said that sounded a lovely idea, but asked her to hold on while I consulted Roddy. Roddy made one of those Italianate gestures he'd picked up, eyes cast to heaven and spreading hands. "It's all the same to me, love. I don't know a thing about it. But if you'd like to go, I'm easy."

And so it was arranged. We would go over in the early evening, to allow time for me to rest and for us all to have dinner before the performance, which, as always in Italy, made a late start. Later Roddy and I decided to make a day of it and take a picnic lunch up into the hills somewhere on the way. That sounded a lovely idea, too.

I was not to know at the time, of course, that the day would hardly turn out in quite the way we had expected.

5

Maria made up a picnic basket for us on Thursday morning — fresh crusty bread, salami, Parma ham, cheese and fruit, and a bottle of white wine in a bucket packed round with ice cubes. I took with me, too, a small bag with a long dress in it, and a pair of evening sandals, to wear to the opera. Steffy saw us off with many injunctions to Roddy to drive slowly and not make me nervous, and we went off giggling about this; as I told Roddy, Steffy, far from practising what she preached, had almost reduced me to a jelly of fright when she had driven me home from the hospital.

"Then you really are scared?" Roddy said.

"I'm afraid so, up to now, anyway."

"We shall crawl," he promised. "We've got all day, anyway." And he really was good about it, though it must have tried him somewhat to creep along the Gardesana at about forty kilometres an hour and put up with the procession of overtaking cars.

It was another beautiful morning; well, in Italy in early June, with very few exceptions, every morning is a beautiful morning. I rode along beside Roddy, the breeze of our passing ruffling my hair, like someone in a dream, or rather, perhaps, like someone in a film. Except that we weren't tearing along as if our lives depended on it, as people always seem to do in films, the whole thing had a film-like quality. There was the rakish, powerful car and the rakish, tanned, attractive man at the wheel, and there was the girl beside him which was me. No doubt we looked the sort of couple which would be the envy of others; young, idle, rich, successful, with nothing on our minds except the pursuit of pleasure and our delight in each other. And it really did seem quite like that to me too. I had, perforce, to put my worries on one side; any hopes I had had of talking to Roddy about them had come to nothing as he wouldn't listen. "Don't think about them," he said cheerfully, "think about me instead." And, I must admit, it wasn't all that difficult to do that . . .

Traffic was heavy, at least in the direction in which we were travelling. After a while Roddy said with mild irritation, "Can't think what's with that chap in the Volvo. I've waved him on half a dozen times but he won't go. There's plenty of room, after all."

"Perhaps he doesn't like driving fast, like me," I said. I looked back through the rear window at the grey Volvo behind us. A couple of other cars, honking irritably, passed him, closed on us, pulled out and went by. The Volvo remained in the same position. The driver, I noticed, was alone in the car, which had an Italian registration number; for some reason, I hadn't the faintest idea what, I made a mental note of it.

"Hate people hanging on my tail," Roddy said. I laughed. "I don't suppose they often get the chance. Don't we turn off here, somewhere?"

"In a minute. We'll lose him then."

"Roddy," I said, "I've been thinking . . ."

He flashed a grin in my direction and said, "You're not supposed to do that."

"Well, I know. But it's just struck me that we're not awfully far from Denzano. If we could, I'd like to call at the hospital."

"Whatever for? I should have thought you'd had enough of that place."

"I want to ask them something . . ." I gave him a quick look and added humbly, "I know it's a bore. But I want to ask them if they remember what I was wearing when I was taken in there."

"What you were wearing? Oh yes. Your thing about the dress."

"I expect it all seems silly to you, but it's important to me to know."

131

"Hang on a minute," Roddy said. He signalled a left-hand turn and pulled out on to the crown of the road, and a stream of traffic, including the Volvo, passed us on our inside right. Roddy drove up the side road a short distance, pulled on to a grassy verge and parked.

"Now look, love," — he sounded patient. "They won't remember, you know."

"You think not?"

"I'm sure not. Jo, it's weeks ago. Besides, they won't understand what you're on about anyway — I'm not even sure that I do. And if you do find out, what good will it do?"

"I don't know. I just think it would help me to know what happened."

"We *know* what happened," Roddy said irritably.

"I'm not sure we do, you see."

A car came by. My attention was caught because it checked its speed as it came level with us. I heard the gear-change and the rising engine note as it picked up again. It was the Volvo I had seen before; as it went away in a cloud of white dust, I once more noted the number. He couldn't have turned when we did, I thought, there was oncoming traffic and Roddy had executed a very swift and smart manoeuvre. He must have turned back after he'd seen us leave the highway . . .

"There's that car," I said. "The one that was following us."

"Following us? You mean the one that was behind us."

"Yes," I said oddly. "I expect that's what I mean."

"*Joanna,*" Roddy said, "are you cooking something up?"

"No . . ."

"Well then. What about this hospital business?"

Sufficient, I thought, unto another day; and I was getting on Roddy's nerves.

"Forget it," I said.

"Good. That's my girl." He leaned over and kissed me lightly, and started the engine. "Come on. We'll go and find somewhere to have this picnic."

From the point where we had turned off the highway the road climbed steeply, the Porsche taking the gradients in its stride. The view on either side of us opened out. We passed a small farm, vines growing on the terraced slope below it: whitewashed buildings, rows of ripening tomatoes, gourds and zucchini, skinny chickens foraging in the yard, tethered goats. Beyond the farm the land was open, too high, too dry and barren for cultivation. Here were a few scrubby trees, the ground covered with thin grass and underbrush, the only sign of life a few sheep scraping a living from the arid pasture. Here and there outcrops of rock were beginning to show. Roddy ran the car off the road and parked once more, and we took the picnic basket and climbed round the shoulder of the hill until we could see the lake once more.

We made our way towards a small clump of trees bent every which way by the prevailing wind; at least, we could get a little shade there. At their foot was a quite broad hollow, scooped, as it were, out of the side of the mountain. There the grass grew thick and lushly green, watered by the dew which gathered in the hollow and protected by the trees' shade. "Just the place," Roddy said.

I looked at it with a puzzling, unplaced feeling of doubt. I couldn't think, what was wrong with it, why we should not spread our rugs and cushions there and eat and sleep, maybe even make love, out of sight of the road with probably not a soul for miles. But, of course, as I couldn't offer any logical explanation I said nothing.

We finished up every last bit of the picnic and drank all the wine, and the wine and the bright noonday combined to make us sleepy. We lay there in our hollow under the trees' shade, my head on Roddy's shoulder, and let time slide by. Insects hummed; once a car roared up the hill, and once we heard the slow clop of hooves and the creaking of cartwheels. A lizard came out on a rock near us, sunned itself and vanished. The sky and the lake and the sunbaked hillside ran together in a shimmering haze.

"Christ!"

I was thrown off violently from Roddy's shoulder as he sat up, clutching his arm. I just saw the small, greyish-yellowish shape with the wavy black band down its back, slithering away.

Now I knew why I had had the feeling of doubt about the lush green hollow. At some unrecalled time, I must have been warned about such places because they are the habitat of snakes. Foolishly, neither of us had given a thought to this common hazard of the Italian countryside. Roddy was greenish-white; he sat there uttering a steady stream of curses, breaking off to ask, "Did you see it? What do we do?"

I reacted it seemed, automatically. *Be calm. Keep him calm.*

I said quietly, "Yes, I saw it. It was a *vipera* — an adder."

"What!"

"It's not all that bad, darling. We just have to get you to hospital as soon as we can —"

"But don't we do something now? A tourniquet, or something?"

"Not for adder bites," I said. I stood up and took hold of his other hand, pulling him to his feet.

"Now hold your arm steady with your other hand, that's it. It ought to be splinted but there's nothing here to do it with —"

"How do you know that this is right?"

"I don't know how I know, Roddy. But I do. Now let's get down to the car. Slowly."

"I can't drive like this —"

"Of course not. I shall. We'll leave these things, we can come back later and pick them up."

He stared at me oddly and said slowly, "You are some lady, Jo, you really are."

"Never mind about that. Come on."

We reached the car and I helped him into the passenger seat, fished for the ignition key in the pocket he indicated, and switched on the ignition. The engine whirred momentarily, coughed and died.

"What have I done?" I exclaimed, dismayed.

"Nothing. You haven't done anything. We're out of petrol."

136

The last straw. We looked at each other; Roddy managed an apologetic grin. "Forgot about it. Filling her up. I'm sorry —"

"Don't be sorry. We've got to think what to do. I shall have to run back to that farm we passed —"

"That was miles back, you don't realize. We'll have to wait for someone to come by. Hang on, isn't that something coming now?"

He was right. Through the limpid air came the sound of a climbing car. I was out in the middle of the road in a flash, ready to flag it down. As soon as it was in sight I began to wave frantically. The car slowed, slid to a halt beside me. A middle-aged man was driving, a woman of about the same age in the seat beside him. Tourists.

The driver leaned out and looked at me enquiringly.

"Please," I said. "Oh, please!"

He said carefully, in heavily accented English, "You have trouble?"

Of course I ought to have thought, but at that moment my capacity for thought was limited. I began, rapidly and in English, to explain. My friend, snake bite, no petrol, hospital . . .

"Wait," said the man. "Please, speak slowly. I do not understand."

I said desperately, *"Parla italiano, signore?*

137

Est-ce que vous parlez français?"

He shook his head. "*Nein, nein.* English only, a little."

The woman in the passenger seat said, "*Was ist's, Karl?*" and he turned and said something and she nodded. The man had a blunt, square face, brick-red with sunburn, below thinning, fairish hair streaked with grey. The woman was plump, with a pink-and-white faded prettiness. . . .

As I looked at them, it happened, another nightmare: *they were two different people.* The two bland faces changed before my eyes as if seen in a hall of distorting mirrors; they expanded, advancing on me, enormous, sinister, inexplicably menacing . . .

The hallucination passed. I suppose it only lasted a few seconds. I got myself together again and there they were, the right size once more, two middle-aged tourists, mildly puzzled, amiable, totally unremarkable.

As I know now, my German isn't very good; I understand it well enough, but I've never been fluent. With an effort I made them understand and anyway, by the time they had got out of the car and seen Roddy, the situation jumped to the eye.

The woman was clucking and exclaiming in a commiserating sort of way. The man turned to me briskly: "We have need of a *notverband, nicht wahr? Moment,* I have it . . ."

I had no idea what a *notverband* was, but he was already scrabbling among the gear in the back of the big station wagon and came up with a piece of wood about eighteen inches long and two handkerchiefs. A splint, of course. With a staggering competence and speed he had Roddy's arm splinted and had helped him into the back seat of the station wagon. "Now," he said to me, "there is need for hurry, yes? We take you both to the hospital. There we leave your friend. Then we buy petrol, and you ride with us back to your car? You drive, Fraülein?"

"Oh yes, I do . . ."

"Also gut. Kommen Sie."

I got in beside Roddy and as we got going the driver said over his shoulder, "You know where is hospital?"

Roddy said, "Denzano will be nearest." His voice was strained, but he was holding up pretty well so far. "Have you a map?"

"Ja, ja. Ein Moment."

He fished in the glove compartment, handed the map to me. The route, thank heavens, was simple and straightforward. Roddy seemed to relax, and slumped against my shoulder.

I hadn't realized that the woman was looking back at us, watching us keenly. She said something quickly which I didn't grasp at first, and then it came to me: "He must not sleep." A vacuum flask appeared. With difficulty, as her husband was taking the mountain road at about eighty miles an hour, she poured some black coffee, handed it to me. "Drink," she said. "He must drink." Her round lined face, flushed with heat under a linen sun-hat, was kindly, concerned. Why had I ever thought it otherwise?

Roddy drank the coffee and I took the cup and handed it back. With effort I found enough words to make a friendly gesture: 'You come from Germany, *meine Frau?*"

"*Ja, aus Düsseldorf* . . . we arrive in Italy only yesterday."

So they were ordinary tourists, nothing more, just arrived, and it was next to impossible that I had ever seen them before.

Maybe it was fortunate that I didn't have much time to think about it, being frantically anxious to get Roddy to hospital as quickly as possible, and equally terrified by the speed with which we were going there. However, we arrived safely, and in no time at all, it seemed, we were racing up the drive to the hospital entrance.

Once in the casualty department, action was swift. I had to go in with Roddy to interpret for him. The doctor questioned me closely. What did the snake look like and how big? More than a metre long? A horn on its head?

"No, no, nothing like that. A wavy black band on the back, but this was more like spots at the top part. And it was little . . . not more than half a metre long . . ."

"Ah," said the doctor with satisfaction. "*Vipera ursini*, the Buonaparte. The least potent of all the *vipere*. You are fortunate, signore."

"What's he saying?" Roddy asked.

I explained. Roddy's look of relief spoke for itself. The doctor laughed, and patted him on the shoulder. "Naturally, in case of error, the treatment is the same as for a more serious case. But this should be a matter of a few hours' discomfort only."

"How long have I got to stay here?" Roddy asked.

A couple of hours or so, they said, for rest and observation. When I had passed this on, Roddy said at once, "You'd better go back and get the car. Get those people to take you. They said they would."

"Yes. All right."

"You're sure you can manage?"

"Of course I can manage," I said, with a confidence I did not feel, and went out to find the two Germans, who had settled themselves placidly in the waiting room, apparently not at all put out by the disorganisation of their plans. They waved my thanks and apologies away: "No, no. It was nothing. All will be well with your friend? Good, good. That only is important. Now, Fraülein, your car. We go to buy petrol, yes, and return?"

I said I wouldn't trouble them; I would hire a car in Denzano and go back in that to the Porsche. But they wouldn't hear of it, and soon we were in their car once more, going back the way we had come.

Now I was alone with them.

As we climbed back along that long, hilly, switchback road, I sat by myself in the back of the car while the German couple chatted placidly in their own language. I had a tight grip on my imagination now, but all the same, riding alone with these two strangers, I was far from being at ease.

The woman turned and said something to me. I thought I understood what she said, but it couldn't be. Her husband said in his halting English, "My wife is saying, she has met with you before."

"Met me? But I'm afraid I —"

"It is not quite right what I say, no? Met with you? She has *seen* you. But you would not have seen her, I think." He chuckled in a cosy way, as if mocking me.

I said hoarsely, because my throat was tightening, "What?"

"On . . . the . . . I do not know the English . . . the *Fernsehapparat.*"

"*Fernsehapparat* . . . oh! Television! You mean the television!"

"Television," he nodded. "Yes. I must remember. Television."

The woman spoke again and he translated. "A costume drama, is that right? You are an actress, yes?"

"Yes. Yes, you're quite right . . ."

They got quite excited then, and said that it was wonderful to meet me. The man interpreted once more for his wife. "The dresses, she says, were very beautiful and you are very beautiful too."

"Oh . . . thank you."

The car slowed, came to a stop.

"It is such a pity," he went on placidly, "that, after all, you have to die."

My blood ran cold.

The woman's face was still turned towards me. She could see my expression, and although she spoke no English she must have caught the drift and was, perhaps, intuitively quicker than he was. *"Karl,"* she murmured, and something else I couldn't catch, and the man said quickly, "I say it not right again, I think. Are you not beheaded? In the play?"

"Oh yes! Yes, of course."

"*Nine Days a Queen,* it was called, I think. My wife says it was very sad and she shed much tears."

"I hope," I said idiotically, "not too much," and burst out laughing and they laughed with me. My laughter, I'm afraid, was a touch hysterical. Then I looked round and there, of course, was Roddy's car.

The man put the petrol in the tank for me. They walked with me to where we had left our picnic gear and helped me carry it back. Then they turned their car and waited to make quite sure I could get the Porsche started. We all shook hands and I thanked them again, and they drove away. It seemed terribly ungrateful, but I was extremely glad to see them go.

I put the Porsche cautiously into gear and started back in the same direction. Driving a car of this calibre for the first time is rather, I imagine, like riding a mettlesome racehorse when you've only been used to a riding-school hack. A touch on the throttle and the Porsche seemed to spring away with me, intent on having its head. I was so absorbed in mastering it that I almost failed to notice the car parked among some trees, half a mile on.

It must have been waiting for me to pass. In the mirror I saw it swing out on to the road and begin to follow me down.

It was the grey Volvo.

Of course, in the tourist season there are, no doubt, thousands of Volvos speeding along the roads of Italy. It didn't have to be the same one. But it was, of course. I knew the registration. It had been there in the trees, hidden. Waiting for me?

It didn't have to mean anything. But I didn't argue with myself about that. I followed my instinct, thanking God for the Porsche and its powerful engine. In some mysterious way fear gave me the confidence to handle the car. I went up through the gears as if I had been driving it for years, put my foot down, and down the zig-zag road I went, like a bat out of hell.

It was a miracle, really, that I wasn't killed. For all I knew I had never driven so fast in such conditions before, and perhaps what saved me was the great car itself and its delicate and responsive steering. Once I took a bend too wide and knew, as I took it, that there would have been no future either for me or for oncoming traffic, if there had been any at that moment. It didn't bear thinking about and I didn't, at the time. But I was lucky. The steep, snaking road came to an end at last; I came out on to level ground and the T-junction which would lead me on to the main highway. Right to Denzano, left to Verona. There was no sign of the Volvo and I relaxed.

A few miles further on I came up with the scene of an accident. It didn't seem to be very serious except to the two cars concerned, one of which, slewed sideways across the carriageway, looked considerably battered. The two drivers, quite unhurt it seemed, stood in the middle of the road having one of those violent and noisy altercations typical of the Italian motoring scene. Drivers in the opposite direction, fingers on their horn buttons, leaned out of their windows and shouted abuse too. The air was filled with klaxons blaring and men yelling. At any other time, I would have found it wildly funny.

Only, of course, one couldn't get by.

A queue of cars formed behind me. A police car, a breakdown van, appeared. The battered car was lifted out of the way, the other manhandled to the side of the road; we were waved on.

I was getting tired and knew that my concentration was flagging. I began to take things more gently. I had lost the Volvo, I was sure, and anyway I was on the home stretch, so to speak.

Several cars pulled out and passed me. After a while I looked in the mirror again and there the Volvo was once more. There could be no mistake. Steadily, relentlessly, keeping the same speed as I did, he came on, following me like the hound of heaven.

I went down the hill into Denzano, which was milling with people as before; they wandered about, crossed the street without looking, stood right in the middle of it, chatting, arguing. I crawled carefully through the square, out of the town, up the hill to the hospital, my eyes seeking the mirror every few seconds.

He was still there.

I reached the hospital gates, turned into the drive, drove round the side of it to the car-park. There were only two spaces left, side by side. I drove into one of them, killed the engine, and got out.

As I did so, the Volvo rolled quietly round the corner, into the car-park, and came neatly to rest in the space beyond mine.

Unhurriedly, the driver got out in his turn, locked his car and turned, though not, it seemed, deliberately, to face me.

I didn't stop to think. I said furiously, "Why are you following me?"

He was wearing dark glasses, but, rather curiously, took them off at that moment, as if to see me better. He was a singularly colourless individual, about thirty-five I should think, wearing the type of standard leisure clothes men wear anywhere in Europe: a patterned shirt, light fawn trousers and jacket. His eyes met mine with a look of indifference mixed with faint surprise.

He said dryly, *"Mi scusi, signorina. Non capito."*

This effectively took the wind out of my sails. Without realizing it I had spoken in English. I said it again, in Italian.

He said, "I don't understand, signorina. I am not following you."

"I don't know why you bother to lie," I said. "You've been following me all day . . ."

He smiled coldly. "I could hardly have done that. While I can well understand the temptation to follow a young lady such as yourself —" he made me a little bow — "I have not done so. I am a very busy man —"

"Then what are you doing here?"

"I am a doctor. I am here to visit a patient. Now, if you will excuse me —" He moved past me, determined, it seemed, to bring this absurd conversation to an end. "Good-day, signorina," he said politely, and walked

148

rapidly away, leaving me staring after him.

I went into the building and asked for Roddy. I was directed to a two-bedded room where I found Roddy resignedly trying to rest. The other occupant, an enormous man with a leg in traction, was enjoying an extremely noisy siesta. He lay on his back, fast asleep, snoring reverberantly. The situation was not, I felt, exactly Roddy's style. If he were ever ill, no doubt that would mean a room in a private clinic, a bevy of nurses anticipating his slightest wish, and altar-pieces of flowers sent in by anxious fans. However, he seemed cheerful enough, looking up with a grin when I put my head round the door.

"You've been quick," he said.

Quick? I was astonished. It seemed like hours to me since I left him, returned to the car with the Germans, fled from the man in the Volvo. Probably the whole thing had not taken longer than forty minutes.

"You managed the car all right?"

"Oh yes, fine . . . How do you feel?"

"All right, really. The arm still hurts, but I'll live. They're going to let me go in an hour or so. Which I shan't be sorry for," he added, nodding at the gargantuan snorer.

"What's the matter with him?"

"Broken leg. Seems a very nice chap when awake — he doesn't speak any English — but

I can't help feeling sorry for his wife, if he's got one. Imagine having to contend with that every night in life!"

We chuckled comfortably. It was so ordinary there, so completely normal, the plain hospital room, Roddy close to me, smiling at me, the snoring man with the broken leg.

"What shall we do about the Castelanis?" I asked. "I don't suppose you feel much like socializing now. And there are those opera seats."

"Well, I don't know. I'm game, if you are. But perhaps you should phone her, anyway."

I said I would do that now, and went out to find a telephone. I recalled, suddenly, my argument with Roddy earlier in the day. We had come to the hospital, after all. Just at that moment a tall figure in the white habit of the Order came round the corner. I looked up into the placid bespectacled face beneath the white coif and exclaimed, "Sister Luisa!"

She peered at me for a moment without recognition. Then her face cleared and she said warmly, "Forgive me, my child. I did not know you for a moment. Alas, it is sometimes so with patients, there are so many, and we only see them when they are ill —"

"Of course. I understand."

"You look very well. That is good. You are quite recovered?"

"Physically, yes, I'm fine. But my memory is not much good, I'm afraid. Just flashes, now and then."

"Oh yes, your memory. It will come. Rest, relax, and trust in the good God . . . but I, too, am forgetting. Why are you here today?"

I explained about Roddy and she clicked her tongue sympathetically.

"We were going to visit friends in Verona this evening and I'm not sure whether we had better go, now. Is there a telephone I can use?"

"Of course, of course. Follow me."

As we walked together down the corridor I remembered the dress, and saw my chance.

"Sister, as I'm here . . . and if you have a moment to spare . . . there's something I'd like to ask you. Something that would help me."

"Why not? That is what we are here for. Here is the office. Come."

In the office a lay sister was sitting typing; Sister Luisa nodded at her and murmured something and the woman got up and went away. Sister Luisa waved me to a chair and sat down herself, settling her hands comfortably in her wide white sleeves. "Now, what can I do for you?"

"There's something I need to know about the night I was brought in here, after the accident. What was I wearing?"

"What were you *wearing?*"

"Please," I said quickly, "I know it sounds unimportant . . . ridiculous, even. It's a long story, too complicated to explain, but it's important that I should know. It's connected with what happened before, you see. Before the accident."

She rested her eyes on my face with a puzzled look. She said slowly, "I fear that would be very difficult. It is many weeks ago, you understand, and in an emergency who would remember such a thing?"

"Somebody might. Whoever was on duty that night? Couldn't you ask them? Please?"

"I have no recollection of who received you," she said. "I should have to consult the duty rota —"

"Then would you? I know I'm being a nuisance, but it means a great deal to me."

"Very well." She sounded, somehow, rather less affable than she had been. I waited while she brought out a large ledger-like book and began to look through it. It seemed a very long time before she said, "Ah, here it is. But I cannot help you, I'm afraid. The sister who was on duty that night has been transferred to another house of our Order in Rome."

"Oh! Then . . . couldn't I go to see her

there and ask her?"

Sister Luisa said drily, "We are an order of nuns, signorina. Members of our Order cannot be approached casually by members of the public. Apart from the fact that the request you want to make is such an odd, indeed a trivial one. However," she added reluctantly, "I will give you the address of the Mother Superior and she can decide. Though without a more adequate explanation —"

"Don't you see," I said desperately, "there isn't any way I can explain properly? Just *because* I have forgotten everything? Things have happened since I left here which make me suspicious about what took place before I had the accident. Other people's accounts of what happened don't add up. I was supposed to have left a house called the Villa Flora after a party, wearing an evening dress. I have reason to believe that I was not wearing that dress when I had the crash. I've found it at home, and it's not torn or blood-stained . . ."

"But how do you know that this was the dress you were wearing? Has anyone confirmed that?"

"No . . ."

"Well, then . . ."

"It was thrown in the back of the wardrobe, crushed, crumpled into a ball, as if I'd been angry. I left the Villa Flora after a quarrel

. . . it's just the sort of thing a woman would do in those circumstances, but I suppose I can't expect you to understand that."

"My dear child," Sister Luisa said, "on the contrary. I was twenty-six years old when I took my vows. I have lived in the world and know very well what it is to go to parties, to dance, even . . ." she smiled . . . "even, yes, to quarrel with a man one likes too well. All of that I understand. What I don't understand is the significance of this to you."

"It's significant only because if I wasn't wearing the dress at the time of the accident, something must have happened in between. I don't remember but I *feel* it . . . a feeling of . . . of evil."

"I see." For the first time I had got through to her. "But surely . . . your friends . . . don't you trust them?"

"They've told me what they know. There may be things they don't know."

"Yes." She was silent. I felt tension winding up in me.

At last she said, "You believe that if you were to know the nature of this evil, it would help you?"

"I suppose so, yes."

"Supposing," said Sister Luisa, "that this is a material matter, external to yourself. You might know the facts — and facts, signorina, are not the same as truth. To know something, and yet still not be able to remember it — how would that help you? What you need and desire most is to recover your memory, am I right?"

"Yes, but —"

"You have a great affliction," she said. "And because you are young and wilful you struggle and rebel against it . . . The forces of darkness are very devious, my child, and the evil of which you speak may exist nowhere but in your own heart. I beg you, don't fight your affliction. Be at peace, watch and pray, wait trustfully for God to lift this burden from you, and all will be well . . . Here is Sister Justina's address in Rome. Now, I will leave you to make your telephone call. May the Holy Spirit go with you and comfort you."

She rose and I rose with her. I felt confused, rebuked, a silly schoolgirl in the headmistress's room. There was nothing to say. She made the sign of the cross over me, and went away.

6

Kate was warmly concerned and sympathetic, but wouldn't hear of us crying off. "From where you are, it's a shorter journey to us than to go home, and you were going to stay over anyway. And don't worry about the opera, we can decide about that later and if Roddy doesn't feel like it, Giorgio can take the tickets back — when Pavarotti's singing there's always a crowd outside trying to get last-minute seats. So just come whenever you're ready, love. You're doing the driving, I suppose? Well, mind how you go, you'll just about be getting into the rush hour."

Did she but know, I had done more scarifying things with that car already today than just drive through the rush hour. When Roddy and I at last left the hospital, I couldn't prevent myself looking at once for the grey Volvo. It wasn't there, of course — a quite different car was parked in the space beside the Porsche. As I drove carefully towards Verona, Roddy beside me with his arm in a sling, I couldn't help looking again and again in the mirror. But the grey Volvo had vanished and I never saw it again.

The house in which the Castelanis had their apartment was lovely, a small palazzo approached from the street through a stone archway, which led into an enclosed paved garden in which a fountain played, and flowers bloomed in baskets hung from the external stone balconies of the upper floors. Kate and Giorgio had most of the ground floor; the rooms were high and cool, and the thick walls muffled the sounds of the Verona traffic, so that they were only a ceaseless murmur, coming, it seemed, from afar.

Kate was not quite what I expected. Her voice and her bubbling chuckle had given me the impression of a small person, rather plump and cuddly. In fact she was in her early thirties, tall, lithe and skinny, with a strong humorous face, a generous mouth, and eyes surrounded already with fine laughter-crinkles. She greeted me with such affection that I felt like an imposter, and I felt this even more so when a small girl burst into the room and threw herself into my arms. "Auntie Jo! Auntie Jo!"

Heavens, I didn't even know what her name was, but I said warmly, "Hallo, there, love," picked her up and hugged her. She giggled, and reached up to run her fingers through my hair. "Your hair does look funny. You've had it cut off. Why have you had your hair cut off?"

"Because I had a cut on the head, and they had to sew it up."

"Where? Where did they sew it up?"

I felt for the scar, and showed her.

"Ouch!" she squealed. "How horrid!"

"Lisa," said Kate, "Auntie Jo's not been well and you mustn't worry her. Get down, now, and behave yourself."

Lisa. Well, that was one problem solved.

Giorgio was not yet home. We sat for a while drinking the long cold drinks which were immediately forthcoming, and I let Roddy do the talking. After a while Kate led us down a long corridor to what seemed like a separate guest suite, two rooms with a bathroom between. In each room was a fresh cotton robe of appropriate size, the kind Italians habitually wear around the house in the heat of the day, or for the siesta. In the bathroom were immense fluffy towels, bath oil, a selection of cosmetics for me, even new toothbrushes, in case, as she said, we had forgotten anything.

"Now," she said briskly, "you've both had rather a fraught sort of day, so have a shower or a sleep or both if you want, and I'll call you when dinner's ready."

When she had left us, Roddy and I looked at each other and grinned.

"A nice lady," I said.

"What did I tell you? Don't know about you, but I'm going to take her advice and have a nap. See you later, love."

It seemed good advice to me, too.

I must have slept for an hour, and woke refreshed, to the sound of voices, a burst of laughter, mingled with music softly played. I got up and showered and put on the long dress and the strappy evening sandals I had brought with me, and combed my hair, which despite Lisa's frank comments, was looking a good deal better than it had.

I went out and down the passage, following the music and the voices: when I reached the living-room door it was only men's voices I could hear, Roddy's and another which I supposed was Giorgio's. I didn't feel quite like facing Giorgio yet, and they hadn't seen me. So I drew back, and began to cast around for the kitchen, locating it at last by the faint clatter made by someone cooking. I opened the door and went in.

The kitchen was beautiful, cheerful and inviting with wood panelling and touches of brilliant yellow. Kate, wrapped in a big white apron over a long dress, was busy at a large hotplate. She heard me, turned and smiled. "Oh, there you are, and don't you look lovely! Did you have a sleep?"

"Yes, thank you. I feel fine. Can I do anything to help?"

"I don't think so, really thanks, but do come and talk to me while I cook . . . look, why don't you just go and say hallo to Giorgio, get him to give you a drink and one for me, and bring them back here?"

There was no way out of that one, so I nodded and went back to the living-room and went in and smiled and held out my hand to a man I didn't know at all: a big, dark man, rather slow-moving, solid and mature. I liked him at once, but it was strange to have him warmly greeting me as an old friend. I managed well enough with the small change of conversation, and Giorgio poured the drinks, and I escaped back to the kitchen again.

Kate, wine bottle in hand, was making a sauce. The most delicious aroma came from it, and I began to feel very hungry. When she turned from the stove and picked up her drink, I took a deep breath, and plunged. "Kate, I've got something to tell you."

It didn't take long.

Kate put her drink down as if afraid of spilling it. She said slowly, as Roddy had done that first time, "Oh, my God."

"I'm terribly sorry. I can't help it."

"Darling, of course you can't, and why should you be sorry? But you said, you've forgotten everybody. Even Roddy?"

"Even Roddy. Of course, we've sort of got together again. Started again. But it's difficult, even with him. Look, Kate, I didn't want anyone else to tell you about my trouble, that's why I've sprung it on you like this. I wanted you to hear it from me, not . . . not coloured by other people's opinions of me, or warnings . . ."

"Warnings?"

"Well, you know the kind of thing, take it gently, she's not quite herself these days, she imagines things. Well, maybe I do, part of the time. But things have happened. Frightening things. I don't know what they mean, except that something's wrong . . ." Saying this, I watched her, waiting for the usual bland look of patient incredulity. But, thank God, it was not there. Kate's expression conveyed only total attention, and a deep concern for me.

At last she said quietly, "When you say something's wrong, you mean that you may be in some sort of danger?"

"I don't know. It's possible. Right now what I need is to talk to somebody who'll really listen and take it seriously, not fob me off with a lot of . . . of flannel."

She grinned. "If that's what you want, love, you've got it. And no flannel, I promise. I don't know about this evening . . . we won't be able to get rid of the men . . . but tomorrow morning, perhaps? We're always up early. Giorgio is generally at the office by eight, and he takes Lisa to nursery school on the way. Roddy can have breakfast in bed and that will give us some time to talk. How would that be?"

"Fine," I said gratefully. "I'm sorry to burden you with it all, but I don't know who else to turn to —"

"Don't be a nit, darling. We've been friends since way back, and what are friends for, after all? But there's just one thing, Joanna — What about Angelo?"

"What about him?" I said drily.

"Oh, I know, I know . . . you don't get on. But if there's any real trouble going, I'd back Angelo against anybody to cope with it. He's the most resourceful man I know. Giorgio and I have a very particular reason to be grateful to him."

I waited.

"The reason," Kate added, "being down that corridor, fast asleep in bed with her teddy-bear, thank God."

I stared at her. "You don't mean . . ."

"Kidnapped," she nodded. "Three years

ago. They snatched her one night when we were out at a concert and a baby-sitter was here, and we got these awful telephone calls, threatening to kill her if we didn't pay or if we went to the police. I don't think either Giorgio or I showed up well under that sort of strain. I was beside myself, and Giorgio — well, you've seen him, he's a strong man, wouldn't you say? He wasn't then. Because it was Lisa, he went to pieces. And then Angelo turned up, quite by chance . . . we didn't try to hide it from him, and he just took over, took hold of the situation. It was a frightful time, but we got Lisa back unharmed and the gang was trapped as well. Don't ask me how it was done; some of it was quite outside the law, I think, so we don't talk about the details. Some of them we never knew, anyway. But I don't think it was exactly kid-glove stuff." She smiled reminiscently. "Angelo . . . a tough cookie, that one. He risked his life for us, but the odd thing is that in a weird sort of way he was enjoying himself . . ."

"Enjoying himself?"

"Oh, don't get me wrong. He was kindness and understanding itself to us, but at the same time I just had this feeling that working out what to do, outwitting the enemy, was an awful kind of fun for him, an outsize challenge. I remember looking at him once, meeting his eyes, and he looked so cold and intent, a sort of God-help-you-if-you-get-in-the-way kind of look. I remember thinking, thank heaven he's on our side."

"Yes," I said, "I can imagine." I did my best to hide my deep disappointment that Kate was not, after all, the uninvolved and trusty friend, mine alone, to whom everything might be confided. In one particular, at least, she was prejudiced. Something of that feeling must have come through in my voice, as she exclaimed, "You don't seem very encouraged. I just meant that there's somebody absolutely reliable and resourceful there, who . . ." She broke off and added, "Oh, dear. It's still that silly business, isn't it?"

"What silly business?" But I was thinking about what she had said. About Angelo's look, which I knew so well. *God help you if you get in my way* . . .

"Well, like I said," said Kate, "you don't get on. I don't believe either of you know what it's about, but I bet I do." She was looking at me with a triumphant sparkle in her eyes.

Matching her light tone I said, "Well, so what is it?"

"It's just a plain case," Kate announced,

"of sexual antagonism."

"Sexual antagonism?" I stared, and burst out laughing. "Oh, Kate, really!"

"All right, all right," said Kate resignedly, "I give up on that one. But it's nice to hear you laugh. I'd better get this dinner dished up. Look Giorgio doesn't know about your trouble, yet, does he? Do you want to tell him, or shall I put him in the picture later?"

I said, "I should think we might let it ride for now, don't you?"

We left it there. Later, I thought, I should have to work out how much more, if anything, I was going to tell either of them.

We dined by candlelight; Kate's cooking fulfilled all its promise; we drank a really good Valpolicella and commiserated with Roddy who was not allowed any. Not that Roddy really seemed to care about the lack of wine, as he clearly had his own source of exhilaration, the reaction from fright. He had never showed fear, except in his shocked pallor, but I knew, and felt a special tenderness towards him as he joked and clowned over his efforts to eat spaghetti with his left hand, which had us all giggling. The feeling of tenderness deepened when he insisted that we kept to our original arrangement and went to the opera. "This is Joanna's first big day out and it's been spoiled for her enough already." He gave me a loving, heart-melting look. "I feel fine, and I'll stay fine so long as nobody bumps into me."

"I suppose," said Kate, "you might be recognized —"

"Oh, I doubt if that would happen here," said Roddy, but I could see he was pleased with her for having thought of it. He had an open, rather child-like vanity which was, somehow, part of his charm. That was the hallmark of his personality, this open directness, all his faults on view as well as his virtues, and I couldn't help mentally contrasting him with Angelo, that most complex and unpredictable of men . . .

With dinner over and still plenty of time to get to the Arena — "We can walk," said Kate. "It's not more than seven minutes away from here" — we lingered at the table with our coffee. Kate and I were having a comfortable feminine chat about clothes, which seemed to me a new and delightful occupation. The men were talking, or rather Giorgio was talking and Roddy listening, about the situation in the country, crime, the police . . .

I became alert suddenly to what he was saying.

166

"Of course they're overstretched, one has to appreciate that. The whole system's breaking down. Bombings, kidnappings, shoot-ups in the street, who's going to have time to investigate even an ordinary murder, if it doesn't look as if it's politically motivated? There's been a lot of fuss about that Lady of the Lake case, but once it's lost its news value I daresay we shan't hear any more of it."

"Giorgio," said Kate, "do we have to talk about all this?"

"Who's the Lady in the Lake?" I asked.

Giorgio said, surprised, "Don't you follow the news, Joanna? It was on television last night. She was picked up almost at your back door."

"Giorgio," said Kate again.

She looked at Roddy, who seemed to pick up an unspoken message and said quickly, "I don't think Joanna's been bothering much lately with what's been happening in the outside world. She's been taking things quietly."

I smiled. "I'm not taking things quietly now. And Giorgio hasn't answered my question."

"I can't do that," Giorgio said. "Nobody knows who she is. Some fishermen picked her up in their nets, the night before last it must have been. The body had been stripped, and she'd been in the water some time, so . . . But there was one very small clue. She was wearing an earring. Just one. I suppose the killer overlooked it. She must have lost the other before she was killed."

"It's an odd thing about that earring," Kate said. "It was a stud earring, they said, the kind which clips on. How many Italian women wear them? You see little girls of six or seven here with sleepers in their ears; they have them pierced young."

"Is it thought, then," I asked carefully, "that she was a foreigner?"

"Oh, not necessarily. She wasn't local so far as anyone knows. It's thought she was murdered somewhere else, brought to the lake and dumped, poor thing."

"How was she killed?"

"Strangled."

"This is an awfully dreary conversation," Kate exclaimed. "And if we're going to this opera, it's time we made a move."

There was a full moon that night. It hung in the sky like a great golden bauble, seeming so close in that clear blue air that you felt you could reach out and touch it. It was the first time, for me, that I had actually walked on a street, and even as I was, surrounded by friends, it was a nerve-tightening experience, especially when

Giorgio guided us into a dark, high-walled alley; a short cut, he said. When we turned into it it was dark and empty, but almost immediately there were footsteps behind us, ringing on the cobbles, and I couldn't stop myself looking back; only to see a quartet of people, two men, two women, the women dressed to kill, bound like us for an evening out. All the same, when we came out into the Piazza Bra', the great open space which surrounds the Arena on two sides, I felt relieved.

Inside, the amphitheatre was already more than half full, a golden bowl of light, open to the night sky. The tiers of seats were rapidly filling up. All around us, as we settled ourselves in our seats, was the buzz of excitement and anticipation; and presently the first burst of applause as the conductor of the orchestra walked in and bowed and took up his baton. The lights in the vast auditorium went down, giving the yellow moon back its pride of place in the sky. There was a great hush as the overture began.

Il Trovatore has arguably the silliest libretto in opera, made all the more nonsensical, I suppose, because most of the action takes place before the opera begins, and goodness knows, all that is absurd enough. Of course, it doesn't matter: the music is the thing. Hackneyed it may be, because so much loved, often repeated, and therefore familiar. Familiar, too, to me. It came to me like the voice of a friend.

The Leonora was slender, young, and beautiful, and sang angelically; Pavarotti . . . well, what is there to say about Pavarotti that has not been said a hundred times already? The two of them, backed by a splendid company, carried me away, took me out of myself as they say, and my fears and anxieties faded as I became wrapped up in the absurd story transmuted by the music into a truly tragic tale of doom-laden and romantic love.

For the first three acts, that is. The third act came to an end. We hadn't moved during the previous intervals, because getting out of the Arena and back again tends to be a slow business. But this time Kate got up decisively: "Giorgio, it's terribly hot in here. Could we go for a drink, do you think?"

Fortunately we were near the gangway and not too far from one of those cavern-like exits. We got out quite quickly into the clearer air of the Piazza. People stood about near the entrance, smoking and chatting; we made our way through them towards the nearest bar.

As we did so, I saw him: the driver of the

grey Volvo. He was talking and laughing with a group of people. I was only a few feet away from him as we went by, and I met his eyes. Well, we had met before that day. On impulse, I acknowledged his presence with a little nod. He stared back at me with a total lack of recognition, and then, rather unflatteringly, did a double-take and made a jerky little bow in my direction.

Roddy said sharply behind me, "Who's that?"

I said without thinking, "The man in the grey Volvo."

Kate said eagerly, "Jo, you've recognized somebody?"

"Not really, I'm afraid. I never saw him before today."

Roddy said, "But we didn't see him . . ."

Giorgio, whose attention was on getting us drinks as quickly as possible, said, "What are you going to have, Joanna?"

"Just *espresso* for me, please." I would really have preferred a cold drink, but I felt I needed that strong black mouthful, a stimulant to get me through this conversation, which I regretted having started.

"We didn't see him," Roddy repeated. "He just went by in the car. Joanna, you're not starting all that again, are you?"

"Starting all what again?"

Kate and Giorgio, I could see, were going to regard this as a private argument. They looked into the middle distance and didn't say anything.

Roddy said, "All that stuff about him following us."

The words and the tone stung me. Was he, too, beginning to look on me as either crazy or childish.

I said coldly, "He *was* following us. Following me, anyway. When I was bringing the car back he was parked a little way along that road, among some trees. As I came by he pulled out and followed me down, right to the hospital, and parked in the space next to mine. So I spoke to him. Asked him why he was following me."

"And what did he say?"

"He said he wasn't. That he was a doctor visiting a patient."

"Which he probably was. That ought to have satisfied you, surely."

"Well, it almost did, at the time. But now, seeing him here . . ."

"Joanna," said Roddy. He looked and sounded as if he were holding hard to patience. "Thousands of people come to this show every night. Probably he lives here, anyway. And how could he have come tonight on your account? The place must have been booked up weeks ago, with this big tenor singing. It's a coincidence, it's got to be."

I looked at the line of worry between Kate's brows and accepted with resignation that Roddy had probably destroyed whatever confidence there had been between her and me. Quite without meaning to, of course.

I got myself together and said firmly, "Yes. I'm sure you're right." I caught her eye and smiled. "Like Roddy says, I imagine things. Don't give it another thought, any of you. Isn't it almost time we went back?"

So we went back, and found our seats again, just in time for the opening of the last act. Love, revenge, sacrifice, and death. Manrico in his prison, the tolling of the bell. Leonora singing her lament outside, backed by the monks' chorus, unseen, chanting the *Miserere,* that well-loved tune, sad and ominous, yet strangely jaunty in its construction, like some sort of medieval dance; and then the tenor's great voice coming from the tower: *"Ah, Che la morte ognora — E tarda nel venir a chi desia a morir . . ."* Ah, how slow is death in coming to him who longs to die . . . A golden parabola of sound that brought the audience to its feet. They clapped madly, they shouted *bravo, bravo, bravo,* so that the opera came, perforce, to a full stop while the jailer absurdly had to let Manrico out of the tower so that he could come and acknowledge the applause . . .

After that, the rest of the opera tends to come rather as an anti-climax, but they had lost me, anyway. The words and the music of that last act had done their work already, opening up the thoughts I had been suppressing all that evening.

On the stage Leonora was singing mellifluously in her death agony, Manrico was dragged off to the scaffold, Azucena triumphantly cheated the stake. Afterwards they would all dash to their dressing-rooms, take their make-up off and retire somewhere to have a well-deserved late supper.

I was thinking about a real death. The woman in the lake, for whom death had not been delayed. Who, one had to suppose, had not, unlike Manrico, desired it. The woman with the earring. I had no doubt whatever that I had its fellow in the jewel-box in my room at Steffy's villa.

The opera came to an end, the principals, magically resuscitated, took their bows, I joined with the others in the tumultuous applause.

On the way home, and later having a nightcap in the big cool living-room of Kate and Giorgio's flat, I made a big effort to be chatty and sociable, to show I hadn't a care in the world. But I was very tired after that eventful day, and soon thankfully admitted to it and retired to bed. Roddy stayed talking with the others. Perhaps they were talking about me; I didn't really care very much if they were.

However, it wasn't very long before Roddy knocked softly at my door and put his head round it. "I thought you might be asleep."

"No, no. Come in, Roddy."

"Are you okay?" he asked.

I said brightly, "Yes, of course. Are *you* okay? How's the arm?"

"Still there. It'll be better by the morning, I should think." He sat down on the bed and took my hand in his. "Joanna, I'm sorry about tonight. I shouldn't have taken you up like that, about the fellow in the car. Not in front of the others."

He spoke with such gentleness that I was totally disarmed, the determination to keep my troubles to myself dissipated. After all, I desperately wanted to share them.

I said eagerly, "Oh, darling, it's all right. You were probably quite right anyway. It's not that that worries me."

"Something does. You've gone broody again, I can tell. Oh, lord, I suppose it's that story Giorgio told us about the woman in the lake. That bloody earring . . ."

I nodded. "You knew about her, didn't you? Before tonight? I wish you'd told me."

"Oh, come on. You can't really think there's any connection?"

"I'm afraid I do," I said.

"Now look here," said Roddy. "Supposing . . . just supposing . . . the earrings matched. There are probably thousands of them. Didn't you hear Angelo say it was a cheap mass-produced thing?"

"Yes. But it isn't, Roddy."

"It isn't? Then why should he say it was?"

"I don't know. Perhaps he just doesn't know anything about jewellery. But it isn't a cheap mass-produced thing, I do know that. It's onyx, set in gold, and there are little diamonds round it. I feel I ought to do something about it. Go to the police with it —"

"The *police?*"

"Isn't that what you're supposed to do, if there's been a crime, and you know something that will help?"

"Oh yes," said Roddy drily, "and what do you know?"

I was silent.

He said forcefully, "You're not thinking straight, love. Supposing the earrings do match, and they are valuable. That will link you with this affair — in the police mind, anyway — and right away they'll ask questions which you won't be able to answer. So then they'll start putting you through it, and you won't be able to help them, and will get horribly upset into the bargain. It could set you back for months, just as you're getting on so well. And how could you be involved? The whole idea's ridiculous."

"Yes," I said. "I suppose you're right."

"That wouldn't be the end of it, either. The press would get on to it and we should have a load of unpleasant publicity on our hands — and it wouldn't be only you who'd be involved in it . . ."

"No, that's true. Well, of course I wouldn't want to make trouble for anyone else."

"You wouldn't be able to avoid it," Roddy said. "And you've nothing to go on, anyway, except that the damned thing's got bad vibes; and that could mean absolutely anything. The very best thing would be to get rid of it, you know. Throw it in the lake, or something."

"Yes. Well, perhaps I will."

"And you won't do anything daft, now, will you, like rushing off to the copper shop with it?"

"No. Really. I promise."

"That's my girl," he said, and leaned over to kiss me lightly. "We've both had a hell of a day one way and another, and my arm's playing up a bit. I think I'll hit the hay, sweetheart. See you in the morning."

"Of course. Good-night, Roddy."

He went away and left me, and I switched off the lamp and lay there in the darkness, listening to a church clock not far away, tolling out the hour; recalling Roddy's vehemence, and still more the look of profound relief in his eyes when I promised to do nothing: like a misprint which destroys the sense, or a false note in a song.

Kate kept her promise and we breakfasted alone next morning. It was still quite cool; we sat drinking our coffee at a table drawn near the windows, open and unshuttered. Beyond them, the courtyard where the fountain plashed was still a deep well of shadow. Kate said she had taken Roddy his breakfast, together with the morning paper, which amused me. "I don't know what he'll make of it. He doesn't read Italian."

"Oh well, he can look at the pictures," said Kate, as if Roddy were a child. She looked relaxed and happy; in the simplest of blue cotton dresses, the colour bright against her tanned skin, she had an unstudied elegance. All around her was her home: nice old pieces of furniture, good pictures, beautiful rugs, all of it combining gracefully with contemporary comfort, everything used and loved and not for show. There was Giorgio at his bank and Lisa at her kindergarten: beloved people and her own; and I felt a sharp twist of envy of them all until I remembered that they, too, had had their fill of anguish, anxiety, and despair.

"Another cup?" she said.

I nodded. "Please." Her eyes met mine: honest, candid eyes. There were not overtones or undertones here, just a friendly affection and a wish to help. Yet even here there was a snag, a bias: Kate's unequivocal respect for Angelo, her gratitude to him.

"Well?" she said gently, pouring out the coffee.

I said with a sigh, "You're going to find all this pretty weird, you know. Especially after that argument I had with Roddy last night . . ."

"Oh, Roddy," said Kate with a grin. "He's a man. Men are always talking about being logical when what they mean is *literal*. Especially when whatever it is, is connected with what goes on in one's head. And if the head is a woman's so much the worse. Look, Jo. I don't think it's likely that you're fantasizing, but even if you are, there's got to be a reason for it."

"Yes," I said gratefully. "That's how it seems to me too. You are a comfort, Kate."

"Well then, spill the beans, my love, and we'll see what we can make of them."

So I did; up to a point, anyway. I would have liked to tell her everything, but inevitably there was a censor at work, selecting, editing the story, eliminating anything which would connect with my unease and suspicion about Angelo. Thus I didn't mention the dress, or my conversation with Sister Luisa. I suppose I wasn't entirely consistent about this either. I had never told anyone before about my feelings about the lemon garden, but about that I spoke, though with an effort, for the first time.

Kate didn't interrupt. She sat quietly, nodding now and again, letting her serene gaze wander sometimes to the fountain and the flowers outside.

"Well, there it is," I ended. "And a proper load of nonsense it must sound, I should think. To anyone hearing it all at once, like this."

Kate shook her head. "No. Puzzling, bewildering, even. But not nonsense. Piecing it together . . . well, that's something else again and I'd be a fool to say I understand it any more than you do." She looked at me gravely. "Look, this is how it seems to me. It's pretty well useless to keep trying

180

to remember or trying to work out what it's all about. What you need to do is to act, darling —"

"You mean, like about the earring? You think I should go to the police?"

"No, not that. I think Roddy's right about that, for the time being anyway. You can't help them, and doing it certainly wouldn't help you. I think you should get some better advice than you've had up to now. Medical advice. No, don't look like that. It's quite obvious that the psychiatrist you saw before was no good for you at all, or else you weren't ready for that sort of treatment. But there's somebody in Rome who *is* really good: Dottore Luciana Fratelli — I'll give you the address. She's lovely — warm and kind and sympathetic and she won't bully you or make you feel small as some of them do. I've been to her and I know."

"*You* have?"

"After Lisa was snatched — when we got her back, I mean — I had a breakdown. A lot of it was guilt, of course. If only I hadn't left her, if only I'd been there, you know the kind of thing. I was really quite sick for a while. Well, of course I know amnesia's different, but I'm sure she can help you too. Apart from going to see her, there's one other thing I'm going to suggest. The lemon garden. Have you ever been in it?"

"No. That is, not to my knowledge. I haven't dared."

"I see. Well, I think you must, Jo. I really do. Even if it frightens you. I don't think for a minute that anything had happened there . . . in Steffy's garden, I mean, is it likely? But there must be some association of ideas there . . . which it might trigger off." She hesitated. "Look, I know it's risky, giving this sort of advice, when one doesn't really know much about it, and of course I don't. But I do know you. You're being very brave about all this, and that's what I'd expect, because you're a strong person . . ."

Without thinking, I blurted, "Angelo says I'm an insufferable little rich bitch. Or used to be, anyway."

Kate stared and burst out laughing. "Oh Joanna! He didn't really say that?"

"He certainly did," I answered rather grimly.

"Darling, he's just putting you on. Of course you aren't an insufferable little rich bitch . . . well, rich I suppose you must be, now. But a bitch? Insufferable?" She looked at me doubtfully. "You didn't take it seriously, did you? He doesn't mean it, you know."

"No. I suppose not."

Kate sighed. "I do wish you two were better friends. He could be an absolute tower of strength to you right now . . ."

"Perhaps. But the fact is that he isn't. Look, Kate, you've been awfully kind and helpful and I am grateful, really I am. But just do me one more favour, will you, and leave off about Angelo? He's somebody else who thinks I'm fantasizing. And please don't discuss me with him, either."

Kate looked grave, even a little upset. "I wouldn't do that. Everything we've talked about today is in confidence, as far as I'm concerned."

"Well, thank you. And I will do as you say — go and see this doctor. I'll go to Rome as soon as I can."

Kate brightened immediately. "Good. That's fine. Roddy could drive you down, couldn't he? If his arm's better?"

"I don't see why not," I said.

Roddy didn't take me to Rome, though he agreed to readily enough when I suggested it on the way home from Verona later that morning. He seemed to be quite recovered, and was very cheerful; he made light of the snake-bite episode to Steffy when we got back, and was warm in his praise of my reaction to an emergency.

We had lunch, Steffy retired to her room as she always did at that hour, and Roddy and I remained for a while on the terrace. Presently the telephone rang. Maria had gone home and I got up to answer it, but Roddy stopped me. "It's probably for me. I'll go."

He was a long time on the telephone. Sitting there alone, I remembered my promise to Kate: to visit the lemon garden.

It was still early afternoon and the sun was striking downwards in a blaze like hammer blows. The day was absolutely still, with no breeze coming from the burnished surface of the lake. I walked across the rusty lawn and through a little shrubbery and into the lemon garden.

Angelo had said that Steffy tried to keep it up, but by the standards of lemon growers it was neglected. Still, who would have wanted it to be like a grove cultivated for commercial purposes, the trees crucified on a wooden frame? In Steffy's lemon garden they grew every which way, not having been pruned or trained for a long time, I guessed. Even so, though nobody could have harvested a saleable crop from them, the boughs bore ripening fruit: small, still streaked with the green of their immaturity, but here and there a pure pale gold, giving off, in the dry brilliant heat, the tang of their inimitable perfume, not the same as the heavy, intoxicating fragrance of the lemon blossoms, but a sharper scent, acrid and sweet at the same time.

I breathed it in, that fragrance, and felt the beginnings of panic. I didn't try to fight it off; if panic was the price of knowledge, so be it. I walked slowly into the middle of the lemon garden and let it take me over. It was as if I were saying to it, *tell me. Tell me your secret, no matter how bad it is. Tell me now* . . . I tried to open all my being to it; to the shape of the trees, the lantern-like glow of the ripening fruit, the hot fragrance, the unmown grass in which a few wild flowers lingered . . .

Yes, it was there, the sense of evil, of an indefinable menace. But nothing more. The lemon garden, silent, sinister, and unyielding in the afternoon sun, kept its secret.

"Joanna! Jo, where are you?"

Roddy's voice. He was coming out to look for me. I walked out of the lemon garden to meet him on the lawn.

"You shouldn't be out here this time of day," said Roddy. "What are you doing, anyway?"

"Just having a wander round," I said lightly. "What's up?"

"That was Kornerup on the phone. Ringing from Stockholm."

"Kornerup?"

"The film director."

"Oh?" Someone important, obviously. I said, smiling, "He's got some wonderful new project and he wants to see you."

"How did you know?"

"I didn't. It jumps to the eye. So what's happening?"

"I've always wanted to work with Kornerup," Roddy said. "He's the best there is."

"Better than Frank?"

"Better than Frank and that's saying something." He looked at me doubtfully. "Darling, I don't want to leave you —"

"But you're going."

"Well . . ." He looked embarrassed, wanted me to release him, I could see, to let him go away with a clear conscience. I fought back a feeling of being let down, deserted. It was his career, after all, and my problems were neither his fault nor his responsibility. I kept the smile on my face and said, "Well, go on then, love. I expect I'll be in Rome by the time you get back and we can get together again there, can't we? I might have sorted myself out by that time. You never know."

"Oh, Joanna," he said, "you're lovely." We were walking back towards the house;

he put his arm round me, dropped a kiss on the corner of my eyebrow.

"When are you leaving?" I asked cheerfully.

"Tomorrow. There's an early flight, nine o'clock."

So he had booked that, already, before he spoke to me. Oh well.

"You'll be all right, won't you? You won't do anything silly?"

"About what?"

"Oh, I don't know. Anything."

The earring, he meant, I suppose. I didn't take it up; this was another thing I didn't intend to talk about any more.

It seemed very quiet at the villa after Roddy left. Steffy and I were now alone there, except for Maria during the day, for the first time since I left the hospital. Well, what of it? Steffy had lived in that house for years, sleeping alone there at night and nothing had happened to her.

With nothing much else to do we watched television that evening. An ancient film creaked its way to its predictable end, and then the news began.

This was unrelievedly depressing. There had been another bombing in Rome. A confused street scene appeared; vehicles on fire, water streaming from firemen's hoses, blasted windows and doorways, police, stretchers, ambulances, most of whatever horror there was hidden from the cameras by the police cordon: just one shattering close-up of a woman being helped away, streaming with blood and staring in a state of shock. Then there was an interview with the Minister of the Interior, looking grave and making an official statement. Then a long piece on the state of the economy; the foreign news, the Middle East, Africa, Europe, a general election going on somewhere; and finally, the local news.

Oddly, the scene before us was now almost exactly the one we saw every time we looked out from the terrace towards the lake. There was the small promontory curving away to the right. There was the village across the water, the shingled roofs, the church, the white hotel. The news reader was reciting some bromide about the woman found in the lake. She had not yet been identified but police were pursuing their enquiries . . .

Stephanie said suddenly, "I think we've had enough of this." She got up and switched off the set, then looked at me doubtfully. "Unless you wanted it, Jo?"

"No," I said. "That's all right. I don't want it."

7

"Rome?" said Steffy, as I had known she would. "Darling, you can't do that."

"Why not?"

"Rome's the last place you should be just now. It's dangerous. These bombs and things . . . you saw that bit on the television last night."

"Oh, Steffy dear! There must be thousands of people going about their business in Rome who've never been within miles of a bomb. You have to take some risks in this life and . . . well, I just need to go to Rome. I'll be all right. There's this flat I took while I was there . . . Roddy told me about that. I've found the papers, and a set of keys; I'm not due to give it up until the end of June."

Steffy frowned; perhaps, I thought, this display of independence made her uneasy. I went on cheerfully, "I've lots of people to see in Rome, Steffy; maybe one or two will jog my memory somehow. And there's the film, too, of course: I'd like to see how it's turned out. They should be able to show me a rough-cut, at least."

Steffy's face cleared a little. "Oh well, if

you must go, you must. I can't stop you. Look," she added, "I could come with you. We could drive down."

I had a mental vision of enduring Steffy's driving all the way to Rome. "I don't want to go by road, Steffy. And it's sweet of you to suggest coming, but I really want to go by myself, if you don't mind."

"Well, how will you go?"

"I haven't really thought . . ."

"You could fly."

"I could . . ." But I didn't want to fly. "I shall go by train," I said.

I packed only one small suitcase to take to Rome: Steffy said she was sure I would have left some clothes in the flat, and anyway, as she also said, I could always buy some. It struck me then how little I was familiar with the mechanics of ordinary living; so far as I knew I had never been in a shop and chosen clothes, handled money, though maybe I didn't do too much of that anyway — I had a wallet full of international credit cards. I had to sort all that out before I left: what papers to take, my passport, my work permit; an address book full of names and telephone numbers I had never heard of; some money, of course. I packed the jewel-case, too, in which the single earring, which might mean so much or nothing at all, was securely locked. I was just about to close my suitcase when I came across the brown wig Steffy had bought me to wear when I left hospital, and put that in too. It might, I thought vaguely, come in useful some time.

The day I left Steffy insisted on driving me to Milan and seeing me off. After a dashing and harrowing performance on her part on the autostrada, we arrived at the station with a more than necessary amount of time to spare. We secured a porter, gave him the number of my reserved seat on the Rome train, and surrendered my case to him. Steffy went away to park the car.

"There's a café just inside," she said. "I'll meet you there."

As one comes into it out of bright sunlight, Milan Central is a dark cavern ringing hollowly with the sound of loudspeaker announcements, the rattle of porters' trolleys, and the rush of feet hurrying from here to there. I found the café and sat down to wait for Steffy.

I ordered coffee and looked around me idly. Then, momentarily, I froze. Some little way from me, sitting alone at a table, was the man who had spoken to me in the café in Denzano, that first day.

At least . . . it was somebody very like him. I couldn't see the scar on his cheek from where I was sitting, but he had the same lean, dark, wolfish look, and it seemed to me that his very pose, his way of sitting and moving, had been imprinted on the retina of my eye that first time, and could never be obliterated.

He glanced towards me. Inevitably, he had dark glasses on. So had I, and the scarf over my hair hid it completely. If it were he, he probably couldn't recognize me. Certainly he didn't seem to. He turned his head after a moment, picked up a newspaper from the seat beside him and began to read it.

The coffee came and with it Steffy, her high heels clacking as she hurried along. She had just sat down when the man leisurely finished his cup of coffee, folded his newspaper, got up, and strolled away. Of course. He was a perfectly innocent citizen, not the same man at all . . .

I didn't say anything about it to Steffy, who was looking at me over her coffee cup and saying sadly, "I wish you wouldn't go."

"I know," I said. "And I'm sorry. You mustn't worry about me, Steffy. I've just got to take hold of things somehow — take hold of life."

"But you need rest —"

"I've had lots of rest. Now, I want some action."

I didn't say what kind of action, because I didn't know, and she didn't ask me. We drank our coffee and went to find my train.

The train wasn't in yet, but the platform was already crowded. Of course, it was almost midsummer, by now, the holiday season getting under way. All around us was a babel of tongues. I heard, quite close to me, a woman's voice speaking in English with a flat Midlands accent: "Bob, are you sure this is the right train?" A masculine mumble answered her and she said fretfully, "Well, why don't you ask, there's a Cook's man just over there."

Stephanie and I exchanged grins. I looked round at the young woman who had spoken and then looked again. Her face was extraordinarily familiar to me; I had an absurd urge to speak to her, to say, *Look, I can't remember your name, but we know each other, don't we?*

Another of my aberrations. It happened all the time.

"We're still too early," Steffy said. "You've got a reservation. We could have strolled along at the very last minute when all this lot had got themselves settled. I don't like your having to stand about like this."

"I'm all right," I said. I felt uncomfortable about Steffy having to stand about; I thought of telling her not to wait to see me off, but knew this would have no effect at all. She was determined to look after me until the last possible moment.

The porter had dumped my bag at the spot where he expected the Pullman would be. Steffy tipped him and he nodded dourly and went away. The crush of people on the platform grew thicker.

The train came in, sliding majestically along the rails beside us; it had hardly come to a halt before the rush began. For some reason a peculiar sort of urgency and panic attacks Italians when they are boarding any kind of public transport, and it was no different that day. The platform, crowded before, became a press of struggling, jostling bodies; suitcases were banged against one's legs, as people pushed forward, crying *'Permesso, permesso'.* They might have been escaping from a fire.

"Oh God," said Steffy, "this crazy country. The best thing is to stand quite still and let them get on with it. That's your coach there. They'll sort themselves out soon."

So we waited, while people were squeezed and propelled into the waiting train. Then, quite suddenly, the crowd recoiled. It was like a wave coming up a beach: it pressed forward and was then irresistibly, it seemed, sucked back again, so that there was a space on the platform near the entrance to the first-class coach.

Almost simultaneously, we heard the scream.

It resounded and echoed up into the high girders of the station roof, a blood-chilling shriek of horror.

I could see now who was screaming. It was a woman standing on the steps of the first-class coach. She was a typical young Milanese matron of the middle class, expensively dressed, with a sulky handsome face which was now greenish white with fear and shock as she stared down at something on the platform; something which lay, silent and still, at her feet.

It was the body of a woman. In the instant before the crowd surged forward again and hid her from my sight, I recognized her by her clothes and the colour of her hair.

It was the English girl with the Midlands accent, the one I had noticed. There was a knife, buried up to the hilt, in her back.

Stephanie had seen her, too. She clutched my arm, so tightly I found a bruise on it afterwards; she was whimpering, "Oh, my God, my God . . . Joanna, don't look, don't look." There were cries all round us: "*Che*

195

succede? Qu'est-ce qu'il y a? What's happened?"

The woman on the steps of the coach was sobbing hysterically. An elegant young man in a pearl-grey city suit lifted her down; she collapsed in his arms and he began to move through the crowd, supporting her, saying in a sharp authoritative voice, "Make way, please, my wife needs air."

"And she isn't the only one, chum," Stephanie muttered. "Are you all right, Jo?"

"Yes," I said. "I'm all right." It had all happened too quickly for me to grasp it properly. "She's dead, isn't she?"

"It looked like it, I'm afraid. But how could it happen like that? In front of all those people?"

"Very easily, signora," said an elderly man standing near us. "In a crowd like this — she would not even fall you see, to begin with, because of the pressure of the people round her. And for someone who knows how . . . a knife between the ribs, it is neat, quick and silent. A gloved hand on the knife . . . the knife stays behind . . . and everyone is too absorbed in fighting their way on to the train to notice what is happening."

"But whoever would want to kill a girl like that?"

The man spread his hands. "I know no

more than you, signora. A revenge killing, perhaps? Who can tell?"

I found my voice. "But it couldn't have been anything like that! She was an English girl, a tourist!"

The man stared at me, his interest sharpening. "Is that so, signorina? You knew her?"

"No, I didn't *know* her. We just happened to pass her on the platform a few minutes ago. Noticed her because . . ."

For a moment I could not go on. *Because she looked like me.* Now I knew what it meant, that strange sense of closeness and familiarity when I looked at her. It was simply that I saw someone who might have been my sister. Not an identical twin, a replica, but like enough; the features, the eyes, the red hair. My throat closed. Neither Stephanie or the man who had spoken to us found anything odd about my long hesitation. We were all upset, finding it difficult to put words together. I said at last, "She was speaking English, you see, and she was grumbling at her husband. It rather amused us, that's all."

Steffy said quickly, "Joanna, you look awful. I think you'd better call this trip off. Don't go today, dear. It will be too much for you."

"I don't think," said our companion drily, "that any of us will go anywhere for the

197

moment, signora. Here come the stretcher party and the officials. And the police." He added in a resigned voice, "This train is going to be very late leaving. If it leaves at all."

The officials and the police arrived none too soon, with the crowd getting out of hand, the air echoing with cries of "Where is the assassin?" and women exploding into hysteria like fireworks. But quite quickly order was restored, people consented to be shepherded, coralled behind a barrier swiftly put in place. Somehow, perhaps because we felt too stunned to move, Steffy and I found ourselves on the edge of the crowd, near the barrier, so we could see everything: the girl on the ground; a doctor kneeling beside her; the young husband, a dazed, helpless figure. Quite soon they took the girl away. As they lifted her on to the stretcher, one of her shoes fell off, a small, wedge-heeled sandal. The husband bent down, mechanically and picked it up; he walked away like a sleep-walker after the stretcher bearing his wife's body, holding the shoe in his hand. A strange sound, like a collective groan, rose from the watching people. I felt a sob rising in my own throat and held on frantically to my self-control.

Steffy said, "Jo, let's go and find your

seat. We can at least sit there for a bit, and find out what's going to happen."

The compartment was empty. Stephanie sat down opposite me. Her customary air of gallant youthfulness had completely disappeared. She looked what she was, a little elderly woman, her skin a greyish parchment colour except where the rouge stood out, like flags of fever, on her cheeks. Her eyes stared haggardly at me. Probably, allowing for the difference in our ages, I looked much the same myself.

"I suppose," she said after a moment, "they'll keep us all here until they've questioned everybody."

"I suppose so."

"It's so *horrible*," Steffy said. "That poor girl — on holiday — who would want to kill a girl like that?"

Nobody, I thought, nobody. It wasn't meant for her. My skin crawled, thinking of the killer who was now walking calmly away from the station, or standing in a bar somewhere having a drink, his assignment accomplished. It must take strong nerves to do a job like that, to thrust the knife neatly and quickly home, knowing exactly where to strike; to stand still, perhaps, while the crowd pushed forward, then extricate yourself; *walk, not run,* down the platform, across the booking-hall to the exit. He would be pleased with himself, this man with the strong nerves and the expert killer's hand, completely callous, thinking of it only as a job completed for which, later, someone would pay him. In notes, of course. Old notes, small denominations.

Unless, of course, they found out first that he had made a mistake.

They. Who were they?

Someone was making an announcement over the tannoy which we didn't catch. We continued to sit there until the door from the corridor slid back and a voice said, "Tickets please, ladies." The man who stood there was not a ticket collector, but a young policeman. Stephanie said, "I'm not travelling."

"In that case, signora, will you be so good as to alight from the train. Persons who are not travelling will be interviewed on the station. For the convenience of passengers, an inspector will travel with the train."

Stephanie said, "That's very unusual, isn't it?"

"The circumstances are unusual, signora. There were a great many people on the platform when this crime was committed, and naturally we must check everyone."

"Of course." Stephanie hesitated. "I suppose . . . she really is dead?"

"Beyond doubt, I'm afraid, signora. Now, if you please . . ."

He stood aside politely for Steffy to leave. She looked at me beseechingly. "Joanna, don't go. Come back with me. Please."

For a moment, I wavered. To go home with Steffy, to sit in the garden, peacefully and safely . . . safely? I was no more safe there than here; and anyway I longed to put as many miles as possible between me and the spot where all the terrors were. "Jo?" said Steffy again.

I said gently, "I've got to go, Steffy; I'll be all right. Truly."

She sighed. "Oh well. If you must." I got up to see her off the train and she hugged me. "Take care. Ring me tonight . . ."

"Of course. And thanks for everything, Steffy."

She got out of the train, and I went and peered over the top of the window in the corridor to have a last word with her. She looked small and lonely standing there. There were only about thirty or so people on the platform now, the exit still barred by police. They stood about, looking self-conscious and at a loss, temporary prisoners as they were.

I said urgently, "Steffy, don't go straight home when you get out of here. Have some lunch, do some shopping, take your mind off all this."

She shrugged her shoulders and grinned up at me. She was saying something I couldn't catch when the train began to move. She was waving good-bye, not as English people wave good-bye, shaking their hands about, but with that charming, typically Italian gesture: the palm turned towards you, the hand opening and shutting like a butterfly wing. I waved back. The platform snaked past us and Steffy was lost to view. I turned back into the compartment.

The elderly man who had spoken to us on the platform was sitting there, in the seat opposite to mine. He sprang up politely as soon as I entered. "We meet again, signorina!" He seemed delighted. "Allow me to present myself, Luigi Paraduca."

I forced a smile and told him my name, which fortunately he had clearly never heard of, and we shook hands.

"A terrible affair," he said, settling himself comfortably. He spoke comfortably too. We were alone in the compartment; some of the other seats had reserved tickets on them, but they hadn't been taken up.

"I wonder where he is now," said Signor Paraduca.

"Who?" I said. Though I knew whom he

meant, of course.

"The assassin. It has just struck me. We assume that he made his escape from the station. But he could just as easily be on the train."

"On the *train?*"

"Why not? Doubtless he would have the necessary tickets, papers, a story to cover his journey. There is no reason to suppose that he looks the part — of a murderer, I mean. And, indeed, how does a murderer look? His only problem, it seems to me, would be to dispose of the gloves."

"The gloves?"

"He would have been wearing gloves, of course. He left the knife behind, did he not? He could not leave fingerprints on the handle. But who would be wearing gloves in this weather? He would have to get rid of them. But that is easily done. A visit to the toilet, the gloves dropped out of the window. If he did his job properly there would be little blood, you see . . . So once that was done, his troubles would be over." Signor Paraduca, who had, it seemed, a rather morbid sense of humour, chuckled. "He could be sitting quite peacefully somewhere. In this very coach, perhaps. A respectable citizen, travelling to Rome on business. *Chi sa?*"

I stared at him in silence, and after a moment he smote his forehead and exclaimed,

"My dear young lady! I am a fool, an idiot! You look quite pale! I read too many detective stories. Forgive me."

"Please," I said, "it's nothing."

But the floodgates of Signor Paraduca's remorse and reassurance were opened and he had to explain to me in detail how there was nothing to fear, even if the killer were on the train his task was done, he was now harmless. "Like a bee," he added with a final flight of fancy.

"A *bee?*"

"When a bee stings, its task is done, the sting is torn out —"

I said drily, "And it dies, surely? I'm afraid we can hardly hope for that, with this gentleman, can we? I think, if you don't mind, I'd rather not talk about it any more."

"Of course, of course! We will dwell on happier things —"

I couldn't very well say that I wished he would keep his mouth shut and not dwell on anything. It was almost a relief when the compartment door slid back and someone else came in.

The newcomer was a little, dumpy, elderly woman. She entered the compartment with some difficulty, as she had a heterogeneous collection of luggage: a suitcase, a large polythene bag stuffed to overflowing, a straw skip tied together with string. She began to lump all these into the compartment, puffing and sighing and making little exclamations in a language totally unknown to me. Signor Paraduca gallantly got up to help her, and it was some while before all the bits and pieces were stowed away and she threw herself back into her corner with a sigh of relief, a beaming smile, and more chatter which was, one had to suppose, expressions of gratitude. I wondered about her a little; she didn't look really like somebody with a first-class ticket, but probably, on this trip, nobody was going to bother whether you travelled first or second so long as you were satisfactorily accounted for. She was an odd-looking little body, wearing a button-through cotton dress, sensible sandals, and on her head on this warm day a woolly knitted cap from which a few wisps of greying hair escaped. She had thick glasses through which she peered with myopic benevolence.

Signor Paraduca, with the typical Italian affability with perfect strangers, made an effort to communicate with her and got nowhere. I think by this time he must have felt the entertainment value of both his travelling companions was nil. He fumbled in his brief-case, drew out one of the *gialli* to which, as he had explained to me, he was addicted, and was soon immersed in it. He didn't read for long. The paperback slipped from his hand, and he was asleep.

I took a mirror from my handbag, and looked at myself. I tucked my hair carefully away under the scarf and replaced my dark glasses: the unintended disguise which had saved my life, and wrecked the lives of two innocent people. The killer, perhaps, was not very bright the — hair would be the thing he would look for. In other ways there was a difference between me and the girl who had been killed, alike though we were: that curiously finished, modish look which is the hallmark of women with an actor's training. People ask you how it's done and it's quite difficult to explain: something to do, I suppose, with the way you hold yourself and wear your clothes. The girl who had been killed wasn't like that. She had looked untidy with travelling, and rather tired. Well, now she would sleep for a long, long time . . . I thought about them, the two of them, starting out on holiday, cheerful and excited; about the bewildered boy with his wife's shoe in his hand; and wept.

I was furtively wiping away a tear which ran down my cheek past the rim of my glasses when I saw that the old woman opposite was watching me behind her own thick pebble-lenses. It seemed to me for a moment, one of those moments either of delusion or illumination — which? — that the eyes behind the big lenses were those of quite another person, shrewd, attentive, aware.

But I was not having that. I would not allow her to become part of my nightmare. I finished wiping my eyes without any pretence and looked at her with a slightly deprecatory smile. She smiled back and was at once as she had seemed before, an innocent, elderly woman, well-meaning, kindly, rather stupid. She shifted along the seat until she could reach over and pat my knee. She pointed back the way we had come and said laboriously, *"Milano . . . Male. Triste."*

Well, bad and sad it certainly was. I nodded. *"Si. Tristissimo."*

That looked like being the extent of our communication. The young policeman I had seen before reappeared and asked for our papers. He had to wake Signor Paraduca up, but nodded at the old lady and said he had already seen hers, thank you. I handed him my passport, wrote down for him my address in Rome; answered his questions carefully, minimally. No, I had seen nothing of the incident itself, just the lady who screamed, and then the girl lying on the ground. Paraduca said much the same. I thought about what I could have said, and stayed silent.

The train rattled on. The compartment was hot and airless and when we stopped in Bologna I longed to get out and stretch my legs on the platform, but my nerve failed me. I felt moderately secure in the compartment with the two elderly people who had both dozed off again after the policeman left us, woken briefly when the train stopped, and relapsed once more into somnolence.

When at long last we pulled out of Bologna I became conscious that I needed to go to the lavatory. I went on sitting there, thinking about it, about the necessity of walking down the train by myself. Paraduca's words rang in my head, *perhaps he is on the train*. On the train, on the train . . .

Yet, what was there, really, to be afraid of? The sting was drawn, as Paraduca had said, the knife left behind, the task done, for all *he* knew; and there were police on the train. It was absurd to be too frightened to answer a call of nature.

I got up and started down the train. The first toilet, at the end of the coach was occupied. I went on through the next, second-class, coach. This was crowded, every available space filled with suitcases and rucksacks. People sat on the luggage in the corridor, stood looking out of the window, smoking, eating, drinking beer or coca-cola out of tins. All around me was talk of the murder — it was in several languages, but the Italians talked the most. In the genial habit of the country they chatted away exhaustively to complete strangers. The talk was cheerful, speculative; the thing now no more than a stimulating talking-point.

I wove my way past them, occasionally tripping over the luggage; *permesso, permesso.* Some of the young men looked at me with an air of appreciation and became alertly civil: *scusi, signorina, venga, venga.* One, less civil, snatched his chance to pinch my rear end as I went by. I tried to ignore it and look dignified. In a way I didn't resent it too much. Outrageous, insulting it might be, but commonplace at least, thus making everything seem more normal.

Then I saw him, the man who had been having coffee on the station.

The man in the seat next to him said something and he turned his head, he nodded and I saw the narrow lips curl back in the wolfish grin I remembered, and the long, thin, white scar on the cheek. I hadn't been wrong, after all. This *was* the same man, the man who had threatened me.

He looked perfectly relaxed, his hands folded in front of him. Long, narrow-fingered, sinewy hands. The hands of a killer?

It sounds from this account as though I had stood still and stared at him, but it wasn't like that. The bewildered thoughts went through my head as I hurried on to the end of the coach where, thank heaven, there was a toilet disengaged. I went into it and shut and bolted the door. At least while I was in this airless little box, already none too clean, nobody could touch me, I was safe.

It seemed to me now that ever since I recovered consciousness after the accident — or, at least, after I found the earring — I had lived in a kind of no-man's-land between the normal and the paranormal. Some of my terrors had been imaginary, but it was like Kate had said: there had to be a reason why I imagined them. I had believed all along that I was in some way threatened, and now I knew that was true. Somebody wished my death. He . . . she? Or they? . . . had made one mistake, which they would soon find out. They'd make sure they didn't make another, and there was no way I could protect myself *unless I knew why*. Knowing why meant remembering. To do that I had to relax, that's what everybody said. Relax, and it will come. Relax, and death would come. Double jeopardy, wasn't that what it was called?

One thing was plain. I couldn't hide myself in this filthy little hole all day. The door handle had been rattled several times. I heard muttered imprecations.

I unbolted the door and walked out.

He was there, waiting for me outside. The train lurched, and I was thrown into his arms.

All natural enough, of course. I lost my balance, he happened to be there and gallantly grabbed me and saved me from falling, that's what it would look like to anyone else. To me it was like falling into a trap, with those sinewy hands gripping my arms, the face with the wolfish grin and the scar close to mine.

He said, "So we meet again, Mees."

I tore myself free and made to pass him, but he blocked the way. "Is it not time for us to have another little talk, Mees? Last time, we were interrupted. But now you are alone, isn't that so? Travelling to Rome? So am I. Isn't that a coincidence?"

I heard a sound behind me. I saw his attention switch from me to whatever was there at my back. I turned to look.

It was the old woman in the woolly cap. She had come out of the other toilet, I suppose, but to me at that moment she seemed to have popped up, rather frighteningly, out of nowhere. She and the man looked at each other, he through his dark glasses, she through her pebble-lenses, almost as impenetrable. Both were smiling. She was on one side of me. He was on the other. She blocked one way, and he the other.

The door at the end of the coach opened and a policeman came through it. The old woman, still smiling, said something like, "Excuse," and made to pass by. She even pushed me a little. The man with the scar glanced round, saw the police uniform approaching, stood back to let the woman pass. I moved quickly in front of her and started back down the train with her following close behind. A steward passed me announcing lunch and I went straight through into the restaurant car.

The rush for lunch hadn't yet started and the restaurant car was empty.

"A table for two, signora?"

I was nonplussed; then I realized that Woolly Cap was still close behind me. The steward was already pulling out a chair at a table for two. I shook my head. "No, I am alone," I said and I firmly made my way to a seat the other side of the gangway. The larger tables for four had seats with high backs to them, and I felt more secure there, on the inside, next to the window. The old woman consented to be placed where the steward wanted, at one of the small tables, where, nevertheless, she could still see me, and I her. Whenever she caught my eye she smiled and made a little bobbing bow. This made me feel both foolish and uneasy, and I steadfastly avoided looking at her after that.

I had been hungry, but since the encounter with the man with the scar my appetite seemed to have disappeared. I ordered an aperitif, some soup. People began to shoulder their way into the restaurant car; the train swayed and rattled and the cutlery rattled with it. A youngish couple and a stout man who seemed to be with them came and sat at my table, the stout man next to me, leaving me little room to move, but providing a welcome bulwark. They all talked French. I pretended not to know any. I didn't want to talk.

The train slid into a station; a voice over a loudspeaker announced mellowly, "Firen-ze . . . Firen-ze . . ."

People began to get off the train, collect their luggage together, mostly handed by helpful fellow-travellers out of the windows.

Soon they were walking past the restaurant car, on their way to the exit. I watched them idly.

Then I saw Signor Paraduca. I thought for a moment he had just got out of the train to stretch his legs, but no; briefcase in one hand, a suitcase in the other, he walked briskly away down the platform. I watched him until he was out of sight, surprised and puzzled. Surely he had said he was going to Rome? At any rate, he had certainly never said a word about Florence. This circumstance bothered me for a little while, but not for long. I had too much else to think about, both what had happened and what was about to happen: an interview with the police. I didn't want to talk to them, but knew, now, that I must. Commonsense, my sense of self-preservation, told me I must. . . .

The inspector was quite young, and rather good-looking. He got up politely when I came in and waved me to the seat opposite him. I sat down and the policeman who had escorted me sat down next to me. Absurdly, I felt trapped — absurdly, because, surely these people were on my side, were my defenders?

"You wished to see me, signorina? You have information for me?"

His voice was curiously light and hard; it went with the rest of him. For an Italian his eyes were unusually light-coloured, a pale cold grey, startlingly impressive in a dark-tanned face. They seemed to look right through me; *don't bother to lie to me, lady, I shall know if you do.*

I said yes, I did have something to tell him. He held out his hand. "Your papers, please."

"But I've already —"

"I know that, signorina. I would still like to see them."

I handed over my passport and he examined it carefully. "Will you oblige me by taking your glasses off signorina? And the scarf you are wearing?"

I took them off. Surely he would see it now, the likeness?

But he merely looked again, back and forth, from me to the passport photograph, and added pleasantly, "You are an actress, signorina?"

"Yes."

"You have been working here in Italy?"

I explained about the film.

"Then you will have a work permit?"

"Oh yes, of course, I'm sorry." I found it and gave it to him.

"I see. Yes. This is all in order. Thank you. Now, what do you have to tell me?"

I took a deep breath. *"Signor Ispettore . . .*

215

I think that the . . . the killing of this young woman may have been a mistake."

"*A mistake?*"

"Yes. I think she was mistaken for me. Killed instead of me. We were very alike. We both have . . . or had . . . red hair."

"How do you know that? That you were alike? Did you know her? Had you seen her before?"

Well, I certainly had his attention now, all of it.

"No, I didn't know her. I saw her on the platform, before she was killed. I noticed her . . . well, I noticed the likeness. To myself. And there was the hair, of course."

"Ah yes, the hair. So, signorina. The murder victim had red hair. You have red hair. So, you conclude, the killing was meant for you, *vero?*"

"Yes . . ." Was he mocking me?

"Have you any reason to believe that anyone wants to kill you?"

"Well . . . not exactly. Look, if I begin at the beginning, will you listen to me?"

"Yes, of course, signorina. But I would ask you to make it brief. I have much work to do."

"Two months ago I had a car accident. After it I suffered complete amnesia . . . loss of memory . . . ."

"Ah, yes. I know what amnesia is, signorina. You have now, I assume, recovered from this malady?"

"No. No I haven't. I still don't remember anything before the accident. But since then, since I came out of hospital, things have happened . . ."

I told him about the man in the Denzano café. I told him about the Frightener. I never got to the woman in the lake, or the earring; before that I was already stumbling over my narrative, conscious of how thin, how absurd it all sounded. At one point I looked up and intercepted, not a wink exactly, but a swift glance of complicity, of understanding, between the inspector and his subordinate. It was also possible, that in someone of my profession they might see it as a publicity-seeking ploy. Either way, my credibility rating was zero.

I broke off and added hopelessly, "You don't believe me, do you?"

The inspector suddenly became quite jovial. He said cheerfully, "Oh, come now, I didn't say that. But your interpretation of these events may be at fault. You say, someone wants to kill you. *Who? Why?*"

"I don't know . . ."

"Exactly. And until you can provide the answers to those two questions, signorina, your theory must remain somewhat . . . if I may say so . . . insubstantial."

"I see. So you won't accept that I may be in danger?"

"Signorina, these days we are all in danger. And especially, I would say, in Rome. Why are you going there?"

I said coldly, "You are doubtless a practical man, *Signore Ispettore,* so you won't understand what I'm talking about. I'm going to Rome to get further medical — or rather, psychiatric — advice. But also to meet people I used to know there, who may help me to remember. When I remember, no doubt I shall know the answer to your two questions. If I'm still alive, that is."

I spoke crisply, saw his face change a little, and he said more gently, "Signorina, if you feel yourself to be in danger here, I would strongly advise you to return to England."

"I can't do that. I may be no safer there than here. And it is here in Italy that the answers are." I stood up, and added, "They may also provide the answers to why this girl was killed today. I don't expect you to accept that. Or to protect me. And I'm sorry to have wasted your time."

He was making notes. He underlined something neatly; looked up at me, his eyes unreadable. He said politely, *"Buona sera, signorina.*" The other policeman stood aside for me; I went back to my seat. I took out one of the magazines I had bought that morning and tried to concentrate on it. At intervals I looked out of the window at the golden countryside switching by.

The road to Rome seemed to go on for ever.

We were late getting in, of course. It was already dark and the Rome terminal ablaze with light. It has been said that the building of this station was the one good thing done in Mussolini's day and I can believe it. So much glass was used in its construction that after dark it resembles a great crystal, with light reflected dazzlingly on all its surfaces. In spite of my fears, I could still look at it with delight.

Porters seemed hard to come by and I lumped my case out of the train and started down the platform carrying it. I looked back once or twice for the man with the scar, but there was no sign of him among the jostling crowd. I trudged on, thinking about what I had to do next. Find a taxi. Give the driver the address. Put my key in the door of a strange flat. A dark, empty flat. Fumble for the light switches. Wander about the rooms, checking the windows and the doors. Go to bed at last and turn the light out and lie there in the dark.

"Signorina Fleming?" A woman's voice spoke beside me. I said mechanically, *"Si, sono io,"* and then checked, turning to look at her. She was young and pretty and gracefully dressed in a skinny dark top and swirling colourful skirt. She smiled and put out a hand. "I am Carlotta Neri. Frank sent me. Welcome to Rome."

A bit bemused, I shook the proffered hand. "Frank sent you?"

She nodded. "He said I was to meet you off the train and see you back to your flat. I've a taxi waiting outside . . ."

"How very kind of him," I said.

"Oh well . . . it is not very pleasant, is it, to arrive after a journey with nobody to meet you and having to do everything yourself? I'll take that, shall I?" She reached for my case and I surrendered it willingly. We walked on together down the platform.

"Did you have a good journey?"

"Yes, quite comfortable, thanks . . ." I couldn't talk about what had happened, not just now. "How is Frank?"

"Frank's fine, he sent his love and said to say he'd see you in a day or two . . . *What is it? What do you want?"*

Her voice had completely changed; it sounded

220

so sharp that for a moment I was bewildered. Then I realized that she was no longer talking to me. She was speaking, heaven help us, to the little woman who had been with me on the train, who must have been waddling along behind, trying to catch us up — who was now trying to wrest my case out of Carlotta's hand. She was talking as rapidly and unintelligibly as ever. Eventually I heard her say, *"Mia, mia . . ."*

I said firmly, "I'm sorry but that really is my case."

"Errore," she said. "Mia." She grabbed at the case again and the two women wrestled with it, both of them getting rather red-faced. People paused, staring; some of them were laughing. I said to Carlotta, "I think you had better leave this to me. This lady was on the train with me. She doesn't speak Italian."

Carlotta let the case go. I put my hand gently on the old woman's arm and smiled at her. "Please," I said placatingly, "I will open it," and followed this with a bit of dumb show indicating what I proposed to do. I got my keys out and waved them at her: *my* keys, *my* case. I opened the case and showed her the label inside, lifted up one or two articles of clothing, clearly not hers. Then a strange thing happened. I heard a voice saying in clear, very precise, English, *"Don't go with her. She's a phoney."*

It was so clear, so real, that I looked round to see who could have spoken; but I could see no one, only Carlotta looking exasperated and the old girl now nodding and smiling and apologizing volubly. I had to suppose that she was apologizing.

Carlotta smiled and shrugged and picked up the case again, just as the crowd was parted by somebody bursting through towards me, shouting.

"Joanna! Joanna!"

It was Angelo. He reached us, towering over us; he looked angry.

"Angelo," I said, "What are you doing here?"

"Meeting you. Steffy phoned me. Where's your case? I'll have that, thanks." He took it out of Carlotta's hand; he didn't look at her again, or speak to her. He spoke only to me. "Come on. I've got my car outside and it's parked where it shouldn't be, so we'd better hurry."

I said doubtfully, "Angelo — this lady very kindly came to meet me. Frank sent her."

"What lady?" said Angelo.

I looked round. The woman called Carlotta had gone, as if she had literally vanished into thin air. The old woman was waddling down the platform in front of us, laden with her bits and pieces of luggage; then she, too, disappeared in the crowd.

Angelo stood there looking down at me. He said grimly, "You *are* a little fool, aren't you?"

8

Rome was noisy, frenetic, traffic-bound, smelling of petrol and diesel oil. Rome was a glittering succession of squares and statues and the palely golden cascades of illuminated fountains, a great city at night, full of romantic promise. Rome was a dark mystery, full of menace, threatening bombs and gun-fire and kidnappings . . .

From one of which, allegedly at least, I had just escaped.

Angelo wove his way efficiently through the heavy evening traffic and for a short time neither of us spoke; the kaleidoscope of Rome passing by, the unravelling of the tangled skein of bewilderment in my mind, took all my attention.

After a while Angelo said drily, "What did she say to you?"

"That woman? I told you — she said Frank had sent her to meet me."

"How did he know you were coming? Did you tell him?"

"No . . ."

"Well, then. What else did she say?"

I tried to remember. "Not very much . . . I asked her how Frank was, and she said

224

he was fine and sent his love and he'd see me in a day or two."

"Frank isn't fine," said Angelo. "He's in a clinic, having treatment . . . Stabilization, I think they call it. He's a diabetic. Didn't you know that?"

"No."

"Perhaps your little friend at the station doesn't either. Not that it would have mattered, of course, if you'd swallowed her story."

"But why?"

An attempted kidnapping, after an attempted murder . . . it didn't make sense. Or did it? I hadn't yet mentioned the murder and I had not forgotten that I didn't trust Angelo. Kidnappings, I thought. I am here with him in his car. He has, so to say, rescued me. A set-up, to establish my confidence in him? There was nothing I could do, now, except to continue to sit beside him while he took me heaven knows where.

"Why what?"

"Why would anyone want to kidnap me?"

"That's a silly question," Angelo said. "It surprises me. You never used to be stupid. You're a rich woman, or have you forgotten?"

"Yes," I said slowly. "I hadn't thought of that."

Then, to my surprise, Angelo reached out and put his hand over mine and said gently,

"Poor Joanna. That affair this morning must have upset you a lot. Steffy was in a terrible state when she telephoned . . ."

"Yes, well, she was, of course, at the time. Everybody was." I added carefully, testing the ground, "It seems such a senseless business. The girl was English, a tourist . . . we'd heard her talking . . . Who would want to kill somebody like that?"

"Who knows?" said Angelo. "One of those terrorist demonstrations, perhaps? We can get anybody, any time, and you can't touch us?"

"Do you think that's really possible?"

"It's possible," said Angelo. "Here we are."

He turned the car into a square and stopped outside a flat-faced, massive building near the corner. I looked up at it: wide steps led to a heavy door of carved wood. It looked blind, enclosed, like a prison.

I got out of the car quickly, and started towards the corner of the square.

The corner was not far away; the name of the square was there. Yes, it was the right one. I walked back to the car, looking up at the house; yes, the number was right.

Angelo was out of the car by now, my case in his hand.

"What's the matter? What are you doing?"

"Just checking," I said.

"For God's sake!"

I looked at him. I said drily, "You told me I was a fool to trust that woman on the station. I'd better get into practice, hadn't I? Not to trust anybody?"

"She was a stranger," said Angelo.

"My dear Angelo," I said, "so far as I'm concerned, so are you."

He nodded and said in a voice as dry as my own, "You have a point there. All right."

I reached for the keys in my bag; as I did so, Angelo took a set of keys from his own pocket and set about opening the street door.

"You've got keys to my flat?"

"Of course I've got keys to the flat. I've been keeping an eye on it for you. Had the place cleaned. Seen that the fridge is filled."

"Oh," I said blankly. "Thank you."

"Well, I'm glad you approve of that, at least."

He opened the door for me to enter: inside was a cold marble entrance hall, totally impersonal; marble stairs led to the upper floors; there was an old-fashioned lift, with a black grille picked out in gold. I stood inside the hall, looking about me.

"Rings no bells?" Angelo said.

I shook my head.

227

"Oh well. Perhaps the flat will." At that moment the lift, called from above, ascended from our sight.

"It's only one floor up," Angelo said. "We can walk."

The flat was quite attractive, furnished in the cool bare style characteristic of city apartments in Italy. I had expected to find it empty and still but it was perfectly plain that someone was in occupation. The lights were on; the unshuttered windows were open, letting in the night air and the hum of the city; music played; there was a faint smell of cooking.

A door, to the kitchen I supposed, opened, and a woman came out.

"Oh, there you are!" she said cheerfully. She was young and pretty, with short blonde hair, rather a big girl, lithe and athletic.

I looked at her, dumbfounded.

"Joanna," said Angelo, "this is Penelope Dean. Penny, this is Joanna."

Penelope exclaimed, "I don't really need an introduction — I've seen and admired you already. From afar, so to speak. Hallo, anyway."

Smiling, she held out her hand to me. I didn't take it; I said coldly, "How do you do." She let her hand fall and blushed painfully.

Angelo said, "I've got Penny to come and

228

look after you, Joanna."

"Look after me?"

"Do the cooking and shopping — all the domestic things. And provide a bit of company too I hope." There was something coaxing in his tone, like somebody talking to a child.

I said, "Excuse me." I went over to the other door in the room and pulled it open.

"Do you want the bathroom?" Angelo asked.

I felt a fool, plunging blindly around the place while they stood there watching me, mocking me, perhaps.

Penny said timidly, "Your bedroom's through there on the left."

I found it and shut the door behind me. I stood in the middle of the room, trembling, shaking rather, eaten up with rage, saying to myself, *How dare he, how dare he!* After a bit there was a knock on the door.

"Joanna." It was Angelo's voice.

"Go to hell," I said.

"Joanna, I want to talk to you. Let me in."

"The door's not locked," I said.

When he came in I didn't look at him. He said flatly, "You're angry with me, aren't you?"

"What do you expect?" I burst out. "This is my apartment — my home, for the time

229

being, anyway. What do you mean by introducing a strange woman into it without even asking me if I want her here? What's she supposed to be — a nurse? A jailer? You've been keeping an eye on the flat and now I'm here she's going to keep an eye on me, is that it?"

"Joanna," said Angelo. He sounded perplexed. "What are you talking about?"

"You know perfectly well what I'm talking about. You had no right to bring her here. To . . . *install* her like that. Without even asking me."

"How could I ask you," said Angelo reasonably, "seeing that I didn't know you were coming until today? Look here, Penny's just a nice young Englishwoman who's working her way round Europe and improving her languages. She was broke and at a loose end, so I grabbed her for you. She's intelligent and tactful and she knows the score. She'll run the flat and act as companion and confidante when you want that. When you don't she'll keep out of your way. All right, perhaps I've jumped the gun, bringing her here before you arrived. But that isn't her fault and she's spent a lot of time cooking us a nice meal. Of course, as you say, this is your place. You can turn her out. Are you sure you

230

want to? Do you want to stay in this flat all by yourself?"

Unerringly, he had found the sore point. To be alone there, at night . . .

I felt myself weakening. I said rather feebly, "I don't know her."

"My dear girl," said Angelo, "as you said yourself you don't know anybody really, do you? But if you're going to relate to people at all, you have to take some of them on trust; those, at least, who have got names and a bit of supplied background. Who don't walk up to you out of the blue on railway stations. All right, perhaps from where you stand there's not a lot of difference. If that's the way you feel I'll walk out of here right now and take Penny with me, and you can have your dinner in state all by yourself. It's up to you."

I had already learned that in argument Angelo was a master in the art of making the other person feel foolish, unreasonable. I was very tired, for the stresses of the day had caught up with me; I didn't want to be alone. It was easier to give way.

I went back into the living-room where Penny, fiddling with the table arrangements, looked forlorn and uncomfortable. She really did seem quite a nice girl. But then, the woman on the station had seemed nice enough . . .

Well, there it was. It was like Angelo said, I had to put my trust in somebody. I went up to Penny who said at once, "Miss Fleming, I feel I should apologize. You must think I'm intruding. If you'd like me to leave —"

"Look," I said, "I'm sorry if I seemed cross. I've had a very trying day and I'm awfully tired. And it's very nice of you to have cooked the dinner. Have I time to have a shower and change first?"

"It'll be ready in about ten minutes," Penny said, brightening.

"Fine. Perhaps Angelo could fix us all some drinks meanwhile. Oh, and by the way," I added with a smile, "my name's Joanna."

I would have been better pleased if I had not caught, out of the corner of my eye, Angelo's benign nod of approval at this last remark; as of a father whose little girl has been naughty and quarrelsome and is now being good once more.

After this inauspicious beginning it was quite a pleasant evening. Angelo opened a bottle of wine. Penny, relieved, I supposed, not to be regarded any longer as an interloper, expanded and became vivacious and quite funny; in the course of her wanderings she had had a lot of experiences, some amusing, some hair-raising. During one of her stories a small cold thought dropped into my mind; she was a bold and capable girl. Physically strong and powerful, too. I recalled Kate's words about Angelo: good to have on your side but God help you if he wasn't . . .

Angelo left quite early, saying he was sure I would want to get a good night's sleep. Unreasonably, as I didn't trust him, I was rather sorry to see him go. Acting the polite hostess, I saw him to the door. Standing in the hall he said, "Take care. And I mean take care, seriously. Those people might try again."

I didn't ask him which people.

"Talk to Penny about it. Get her to answer your telephone and the door . . ."

"That's all very fine," I said drily. "You don't suppose I'm going to stay in the flat all the time, surely? Turn it into a fortress?"

"No, not that. When you go out, take Penny with you. Don't take taxis. Get yourself a car and a chauffeur — you can afford it. I can fix that if you like."

I did not want Angelo fixing anything else for me, but I nodded and said, "That's all right. I can get the studio to do it. And as for not going out alone — I've come here to try to recover my memory. I shan't do that by wrapping myself up in a cocoon. It's like you said — I have to take some risks."

"That's not what I said," said Angelo; but he didn't enlarge on it, and went away.

Penny was in the kitchen washing the dishes when I returned from seeing Angelo off. I leaned against the doorpost, looking at her back as she stood at the sink — a long, strong back. Her brown arms, I noticed, were muscled. I stared at them, wondering who or what she really was.

She became aware of me after a moment, turning with her bright, rather too ingratiating, smile. "Can I get you anything?" she asked. "A nightcap, perhaps? Some milk?"

"Penny," I said . . . I advanced further into the room and looked at her very directly . . . "if you're going to stay here with me I think we'd better understand each other. Let's get it straight — I am not an invalid. I don't have to be eased off to bed with cups of milk. I've just got a problem that nobody can solve except me, and that's what I've come to Rome to try to do."

"Yes, of course," said Penny. "I do understand. I'm sorry if I did the wrong thing just now. I will try not to . . ." She looked at her hands, covered with detergent bubbles. "And if, you know, you want to talk about things . . . if it would help . . . well, I hope you'll remember I'm around."

I couldn't really see myself confiding in Penny, but I said, "Yes. Thank you. Perhaps I will some time."

I locked my door that night, quietly, so that Penny wouldn't hear. As might have been expected, I didn't sleep very well. A mosquito zoomed about the room for a while, and I switched on the light and got up to swat it, and lay down again, stiffly braced, as it were, against the realities of my situation: which were that if I were to stay alive, I had to do more than try to remember. I had to find out what was going on. I realized, as I lay there sleepless, what a fool I had been to run from the man with the scar. Unpleasant, sinister character he might be, almost certainly a crook; but he didn't want to kill me. Intimidation, blackmail, rather than murder, seemed to be the name of his game. That meant he *knew*, knew what? Something about me — something bad? I didn't care about that any more. However bad it was, knowing it had to be better than being dead.

Exhausted, I must have slept at last, but I woke quite early, stiff and aching with the tensions with which I had gone to bed. The warm sunlight filtered through the shutters;

the flat seemed very quiet. I got up and wrapped a robe round me and carefully unlocked the door and made my way to the bathroom. I passed the open door to the second bedroom: the unmade bed was empty. I couldn't hear movement anywhere in the flat, but I spoke her name aloud to make sure: "Penny?"

No answer. She must have gone out. I went into the bathroom which was large and luxurious, with a big window overlooking a side street. The shutters were pulled back and I could see the street, bright with the coloured awnings of market stalls. It was all cheerful, colourful and busy — Rome housewives do their shopping early, before the heat of the day. I could hear traffic noises and the sounds of stallholders calling their wares. The air was still cool and fresh and the sun shone down like a benediction. For a moment, standing by the open window, I forgot my terrors. This was Rome in the summer time, *il bel stagione,* the beautiful season as the Italians so gracefully call it. I was young, I had money, I could do anything I chose . . . For a moment, I was light of heart, and then, only too quickly, the shadows closed in again.

I thought longingly of a bath, and decided to defer it. I was alone there and so had the opportunity to . . . well, look around, find out . . .

I went back and stood in the doorway of Penny's room. It was untidy, the dressing-table a jumble of cosmetics: yesterday's underwear sprawled on a chair, shoes lay as if kicked off.

I had never, so far as I knew, searched anyone's room before. I was not sure, even, how it was done, I certainly didn't know what I was looking for, and I was scared she would come in and catch me at it. I looked around first of all for papers, photographs, letters . . . not, I told myself that I would have read her letters, it was all just to give me an idea of what sort of person she was. Then I realized that of course she would have her handbag with her and the personal documents would be in it. So that was no good. Irresolutely, I opened the drawers of the dressing chest. There wasn't much in them, clearly Penny travelled light. Bras, briefs, unopened packets of tights, T-shirts, sleeveless cotton tops, and that was about all. I was going to shut the second drawer again, when my eye was caught by something, a mere glimpse, something hard and shiny. I put out my hand, very gently, and lifted the various scanty nylon garments that lay on top of whatever it was.

A gun.

I stared at it. I knew nothing about guns. I supposed it was a revolver. It was small, small enough to be put in a woman's handbag. It lay there, gleaming malevolently at me.

I dropped the clothes carefully back over it. I shut the drawer very gently, as if the slightest vibration might make it go off.

I didn't really want or need to see anything else in Penny's room. I looked around quickly and it certainly didn't look as if I had disturbed anything. I felt I needed a strong cup of coffee and went to the kitchen to make some.

Penny had evidently done some of the shopping. The kitchen table was covered with groceries, vegetables and fruit, but no bread. She must have forgotten the bread and gone back for it. I got the coffee started. Jumpy and restless, needing something to do, I began to put the food away, or rather, to try to find the places where it went. There was some green stuff wrapped in an old newspaper. As I picked it up a headline caught my eye. *"Lago di Garda — Elena Menotti found dead."* I put the salad down on the table and unfolded the newspaper carefully.

It was the front and back page of the Rome paper *Il Messaggio,* about four days old, the second lead story:

The body found in Lake Garda has been identified as that of our own Elena Menotti, a member of the staff of this newspaper. Anxiety has been growing about Signora Menotti who has been missing for some weeks after her failure to return to duty after her vacation . . . Signor Bernardo Menotti, her husband, from whom she had been living apart for some time, identified the body after his return from a business trip to the Far East yesterday . . .

Identification had been difficult owing to the ravages caused by immersion, and one of the curious features of the murder is that Signora Menotti's killers, who apparently robbed her of everything else, failed to notice the very distinctive earrings which she wore, one of which was still attached to her body. This earring, of onyx and diamonds, was one of a pair specially made and given to her by her husband as an anniversary present some years ago . . . Unusually, Signora Menotti had never had her ears pierced and the earrings were of the stud or clip-on type. It was the earring which caused Signor Menotti to believe that this was the body of his wife, and a comparison with dental records had since confirmed the identification.

The police are pursuing their enquiries.

The story continued on the rear page. Appended to it was a rather florid obituary, and an announcement of a memorial Mass to be held at the Church of St Michael of the Angels. Date and time were given: a Thursday, I worked it out: tomorrow.

I turned back to page one, remembering that the report had been accompanied by a photograph.

Elena Menotti looked out of the page at me with a wistful smile. Not young, in her late forties perhaps. An attractive, large-eyed face, rather worn, with the remnants of beauty. If I had known her, I thought, I would have liked her, been drawn towards her.

I didn't know her.

But I must have done. I had her earring . . . custom-made, valuable. Onyx and diamonds. The description was exact. It was in the jewel-box in my room.

I heard the front door open, Penny's footsteps. I folded the paper as quickly as I could and thrust it into the pocket of the robe I was wearing.

Penny carried a loaf, rolls, a handful of today's newspapers.

"Oh, you're up!" she exclaimed cheerfully. "I was going to let you sleep on and bring you breakfast in bed . . . had to dash out again, forgot the bread . . . look, I'll see to the breakfast, you go and sit down, and have a look at the papers . . ." She had brought today's *Il Messaggio*, yesterday's *Daily Telegraph* and *Le Monde*. "I thought," she explained, "that you might like to catch up on things a bit."

"That was thoughtful of you, Penny. Thank you." I did as she said and went away with the papers into the living-room. There was nothing more about Elena Menotti in *Il Messaggio*. Her death was not even a nine days' wonder, poor woman. I skimmed the headlines of the other papers and thought about Elena and the earring and Penny's gun.

Penny clattered about in the kitchen and came bustling in with a tray of coffee, fruit, fresh rolls, butter, and apricot jam. She poured the coffee and chattered cheerfully about trivialities. She had on a skimpy cotton dress and her long brown legs were bare. In the clear morning light she seemed very young, fair and fresh and candid, like a healthy schoolgirl. Angelo's creature. I wondered briefly what she would say if I asked her straight out why she kept a gun tucked away in her underwear. I wasn't sure I had enough nerve for that yet. And, anyway, at the moment

241

I had something else on my mind.

I was thinking what to do about the earring.

I remembered Roddy's argument, which had seemed sensible enough at the time, mainly because I wasn't sure it was the right earring. Now, I knew that the description of the earring tallied exactly with the one I had. So I had to go to the police this time. Heaven only knew what it would lead to. But I had to do it, just the same.

After breakfast I went to my bedroom and shut the door behind me. I took the locked jewel-box out of the make-up case I had carried it in. I took out the tiny ring case inside and opened it.

It was empty.

The earring had gone.

I couldn't accept at first that it had really disappeared. I hunted through the jewel-box and the case I had carried it in, and after a while I knew it was pointless to keep looking. It had really gone.

I had put it away so carefully that night, the night I had worn it. I had locked the box and hidden the key, and nobody had seen me do it.

Well, that wasn't quite true. Roddy had seen me do it.

Roddy?

Roddy hadn't wanted me to take the earring to the police.

But Roddy had left for Stockholm days before I started out to go to Rome. Surely, if it had been he who had taken it, I would have missed it, since that time . . .

But, of course, I shouldn't have done. After that one evening, when it had been a feat of endurance to wear it, I had locked the earring safely away and never looked at it again. And that meant, that since the night I actually wore it, anyone could have taken it any time.

Penny came knocking at the door. I thrust the jewel-box into one of the dressing-table drawers and called to her to come in: she appeared, almost hidden behind the enormous bouquet of flowers she was carrying.

"These just came for you," she said.

I stood looking at the flowers as if they might bite. Who, after all, knew I was in Rome?

"Aren't they *lovely?*" Penny said. She sounded impressed. "There's a card here somewhere." She handed it to me. I read: "*I hear from Stephanie that you are in Rome — welcome back. As you see I am stuck in this place in a state of frustrating idleness. It would be delightful to see you if you have nothing better to do. Call the studio — they'll send a car for you.*" It was signed: "*Affection-ately, Frank.*"

Penny was looking expectant, so I said, "They're from Frank Harmer."

"The film director? Really?" Her eyes widened; she was, it seemed, an impressionable girl. "What's he like?"

"Frank? I don't know him all that well, but he's been very kind to me, since I was ill. He's ill himself now. He wants me to go and see him."

"Oh! Are you going? Today?"

"This afternoon, I expect."

"Oh," said Penny again. "Would you like me to come with you?"

I looked at her, smiling. "No, thank you. I think I can manage."

She said unwarily, "But Angelo said —"

I said pleasantly, "I shouldn't worry too much about what Angelo says. I'll be quite all right. If I call the studio they'll send a car for me."

She looked at me doubtfully. "Shall I do that for you?"

"Call the studio? I think I can manage that too, you know. Thanks all the same."

It may seem strange, but at that moment I felt quite light-hearted. The earring was gone and someone had taken it and that had a deadly significance; yet the fact that it had gone was, in a way, a relief. I could not now go to the police, and Frank, with his lovely flowers and the kindly message with them, had come exactly to cue. I was not now alone in Rome; I had someone to turn to: not, I thought that I can burst out with all my troubles to him; if he wasn't well, that would hardly be fair.

I telephoned the studio, and a friendly girl who seemed to know all about it greeted me pleasantly, said of course, Mr Harmer had left instructions; the car would be there any time I wished. We fixed a time, and then a thought occurred to me. "By the way," I said, "what's the driver's name?"

"His name?" She sounded faintly surprised but was too polite and well-trained to ask why I wanted to know. "It's Sandro — Sandro Rossi."

"Thank you. I'll expect him at five o'clock then."

Sandro Rossi, a civil young man who didn't seem overly surprised to have his identity checked, arrived punctually; Penny insisted on coming downstairs with me, seeing me into the big limousine and waving me away. I found her insistent solicitude increasingly oppressive but at least, so far, solicitude was all it seemed to be. Driving through the streets of Rome, the air heavy with the heat of afternoon, I felt more free and relaxed than I had felt at any time since I woke up in that hospital bed in Denzano. I felt safe in the car; I was doing something infinitely ordinary, visiting a sick friend.

The clinic was not a modern building, but was housed in an old palazzo converted for the purpose, in which clinical efficiency and traditional splendour were rather oddly mingled. I was shown into a large ante-room like that of a rather grand private dwelling of a past day: the ceiling was garlanded with frescoes and plaster moulding, and supported by pillars; rugs were scattered on the marble floor. A graceful staircase with a wide curve and shallow treads led up to the floor above. Sofas and chairs were scattered about. There, it seemed, I was to sit down and wait. A few minutes later a tall man in a white coat appeared from an inner sanctum and came towards me. "Signorina Fleming?" A doctor, obviously.

I nodded.

"You have come to visit Signor Harmer, I believe?"

"Yes . . ." I began to feel rather uneasy. "Is anything wrong?"

"No, not exactly. Don't disturb yourself

please. It is simply that I like to have a word with Signor Harmer's friends before they visit him. You see, it was only when Signor Harmer was admitted here that we became aware that there was another problem besides the malady for which he came for treatment. There is a heart condition . . ."

"Oh," I said, "I'm so sorry. Is it serious?"

"Not so serious if he can be induced to take care of himself. No doubt you know Signor Harmer better than we do, so you will know how he drives himself and how reluctant he is to accept that he is in any way an invalid. It is impossible to stop him working, even here. We tried —" he smiled reluctantly — "to take his telephone away, to insist that he rest. But it was clear that would only lead to frustration and more stress, which is very bad for him. What we can do, at least, is to ensure that he has as little excitement as possible. You understand?"

"Yes," I said. "Of course. We should tell him only the good things. Things that will make him happy." But my heart sank; I could not, now, confide in Frank at all.

"Exactly. Thank you, signorina." His smile, now, was genuine.

"I could wish that all Signor Harmer's associates were as co-operative as yourself. I am sure," he added with a little bow, "to be visited by a beautiful young lady, with only happy news to tell, will do my patient nothing but good. Only don't stay too long, will you? Not more than half an hour, perhaps?"

"I'll do whatever you think right," I said.

"Benissimo." He touched a bell on the table in front of us. "And now I will have you shown to his room."

A nurse appeared and conducted me up the graceful staircase; peered through a small peephole in a door; nodded and opened it for me to pass through; closed it behind me.

The room was large, lit with the mellow sunlight of late afternoon as the shutters were thrown back and a french window was open on a balcony brilliant with flowers; a room tastefully decorated and furnished, a luxurious room in a private clinic. Frank was sitting up in bed, telephoning; he wore no pyjama jacket and his powerful torso, with the bulge just above the sheet showing where his pendulous belly began, was very brown against the immaculate white of the bedclothes. He looked up as I came in and smiled and waved me to a seat while he went on talking into the phone.

At least, I think he did. I don't remember properly.

There was nothing in that room to frighten me, least of all Frank. All the same, as I walked in I had another of those awful, irrational experiences, in which a friendly smiling face — in this case a familiar one — was transformed into an expanding, threatening, snarling mask.

I was bewildered and terrified. I wanted to get out of the room but I couldn't move. I stood there trembling like a frightened horse.

A voice said, "Joanna, what is it? What the hell's the matter?"

English. English words . . . They brought me to myself. The hideous vision faded and was gone and there was only Frank, sitting up in bed and looking at me with anxiety and concern.

I stumbled towards a chair and sat down. "It's nothing," I said, remembering too late that I was not supposed to do anything to upset him, and too late to stop the tears which now began to run down my face.

Frank didn't, fortunately, seem to be much upset. He sat there quietly and waited until he could see I was getting myself together again. Then he said gently, "Mop-up time, I think. Here." He reached for the bedside table and handed me an enormous clean white handkerchief; I buried my face in it thankfully and emerged to say wretchedly, "Oh dear. I really am sorry."

"Well, so you should be," said Frank humorously. "You're supposed to come and cheer me up. Never mind. Would you like some tea?"

"That would be lovely," I said gratefully.

"Right. I'll have some sent up. Just relax, now. When it comes you can tell me all about it, whatever it is." He reached for the telephone.

But I didn't want to wait for the reviving tea, because I knew already what had happened to me. When he put the phone down I said, "Frank . . ."

"What?"

"Just now, on the telephone. You were talking German."

"Sure. So —"

"It's happened before."

I explained, remembered it all now so clearly. The mountain road. Two people in a Mercedes car. The woman saying *"Was ist's, Karl?"* Perfectly innocent, inoffensive people as they were, they had seemed to me like monsters. *As soon as I heard them speak.*

"It was so weird," I said. "They were really nice people. Kind. They took Roddy and me all the way to the hospital, and waited for me, and took me to buy petrol and back to the car. There was nothing wrong with them, nothing at all. So, as it happened

250

again with you, it has to be the language that does it. It can't be anything else."

Frank frowned, groping after it. "Let's get this straight. You mean that when you came in here and heard me talking to Bruckdorfer in Hamburg, *I* seemed like a monster, too?"

"It only lasts a few seconds," I said foolishly, and added, not looking at him, "It doesn't mean I think you are one."

"No," said Frank kindly, "I didn't think it meant that. You've no idea why it happens?"

"Not the foggiest. I did wonder if you might — you know, if you could remember anything that had upset me, or whatever."

"Nothing comes to mind. But then we haven't known each other all that long."

"No, I suppose not. Oh well."

The tea came, and I busied myself with it, pouring Frank's — lemon, no sugar and putting it on the bedside table.

"The memory's no better?" Frank asked.

"Not really."

"My poor Joanna," Frank said. "It really is a bit of a swine, all this, isn't it?"

"Yes. It is, rather."

More than a bit, I thought, if only he knew. But, of course, I couldn't tell him, for the time being anyway. I drank my tea, and relaxed a little; Frank looked at me over his teacup and smiled. "You're getting your colour back. That's better . . . I wish I could do more to help you, child."

"You have helped me," I said. "More than I have any right to expect. And I feel awful about worrying you with it today, I really do . . . but, you know, I don't think anyone can help me much more, except a good therapist. That's one of the things I've come to Rome for."

"You've been recommended to one? I never did think that fellow in Milan was much good."

"Yes, well . . . I expect he was all right really, only not for me. This woman really is the tops, I'm told. But she's away just now . . ." I had telephoned the doctor that morning, and received this disappointing news. "She won't be back until next week at the earliest."

"You're going to wait around for her? You won't go back to England?"

"Oh no, not yet. Quite apart from seeing the doctor, I think I ought to stay here for a bit, catch up on things, see old friends, people who were in the movie, that sort of thing."

"That sounds like a sensible idea," said Frank. "Now look, I'll tell you what we'll do. I've every intention of getting out of this place as soon as I can —"

"You shouldn't hurry it," I said quickly. "You've got to be careful —"

He gave me a mildly exasperated look. "Now don't you start. Have they been filling you up with dire warnings about my health?"

"Well . . ."

"I'm *perfectly all right*," said Frank with typical masculine obstinacy. "I'm not going to run up and down stairs or climb a mountain, dammit. But I *am* going to be back in circulation by the end of the week. Then we'll fix a date for you to come to the studio and see the rough-cut of the picture. And I'll give a little party for you —"

I was deeply touched by his kindness, which, after my recent performance, I didn't really feel I deserved. All the same, I shook my head.

"No," I said. "You're not giving any party, Frank. I am. I shall give the party and you, I hope, will come to it." I added politely, "And Carole, of course."

"Carole's gone back to England. She doesn't like sick-rooms." He said it with rueful amusement, laughing at himself; no fool like an old fool. Poor Frank. I hadn't been wrong about Carole. I wanted to show him sympathy without embarrassing him, so I said especially warmly, "You will promise to come, won't you? If you're well enough? Please . . ."

"All right," said Frank. "What else can I say, when you look at me like that? There's just one thing you seem to have overlooked, though. How do you know who to ask?"

"Ah, yes. Well, I would like some help with the guest list. If you wouldn't mind —"

"Well, of course. But I'm not sure I'd be much help. I'd say Roddy would be a better bet for that. He knows most of your friends."

"That would be fine if Roddy were here. But as he's in Stockholm —"

"Stockholm?" said Frank blankly.

"Oh dear," I said, dismayed. If Frank were counting on Roddy for his next picture and Roddy were secretly treating, in Stockholm, with a rival director . . . this was just the sort of thing to give Frank another heart attack.

But Frank merely looked embarrassed. "Darling Joanna," he said gently, "I'm sorry to have to tell you this. Roddy hasn't been to Stockholm, whatever he told you. He has been here, in Rome, for the past week."

I was silent.

"Oh hell," said Frank. "I should have kept my big mouth shut."

I tried to smile. "It's all right. I'm just . . . just surprised, that's all. I can't think why he

254

did it . . . said he was going there, I mean."

"No more can I," Frank said. He looked at me probingly. "You're upset, aren't you?"

"I don't know. Taken aback, certainly. Because I don't understand."

Frank said gently, "I wouldn't pretend to know what Roddy's up to, Joanna. But he's very fond of you. I do know that."

"Yes," I said.

My half-hour was more than up, and I began to take my leave.

"What are you going to do," I asked, "when you leave here?"

"Come to your party."

"No, I mean after that."

"Get away to the mountains. Three weeks from now Rome will be unbearable. Thank you for coming, Joanna." He took the hand I held out, and carried it to his lips. I think, really, he expected me to go to him and hug him and kiss him good-bye, but I couldn't bring myself to do that. I was not good at touching or being touched; except, I thought wryly, with Roddy, about whom surely I had made a terrible mistake.

I went downstairs.

As I crossed the big reception room the outer door opened and someone came through it; halting, taken aback, when he saw me.

I said, "Hallo, Roddy."

He rallied at once, exclaiming, "Joanna! Darling, how lovely to see you! I thought you were still up at the lake. What are you doing here?"

"The same as you, I suppose. Visiting Frank." Remembering the snake-bite, I asked, "Are you well, Roddy? No after-effects?"

Yes, he was disconcerted. He didn't answer immediately, and I added, "From the snake-bite."

"Oh, that. No, not at all. I'm fine."

"Good," I said. "And how was Stockholm? And Kornerup?"

"Oh, fine, everything went very well . . ." Then he saw I knew. "Oh hell," he said. "Joanna, I'm sorry."

"It doesn't matter," I said. "Except that it makes me wonder. Why you had to make up that story."

"Look, Joanna —"

"No," I said, "*you* look. I said it doesn't matter and I mean that. Whatever there was between us before . . . before I was ill . . . I wouldn't want to hold you to that now. You're free to go wherever you want so I can't see any point in lying about it. That's all."

I turned to go, but he stood in my way. "No, Joanna, wait. Let's go and have a drink somewhere. We must talk. I want to explain . . ."

I looked at him. "You've come to see Frank."

"He isn't expecting me. And they probably won't let him have another visitor anyway. Joanna, please."

I said with a sigh, "I've got the studio car outside and I'm going home in it. You can come too if you like."

He grinned. "That's better. You can give me a drink at home, can't you?"

"All right." I didn't tell him Penny would be there; that would keep. For the first time, I thought of her almost as a friend.

In the car, he reached out to close the screen between us and the chauffeur's seat. Traffic was heavy; all Rome was coming out on the streets after the heat of the day, the shops open again after the siesta. The mellow apricot light was fading, and soon darkness would fall and the summer night in the city would burst into glittering life. It lured me, that glittering life; I thought for a moment how lovely it would be if I could go home and have a shower, put on a pretty dress, go out with Roddy for dinner and a frivolous evening. But of course I wasn't going to do that. I didn't think, really, I would be going out with Roddy ever again.

He said, "You're looking very well, Joanna. And very lovely."

"Thank you." He took hold of my hand and I let him, though without making any response, and he said, "You are angry with me, aren't you?"

"No, Roddy, I'm not angry. I just don't like mysteries. I have enough of those already."

"Poor love, of course. It was stupid of me. Things . . . they're no better?"

"The memory you mean? Not really." I had no inclination to tell him about the train journey; I didn't want to relive it. But there was one thing I had to say. "They've identified that woman, by the way. Did you know?"

"What woman?"

"The one in the lake."

"Oh lord," said Roddy. "Are you still worrying about that?"

"I have to," I said. "I did have the earring, you see. The description in the paper tallied with it exactly."

"So," said Roddy carefully, "you still want to take it to the police?"

"I can't do that," I said. "I haven't got it any more. Somebody took it."

"What? Stole it, you mean? But who would do that?"

"I don't know. I thought perhaps you had."

258

"Me! For God's sake, Joanna!"

"Well, you didn't want me to do anything about it, did you? You thought it would be a hassle —"

"I did think it would be a hassle, and very bad for you, and that's all there is to that. *I didn't take the bloody earring . . .*"

He was shouting; through the glass I saw Sandro's head turn.

"Oh, shush," I said. "All right. You didn't take it. I'm sorry."

"I'm sorry too," said Roddy. His anger had gone as quickly as it had come. He looked at me and smiled and shook his head. "Oh, Joanna, darling, can't you see this is just what it was all about?"

The car was at a standstill, Sandro at the door, opening it; we were home. I couldn't ask Roddy what he meant, not then.

As we entered the flat, I could hear voices, where another argument, it seemed, was going on.

"You mean to say," Angelo was saying, "you just let her go off on her own?"

"Well, of course," said Penny fretfully. "There wasn't any way of stopping her. Unless of course you'd like me to lock her in her room. That really would tear it, wouldn't it?"

I knew Roddy must have heard the words,

as well as I. I didn't look at him; I made a great business of getting my key out of the door, rattling it to announce my arrival. I walked into the sitting-room with Roddy behind me, saying cheerfully, "Hallo, you two. Angelo, you know Roddy, of course. Penny, this is Roddy Marchant."

They had both looked, momentarily, rather foolish as I came in; but for Penny, at least, all embarrassment was swept away by the sight of Roddy. If I had walked in with a golden peacock covered with jewels and presented it to her, she could not have been more dazzled. She blushed, and mumbled something while Roddy, who had picked up a lot of pretty Italian tricks in Rome, bent gracefully over her hand and kissed it.

Nobody had much to say. Roddy was as disconcerted to find Penny and Angelo there as they were to have us walking in on their conversation. For the moment I seemed to be in command of the situation, and made the most of it, brightly offering drinks and news about Frank's state of health. Angelo said hastily he had only looked in for a minute, refused a drink, and left. Penny had one, but took it away to the kitchen, murmuring something about dinner, shutting the door carefully after her. Roddy and I were left alone once more.

260

"Who's the girl?" Roddy asked.

"Just a girl. Angelo's idea. He seems to think I ought to have someone with me. She housekeeps, does the cooking —"

"Oh. Not a friend of yours, then?"

"I never saw her before yesterday."

"I see. It doesn't sound as if you like her much."

"She's all right," I said. I could see how his mind was working: poor Joanna, there really is a problem if they have to instal a . . . what? A nurse? Or a keeper?

"What did you mean just now?" I asked. "In the car? We'd been talking about the earring, and you said, 'This is just what it's all about'?"

"Oh! That. Well . . ." He was turning his glass round and round in his hand. Then he looked up, and met my eyes, and grinned ruefully. "I feel a heel," he announced.

"Well, don't. I told you. There's no obligation whatever, Roddy. Only you did say you wanted to explain."

"Yes. Well, it's simple enough, really. It all got too heavy, darling."

"Too heavy?"

"The whole bit. I mean, I know you can't help it — but it's just the way you are right now. Imagining things. Thinking people are following us. Worrying about a dress you

261

might have worn or didn't wear, or an earring you picked up somewhere. Getting all intense about them. I did try to understand, honest. But I suppose I was fagged out with all those weeks of filming in the heat, ending up with a bloody snake-bite . . . I don't know. I just got fed-up. Wanted to get out from under for a bit. I couldn't do much to help you, after all, and . . ."

"It was a drag," I said sympathetically. "All right, Roddy."

"I should have told you straight out, I suppose. But I didn't like to do that. I didn't want to hurt you. And anyway I never meant to stay away long. I should have come back —"

"Of course," I nodded. "When I was well again. After all, I might get my memory back any time. And then I'd be the same Joanna. The one you knew before all this happened. That's it, isn't it? I'm not the same, am I?"

"Well, you didn't seem to feel the same about me, and . . ."

"And that night really wasn't such a wild success, was it?"

"Well . . ." he looked up, grinned reluctantly, and said, "You're not having me on, are you?"

"Of course not. I do understand, really I

do. It's difficult for people, I can see that."
And especially, I thought, for you: a little
boy still, inside that radiantly powerful masculine exterior; my problems got in the way
of your egotism. But at least my vague suspicions had been done away — Roddy did
not belong in this scenario. The only thing
was, I knew now that I could never confide
in him again.

And, except for Kate away in Verona, that
left, precisely, nobody.

9

The following morning I got dressed to go to Elena Menotti's requiem. The wardrobe at the flat seemed just as full as the one in Steffy's villa — where and when had I got around to buying so many clothes? I found a dress which I hoped would do, black linen with a yoke embroidered in white, and a black lacy shawl to wear over my head and arms.

I put the dress on and pinned back my hair so that it lay close to my head. Then I looked out the brown wig and put that on and combed the dark tendrils over my forehead. Now the dark glasses, and the shawl . . . surely in this get up I could pass unnoticed in a crowd? I looked in the mirror again, and still wasn't satisfied. My stance and the poise of my head was wrong. I still looked polished, groomed, sophisticated.

Well, I was an actress. This was the time to prove it.

I let my shoulders slump. I relaxed the muscles of my stomach and pushed it forward, and let my head drop forward too. Ah, that was more like it. I walked to and fro in front of the mirror with a slight waddle;

someone watching me might have thought me a few months pregnant. I could have been some young Italian widow, walking weeping after the coffin, supported by a tender posse of brothers.

Penny knocked and called, "May I come in?" and didn't wait for an answer. She was there, inside the door, staring at me in amazement and exclaiming, "What on *earth* are you doing?"

This really was a bit much, but I bit back a sharp retort and said pleasantly, "Getting ready to go out. To a funeral, actually."

"But you don't know anyone who's died —"

"Oh come," I said, "how can you know that? It isn't actually a funeral, by the way — it's a memorial service. For someone who may have been a friend of mine. Going along there may help me to remember. So . . . I thought I'd better wear black. And the wig is just camouflage."

"Oh . . . I see. A memorial service? Won't that be rather upsetting?"

"Not while I don't remember the person, no, I shouldn't think so."

"Let me come with you," said Penny.

"That's very nice of you, but I don't really think I need my hand held . . . Thanks all the same. Anyway, I've got the studio car again today. It should be here in a minute."

"Joanna," Penny said, "I wish you'd trust me."

I looked at her. She looked right back at me with her candid blue eyes. She looked innocent and anxious, out of her depth. Disarming.

"My dear," I said nicely, "of course I trust you." The doorbell rang and I added, "That'll be the car now, I expect."

Once again Penny insisted on coming down to the street with me, to see me into the car and wave me away. Through the rear window I saw her turn back into the building, and at once made a loud exclamation of annoyance.

"Signorina?"

"I've forgotten something, Sandro. I'll have to go back. I'm sorry."

Sandro made no comment, made a ruthless U-turn to the vocal indignation of two other drivers, and once again we were back outside the apartment house.

I had my keys ready. The lift was there and I went up in it. I took off my shoes, and crept silently and quickly along to the door of the flat. I opened the door quietly.

As I expected Penny was on the telephone. I was lucky — it seemed she had only just got her number. She was exclaiming in a harassed tone. "Where have you been? I've been ringing for ages . . . look, she's just gone out again. She's going to the Menotti memorial service. Yes. Well, if you are, that's all right then. Listen, she's wearing a dark brown wig —"

I didn't wait to hear any more. I closed the door noiselessly, put my shoes on again, and hurried back to the car.

I could think of only two things. One was that I had never mentioned the name Menotti to Penny. The other was that the wig was now worse than useless.

I leaned back in the corner of the car, hoping that Sandro wouldn't see me. I took the wig off and thrust it into my handbag and draped the shawl over my head, hiding as much of my hair as possible. It was the best I could do.

That morning, up to then, a sort of spurious confidence had possessed me. Now, once more, I felt terribly vulnerable. I had three choices: to go to the church as I'd planned, to return to the flat, or to ask Sandro to drive me around the city to see the sights. None of them seemed a good idea. None of them seemed any safer than the others. It was simpler to go on doing what I had planned in the first place.

The Church of St Michael and the Angels, like so many Roman churches, seemed too large for the buildings round it. A tall campanile reached for the sky; the façade occupied the whole of one side of a small and unremarkable piazza.

I was early. There didn't seem, as yet, anyone else going in. I asked Sandro to return for me in an hour, and he drove away.

When I entered the doorway I realized I was not yet in the church but in a large colonnaded portico, ornamented with statues ground down with the wear of antiquity. Beyond this, to my surprise, there was greenery and sunlight. More columns, an arched covered walk between two patches of garden brilliant with flowers and carefully tended; and so into the church itself.

Inside, it was vast, and dark compared with the light outside. There were candles on the altar and in the sconces provided for people who light a candle for someone's soul. A few shafts of sunlight with dust motes dancing in them, filtered through stained glass. I was struck by the twilight chill.

Instinctively I genuflected and crossed myself . . . someone must have taught me to do that, long ago. Then I stood irresolutely in the nave, wondering what to do. There was nowhere to sit down and it did occur to me that if the service went on a long time I might not be able to stand for so long. But that, after all, was the least of my worries. What I needed was to be somewhere I could see people, to recognize something, anything, which might tell me what my connection with Elena Menotti was.

I also needed to be somewhere safe, if possible. At the side, with my back against one of the great pillars, that would be best.

The organ was playing softly, as if the organist was playing for his own pleasure. I found my niche and stayed there a little while, while the cool peace of the place, its large echoing spaces, the music, sonorous yet muted, seemed to still my soul like gentle fingers on an aching head. After a bit I left my place and went up to where the candles glimmered and guttered in the sconces. I put money in the box and took a candle and lighted it from one of the others. A candle for Elena. But I uttered no prayer, unless what I was thinking could be called a prayer: *Elena, tell me. Tell me what happened, and why you haunt me.*

People were beginning to drift in now. I went back to my chosen place and drew my shawl closely round me, and watched them.

Elena's colleagues. Elena's friends. Men in black ties. Women, some of them very elegantly dressed, wrapped, however, in the inevitable shawl. They filed in in increasing numbers now, but even so seemed a small gathering in that large building. I watched them and searched the rows of grave faces, but not one of them aroused the slightest echo of memory.

The organ voluntary drew to its close. There was a moment's pause and then the music began again, in a different key and to the sound of chanting voices. The priest, the choir, the acolytes entered in procession. The smell of incense filled the air.

I could not follow the Latin liturgy, but it didn't matter. I stood or knelt when others did and continued to watch the congregation as well as I could.

This was quite easy as most of them, naturally, were not in the least concerned with me. Then, quite suddenly, I became aware that someone was watching me.

He was a young man, quite nice-looking, and there was nothing at all sinister about him. He looked at me with interest, not attending to the service at all. Our eyes met; he smiled, and inclined himself in the faintest sketch of a bow. Was I supposed to know him? Or was he, for heaven's sake, trying to pick me up in the middle of a church service?

I let my eyes slide indifferently past him, turning my head away. A lot of good that did me. Because then I saw another pair of eyes watching me, eyes that I knew only too well. At the back, overtopping the people round him, stood Angelo. He wasn't paying any attention to the service, either. He, like the other man, was watching me. Not, however, like the other man, with pleasure; he looked grim, implacable.

The priest, turning from Latin to the vernacular, spoke of our sister Elena, hideously and mysteriously done to death without preparation for eternity, unconfessed and unshriven; he prayed for her soul and invited us to do likewise. A woman near me wept into a lace handkerchief. At last it was over and the congregation began to leave.

I stayed where I was, letting them go. In a situation like this, if one had a choice it might be the wrong one. I would be all right if Sandro had returned with the car. If he hadn't, I had no idea what to do next. I stood there in the empty church, hesitating, changed my mind, and went out.

The people were moving away now, in ones and twos, in groups, talking and laughing in reaction from a solemn ritual. They had prayed for Elena and some had wept over her, but now they would take up their own lives again and forget her as soon as they could. I thought, I shouldn't have come here. It solves nothing.

"Signorina!"

It was the young man who had smiled at me. Of course. Why was I such a fool as to think he would just go away?

"It is Miss Fleming, isn't it? Joanna Fleming? Pardon the intrusion," he said, and sketched his little bow again. "Nicolo Parisi. *Il Messaggio*. At your service.

A reporter, of course. Elena had worked for *Il Messaggio*. The place would be swarming with newspapermen. Why hadn't I thought of that?

"You have quite recovered from your accident?" His black eyes were sharp, he scented a story: Why Joanna Fleming, a British film actress, should be at the memorial service for a relatively obscure Italian journalist . . .

For a wild moment I wondered whether it wouldn't be the best thing to tell him everything. Let it be plastered over the front page. Tell the world, tell Them, whoever they were . . .

Tell them what?

I stared coldly at the young man. I said in English, "I don't understand. Excuse me."

He looked momentarily taken aback, and then, to my horror repeated everything he

272

had said before in hesitant but passable English. Adding craftily, "This was a terribly sad thing, wasn't it, Miss Fleming? About poor Elena? She was a friend of yours?"

I began to say, "My name's not Fleming and will you please leave me alone . . ." But I never finished the sentence. Angelo was there. We were still standing in the covered walk where the flower garden was and Angelo must have been waiting, I suppose, in the porch. He came strolling back, nodded and smiled at me, said pleasantly, "Hallo, Clair," and put his hand on the young man's shoulder. "Could I have a word with you, Nico?"

Parisi began to protest.

"A word," said Angelo, smiling still. He wheeled the young man away and began to walk with him out of the building, talking rapidly in an undertone. At the entrance to the porch they stopped, Parisi made a shrugging gesture, half despairing, half laughing. They seemed, astonishingly, to be in agreement. Then Parisi disappeared and Angelo came back to me.

I said, because I could do no less, "Thank you." I began to walk out of the building.

"That's all right," said Angelo, keeping pace with me. "Not that you deserve to be rescued. Just what do you think you're doing here?"

"I might ask you the same question," I retorted.

"I knew Elena," Angelo said. "Same line of business. I even worked for the same employer for a time. *Il Messaggio,* I mean."

"You *knew* her?"

"Of course I knew her. The point is, however, did you?"

"I don't know," I said. "That's why I came."

We were in the portico, and I was looking out into the piazza for Sandro and the car.

Angelo said shortly, "It was an idiotic thing to do."

I wasn't really listening. I walked out into the sunlight; Angelo came with me. I looked round again, but the car wasn't there. The only vehicle in sight, actually, was a Volkswagen van on the corner, with its engine running as if it were waiting for somebody. I remember noticing the man sitting next to the driver, his head turned towards us. I saw sunlight glint on metal and thought, annoyed, he's taking a photograph.

The next instant an extraordinary thing happened. Angelo sprang on me like a tiger. He attacked me, that's what it felt like. He flung me to the ground, pinning me down with his weight. As he did so I heard two or three thin, sharp sounds, like metal on stone. The Volkswagen engine roared, then faded as the van drove away.

Angelo got to his feet, pulling me up with him. Bruised, dusty and dishevelled, I demanded angrily, "What are you *doing?*"

"Here," said Angelo. "Look."

I stared at the stonework of the column just behind where we would have been standing. Three neat, newly made holes told their own story.

I couldn't speak.

"It's all right," said Angelo. "They've gone."

I found my voice. Bewildered, I said, "You saved my life."

Angelo stared at me. His eyes had never looked blacker; he had never seemed to me more Latin, more violent, more formidable. Yet, when he spoke, he spoke softly.

"Holy Mother of God," whispered Angelo reverently, *"why wouldn't I?"*

We found a café just off the Piazza del Populo, noisy and busy, and a table as far away from the door as possible. Angelo ordered coffee and brandy.

We had got away from the scene of the shooting with surprisingly little fuss. Nico

Parisi had gone — he would, I reflected, be furious to have missed it all. A few people saw what happened, came hurrying over to see that we were all right, but really the whole thing was accepted with extraordinary casualness. This surprised me, because there were newspapermen among them, but Romans were becoming accustomed to an atmosphere of violence and according to Angelo, this sort of incident — in which, after all, nobody had been hurt — would merit two lines at the bottom of a page, if indeed, it got reported at all. One man had taken the number of the van and gave it to us, remarking that he was afraid it wouldn't be much use, the van would almost certainly be found abandoned. "I suppose you'll report it, won't you?"

"Oh yes, we'll report it," said Angelo without asking me, "but my guess is, nobody will be much interested."

He was right, they weren't. The police in the local quarter where Angelo and I went to tell our story listened, politely enough, and wrote everything down, but made it perfectly clear that they didn't really want to be bothered.

As I had done on the train, I gathered my courage together and tried to explain what I thought to be my connection with it all, but once again I didn't get very far. Why do you think your life is threatened, signorina, have you an enemy, do you know who it is? Well, no, you see, I had this accident, and I lost my memory . . .

It isn't easy for an Italian face, normally so mobile and expressive, to look wooden, but wooden was exactly what those policemen looked. With two witnesses in front of them, they had to concede that the shooting had actually taken place. They soon decided that Angelo, not I, had been the target. The senior of the two policemen knew his name. A writer, a publicist . . . such men, he said, nodding sagely, often made enemies . . .

We came away.

In the café, waiting for the drinks, we sat and looked at each other. Angelo looked solid and reassuring, sitting there. My terrors, both fancied and real, had made him into a sinister figure. Now my eyes were opened and I felt a warm flood of relief not unmixed, however, with embarrassment.

The barman brought the drinks and went away again.

I had to speak first. I had to.

"Angelo," I began.

Angelo smiled. "Drink your brandy, *cara*. Then we'll talk."

He watched me while I drank some of the brandy and started on the coffee. After a bit he nodded. "You're getting your colour back. That's better . . . How do you feel?"

"All right. Fine, even. Angelo, I'm sorry I misjudged you."

"Oh well," said Angelo comfortably, "we got our lines crossed, didn't we? This amnesia thing, Joanna — nobody knows much about it, do they? Even the doctors. Steffy and I — we didn't know, really, what we were supposed to do. We had it impressed on us that psychologically you were fragile, vulnerable. You mustn't be excited or over-stimulated —"

"My God," I said softly, "I've been over-stimulated and frightened out of my mind nearly. And everybody thinking I was deluded —"

"I didn't think you were deluded."

"Then why . . ."

"Why didn't I say so? With this misguided approach we had, what was I supposed to do? Tell you that yes, someone was out to terrify and threaten you? I was engaged in Operation Reassurance, remember —"

"You didn't do it very well," I said. "You were so disagreeable, bad-tempered —"

"I was worried," said Angelo simply.

I stared at him, and we both burst out

laughing. Suddenly I found I couldn't stop. The laughter changed into gulping sobs; I was whimpering under my breath, "I don't want to die. I don't want to die —"

The barman, setting out slabs of cassata on little glass plates, stared at us without much interest. Italians have a low emotional ignition point. No doubt he had seen it all before.

Angelo took both my hands across the table and gripped them tightly. "You're not going to die, Joanna. Joanna, are you listening? *You're not going to because I won't let you.* Just hold on to that, now, and we'll talk, and try to get to grips with this thing. All right?"

I got myself together somehow, and wiped my eyes, and tried to smile. "I'm all right now. Angelo — what happened today — you know it's not the first time?"

"Nor the second," said Angelo.

"What? You knew about the girl in Milan — that it was meant for me? Then why didn't you say so?"

"This misguided approach again. I wasn't sure, you see, that *you* knew. Steffy didn't; she saw it as a very distressing episode that would be bad for you. So I didn't want to frighten you more than I had to. By the time I met you, they'd had another go."

"You mean the woman on the platform in Rome? The one who said she'd come from Frank — that it's connected? But how can you know that?"

"Because it doesn't make any sense otherwise. Too much of a coincidence. Someone must have realized a mistake had been made, so a second plan was put into operation. That's when I came along, just in time, thank God."

"You mean they would have kidnapped me and not let me go again ever?"

"I'm afraid that's just what I do mean . . . don't look like that. It didn't happen."

"But I don't understand. How could they know that they'd made a mistake?"

"Someone on the train, perhaps. Who recognized you? Someone you talked to? The train stopped in Florence, didn't it? Whoever it was could have got off there and telephoned. What's the matter?"

I said slowly, "Someone in my compartment did get off in Florence. An elderly business man . . . Paraduca, he said his name was, and I told him mine . . . a terrible talker but very friendly . . . it couldn't be him?"

"It sounds only too likely, I'm afraid."

"My God. He seemed such a nice old boy. It never occurred to me to suspect him. Anyway, I was frightened by so many other things . . . the other man, for instance."

"What other man?"

"The man who talked to me that day in Denzano, the day I came out of hospital. He was on the train too —"

"Yes. Well — I doubt if you were in any danger from him, you know. What *he* did sounded like a try-on for money. You don't kill the goose that lays the golden eggs."

"No . . . well, I didn't think of that, at the time. Then there was that woman, too, of course. A fussy old thing, all over bags and parcels. I don't know where she came from. She didn't speak any language I know. But that's odd, too . . . she helped me, in a way."

"She helped you?"

"Twice, actually. When the man from Denzano tried to talk to me again she came up, and sort of interrupted. And then, on the platform when we got there, when that woman turned up and said she'd come from Frank, the other old dear came fussing round making out I'd got her bag by mistake, ridiculous really, her bag wasn't a bit like mine. Anyway, she held things up, and then you came . . ."

"Yes," said Angelo with satisfaction, "she held things up, didn't she? That's what she was there for."

I was bewildered. "You've lost me," I said.

"You mean you know her?"

"Lise Hempel. Your guardian angel. Austrian by birth, I believe, but the complete polyglot, speaks Italian and English as well as you or me. I expect she was talking Portuguese . . . as good a cover as any. I thought a woman would be better for that trip, after you rumbled poor Mario in the hospital car-park."

"You mean, they were both there to look after me?"

"That's right —"

"He said he was a doctor —"

"He had to say something, didn't he?"

"I thought I'd shaken him off and then I saw him at the opera . . ."

"Yes. Well, that was, so to speak, legitimate coincidence. He was actually at the opera for his own pleasure. He rang me to say that you had safely arrived at Katie's place, it looked like you'd be safe enough there till morning, and he had a date with his wife, a wedding anniversary, and *Il Trovatore*."

"Oh dear. It all seems silly now. But I was terrified when I realized he was following me. I tried to lose him . . ."

"So he said. He was impressed by your driving, by the way. But he miscalculated — he didn't realize how conscious of danger you were. We've made our mistakes, you see, as well as the enemy.

"Let's get this straight," I said slowly. "You've had someone watching over me, all along? You arranged it? Penny, too?"

He nodded.

"But why? I mean, before the train, nothing had happened . . ."

"Enough had happened to make me uneasy about you. Steffy told me about the chap in Denzano, your first day. Then there was the Frightener —"

"I never thought you believed me, about that."

"Oh yes, I did. Not at first, perhaps. But certainly after I found the tyre marks."

"Tyre marks?"

"Bicycle-tyre marks, on the grass under your window: that's why you didn't hear him going away. And if you've wondered how he got up to your room, two fairly tall men, one on the other's shoulders could manage it easily. It looked as if it was no time to take risks, so the morning after that episode, I went into Milan and arranged a bit of surveillance."

"Good heavens. I had no idea . . . Angelo, what's it all about? Who are they?"

"I wish to God I knew," said Angelo. "I was hoping that by now you might, but as you don't, we'll have to find out, won't we? There's one thing, at least, we do know. That the reason for all this has got to be something you don't know you know. You're a human time-bomb, my love, liable to blow up any minute, and therefore very dangerous to somebody; which is why they've made three attempts so far to defuse you."

The café was filling up; it was the lunch hour and workers from neighbouring offices were crowding in for coffee and drinks and snacks. Two young men shouldered their way in, nodded perfunctorily at us, said, "*Permettono?*" before sitting down, without more ado, at our table.

"We'd better go," said Angelo. "We can't talk here any more and we could do with some lunch."

"I don't want to go to a restaurant," I said quickly.

"In that case, it's a choice between your place and mine."

"It had better be yours, then. I don't feel like meeting Penny again just yet. I owe her an apology."

"Never mind about that. She'll understand. *Andiamo.*"

Angelo's apartment was in a modern block, high above Rome. We went up seven floors and entered directly into a large room which in some ways looked more like an office than a living-room. The walls were lined with books and reference files and card indexes, except for a section given over to electronic gear: cassette recorder, radio, television, amplifier, and a deck for records. Angelo flipped a switch as he went past it; the buoyant splendour of the "Jupiter" symphony filled the room.

I stood in the middle of it, looking around. Through a door there was a glimpse of a small efficient-looking kitchen; there was another door which presumably led to the bedroom and bathroom. There was a desk in the room, with a typewriter on it; a big, comfortable-looking sofa covered in black and white striped material, a chair to match it; the wood floor was strewn with brilliantly coloured rugs. The whole effect was more Scandinavian than Roman, spacious, comfortable and yet functional. A place to work and sleep, a base, so to speak, for a thinking man who was yet a man of action.

"Make yourself at home," said Angelo, and went off into the kitchen. I wandered around a little, looking at the books: large, formidable works, most of them, in several different languages, on science and politics and philosophy. There were volumes of press-cuttings, a shelf of books in various editions, Italian, American, French, all of which bore the name *Angelo Valente*. One, in a bright dust jacket, seemed to be a novel: I took it out, found a rather stern picture of Angelo on the back of the cover, and a quote from a rapturous review in the *New York Times*.

I put it back thoughtfully: I had had little idea about all this, it was a different world. In that room, with the door safely shut behind us, I felt a relaxation of the spirit that was quite new to me. Nobody who wished me ill could reach me here.

I put my head round the kitchen door. Angelo was taking food out of the refrigerator: veal escalopes, eggs, material for salad.

"Can I help?" I asked.

"Can you cook?" Angelo countered. He had the escalopes on a board, and was thumping them with a broad-bladed knife.

"I've no idea —"

"Probably not. I don't suppose you learned anything useful at that elegant school your devoted grandpa sent you to."

I didn't like this very much; it sounded more like the abrasive Angelo I had met at first. I said, "Please. Don't be nasty about him."

"I didn't know I was," said Angelo. "Does

it matter anyway? You don't remember him, do you?"

"He's the only person I remember. I dreamed about him, I told you all how I'd dreamed about him —"

"So you did, I'd forgotten. Well, let's hope you'll be able to come up with a few more dreams like that soon. Because by God we're going to need them." He began to beat up an egg. "Here . . . you can make the salad, get it ready, anyway. Just wash the lettuce, and get it thoroughly dry afterwards, otherwise it isn't worth eating. I'll show you how to make the dressing in a minute. Oh yes, and you can get out some wine . . . the big cupboard, over there."

I obediently washed the lettuce and dried it carefully while Angelo dunked the meat in the egg and began, swiftly and efficiently, to coat it in breadcrumbs. It seemed strange to be in this kitchen, helping clumsily to get lunch, with Angelo, of all people.

The salad was made, the escalopes cooked to a turn; we carried the things through on trays and ate from a long coffee table in front of the sofa. I found I was hungry. The good food, the wine, the music flowing peacefully and not too loudly through the room; all this seemed to make the mystery and terror that surrounded me seem unreal and far away.

"It's nice here," I said presently. "I don't know why we didn't come here straight away, instead of sitting in that bar."

"I didn't think you'd come," said Angelo. "I had to establish my *bona fides* first, hadn't I?"

"You did that," I said, "when you saved my life."

"Well," said Angelo, "I couldn't be sure. Had enough to eat? Coffee?"

"Please . . ." As he got up to go out to the kitchen, I added, "Angelo —"

"What?"

"I do trust you, you know."

"Good," said Angelo. "Because it seems to me that you haven't much choice in the matter, really."

When he came back with the coffee, he said briskly, "Now, there are two things we have to consider. The first is how to keep you safe until we find out what it's all about, and the second is to do just that — find out what it's about. About your safety, well, you've a number of choices. None very attractive, I'm afraid. You could do as the police say, and go back to England. Three hours away by plane, and if our friends are that determined, not a lot safer there than here. A much better bet would be a safe house, in some other country — Switzerland, maybe. For you really to go to ground somewhere."

"Into hiding, you mean?"

He nodded. "Just until we've got it all straightened out —"

"You can't get it straightened out without me," I interrupted, "and I wouldn't want you to try. I can't do that, Angelo . . . hole up somewhere, waiting and wondering. Either I'm going to remember, or find out the truth some other way. I know it's dangerous, and I'm frightened, but if I wasn't doing anything I'd be still more frightened, don't you see?"

"Yes. I can see that. But you can't just take your chance, you know. Another possibility is to hire yourself some bodyguards —"

I don't know what expression there was on my face; I didn't know what I felt. I said slowly, "You mean . . . people who would follow me about wherever I went . . . sleep outside my bedroom door . . . that kind of thing?"

"I don't know about sleeping outside your bedroom door. But that kind of thing, certainly. They wouldn't be much use, otherwise."

"I suppose not. Well, if that's what you advise, that's what I'd better do, isn't it?"

Angelo said, "Did I say that's what I advised?"

"No, but . . ." I made an effort, looked him in the eyes, and said firmly, "Look, Angelo. I'm very grateful for everything you've done for me, but there's no real reason why you should go on being involved. As you say, I can hire myself some protection and, and take it from there . . ."

He didn't say anything: he just looked back at me with a totally unreadable expression. I floundered on, "I mean, the whole thing is dangerous. I've no right to let other people risk their lives for me . . ."

"No," Angelo agreed equably, "but then you're not going to *let* them, are you? They'll do it, or not, as they choose. And if they do choose, what are you going to do about it? No, wait," he added as I opened my mouth to speak, "just listen, Joanna. I suggested hiring a professional bodyguard because you have the right to know what the choices are. You could do that if you still didn't feel that you trusted me . . . or Penny."

"But I do."

"Now you do, maybe. Up till an hour or so ago you were highly suspicious of both of us. Well, anyway . . . You may have a lot of talent for all I know, but in ordinary life, my child, you're not much of an actress. You don't need to tell me what you thought of the bodyguard idea. Your face was a dead give-away. You'd simply hate it, wouldn't you?"

I looked down and mumbled, "Yes. But I don't know why, really."

"It doesn't matter why. If you don't want them, *cara,* you don't have to have them. Only, instead, you'll have to promise to be very careful. There will have to be the most disciplined, organized team work. Between the three of us: you, Penny and me."

"Oh, yes," I said. "Penny. With her little gun." Angelo stared, and I giggled faintly; I felt, suddenly, a little light-headed. "I went through her things," I added. "While she was shopping."

"Did you now," said Angelo. His lips twitched.

"Well," I said defensively, "Operation Reassurance wasn't working too well just then. Like you said, I was suspicious. More so, when I found that thing. Did you give it her? The gun?"

"As a last-resort precaution. She doesn't need to carry one, really. A Karate black belt, no less."

"Did she just tell you that, or do you really know?"

"Really know. I did a work-out with her in a gym not far from here. A somewhat humbling experience, I must admit." He grinned cheerfully.

"I see. Angelo . . ."

"What?"

"I still don't really see why you should do all this for me."

"Don't you?" said Angelo drily. "It's simple enough. Common humanity demands it, for one thing. Then there's Steffy, who loves you very much. If I let anyone harm a hair of your head, she'd never speak to me again. And for me personally there's the challenge, . . . as well."

"The challenge?"

"It's an intensely interesting puzzle, don't you think? The kind of thing," he added coolly, "that I really can't resist."

I said quietly, "I see. But that hardly applies to Penny —"

"Oh yes it does, in a way. She likes the excitement, you see. And there's an element of glamour in it for her. If it didn't have the wrong sort of connotations, I'd call Penny an adventuress. Someone who loves adventure, I mean." He smiled; fondly, I thought.

"Yes," I said blankly. "So what now?"

"You can start by answering some questions. What do you know about Elena Menotti, and why did you come to her requiem?"

"Then you do think it's got something to do with her?"

"At the moment I don't think anything and I'm asking the questions. What do you know about her?"

"Nothing, except what was in the newspapers and on television. So far as I know, I've never met her or seen her in my life. Only, I had her earring. Or I thought I had it."

"Had it? Where is it now?"

"It's gone. Somebody took it. I thought . . ."

He said drily, "That I'd taken it? Or Penny?"

"I didn't know what to think. It's gone, anyway. I was going to take it to the police when I first heard about Elena when I was in Verona, at Kate's. She was just an unidentified woman then, but something was said about the earring, and I said to Roddy I wanted to take it and he persuaded me not to."

"Did he now," said Angelo.

"Roddy said they . . . the police . . . would start harassing me about it, because I wouldn't be able to explain how I came by it. And, of course, it didn't have to be the same one, it hadn't been described, not then. Anyway, I put it . . . the one I had

. . . in a little ring case and locked it up with my other jewellery and I had them all in my handbag when I came to Rome. When I looked for it, the morning I read about Elena in the paper . . . it had gone. And it *was* the same, Angelo, I'm sure it was. Onyx and diamonds, they said . . . you remember, you saw it."

"Yes," said Angelo merely.

"So if it was the same one, *how did I come by it?* That's why I went to the service. To see if there were anything, anyone there that would remind me, trigger off something. Even though I'm terrified of remembering . . . because if the earrings are the same, then I'm mixed up, somehow, in her death . . . I feel sometimes as if . . . as if I'd done something so bad that I suppressed it absolutely . . . something terrible . . ."

"*Joanna,*" said Angelo, "whatever else happened, it couldn't be that. My dear girl, Elena was strangled. You're not suggesting that you might have wrung her neck and thrown her body in the lake, are you?"

"No . . ."

"Well then. Apart from other considerations, that's not physically possible. She was bigger than you, anyway," he added with a wry grin.

I shuddered. "Don't make a joke of it."

"I'm not. Just stating facts. And if this *is* anything to do with Elena — and remember it doesn't have to be — then the chances are that you simply saw it happen. And the thugs who killed and robbed her, and threw her in the lake, know that you saw it happen."

"Yes. I suppose that's possible. But when, where?"

"Ah, that's what we have to find out. Incidentally, why did you come back to Rome? Because of Elena?"

"Oh no, I didn't know who she was, then. No. I came to Rome to see a doctor, for one thing, someone Kate told me about. But she's away just now. And I thought I should try to meet people, people I'd known when I was here before. But most of all, I came to see a nun."

"A *nun?*" For the first time, Angelo seemed disconcerted.

"She was the nurse on duty in the casualty department when I was brought in after the accident. I asked them what happened that night, but the only person who could tell me, this Sister Justina . . . she's been transferred to another convent here in Rome. They weren't sure I'd be able to see her, but I did get the address."

"I see. What do you want to ask her, exactly?"

"About the dress."

He was quick, no doubt about that. "Ah yes. The dress you found at the back of the wardrobe."

"That's right. Angelo, you saw me at the party. Was it the same dress?"

"I think so, though I couldn't swear to it."

"You didn't say —"

"Didn't want to complicate things. You were very excited and strung up that night . . . all the same, I made a mental note of it. So what have we got? If you were wearing this dress at the party, then you were wearing it at the time of the accident. But if you had been, it would have been torn and bloodstained, not crumpled up in the back of your wardrobe. So you must have been wearing something else, so you must have changed your clothes, so you must have gone home . . . what's the matter?"

I didn't know how to say it, but I had to. "I thought it all happened there. Whatever it was . . ."

"There? At home? At Steffy's place?"

"Yes. Because of the lemon garden."

"Because of the *what*?"

"The lemon garden. Because it frightens me, like the earring. Like the dress. Only worse, somehow. And it's connected with all that . . . only I don't know how. I thought. . . something had happened there. I thought . . ."

Angelo said in a soft, somehow dangerous, voice, "Go on. What did you think, Joanna?"

I looked up and met his eyes, the black, black eyes in the dark bony face, hard, intent.

"What did you think?" he repeated.

I swallowed and said, "I thought you were mixed up in it, in some way."

"I see. You thought I killed her. Is that it?"

I didn't answer.

Angelo. I didn't know him, after all, this stranger with the tight mouth and implacable eyes. I was alone with him in this flat, where, idiotically, I had briefly felt myself safe. I felt cold, realizing that nobody else in the world knew where I was.

I suppose it only lasted a few moments, that silence, but long enough. I don't know how I looked. I only know that I couldn't have moved or spoken . . . or fled, to save my life, as they say.

The moment passed. Angelo said in a perfectly ordinary voice, "Well, don't look at me like that."

He got up and went across the room to the desk, took a small cheroot out of a carved box that stood there, and made a great business

297

of lighting it. He said with his back half turned to me, "I didn't kill her, you know. I know no more about it than you do. Less, probably, if the actual truth really is tucked away somewhere inside your head."

I found my voice. "Yes, I expect so. I'm sorry."

"Got across each other again, didn't we?" He turned towards me again, and smiled. "It isn't always easy, dealing with you, Joanna. Sometimes you say things in perfect innocence that are hard to take."

Recovering from my fright, I felt an instinct to strike back. "You're not too easy to deal with either," I said resentfully.

"All right, so we're both difficult customers. But if we're going to get you out of this mess, we have to work together . . . and trust each other, don't you think? So what about this nun? Maybe she can tell you what you were wearing, if she remembers. Much more important is what time it was. They must have had that on the record. Did you ask them?"

"I never thought of it —"

Angelo made a gesture of mock despair. "You'd never make a detective, would you? If you really did change your clothes then there has to be a gap in time that isn't accounted for."

"Of course. But I didn't think of it. When

I asked about the dress they weren't all that co-operative. Sister Luisa . . . the one I spoke to there . . . obviously thought it was a very frivolous request."

"You didn't explain why you wanted to know?"

"I did try. I said I felt something bad had happened and that it was something to do with the dress. She said the evil might only be in my own heart. She said I should be patient, and trust in God."

"I see. Very helpful," said Angelo drily. "So we'll have to try this other lady."

"They may not let us see her."

"They'll let us see her," said Angelo.

10

He was right. In the event there was no difficulty whatever. The difficulty was in getting there in the first place.

I was happy, that morning, going out with Angelo. Perhaps it was foolish of me, but my sense of danger was muted by the much stronger, closer sense of being among friends. Angelo had taken me home the previous afternoon and stayed to dinner; it was an awkward moment when I first saw Penny again. We stood and looked at each other grinning ruefully. I had to make the first move. I stepped forward and threw my arms round her; she hugged me back and then we were both laughing and everything was all right. Considering the situation it was a cheerful evening, even a merry one. I was secure within my own four walls, giddy with relief that I was no longer alone.

The next day was Saturday. As we started out towards the city centre it was quite clear that something unusual was happening. Groups of people who did not look like tourists were making their way determinedly towards some central point, and as they began to converge the crowd grew thicker. Police were everywhere on the streets. "What's happening?" I asked. The traffic was held up, being diverted; irritable motorists all round us were shouting, asking each other the same question, while the crowds of pedestrians crossed the street against the lights and harassed traffic police had to come and sort things out.

"It's a demonstration," said Angelo. "I'm sorry, Joanna. I shouldn't have brought you out in this. I did know about it, but I completely forgot it was today; these affairs usually take place on a Sunday. Still, it isn't far; we should get through soon."

"I wouldn't want to put it off," I told him. "Anyway, it's interesting." I looked out of the car window into the faces of the people. As they walked along in the bright sunlight it was plain that they were in no holiday mood; they looked grave, as if engaged in serious business. The men wore black armbands, and the women, even the young ones in their bright cotton dresses, mostly wore a black kerchief on their heads.

"What's it about?" I asked. "They look as if they're going to a funeral —"

"So they are, in a way. There was a coach trip last weekend. Family parties, out for the day. Lots of little kids. Someone put a bomb in it."

"Oh no, how ghastly! Who did it?"

"It's thought some neo-fascist gang. They've become very active lately. Nobody's been arrested so far. It's also thought that the authorities know quite well who they are, but won't act against them —"

"Why not?"

"Why not? This country was a fascist state for nearly twenty-five years. Attitudes and sympathies die hard, even in high places. Hence the demonstration. It's probably coming this way, which means we may get diverted. Look out for our turning; should be along here somewhere."

I had no sooner seen our turning than we were diverted away from it, to the left.

"This means we'll have to park somewhere and walk back," Angelo said. "Hell, I don't like this."

"Will there be trouble?"

"I shouldn't think so. That's not what's worrying me. I just don't like you walking on the street more than you have to . . . oh, no you don't, my lad." This as he slipped neatly into a parking space, thwarting a young man in an old Fiat "topo" who had clearly marked it for his own. He drove off with a crash of gears, shaking his fist at us; I couldn't help laughing. Angelo gave me a quick approving glance.

"You feel better today, don't you?"

"More confident," I said. "I'm not alone any more, you see."

"That's fine," said Angelo drily. "But you can't afford to tempt providence. Stay close to me, and do what I tell you."

"I shall," I assured him. "I'm not *that* confident."

L'Ospedale della Croce Sacra was not really a hospital at all, more like an old people's home. Angelo having talked the porteress into admitting us, we passed through a dark high court into a small garden, where elderly women sat on benches in the shade, knitting and gossiping, and thence into a cool bare parlour, where we had to wait some time before the Mother Superior came to receive us.

I let Angelo do the talking. I was the more ready to do this because the Reverend Mother was a severe-looking lady who would have intimidated me at once, had I been on my own. I watched and listened, fascinated, as Angelo made a dazzling job of softening her up. His manner was a subtle blend of manly respect for a woman of the cloth, a touch of charm, and more than a touch of steely determination; he told our improbable story with a dry precision and despatch which gave it the full force of reality. Even so, she was sceptical; I couldn't blame her, really.

"I am afraid I don't understand, signore. Surely, if your friend is in danger, you should go to the proper authorities? To the police?"

"*Mia madre,*" said Angelo solemnly, "we have no evidence. Not of the kind which would convince the police. My friend has no memory of events before her accident; she doesn't know why these things are happening. The shooting attempt yesterday — I was there, this was no figment of her imagination. What can we say about it? Two men who made off afterwards, in a van, probably with false number plates, or perhaps abandoned a few streets away? I can see you think our story improbable, why shouldn't you? And, of course, the police have enough to do as it is. There have been so many killings. This latest one the worst since Bologna."

"Ah yes. It is terrible, terrible. Little children, injured and killed, who could do such a thing, to these innocents?" Her face beneath the white coif was tragic; I wondered why I had thought her severe. "The workers demonstrate today, I understand. To commemorate the deaths and, as they say, to protest. They would do better to stay at home and pray." She smiled faintly. "And yet I understand why they do it. And you, my child," she added, turning to me, "surely it is not safe for you to go out in public?"

"My friend puts her trust in God," Angelo interposed smoothly. Unreasonably, as I had been glad enough of his initiative in the first place, I now wished he would leave me to speak for myself.

The nun gave us her faint reluctant smile again. "Of course," she said gently. "But you know, signore, the good Lord does not require us to be foolhardy."

"I hope I'm not that," I said. "I'm very frightened, really. But, you see, I have to do things which will help me remember."

"Ah yes, the amnesia. A terrible affliction. You have found no improvement since your illness?"

"Very little, I'm afraid. That's why I so desperately need help . . ."

She seemed to make up her mind. *"Ebbene,"* she said quite briskly. "Whatever help we can give you, you shall have. It may not be much. But I will send for Sister Justina, and we shall see."

Sister Justina could not have been more different than her superior, being much younger, rosy and plump, with a motherly smile and a warm open manner. She remembered me immediately, and some minutes were taken up with her exclamations over me, how well

I looked, completely recovered, yes?

"Thank you, Sister, physically I'm very well," I said. "But my problem remains. You know I lost my memory."

"And it's no better? Never mind, never mind. It will come," she said cheerfully.

"I'm afraid it's more complicated than that. That's why we have come to see you. To ask you to help us."

At first it seemed like a rerun of the conversation I had had with Sister Luisa in Denzano; it sounded, as I spoke, frivolous, ridiculous; I mean, who would care what they were wearing when they'd had an accident?

She did, to begin with, look puzzled. "That would be very difficult. In such circumstances . . . to recall one dress, rather than another . . ."

"A white dress," I said. "A long evening gown."

She sat silent for a moment. Then her face cleared. "But, my dear child, you were not wearing a dress at all. I remember now, because we had to cut them off —"

"Cut them off?"

"The . . . the trousers. Blue, I think they were, of heavy cotton material — there is a special name for them, I think."

"Jeans," said Angelo quickly. "Blue jeans?"

"Yes, of course. That, exactly. And a white top garment, with short sleeves —" Angelo looked at me. "A T-shirt," he said. "Jeans and a T-shirt." We both fell silent. Sister Justina looked from one to the other of us. "This is important?"

I couldn't speak. Angelo said quickly, "Yes, I think it is. It means that she did not have the accident directly after she left the party. She must have gone home and changed her clothes —"

"In the middle of the night?"

"You may well be puzzled, Sister. We understand it no more than you do. Nevertheless, it takes us a step further forward. Because now we know there must have been a gap in time, not accounted for. You have such remarkable recall that perhaps you can help us there too. What time was it, when she was admitted?"

"Ah, now that I don't remember. Late, very late — or rather, I should say, very early. But the records at Denzano would tell you that. Or the young Americans who brought her in —"

"Americans?"

"Did you not know about that? They were driving through the night, to get back to Rome, I think, and found the crashed car with you in it. They put you in the back of their car and brought you in to Denzano. We were concerned about that, for it is often injurious, as you know, for a casualty to be moved by unskilled people. But no harm was done, and of course really they had no choice; it might have taken longer to get an ambulance."

"I suppose you don't remember their name?"

Sister Justina smiled. "Ah, now that would be too much to ask. They were there only such a short time . . . a German name, I think, but I can't be sure of that. Again, they may have some record of that in Denzano."

"Yes. But I'm afraid that won't help us very much. Tourists . . . they are probably back home in the States by now. There's just one more thing, Sister. Do you remember anything about an earring? Just one."

"You mean, were you wearing it?"

"No, not that. I don't wear earrings. I found it in the locker at the hospital. It seemed to have some significance for me, but of course I've no idea what."

She shook her head. "I was very busy, you understand. I would not notice a small thing like that. But I was not the only nurse on duty, of course. Someone else could have picked it up and put it in your locker — and then, perhaps, it was forgotten."

There was no more she could tell us. We thanked her profusely and apologized for taking up her time and left.

It was a test of my endurance to walk again along the narrow street which led back to the main thoroughfare. As he had done on the way there, Angelo had his arm round me, keeping me close to the wall. He was continually alert, watchful, his eyes scanning windows and parked cars. After a minute or so, he said without looking at me, "Are you all right?"

"So far," I said. "At least, I'm glad to know I wasn't wrong. About the dress, I mean . . . At least I know I changed my clothes, that I must have gone home. But why? And what did I do after that?"

"God knows. But it's still a step in the right direction . . . oh, damn, look at this."

We had reached the corner. Down the street the demonstration was marching towards us, taking up the whole of the roadway. A long banner stretched right across the first rank of marchers, carried in their hands: *Abbasso Fascismo! Abbasso Terrorismo! Abbasso Gli Assassini!*

Getting across the road now seemed impossible. Flanked closely by police, the demonstrators were in serried ranks; they walked in silence; there was no sound except the sound of thousands of marching feet. Some of the women carried little bunches of flowers, and everywhere there were small rough-made placards, held aloft. Each had a picture of a man, a woman, or a child. Each one bore a name and the same message:

Bruno Sarti, ci ricordiamo sempre di te!
Maria Lunghi, ci ricordiamo sempre di te!
I Bambini Rossi, ci ricordiamo sempre di voi!
Bruno, Maria, the Rossi children, we will always remember you.

There were many other names. It was unbearably moving, the placards and the flowers and the grave faces of the great, silent, crowd sweeping forward slowly, irresistibly, a vast tide of humanity extending as far back as the eye could see.

"We can't stand here," Angelo said. "We'd better get into a bar somewhere —"

I wasn't listening. My eye had been caught by someone standing on the edge of the pavement, not a dozen yards away.

"There's that man," I said. "The one on the train . . . look, there . . ."

As I spoke, he turned towards us and saw me. For a moment he froze where he stood; then, to my utter amazement, he turned hurriedly away and plunged into the ranks

310

of the demonstrators.

Without thinking, I plunged in after him. I heard Angelo's shout behind me, but there was nothing I could do, once I was in, but become part of the march. Two women, smiling, made room for me between them; my quarry, in that tossing sea of moving heads in front of me, had completely disappeared; he might even have struggled through to the opposite pavement. But I had to be sure.

I began to move forwards, weaving my way through the people in front of me, and this was far from easy; there were black looks, and some mutterings, but I persisted, trying to do it politely, not to push; *mi scusi, camerate, permesso, permesso.* After a few minutes of this my heart began to fail me; I had lost Angelo, I was alone in the middle of this great crowd, and was no nearer finding the man I was looking for: the man who could tell me so much. *The man who knew.* Blackmailer he might be, almost certainly had been at the time of that early encounter. Now, all he seemed to want to do was to avoid me . . . why?

The march came to a halt; we had arrived at a T-junction and police were holding us up so as to let the transverse traffic go through. It was at that point that I heard a familiar irascible voice just behind me: "Joanna, what *do* you think you're playing at?"

It was, of course, Angelo, looking furious. I must admit I was relieved to see him.

"How did you manage to catch up with me so quickly?"

"By the simple process of belting along the pavement and looking out for you. You could have done the same if you'd stopped to think."

I wasn't listening.

"There he is," I said. "Look . . ."

He was still in the ranks of the marchers, only about four rows ahead. I saw him as he momentarily turned his head to see if we were following, perhaps?

"Come on then," said Angelo. Taking advantage of the momentary lull we squeezed our way through the people in front of us. He looked round again, saw us, and would have made a dive for the opposite pavement; but just at that moment the march got under way again, and he was swept forward, as we were. We moved in beside him, marching along.

I said softly, "So we meet again."

He gave me a quick furtive glance, then looked straight ahead. He said, hardly moving his lips, "I do not know you. Go away."

"This is a great change, isn't it? You were keen enough to talk to me before. You were a friend, you said. Who could keep a secret."

He didn't answer. He was pallid under his sallowness; I realized suddenly that he was terrified. He looked quickly from one to the other of us, and eventually muttered, "Nothing to say."

Angelo took a hand, then. "I think you'd better find something to say, my friend. There are enough police here to arrest you a hundred times over. We could charge you with molesting the lady, or snatching her bag, perhaps . . ."

He said, "I have done nothing. You can't do that . . ."

"If not that, we'll think of something," said Angelo cheerfully. "Now we're going to get out of this, and you're coming with us. There's more traffic ahead, we shall be halted again in a minute or two . . . Now. *Andiamo.*"

We slipped out of the crowd and gained the pavement.

Once there he began walking away very fast, seeking to shake us off. We went with him. He looked hunted and watchful, he began cursing, a steady stream of obscenities. I wondered for a moment why he didn't run, but of course to run would have been to call attention to himself.

I said quite gently, "Why won't you talk to me?"

He turned his head towards me; as usual, I couldn't see his eyes, obscured by his dark glasses. With his mouth, he snarled,

"Because I want to stay alive, lady. It is not healthy to be seen in your company."

"So somebody's put the frighteners on you," said Angelo. "Who is it?"

"If I told you that, I could as well tell you everything. But I will not speak. You can't make me speak."

Angelo said softly, "There's money in it." He cocked an inquiring eyebrow at me and I said, "A million lire."

That checked the man in his stride, but he said, with a ridiculous attempt at dignity, "You hold a man's life so cheap?"

"It's my life too," I told him. "Two million." I suppose, I thought, I must have two thousand pounds to spare, from what they tell me. But it was not enough for him, and we compromised on three thousand.

"You can do a lot with that," Angelo told him. "Get right away, leave Rome, leave the country perhaps. Lie low somewhere for a bit. Till all this is settled. As it will be, if you tell us what you know."

There was a pause. Then the man said, "Cash. Small notes."

"Of course."

He hesitated, then said with a return to

314

his snarling manner, "You take me for a fool. It takes time to get such a sum together, and the banks are closed today."

"We can wait," said Angelo. "And the lady's credit is good. Monday evening, then. You know her apartment? I bet you do."

"I will not come there. They know —"

"Who knows?"

"Nobody. But I will not come there."

"All right. We'll come to you, then."

"No!"

Angelo sighed. "Very well. I wouldn't have thought a public place was such a good idea, but you know your own business best. Let's say in the Trastevere, Monday night, six o'clock, corner of Via Mazzini . . . there's a bar there: Gizzi's. We shall be punctual." Angelo nodded, "You'd better be, too."

For a moment I thought he would refuse. Then he muttered, *"Va bene"*; we stood still and let him go. He scurried away with his head down, as people walk in bad weather, and was soon out of sight.

"Well, don't just stand there," said Angelo irritably. He took me by the elbow and steered me into the nearest bar. Then he collected two cups of cappucino and slapped one down on the table in front of me, rather as if he'd dearly like to slap me instead.

"What's the matter?" I asked.

315

"I *said* stay close and do what I tell you."

"Yes, I know. But it was such a stupendous piece of luck, seeing him like that. I didn't think —"

"Not thinking," said Angelo between his teeth, "could get you killed."

"Yes, I suppose . . . but, you see, I felt absolutely safe among those people . . ."

"What you *felt* has nothing to do with it. Can't you see what might have happened? Some opposition group, sneering and jeering at the demonstration — people getting provoked — a fight breaking out, and you in the middle of it. The easiest thing in the world to set up."

"Good heavens," I said feebly. "I thought *I* was the one with the vivid imagination." But in my mind's eye I could see it all happening in just the way he had said; I had, indeed, been very reckless. I said humbly, "Angelo, I'm sorry."

"I don't want apologies," said Angelo irritably, "just a bit of co-operation. I want you to stay home for the rest of this week-end. You'll have to come to the bank with me on Monday, but on Monday night, I'll take the money and meet that little creep by myself."

"No," I said. "No, that won't do."

"Joanna —"

316

"No, seriously, Angelo. If I'm not there, I don't think he'll tell you anything, money or no money."

"Well, you could be right."

"Of course, we don't know if he'll turn up at all."

"He'll turn up," Angelo said. "For that kind of money. We could probably have got away with less if we'd gone on bargaining."

"It doesn't matter," I said. "So long as I've got it."

"Oh, you've *got* it," said Angelo drily, and then laughed. "Don't look so dismayed. Having more money than you know what to do with is the least of your worries."

"Yes," I said. "I suppose that's true. Angelo, what do you think has been happening, to him I mean?"

"Our friend out there? He's gone off you, that's for sure. Perhaps he talked too much. Tried to blackmail someone else — *who*, I wonder? Now he's under threat to keep his mouth shut about whatever it is — and clearly that's what we need to know."

Angelo delivered me back to the flat, went off and didn't appear at all again over the weekend. He was going to be busy, he said. I kept my promise to him and didn't stir outside all the weekend, didn't sit on the balcony, kept away at all times from the windows. Penny had her instructions too: admit nobody to the flat unless either she or I was certain who it was; answer all telephone calls in a likewise non-committal fashion; accept delivery of no letters or parcels. It felt a little, at first, as if we were living under siege, but it was hot to the point of enervation and probably cooler indoors than out. We kept the rooms in a cool green twilight with the shutters drawn; Penny and I pottered about in a state of undress, bare-footed, with only cotton robes to cover our nakedness; we slept through the heat of the day, ate, drank, listened to records, played games of scrabble. Most of all we talked, talked ourselves into friendship. It was strange to compare the Penny I hadn't known and had consequently suspected with the Penny I was coming to know. Instead of the mysterious, somewhat menacing lady wearing a false front of friendliness and bonhomie, there was this fresh and eager young woman, gentle, a bit naive, enormously impressed by me and my friends and the life I lived, or was supposed to live.

She told me the story of her life and I only wished I was able to tell her mine, though she knew some of it, it seemed, from Angelo. I heard about her family, her three brothers (one of whom had been at university with Angelo; hence her introduction to him when she came to Rome), her young sister, only sixteen, the widowed mother, vague, charming and eccentric. I saw in my mind's eye, from her descriptions, a rambling house in the country, badly in need of a coat of paint; the front door always open in summer, leading to a hall littered with dog baskets and wellington boots and cricket bats. Penny and her brothers were an adventurous lot, intensely active and physical, always going off somewhere; one had crewed in the round-the-world yacht race; another, a zoologist, had just returned from a complicated and dangerous trip down the Amazon. Yet, as she told me, for all their adventurousness they all returned, like swallows in due season, to the place where they belonged; to home, to the family.

I listened, fascinated and saddened, to Penny's chatter. From what I knew of my own history — knew, not remembered — there was nothing like that in my own past: the secure background from which one might set forth on a voyage of discovery and return with confidence of a happy homecoming; the jokes, squabbles, sharing; the solid loyalty and affection, never mentioned, but always there. Just Nonno, and a big house, and a silver spoon in my mouth; and what all that had made of me, I had no real idea. That was the big difference between Penny and me. She knew, perfectly, who she was.

Of course, as I've said, Penny didn't see me like that. She told me, quite innocently, that I was "quite different from what she expected". Nicer, that seemed to imply.

I said, smiling, "What did Angelo tell you? That I was the original rich bitch — spoiled, selfish, arrogant?"

Penny went very pink. "Angelo wouldn't say things like that," she protested. "He's very fond of you, and worried about you —"

"Worried," I said. "Yes."

"And he thinks you're very brave —"

"Did he really say that?" In spite of myself, I was absurdly pleased. "I'm not really, you know. Quite a lot of the time, none of it seems real. All the same — fond of me, Angelo isn't. Don't get me wrong — if I do get out of this mess in one piece I shall owe Angelo, and you too, a debt I can never repay. But believe me, he doesn't do all this for me because he's fond of me. He'd do the same for anyone."

"That's what makes him such a wonderful person," Penny said.

"Of course. But he also does it because it's a challenge, don't you think? What about you? Getting involved with me could be dangerous —"

"I know that."

"Then why? You didn't know me. Angelo told me you're broke, but you could have gone to the Consulate, borrowed the fare home. Instead of that you've put yourself right in the middle of a very dodgy situation. I don't think I should let you do it, but Angelo says I can't stop you. So . . . why?"

"It was just that it's interesting," Penny said. "And exciting —"

"A challenge," I nodded. "There you are, then."

"Besides," she added, "Angelo asked me. He trusted me."

At this point she flushed an even deeper pink. I thought, oh dear, she's in love with him, and felt sorry for her. Being in love with Angelo, it seemed to me, could be both a wearing and unrewarding business.

My theory about Penny's emotional state took rather a knock however, that weekend, after a telephone call from Roddy. I was in the shower, and he gave Penny a number for me to ring. She could hardly wait for me to get out of the shower before telling me, all agog.

I said, grinning, "Shall I ask him to dinner?"

"*Would* you! Tonight?"

"If we've got enough to eat —"

"That's no problem," Penny exclaimed. Her eyes sparkled. "Fancy! Having Roddy Marchant to dinner!"

"You like him?"

"Joanna, you know jolly well I think he's absolutely delicious!"

"Dearie," I said gently, "we'll be having him *to* dinner. Not *for* dinner."

"What? Oh . . . !" She giggled, and then seemed to reconsider: "But he won't want me here. He'll want to be alone with you . . ."

"What he wants," I said cheerfully, "is not necessarily what he's going to get."

"Ah. You're going to play it cool."

"You could say that. Which means, as well, no talk about what's been happening, Penny, please. Roddy thinks I cook things up, and just now I don't intend to bother with convincing him otherwise. I want to get him to help me, though. And I'll be asking for your help too. I'm planning to give a party."

"What a marvellous idea! Who are you going to invite?"

"Well, that's just it. People I knew . . . you know, before. There are lots of names in my address book but at the moment they're just names. Roddy can help us sort them out. I thought, you see, that maybe if I could see a lot of them all in one go . . . fit faces to the names . . . someone, something might ring a bell."

"Yes, I see. When are you planning to have it? The party?"

"I thought at the end of the week. Friday, perhaps. If I live," I added with a wry grin.

So I rang Roddy and he came to dinner. It all turned out quite well, really. If Roddy was surprised to find us a threesome with no extra man to balance the numbers, he didn't show it. He was simply his most delightful self, both to Penny and to me. He flattered Penny and teased her in a light-hearted way, at the same time — and don't ask me how he did it — conveying to me the message that it was all being done to please me.

I understood what was happening. I was different now, not a drag any more. I had got some confidence back and, like the good actress I was supposed to be, I could give him a different image of myself: cool, a bit reserved. And that, naturally, represented a challenge he couldn't resist.

Well, I was a challenge to all of them. One way and another.

11

The bank, on Monday morning, received my extraordinary request with astonishing placidity. I produced my credentials and proofs of identity. A telephone call was made to London. I put my signature to documents. At no time did the smooth young man who attended to our business express any surprise or curiosity about why I wanted such a large sum, not only in cash, but in small denominations. As Angelo had said, the lady's credit was good. We came away, at last, with a suitcase filled with paper money. "It doesn't look real," I said. "He won't think we're deceiving him, and refuse to tell us anything?"

"I don't see why he should," said Angelo. "We'll just have to wait and see."

We emerged, with caution, into the street. My hair was black that morning, I wore clothes I had not so far, at least to my knowledge, worn in Rome. Penny had the car outside the bank with the engine running. On the way there she had dropped us off on a street corner; there we had walked into a shop by one door and out by another into a different street, where we had picked up a taxi and driven to the bank. Meanwhile, Penny had driven around for a bit and then come to collect us; a comparatively simple ploy to confuse possible pursuers.

We returned to the flat without incident.

In the evening Penny went out first, wearing, against my protests, a wig the colour of my hair. She collected a small Fiat car Angelo had borrowed for the evening, and returned to pick me up, by which time she had discarded the auburn wig and looked like herself again. We drove without mishap to the forecourt of a large hotel where we left the car. We then entered the hotel and retired for a short time into the Ladies' Powder Room; after which we walked out of the rear entrance of the hotel into a small street where Angelo was waiting for us with his own car.

"No trouble?" he asked Penny. "Followers?"

"None that we could see."

"Good." He nodded at the cars parked in the street and added; "I've checked these. All locked and empty, so none of them is likely to edge out and start after us. Let's get going, then."

We arrived at the café in the Trastevere at five minutes to six, ordered drinks, and waited. Because the cafe was on a corner we could see out from both sides and could also keep the car in our sights. It was asking for a parking fine to leave it where it was, but at least we knew it couldn't be tampered with.

The district was waking up to its evening life, with people coming home from work, doing their shopping, turning into their favourite bar for a drink and a chat. They were drifting in now to Gizzi's, the one where we were. It struck me what a crazy arrangement we had made: were we going to sit there, in public, while he counted the Italian equivalent of three thousand pounds in cash before he told us anything? Or should we move on somewhere else?

For the moment, these questions seemed academic. There was no sign of the man with the scar. Six o'clock. Five past. The minutes dragged.

At a quarter past I said, "He's not coming."

"Hold on," said Angelo. "That looks like him now.

He was approaching us on the far side of the Via Mazzini. We saw him glance across at the café and then move to the edge of the pavement.

There was not much traffic. He waited to let a couple of cars pass, and then still stood there, looking up and down the empty street, before stepping out into the roadway.

That very caution and hesitation were his undoing.

At that moment, in the comparative quiet, we heard someone gunning an engine. The car came, it seemed, from nowhere; as he stepped into the roadway it swerved to mow him down. He saw it, he tried to run, he screamed, the tyres screamed, and then the car struck him, it swept forward bearing his body on the bonnet and then throwing it off, high in the air, and rushing on to leave him to fall in the gutter. A bundle of old clothes, falling through the air. A rag doll.

Pandemonium broke out in the street, with people running, shouting, screaming. A small crowd gathered round the body, hiding it from sight. The car, of course, had gone.

People in the bar were standing up, craning their necks to see, though there was nothing to see now. The barman was telephoning for an ambulance. Outside in the street a car came by, slowing because of the gathering crowd. It stopped, and a well-dressed, greying man got out, went over to the group round the body, cutting a swathe through it with a few crisp, commanding words: a doctor, we had to suppose. The people drew back and made a space for him and we could see him then, bending over the body. He straightened up, shaking his head; in a few minutes the ambulance and the police arrived.

We stayed where we were. There were enough eye-witnesses already and there was no need for us to become involved.

No need to be involved. But we were involved.

A man was dead and it was our fault.

No. My fault.

I thought confusedly about our . . . my . . . duty in the matter, that I ought to tell the police why he was there, why he was killed. *He knew too much, he was going to tell me . . .* tell you what, signorina? . . . *well, I don't know exactly . . . he tried to blackmail me once, only I've lost my memory so I didn't know what he was blackmailing me about, and I wanted him to tell me, only in the end he wouldn't, he was frightened because someone had threatened him . . .*

Rehearsed like that in my mind, it sounded more of a farrago of nonsense than ever. I couldn't do it.

We went on sitting there. Penny put her arm round me. Angelo said, "There's nothing you can do, Joanna."

"No," I said. "I know."

The body was loaded into the ambulance. The police wrote names and addresses of witnesses down in their notebooks, and presently both police and ambulance went away.

"I'll go and have a word with them later," said Angelo. "The police, I mean. See what I can find out about him."

"Oh . . . will they tell you?"

"A press card helps." He nodded across me to Penny. "Time we got her home, I think. Let's get going. With caution."

The remark, made about me, nevertheless made me feel totally excluded: I might have been a child, a pedigree animal, or any other piece of valuable property. To be guarded. Maintained intact. Oh well, that was how he saw me, no doubt.

We drove home without a hint of any kind of trouble. The assassination squad, it would seem, had done their bad deed for the day.

Once indoors, Penny went off at once to start the dinner. I sat silent, staring in front of me.

"Do you want another drink?" Angelo asked.

I shook my head.

"Oh, come on now." He might have been coaxing a child.

I said suddenly, "We killed him. We lured him to his death."

"A little rat," said Angelo harshly.

"Maybe. But a *human* little rat. Whatever he'd done, he didn't deserve . . ."

"You don't know what he'd done," said Angelo. "You don't even know if we did — lure him to his death, I mean. They, whoever they are, may have decided that his time was up. Joanna, we didn't kill him. Greed killed him. Blackmail is a high-risk occupation."

"Yes. I suppose so."

"And, anyway, this isn't any time for lamentations. We have to go on following up what leads there are; this is one of them. Somebody being very anxious indeed that you shouldn't be told whatever it was he had to tell. If we know who he is and something about his background, it might help. The only other lead we have is Elena, so we have to look into her life, her friends, associates, what she did in her spare time —"

"But where would that take us?"

Angelo said gently, "Joanna, you have to take into account the possibility that Elena was not killed by some anonymous thug. It might have been someone she knew. It might, even, be someone *you* knew."

"Someone I *know?*"

"I didn't say that. I said, someone you knew before the accident. You may not have met him again since then. He's almost certainly keeping out of your way. I mean, he'd hardly want to come face to face with you in public and for you to shout, 'Eureka!' would he? On the other hand . . ."

"On the other hand what?"

"Who stole the earring?"

"I don't know. I put it away that night, after I wore it. I locked it away. Everybody who saw me wearing it left next day."

"I did," Angelo said. "Frank did. And the girl, what's her name, Carole." He was, I saw, carefully not looking at me.

"You don't mean . . . *Roddy?* You can't suspect Roddy, you can't . . ."

I saw a movement in his face, which came and went so quickly I could have imagined it. Then he said in the same careful voice as before, "I can understand that you find that hard to accept. But you did say that Roddy dissuaded you from taking the earring to the police."

"Yes. And I taxed him with it. I *asked* him if he'd taken it. If there'd been the slightest bit of . . . of equivocation . . . shiftiness . . . anything, I would have known, I'm sure of it." And I was, but I still didn't, couldn't, tell Angelo that Roddy had lied to me about Stockholm. Another thought struck me: "Besides, I went out with Roddy. For a whole day, in the country. If he wished me harm, he had ample opportunity —"

"Of course. But you must remember that whoever X is, he wants to cover his tracks, not make more."

I didn't say anything.

Angelo looked at me quickly, smiled, and put a hand over mine. "Don't look like that. I don't really think your boy-friend had anything to do with this. And, anyway, there's absolutely nothing to connect him with Elena . . . always supposing that Elena is what it's all about."

"Have you found out anything about her?" I asked.

"Not a lot that I didn't know already. I must tell you one thing . . . I've taken young Nico into my confidence."

"Nico? The man who spoke to me outside the church?"

"That's the one. I was afraid you wouldn't like it. But he's working on the story and can get information which otherwise I'd have to ferret out for myself. I have his solemn oath he'll be discreet . . . he *is* keen, not only professionally. He was genuinely fond of Elena; she took him under her wing when he first started work on the paper. A touch of maternal instinct, perhaps; she had no children. Anyway, he managed to get past her reserve, a little, anyway."

"She was like that?"

"Very much so. Also very highly strung in a repressed sort of way. Difficult. According to Nico she had become increasingly so recently, showing signs of strain under the pressures of working on a newspaper. In fact, at the time she went on holiday, she was due to be fired. That was going to be done when she came back. Only she never came back, poor thing."

"Heavens," I said. "And all that fulsome stuff in the paper and everybody going to that memorial service. How hypocritical can you get."

Angelo shifted an expressive shoulder. "Hypocritical, yes. A trifle conscience-stricken too, perhaps. Which may be why they've put Nico on the story. I daresay they don't expect much to come of it, but it's a gesture of sorts. I must say there's not a lot to go on, from our point of view. Particularly as there's nothing to show she was ever anywhere near the lake until she was put in it."

"Didn't she have a husband?" I asked.

"Yes, she did. I know him too, though not well . . . the marriage broke up some years ago. In case you're thinking he's suspect, he has an unbreakable alibi. He was in Singapore all through the relevant period. He's back now, of course, living in Milan. Maybe he'll be able to throw some light on things; Nico's aiming to see him if he can."

I sighed. "It looks a bit like a dead end, to me."

"For the moment. So we have to come back to you and your quick-change act the night of the accident. Why you were driving about in the small hours, first wearing an evening dress and then in jeans. It's a pity about that couple who picked you up; thousands of miles away by now I suppose —"

"Wait a *minute*." I sat up with a start, staring at him. "An American couple, she said, didn't she, Sister Justina? A German name?"

"That's right but I don't . . ."

"That letter I had, remember? From a man at the Embassy?"

After a brief pause, we said simultaneously: "Cyrus B. Hoffman."

The discovery shook me out of my grief and confusion.

"It's got to be him, hasn't it? *Hoped we would meet under happier circumstances.* It's just got to be . . ."

"Steady," said Angelo. "It may not be. But it's worth trying. Where's the directory?"

Mr Hoffman was at home, and answered

his telephone promptly. A cheerful, youthful voice, an easy manner which quickened into warmth when I said who I was. He was delighted to hear from me, and his wife would be too, he said, and was I quite recovered?

I said I was, adding carefully, "Mr Hoffman, I want to ask you — was it you and your wife who picked me up, the night I had my accident?"

He said, surprised, "Of course, but I thought you knew that —"

"Well, actually I didn't, and I owe you an apology for not replying to your kind note, and thanking you for everything you did."

"Think nothing of it. Anyone would have done the same. Are you in Rome now, Miss Fleming? Francie and I would be so happy if you would visit with us some time —"

"Well, actually that's something I would like to take you up on, Mr Hoffman. I would like to meet you — as soon as possible, really; I have a little bit of a problem you may be able to help me with —"

"What kind of problem, Miss Fleming?"

I sensed his withdrawal immediately, the cautious diplomatic shutter coming down, and added quickly, "It's entirely personal, nothing that will involve any hassle, I assure you. And it will only take a few minutes."

"I see. Well, if it's urgent, perhaps you'd like to come round and have a drink with us later this evening?"

"Thank you. I'd like to do that. I wonder if I could bring a friend with me? He'll drive me, you see, I don't drive myself yet . . ." I was inspired to add, "You may know him, or know of him. Angelo Valente. The writer."

Mr Hoffman, it seemed, was something of a cultural buff. He exclaimed, and said once more that he'd be delighted, and made a joke about two celebrities for the price of one; the conversation ended on a renewed wave of affability.

I was getting used to Angelo's precautions, and waited upstairs while he, accompanied by Penny, went down to the car, checked it out for possible interference, brought it to the door and remained with it while Penny came upstairs to fetch me and escorted me down again. Getting used to them, yes, but they gave me the feeling of being a prisoner, and I knew I could not stay long like this in Rome.

Mr Hoffman and his wife had a flat in the Embassy, which meant that Angelo and I had to run the gauntlet of their security arrangements. I was a bit disconcerted to be — well, welcomed was hardly the word — by a guard of impassive and fully armed GIs at the entrance. We gave our names to an official who busied himself telephoning, and were then escorted outside again, round the side of the building, and hence to the Hoffmans' front door.

Once inside, the atmosphere could not have been more different.

We were warmly welcomed, waved into deep velvety chairs, and supplied with large drinks containing more gin than I'm used to. Mr Hoffman was much as I expected, very much the Embassy whizz-kid, concealing his youth behind rimless glasses. A quite genuine warmth and friendliness combined with the smooth wary shrewdness I had sensed on the telephone. Mrs Hoffman, on the other hand, was not at all my idea of a diplomatic wife, being rather shy and dreamy-looking, with unfashionable pre-Raphaelite looks: even her hair, being long, blonde, and abundant, was appropriately like that of the Blessed Damozel. I took a moment to wonder how she fitted in there, trying to make a home in what the army calls married quarters, on a somewhat more exalted, even luxurious, scale. She had done what she could with the place, with books and flowers, family photographs, pictures of home; she hadn't been there long, I guessed, and was homesick.

We had just got settled when the sound of wailing was heard outside, the sitting-room door was pushed open and a very small person, quite naked and not more than two years old, wandered bewilderedly into the room.

Mr Hoffman, who had just begun saying politely, "Now what can I do for you?" got no further, cast up his eyes, and exclaimed, "Oh, lordy, here we go again!" but he grinned tenderly at the infant just the same.

Mrs Hoffman, looking harassed, murmured an apology. She scooped the child up in her arms, preparatory to carrying him off. I said quickly, "Please. Don't take him away if you don't want to. He's so lovely —"

Angelo, whose lips were twitching, gave me a sudden, warm look which astonished me, and joined in, "That's right. Don't mind us. He wants a cuddle, I expect."

That broke the ice with Mrs Hoffman, whose shyness seemed to disappear. She gave Angelo and me a grateful grin. "Well, if you really don't mind . . . it's easier to get him back to sleep this way. Cy says I'm not firm enough with him, but . . . ."

"You're in good company in this country, Mrs Hoffman," said Angelo. "We're the greatest spoilers of children ever seen. Boys particularly. Which is why we grow up into such arrogant monsters. Ask Joanna."

"I never said you were an arrogant monster," I exclaimed. "What's his name?" I asked Mrs Hoffman, meaning the child.

"David. But of course we call him Davy —"

Davy, having got his own way, lay back contented in his mother's arms. His eyes were large and deeply blue, like hers, with heavy creamy lids about to fall; his eyelashes were ridiculously long and, suddenly noticing me, he gave me a flirtatious glance from under them and turned to snuggle into his mother's breast. He was a rosy golden colour all over, like a hybrid rose. I felt, looking at him, a profound emotion.

He fell asleep quite soon and his mother took him away.

"Well now," said Mr Hoffman, when she returned. "Let's start over. How can we help you?"

"I'm afraid," I said, "it's rather a long story."

By agreement with Angelo beforehand, I didn't say anything about Elena Menotti. I explained about my loss of memory and the attempts on my life, the problem we had in pinning down just what could have happened the night of the accident. That was as far as I got for the moment, as Mrs Hoffman, who had been listening round-eyed to this recital, broke in with exclamations of horror and concern.

Her husband didn't say anything. He was listening to me with polite attention, but I could not read the expression in the eyes behind the rimless glasses. I thought, it isn't exactly that he doesn't believe me, he's reserving judgment.

"Can't anything be done?" Mrs Hoffman asked. "I mean, the police . . . surely you're entitled to some protection . . ."

I shook my head. "It isn't like that, I'm afraid —" and Angelo moved in to support me.

"We've been to the police. We had to report the shooting outside the church. There, of course, she had a witness. Me. But for the rest of it — the amnesia makes a barrier in more ways than one. There's a whole lot more to this story, Mrs Hoffman, than we've told you because we don't want to waste your time. But from a police angle it lacks substance — that is to say, motive. If and when Joanna recovers her memory, we'll know what that is. But we can't afford to wait for that, can we? So we have to keep searching. For anything. Any detail which will give us a lead. Such as what happened the night of the accident."

Mr Hoffman stirred. He said slowly. "Yes, I see. But, you know, we told the local police everything we knew at the time."

340

"Almost everything," said Mrs Hoffman.

He gave her an indulgent, faintly exasperated look. "Honey, what you thought you saw when you were half asleep really doesn't count for much."

Angelo said swiftly, "What was it you thought you saw, Mrs Hoffman?"

Mrs Hoffman glanced quickly at her husband and away again. Her expression had settled into one of mild obstinacy. She said baldly, "I thought I saw the accident happen."

Mr Hoffman ruffled her hair tenderly and smiled. "Sweetheart, your imagination runs away with you, it really does. *I* was driving, and I didn't see anything until we arrived on the scene. And you didn't say anything about it at the time —"

"No. Because I didn't know what it *meant*."

"Please," I said, "please tell us. Whatever it was, it may help."

Mrs Hoffman said slowly, "Cy's right, of course, I had been asleep. But I wasn't asleep *then*. We'd been on leave, up in the Dolomites, and then we'd spent a day or two with some friends who'd come over on vacation from the States . . . they'd taken a villa at Riva. We should have been travelling back that day, and then we decided to stay around — it was so lovely up there — and drive

341

back through the night. So we did that, with Davy fast asleep in the back of the station wagon. Anyway, just where the road goes round that point, what's it called . . ."

"San Virgilio?" Angelo suggested.

"Well, maybe. Just about there you can see right down the road going south, past Bardolino, that way. Of course it was dark, but if there were any lights you'd see them. And I could see those lights coming along, quite a long way away, and then . . . suddenly they were waving about and then they turned as if they were shining upwards instead of along the road in front of them . . . and then they went out altogether. And then I saw the lights of the other car."

"The other car?"

"She's right about that," said Mr Hoffman. "It passed us going north at a hell of a pace, headlights full on, nearly blinded me. Must have gone right past the scene of the accident without stopping. We did tell the cops about that and they said they'd put out an appeal for the driver to come forward, but I don't imagine he did. Anyone who doesn't stop when he sees a smashed-up automobile near the edge of a cliff, isn't going to be helpful about it afterwards. Well, a few minutes later we found you, and the rest you know."

"You saved my life," I said. "I want you to know how deeply grateful I am for everything you did that night."

They both smiled and made deprecatory noises. Angelo, with no debt of gratitude to discharge, brushed all this aside.

"Mr Hoffman, why are you so sure your wife was mistaken?"

"She must have been. It was after three in the morning. The cops reckoned the crash was about a quarter of two. From the watch, you see, Miss Fleming's watch. The glass was smashed, but you could see the time it had stopped."

"A digital watch?"

"I beg your pardon?"

"Angelo," I said quickly, "of course it wasn't a digital watch. Steffy had it repaired for me, it's the one I've got on."

"My point," said Angelo, "is that if it had been a digital watch, it would have stopped only if well and truly smashed, in which case your arm would have been smashed as well, which it wasn't. A watch with an ordinary movement, like that one, could have stopped at *any* time." He turned again to the Hoffmans. "It didn't strike them . . . the police . . . as odd that nobody else had reported the accident earlier?"

"Well . . ." Mr Hoffman said doubtfully,

"I did make that point to them, as a matter of fact, but they didn't find it too surprising. This time of year, so many people on the roads here are foreign tourists, not wanting to be involved in hassles with the authorities, language difficulties, all that. It seems shocking, but I think they figure people are pretty callous these days and they're not far wrong."

"Yes . . . you didn't notice if the engine was still hot?"

"Why yes . . . but then it was a warm night. It wouldn't have cooled so much anyway. I do remember thinking it was just by the grace of God there had been no fire, but presumably the tank wasn't ruptured. Anyway, when you're getting someone out of a crashed vehicle, you don't think of anything but just that."

"No, of course not," I said. "Angelo, Mr and Mrs Hoffman have been so kind, and I don't think we can take up any more of their time . . ."

Angelo took no notice of me whatever. "Just one last thing. Perhaps you wouldn't mind telling me — when you got her out of the car, what was she wearing?"

Mr Hoffman opened his mouth in astonishment. *"Wearing?"* His wife cut in swiftly, "Levis. Sneakers. A T-shirt."

"Quite," said Angelo. "Now when I tell

you that she left a party at half-past one wearing a white evening dress, I think you'll agree that we've got, well, a little bit of a problem." He smiled at Mrs Hoffman and I thought momentarily what a compelling charm he could exert when he wanted to. "I think you were right, you know. I think what you saw from a long way off was the accident itself. Now we have another reason to be grateful to you, Mrs Hoffman."

Mrs Hoffman went a little pink and her eyes sparkled. She said, "Oh, do call me Francie. And let me freshen your glasses."

While his wife was busy at the drinks table Mr Hoffman remained silent. He doesn't like being proved wrong, I thought. After a moment he said quietly to me, "And you don't remember any of this?"

I looked him in the eye and said steadily, "Mr Hoffman, if I did, I wouldn't be here now taking up your time. I still feel a bit bothered about this other car you saw. Could he . . . whoever was driving it . . . have passed by without seeing me? I mean without seeing the crashed car?"

"With headlights on? No way. He must have seen it and gone on by."

"And likewise," Angelo put in, "if the crash happened when Mrs Hoffman thinks it did, he saw it and still went straight on.

As if he didn't want to be identified? Perhaps saw your lights coming, and knew you were almost certain to stop. Or, perhaps, he caused it."

"Caused the accident?"

"Yes, why not? Overtaking, bumping, shouldering Joanna's car off the road? The kind of thing one sees any day in films or on television. It does happen for real, I believe, from time to time."

Francie Hoffman shook her head. "I don't think it can have been like that. Then both lots of lights would have come together, wouldn't they? Coalesced? But the second set were some little way behind . . ."

"In pursuit?" said Angelo. He glanced at me. "Are you all right, Joanna?"

I didn't answer for a moment. I was sick with terror, with panic, I was driving the car faster, faster, taking the bend knowing I wouldn't make it . . .

But this was not memory, but imagination, a reconstruction of what I had just heard. But bad enough. Frightening enough.

Francie Hoffman was right on my wavelength. She put my drink down on the table beside me and said in her gentle voice, "This must be just terrible for you. I'm so sorry."

That sort of sympathy was just the thing most liable to break me down, but I had myself in hand. "Well, thank you. But I'm all right, really. In an awful sort of way I suppose I'm getting used to it all." I spoke briskly and laughed a little; and Francie said she thought I was just magnificent, she really did. Her husband, inevitably, asked why I didn't go back to England, and I had to explain the futility of doing that. However, I added, I didn't think I'd be in Rome for very much longer. "There's one thing I'm going to do before I leave. Give a party."

The Hoffmans looked astonished again, and I said, "Yes, I know it seems an extraordinary thing to do, in the circumstances." I explained, and added, "I'd be very happy if you'd both come, if you'd care to. It's next Friday."

Francie's eyes were sparkling again, and she exclaimed, "Why, isn't that darling of you! We'd love —"

Cyrus Hoffman said quietly, "*Francie*. You've forgotten the Greek reception." He turned to me politely. "That's most kind of you, Miss Fleming. But I'm afraid we have an engagement."

Looking quickly at Francie's disappointed face, I would have taken a large bet that her husband wasn't telling the truth. The message was clear: Cyrus Hoffman was not going to risk having to explain to the Ambassador, or

Head of Protocol, or whoever, why he and his wife had become involved in something of which the outcome was, to put it mildly, unpredictable. I said quietly that I quite understood, and got up to leave; and now that I was actually going even Mr Hoffman was warm in his expressions of concern and good wishes. He came down with us, to accompany us through the grounds and past the guards and back to the car, where he waited with me, looking politely sceptical, while Angelo checked it out once more.

Driving away, Angelo glanced at me and grinned. "Well . . . What did you make of all that?"

"I don't know, really. I mean . . . who's right?"

"Between those two? Oh, she is, almost certainly."

"I don't know how you can say that —"

"Just *because* she's a bit uncertain — if you see what I mean. She's tentative, groping. He's altogether too sure of himself. *She* can't be right, he's got to be. That's something between the two of them, don't you think?"

"Yes, I see. Poor Francie."

"And anyway, what she says fits. The time gap, I mean."

"Yes, I suppose . . . but I'm still confused about that. I mean . . . you said earlier today, before we came down here, that I'd been running round the roads of Italy, but that isn't exactly what I did, is it? I drove along one particular road. I was driving along it in one direction when I left the party and again in the same direction at half-past three, and that doesn't make any sense . . ."

"Unless," said Angelo, "you went back, in between."

"Went *back*? To the Villa Flora? But I'd quarrelled with Roddy —"

"So we understand," said Angelo. I looked at him quickly, but his eyes were on the street and the traffic, and his expression gave nothing away.

"If I'd gone back," I said, "I would have gone back to the party. And I wouldn't have changed my clothes, and people would have seen me."

"Yes."

"What are you getting at?"

"I'm not sure. Perhaps you went back to see Roddy."

"To make it up, you mean? But if I'd done that, he would have told me. Nobody knew I'd had the accident until the hospital rang the Villa Flora next day, they didn't even know who I was at first . . ."

"Yes."

A cloud of menacing possibilities flew up

in front of me and for a moment I couldn't speak. At last I said, "You think all this has something to do with Roddy. You've thought it all along, haven't you?"

"I didn't say that."

"Roddy would have told me. He's as open as the day. He wouldn't deceive me —" But he had, of course, about another matter.

"No. I expect you're right."

I said violently, "I wish to God you'd say what you're really thinking."

"Look, Joanna," said Angelo. He sounded tired. "I can't tell you, because I'm not 'really thinking' anything. I'm not a detective, especially not one of those miraculous fictional ones, all brilliant deductions and inspirational hunches. I'm just plodding along, trying to get together enough facts and possibilities to make some sort of pattern. The kind of pattern which will convince the police, whose job this is, to do something about it. Now and then I try something on for size, make a suggestion to which you might, just might, react. The only way you react to this one is to rush to Roddy's defence. Which, we already know, is natural enough. At the same time, we have to keep you safe, and that is a problem in itself, as we all know only too well." He hesitated, and added whimsically, "Don't shoot the pianist.

He's doing his best."

"Oh, Angelo," I said with a sigh, "I'm sorry."

"Forget it," said Angelo. "Your nerves are on edge, and no wonder. Anyway, I told you before. I don't really cast your Roddy in the role of villain, you know."

"He's not my Roddy," I said.

"Isn't he?" said Angelo.

12

It seemed to me, looking back in some depression over the past few days, that our efforts at investigation hadn't got us very far. We had lured a man to his death, and that was something I was never going to forget, no matter what else I had forgotten; but we had learned nothing, except that someone — who? — would stop at nothing to make sure we learned nothing.

So, what did we know?

That somewhere, some time, on the night I had my accident, I had changed my clothes. Where or why or when exactly, unknown.

That there was a gap in time, unaccounted for, if you believed Mrs Hoffman.

There was little or no gap in time, if you believed her husband. But the fact that I had changed my clothes meant there *must* have been a gap in time.

And there we still stuck, no nearer knowing how long it was or what had happened in it, or who wished my death, or why.

And that was a pretty chilling conclusion to come to. I couldn't put myself in purdah for the rest of my life. I could go home, I supposed, hire myself an expensive bodyguard and go about watched over every minute, like royalty. Or I could simply behave as if there were no danger, and take my chance . . .

Right now, that sort of speculation got me nowhere. What I could do immediately was to stick with the task I'd set myself. The party.

Organising it was less of a problem than I had feared at first. Roddy was endlessly helpful — it did seem that he genuinely wanted to make it up to me for having lied about Stockholm. We compiled the guest list together, after I had explained that what I wanted if possible was a cross-section of all the people who had worked on the picture. That meant film crew, make-up girls, bit-part players, as well as the big names in the cast. Some of the latter I wasn't going to get: it had been one of those movies with a number of character parts, vignettes as it were, played expensively by famous actors who flew in, did a few days' work on the picture, and vanished again. I hadn't necessarily had a lot of contact with them, and most of them were now scattered across the world.

Roddy also introduced me, or rather re-introduced me, to the script girl who had worked on the picture, Dona Perelli. Dona not only knew everybody, but being the kind of shrewd and sharp-eyed lady that script girls have to be — as their jobs depend on their powers of observation — knew a great deal about the relationships between individuals as well. Talking to Dona, I began to get a mental picture of the whole film unit. By and large, it seemed, it had been a happy enough set-up, apart from the tensions caused by Frank Harmer's sometimes unpredictable behaviour; but, as she said, no matter who wanted to kill Frank at lunch-time, they had always forgiven him by nightfall. She spoke about Frank with a wry affection, mixed with a profound respect, and with unequivocal warmth about two other people. One of these was Gina Montefiore who had played my mother in the picture, and the other the English "heavy", Howard Fortune.

Gina had left Rome when the picture was finished but she wasn't far away. She had retired, as apparently she always did when not working, to her family house near Siena. I knew about Gina already, as I had had a charming letter from her inviting me to stay with her there. Between pictures, she said, she reverted to the ways of her peasant forebears, fed the hens, milked the goats, dug the garden, and went about barefoot. At the time I had written to thank her and left it there. Now, I reread the letter and was tempted, but of course I couldn't go. I couldn't make Gina's haven of rustic tranquillity into a target for trouble, which it would become if I were anywhere near it.

All the same, rereading the letter gave me the courage to telephone her. I felt immensely comforted the moment I heard her lovely voice exclaiming, "Joanna, *carissima,* how wonderful to hear from you!" I explained about the party and what it was for, as I didn't see any point in pretending it was just for fun, not to her anyway. She grasped the idea at once. There were few things, she said, which would draw her back to the city once she had left it for the summer, but she would come back just for me. "I have been wondering for so long what I could do to help, and there seems so little . . . *Cara,* have you been in touch with Howard?"

I said no, not yet. Howard was in Paris, it seemed, which seemed to count him out altogether, but Gina said she would telephone him. "I think he will come, for you. He's very fond of you. And anyway, you know how kind he is —" her voice trailed away. "But what am I saying? You don't know how kind he is."

"I'm sure he is," I said, and knew it the same evening when the telephone rang and there he was: no picture in my mind's eye, just another rich voice, a distinguished-British-actor's voice, with the meticulous diction and well-rounded English vowels. "Gina's told me all about it. You want to get us all together to see if it rings any bells, right?"

"That's right," I said gratefully. "But it does seem a terribly long way to ask you to come. I hardly like —"

But he thrust my doubts and protests aside. "Dear child, of course I'll come. It's not so far, and it will be lovely to see you. How are you, anyway, in yourself as they say?"

"Thank you, very well really. Just this problem . . ."

"A wretched business," he said. Just how wretched, I reflected, he didn't begin to know. "Never mind. We'll see what we can do, between us, eh? How's Frank, by the way? Will he be well enough to put in an appearance?"

"He says so. I don't suppose his doctors are going to be very pleased."

"I expect they've given up the ungovernable old devil in despair," said Howard cheerfully. "How are you getting along with him? On some kind of new footing, I suppose."

"I suppose," I said, and laughed. "I mean, I wouldn't really know, would I? Thank you for saying you'll come, Howard . . . and when we meet, don't, please, be offended if I don't recognize you at first, will you?"

Dona Perelli had offered me stills or publicity pictures of all the principals in the film, to help me, as she saw it, but I thanked her and declined. That would have been to defeat the whole object of the exercise, which was to see them all freshly, suddenly, as if for the first time. It hadn't worked with Steffy or Frank or Roddy or Angelo. But it still might, perhaps, with all these people grouped together in a single setting. Perhaps. That's all it was, a slim hope, as I've said. I hadn't had a preview of the picture either, although Frank had offered me the opportunity. That was for a different reason, though — simply that my courage failed me at the thought of going to the studio, sitting in a small dark viewing-room in which even the projectionist would seem like a threat at my back. I would see the picture soon enough, at the premiere; when all this would be over, please God.

Howard said he understood perfectly that I wouldn't recognize him first time round. "Though you never know. One look at my ugly mug and the shock will bring back everything instantly."

I said I was sure he hadn't an ugly mug

357

and he said want to bet, and we said good-bye laughing.

With those two, Gina and Howard, promised, I began to feel better about the whole thing. Now it seemed more like a gathering of friends and less like an experiment. Roddy was certain to come, and Frank almost certain; and there was Penny, and Angelo . . .

But in the end, Angelo wasn't there.

A couple of nights before the party, Penny and I spent some time trying to find something among my things for her to wear. Living out of a rucksack and tote bag, as she had done for months, meant that she hadn't anything suitable of her own. So when Angelo appeared she opened the door to him wearing a long, gauzy, silver-grey dress with floating panels, which completely transformed her.

"Well, well," said Angelo, following her into the living-room. "What have we here? A fashion parade?"

We explained. "I wanted her to go and buy something," I said. "On me, of course. But she swears there isn't time. Anyway, I think that dress will do, don't you? Doesn't she look lovely in it?"

"She certainly does."

Penny smiled. She did, indeed, look beautiful, and knew it. She stretched out her arms and began a slow swirling dance around the room, tripped over the long skirt and was neatly fielded by Angelo, who grinned, kissed the end of her nose, and said briskly, "Right. You look like a million dollars and can hold your own with all those movie people, and you know it. Now perhaps you could both attend to me a bit."

"What is it?" I asked.

"I've had a call from Nico. He's on to something. He wants me to go up there . . . to the north . . . and follow it up. He can't do it, he's been recalled. Just as he thinks he's got a lead, his editor wants him back. Reckons the story's cold, and anyway something more important's come up. As you can imagine, Nico's hopping with frustration."

"What sort of a lead has he got?" Penny asked.

"Well, to start with, Elena was actually seen in the Garda area. Since that picture was in newspapers and on television, a truck driver came forward. He picked her up one evening, he says, on the Verona-Denzano road. She told him her car had broken down. He dropped her off at Denzano and she said she'd try for a taxi there. At that point she vanishes again — nobody in Denzano who runs a taxi had seen her. The truck driver — and he's not involved, by the way, he's been checked out — couldn't be pinned down on the exact date. He did say the lady was nicely dressed, as for an evening date, and that she seemed a bit keyed up and excited. That could mean she was going to meet somebody. It doesn't tell us much more than that, except that it proves she was actually in Denzano, and not just brought from miles away and dumped —"

"I see. Not much of a lead, really, is it?"

"No. But that's not the important thing anyway. Elena had a cottage up in the hills, near a tiny village miles from anywhere. She told Nico before she left Rome that she was going to spend her vacation there. He took himself up there today, and did a bit of nosing around, found an old woman who acted as caretaker when Elena wasn't there. She was very upset about Elena's death and willing to talk. She told Nico that the police had been along and searched the cottage, something she seemed to resent on Elena's behalf. The signora was very quiet and reserved, she said, but always kind and friendly until this last time, when she was rather touchy and irritable. Then the old lady said something which really made Nico prick up his ears. "I disturbed her papers,"

360

she said, "when I was dusting and tidying up, and she was very angry and said never to touch them again and she would have to find a safer place for them." Nico asked if she had told the police about them and got a very tart response: if the signora didn't want anyone to look at her papers, she certainly wasn't going to show them to anybody. And anyway she didn't know any more where they were . . .

"Well. Clearly she wasn't going to part with the key, and Nico could hardly break into the place. He'd declared his interest, and the whole village would be watching. So he went back to Milan to talk to Bernardo: he, after all, would have every right to go and open up his wife's house. The trouble is, Bernardo doesn't want to know. My feeling is that he's convinced Nico's out to uncover some scandal in Elena's past and exploit it. Nico thinks I'd be able to persuade him, God knows why."

"But why does Nico think all this is so important?" I asked. "Papers — I don't get it. They could be anything . . ."

"Love letters?" said Angelo. "Someone in her life? A man nobody knows about?"

"Oh, I see. So that's why you're going —"

"Only partly. I'd made up my mind to go before Nico phoned me, actually. I've been doing some thinking, about this whole business, and I believe that we've been approaching the problem from the wrong end . . . Asking the wrong questions. Who is threatening Joanna? Nobody's going to answer that one for us. The police aren't going to ask questions about crimes which haven't yet been committed. So we have to go for the questions they're asking. Who killed Elena, and why. Who killed the girl on Milan Central Station, and why. Who killed Tony Dorello, and why."

"Tony Dorello?"

"That was his name — our blackmailer. He had a record, by the way, though not for that. A petty criminal, sneak thief, house-breaking, that sort of thing. He was quite out of his class, which maybe was why he got killed, but, you see, although he was killed here, even he isn't a Roman. You first saw him in Denzano; he followed you to Rome. Mostly, what happened didn't happen here but in the north near Garda or in Milan. It's there that most of the murder investigation is going on. Where the police are more likely to listen to us, because they need all the help they can get —"

"They've never listened to me," I interrupted.

"No. But then you've never talked to anyone working on the Elena case. You've never told them about the earring —"

"But it's lost —"

"I saw it too, remember? I could identify it as the pair to the one they have. If they haven't still got that poor girl on ice in the morgue in Milan, they'll have pictures of her. Presented with a picture of you, they'll have to pay attention if the resemblance is that strong. And, of course, there's an independent witness. Me." He caught my eye and grinned. "Don't look so affronted, Joanna. The amnesia's never been any help to you with them — it's a cop-out, suspect in their eyes. I haven't lost my memory and with any luck they may regard me as a responsible citizen with something useful to say. That way, we may establish some confidence and get some co-operation, and God knows we need it. And, anyhow . . . co-operation or not . . . I'm sure, now, that's where the answers are. In that area. Not in Rome. All there is in Rome is the danger." He paused, and said soberly, "Come with me, Joanna."

"Come with you? But I can't, not yet anyway. There's the party . . ."

"Damn the party. You can cancel it. I haven't liked the idea of this thing from the start. It's asking for trouble gathering together all these people whom you don't know, can't recognize . . ."

"Frank will be there," I protested, "and Roddy. You're not suggesting they're phonies? That they aren't who they say they are?"

"Of course not. But will they know everyone who's coming?"

"Pretty well —"

"Pretty well," said Angelo, "isn't well enough."

I said obstinately, "I'm not cancelling, anyway. Gina's coming from Siena, and Howard is flying from Paris. How can I, when they're taking so much trouble just for me? Besides," I added, "Penny would break her heart, wouldn't you, Penny?"

"Well . . ." Penny grinned ruefully. "I should be disappointed, of course." She looked at Angelo and added more seriously, "Don't you trust me any more to look after her?"

"It isn't that. Just too big a job for one. We'll have to get Joanna a bodyguard — just for the evening."

"Angelo, I don't . . ."

It was just as if I hadn't spoken. "May I use your phone?" he said.

And so it was that later in the evening one Dino appeared, to be introduced to Penny and me, shown the layout of the apartment, and told his duties. He was an enormous man with a more than passing resemblance to a gorilla, and very little to say for himself. Penny, wide-eyed, tried to follow the rather one-sided conversation in rapid Italian, Angelo doing most of the talking and Dino responding with little more than a series of grunts. After half an hour or so he took his leave of us politely and left.

"Heavens," said Penny. "Angelo, where *did* you find him? He ought to be a bouncer in a night-club . . ."

"He *is* a bouncer in a night-club," said Angelo with equanimity, "and he's coming here on his night off. He's absolutely straight and less stupid than he looks. He will check everybody's identity and make sure nobody comes bearing gifts."

"Gifts?"

"Parcels. The kind that may explode. He will also frisk the guests — the men, anyway; the women can hardly carry lethal weapons in the clothes they wear this weather —"

"Angelo," I exclaimed, "how can we do this? What will people think? I haven't told them all that part of it, and I don't intend to —"

"You don't have to. Your guests will be less surprised than you think, and less offended. They may even be relieved. In

365

this city nowadays, especially where any celebrities are concerned, this sort of thing is often done, so don't worry. And, Penny . . . your job will be to see that whatever Joanna drinks is poured for her from a bottle from which other people have been served. Right? At least you're not having any waiters; that simplifies things a bit."

I stared at him. "You can't mean it. That somebody who actually knows me, worked with me, could be responsible? Somebody that Roddy and Dona Perelli know? That they could come here and try to kill me?"

Angelo sighed. "Joanna, you're getting danger-happy. Used to the threat. I've no suspicions of anybody you've got on that list, it isn't that. It's just that one has to think of everything, every possibility. You can see that, surely."

I felt horribly sobered. He was right — I had let the threat slide away from me into the world of the unreal and impossible, for a while, anyway.

"Yes," I said. "I see."

Angelo nodded. "All right then. That's fine." In the hall, as I saw him out, he said, "I'll phone you every day. Keep you posted. See you're okay."

"I'll be okay," I said.

He paused with his hand on the door,

frowning. "I don't like leaving you. You're sure you won't change your mind?"

"And come with you? No, really, I can't do that. I'm committed." And yet, as I said it, I wished I could say yes. He didn't like leaving me and I didn't like his going away. I said what was in my mind. "I wish I could. Come, I mean. I'd rather be with you."

"Would you, Jo? Really?" He never called me Jo. His back was to the light and I couldn't see his expression, so I was taken by surprise when he put his hands on my arms and bent his head and kissed me on the mouth. Perhaps the kiss had been meant to be a light caress like the one he had given Penny, or a friendly gesture of comfort, but it didn't turn out like that. I don't know who took fire first, but I do know that I found myself with my arms round his neck kissing him back for all I was worth.

It was he who broke it up. Not letting me go, exactly. More like gently putting me from him.

"Well, well," he said lightly. "Not really intended, but very nice all the same. Goodnight, Joanna. Take care."

He was gone. I was left standing there, my hand pressed against the lips he had kissed and trying to stop myself trembling.

Whether that was with excitement or anger or just plain pique, I could hardly tell.

As so often before, Angelo had made me feel a perfect fool.

I told myself, after that little episode, that it was just as well he had gone away, but I didn't really feel like that. A great bastion of security and reassurance was taken away by his going. Like Kate had said, he was probably enjoying the whole thing, solving the puzzle, meeting the challenge, nothing personal in it at all. But what did that matter? The thing was that when Angelo said to me, *You're not going to die, I won't let you,* I believed him absolutely; and, naturally, I felt a good deal less sure about it when he wasn't there.

The day of the party, Dino, on Angelo's instructions, paraded quite early in the morning, fetched and carried, answered the door, took deliveries, checking everything to make sure it was exactly what it was said to be: that a case of champagne was a case of champagne and it was nothing more. In between times he did helpful waiterly things like polishing and setting out wine glasses; he was deft and neat-handed in spite of his size. In the evening he retired for a short while and reappeared in white evening jacket and bow tie, looking the perfect . . . what? major domo? butler? From the neck down, anyway; there wasn't much to be done about Dino's craggy face which seemed designed by nature to strike fear into anyone's heart. Well, that was, after all, the idea . . .

Penny, not used to Italian social behaviour, had everything ready far too early and looked dismayed when I explained that it was unlikely anyone would turn up much before ten o'clock. She was tremendously excited about the whole thing, a good deal more than I was. Roddy, keeping his promise, arrived earlier than the rest with Dona Perelli in tow. I had made an arrangement with both of them, that they would leave me to try to recognize whoever arrived first, before moving in to identify them.

However, for some I needed no introduction anyway. When a very beautiful and gracious lady appeared — smile-lines round her eyes, the firm and perfect poise of maturity — I had no hesitation and went to her, smiling and holding out my arms. "Gina."

"Oh, Joanna! My dear! Then you do remember?"

We embraced. I stepped back to look at her, smiling and shaking my head. "No, not like that. Not literally. But you just had to be you. If you see what I mean."

"Yes, I think I do. You remember me in your heart, perhaps, as a friend, yes? You look very well, *carissima,* and very lovely. And now here is Howard, who will say all those pretty things so much better than I . . ."

If Gina hadn't said his name I could have made an inspired guess about him too: rugged features, silver wings of hair above the ears, immense charm, all emerging unruffled from Dino's somewhat ruthless welcome. I apologized, and he laughed and brushed the apology aside. "No, no, my dear, no need to be sorry. I think you're quite right. We should all be more security minded these days, especially in this city." He studied me with shrewd, kind eyes and added, "I shouldn't have thought, really, that Rome was the right sort of place for you to be in just now."

"You could be right," I said. "After this evening, I don't suppose I shall stay long anyway. I shall have done what I came here to do."

The room was filling up with people who were my guests, and I hadn't yet greeted any of them. There were some pretty girls and elegant young men and some more workmanlike types, solid and trustworthy looking, who obviously worked behind cameras and not in front of them. I caught Dona's eye and she came over and went round the room with me. Inspired guesses were no good at all here. Dona muttered names and identifications into my ear, so that I was able to greet them and address them by name. They all knew, of course; but it seemed a little better, less shocking and chilly, to do it this way. Everyone was very kind and said they were pleased to see me again and I looked well and they were so sorry about my trouble and they were sure it would all come right soon; and with some there seemed to be a genuine warmth of feeling. All the same, strangers they were when I started talking to them, and strangers they remained.

While I was going through the routine of embracing and handshaking, and now and then having my hand kissed, Roddy must have been watching me. In a lull I found him beside me. "No go?" he asked.

"No go. I think the whole thing is a bit pointless, really."

"All right," said Roddy cheerfully. "So there's no point in it. Who said a party had to have any point in it? Couldn't you just enjoy it for its own sake?"

"Yes," I said, smiling. "Why not?"

"That's better. It's nice to see you smile, and looking really relaxed . . . poor love, you haven't had much fun lately, have you?"

Not much fun. No.

But I didn't say that. I kept my smile, and shrugged in deprecation.

"And a lot of that," Roddy went on, "was my fault."

"We said we were going to forget all that," I protested.

Roddy looked down into my eyes. "Forgotten *and* forgiven?"

The intensity of his look embarrassed me. "Of course," I said, laughing. "I told you."

"So you did," said Roddy drily, "never mind, then." He looked away from me across the room. "The Old Man's arrived, I see. Making an entrance, as usual."

It was not so much, I thought, that Frank made an entrance, but that an entrance was made for him — the inevitable result of his appearance anywhere, a sort of murmur, rustle, movement. People stood back to let him pass and then closed in as if irresistibly attracted. Of course, this room was full of people who wanted to be near him, be seen by him, and better still, *noticed*. For them, this was the point of the party, what they had come for, not for me.

I went to him and took his hands and kissed him and thanked him for coming. He looked older, thinner. His illness had taken more out of him than he would ever admit, that was obvious. I found a high-backed armchair for him and he moved slowly towards it and settled himself into it, as it were enthroned. People who wanted to greet him personally had to approach him to do it and he didn't get up, I noticed, for the women, not even for Gina, so the effect was a little as if they were all doing homage. I added to the effect, I expect, by putting a footstool by him and sitting down on it, thus, no doubt, having the air of a page or handmaiden.

Frank accepted all this performance as no more than his due. I saw Howard Fortune, who had probably seen it all before, grinning at me with mild amusement across the room. I grinned back, but not so that Frank could see. I felt a bit unkind to be amused at all. Performance it might be, but Frank had been all too genuinely ill.

When I asked him, now, how he was, he sighed and said, "Oh well, feeling my age a bit, sweetheart. How about you? Is this gathering of the clans bearing any fruit?"

"None at all, so far, I'm afraid."

"Never mind. It will come."

"So everyone says, but it doesn't. I think I'm getting used to it, now, anyway. I mean, if you have to live with something, you live with it, don't you?"

"Brave girls like you do, certainly." He bent on me a look of fond approval, and I wished, selfishly I suppose, that I had not been warned not to worry or upset him. It would have been a relief to be able to confide in Frank.

I heard the shrill peal of the telephone bell cleaving the party noise. Penny went to answer it and presently came over to me. "A call for you, Joanna."

"Angelo?" I asked.

"No, it's a woman. Kate something . . . Castelani, would it be?"

"Katie!" I exclaimed with pleasure. "I'll take it in my room, Penny, I'll never hear a thing in here."

Kate said, "It sounds like revelry by night down your end. Are you giving a party?"

"I am, actually . . ."

"Well, good for you. Things really are better, then? You're beginning to enjoy life again?"

"Well, not exactly . . ." I realized that she knew nothing about the events of the past week and it was hardly the moment to tell her. "This isn't really a very *party* sort of party, Kate." I explained what it was for.

"Oh, I see. Things *aren't* any better, then."

"Not really."

"Well, look. I rang because I've had an idea that I think might help you with your problem. Or a bit of your problem."

"I see. Which bit's that?"

"The lemon garden," she said.

I was silent.

"Joanna, are you still there?"

"Yes," I said, "I'm here."

"Well, look. You know how you said the idea of it had bad vibes . . . I did suggest, remember, that you ought to tackle it head on by actually going into it."

"I did that. Nothing came of it. Except for feeling horrible, of course."

"I think I know why, now," said Kate.

I was conscious of an almost overwhelming wish to stop this conversation right there, to put the phone down, cut her off. I was sitting on my bed. I took hold of a piece of the bedcover and crushed it in my hand, trying to still my rising panic. I didn't want to speak but I had to speak. When I did it came out like a croak. "Why, then?"

"Jo," said Kate, "are you all right? You sound awfully odd."

"I'm perfectly all right." I had hold of myself now. "What is it you know, Kate?"

"I don't *know*, not for sure. I just think I do. It's not the right lemon garden."

"What?"

"I mean, it doesn't have to be, does it? There could be more than one. In fact, of course, we know there are. Dozens. All over Italy."

"I suppose so," I said dully. "But I don't see —"

She said, "There's one at the Villa Flora."

I said, more sharply than I meant to, "How do you know? Nobody's ever mentioned it —"

"Who would know it was important, if *you* hadn't mentioned it?"

"Oh . . . yes . . . I see."

"I rang up Steffy," Kate went on eagerly. "She knows the people there, or used to, the old man's dead now. She remembers their lemon garden, but of course she's awfully puzzled about why it's important to you."

"Yes. Well, so am I, Katie."

"Darling, of course . . . but listen, the place is empty now and up for sale. The widow's moved away to live with her daughter in Florence. If you're coming back to the lake soon you could go and look at it. Only don't go on your own, will you? That might be a bit upsetting."

"No," I said, "I won't go on my own."

"Promise?"

"I promise."

Kate sighed. "Oh dear. I've an awful feeling I've done the wrong thing phoning you like this, you sound so . . . ."

"I'm all right," I said. "Truly. And you haven't done the wrong thing. It's just that I've got to go now, Kate. Thank you for ringing, I'll be in touch . . . ."

I put the phone down and went on sitting on the edge of the bed, looking at it. Down the passage the party seemed to be warming up, chatter and music and laughter and the tinkling of glasses were getting louder. It was some minutes before I could bring myself to go back to it.

At the door of the living-room the party atmosphere seemed to strike me full in the face: heat and cigar smoke and a mingling of perfumes, wine on someone's breath and somewhere the animal smell of sweat. A room full of people, all talking. I saw them as one might see actors in a motion picture in a foreign language without sub-titles. They stood and sat about in the conventional attitudes of party-goers, a glass in one hand, gesticulating with the other. They were opening and shutting their mouths and smiling and frowning and wrinkling their noses and flashing flirtatious glances and shrugging and throwing back their heads, ho ho ho, in the wide gape of laughter. As I watched they seemed to me like grotesque puppets, not quite so grotesque or menacing as in my hall-of-mirrors nightmare, but bad enough.

Penny appeared beside me. I looked at her and saw she was real, not part of the puppet show. Just a pretty young woman at a party, having a wonderful time. She brought me to myself. The room and the people in it moved as it were into another gear, and I was back in the real world, with a lot of ordinary humans round me.

"I was just coming to see if you were okay," Penny said. "You've been ages."

"I'm fine," I said. I looked into her sparkling eyes and grinned. "Enjoying yourself?"

"Oh yes. And the party's really taken off now, hasn't it? Of course I can't do much about getting next to some of the people here, the lingo defeats me . . . but the others, wow! That Howard, he's really something, isn't he?"

I had to laugh. She had been enchanted with Roddy and now she was enchanted with Howard. Any ideas I'd had that she was in love with Angelo were finally dispelled: Penny's fancy was like a butterfly, flitting around everything attractive on offer.

"He's a bit old for you, love," I said, meaning Howard.

"I like older men," said Penny simply.

"And talking of older men, Frank Harmer asked me to come and find you. I think he wants to leave fairly soon."

"Oh yes. It's terribly hot in here. He must be feeling it."

I went over to Frank. He was talking to Gina who had taken my place on the footstool beside him. She and Frank were talking with the intimacy of old friends. As I came towards them I saw her put an affectionate hand on his arm. Then they both looked up and saw me and smiled.

"Are you all right?" I asked Frank.

"Fine so far, my love, but I think I'd better not push my luck too far. I'd better remove myself fairly soon, I think."

"Whatever you think best," I said. "It was very good of you to come at all, Frank. I really am grateful."

"Not a bit of it. I've enjoyed myself. I think everyone has enjoyed themselves. Gina was just saying what a nice party it is."

"Oh, thank you —"

"But I'm not sure," he went on, "that *you're* enjoying it." His eyes searched my face. "You look rather pale, to me. How long are you planning to stay in Rome?"

"Not long. I haven't much to stay for, after this." I hesitated, made a big effort. "Look, Frank . . . Gina . . . I wonder if you can tell me . . . is there a lemon garden at the Villa Flora?"

"A what?" said Frank.

Gina gave him a look of fond exasperation. "Of course, *caro,* you wouldn't remember, would you? He has this wonderful capacity," she added, turning to me, "of putting out of his head all thoughts of a project once it has been achieved. Yes, there is a lemon garden there, but why do you ask, Joanna? Is it something you've remembered?"

"Not remembered. It just seems to have some meaning, the idea of it. Is there something special about it, the one at the Villa Flora?"

Gina considered. "Not really. It was very well kept . . . I think it had been something of a hobby with the old gentleman who lived there. Of course, it was springtime when we were there, and the scent of the blossom was really beautiful. Still . . . if it has significance for you, Joanna, perhaps you should go back there, and see for yourself."

"Yes. I have thoughts of doing that, when I leave here."

"What are you going to do, when you leave here?" Frank asked.

"I'm not sure, really."

"I don't think you ought to go back to the lake. It's too hot and humid at this time

380

of the year. Hardly better there than here."

I smiled. "Steffy lives there all the year round —"

"Exactly, and it does her no good either. So I have concocted a little plan. Come back with me to the mountains, Joanna. Steffy has promised to come, if you will."

"To your house? In Switzerland?"

Frank nodded. "Roddy's coming too," he added, "and I've tried to persuade Gina, but she has other fish to fry."

Gina's grasp of English idiom must have been less than perfect, because she exclaimed, "Frank *caro,* you use the strangest expressions. What has frying fish to do with my family? I expect to become a grandmother," she added proudly to me, "very soon now. So I must be with my daughter . . . much as I would love to come. But you should go, Joanna. It is ideal for you just now. Cool and quiet and restful."

"Yes, I know," I said. "It sounds a lovely idea."

Steffy, who had stayed there before, had once described Frank's place to me; a house-in-the-air was what she called it, clinging to its high hillside, all space, peace and luxury within, surrounded by upland meadows knee-deep in wild flowers; with, as a backdrop, the glittering silver peaks of the Alps. Yes,

381

a lovely idea — if I got there in one piece. I had other doubts as well. I suppose they all showed in my face.

"What is it?" Frank asked.

"Well, for one thing, isn't it a bit much for you to have a house party just now? I'm sure you should be resting, not entertaining."

Frank laughed. "Dear child, I don't call you and Steffy and Roddy a house party. Besides, I shan't be entertaining. There's a staff there to look after you; you will amuse yourselves. I make an appearance when I feel so inclined. It's true that Roddy and I have a new project to discuss, a very promising new script, and you could be involved in that as well. But it won't take all our time, and for the rest . . . nothing but beautiful idleness for us all. But you said 'for one thing'. What was the other thing?"

I didn't want to have to say it, especially as Roddy had strolled over and joined the group. I said carefully, "It's just that I've had some unpleasant experiences, during the last week or so. It would be irresponsible of me not to warn you."

"Warn us?" Gina exclaimed. *"Cara,* what can you mean?"

I said, baldly, "I think someone is trying to kill me."

Nobody said anything.

"I'm serious," I said. "It's not just a sick fancy, whatever you may think. Angelo knows about it. Someone tried to shoot me and he saw it happen. He saved my life, in fact."

The party chatter went on round us. Roddy looked shaken, Gina bewildered and horrified. And Frank? Grave, concerned, certainly. I couldn't be sure whether he really believed me or not.

I stumbled on. "I'm safe enough, you see, between these four walls. But I can't stay in them all the time, or for ever, and I don't intend to. But from the time I leave here I become a target again, and you might be involved. I thought it only right to let you know what the score is."

Roddy burst out, "Why the hell didn't you *tell* me?"

Frank lifted an authoritative hand and said quietly, "Shut up, Roddy." He smiled at me, and said gently, "You don't really think that any one of us would run out on you when you're in danger, do you?"

"No," I said. "But that's not what I meant, I'm thinking of you —"

"We all know what you meant," said Frank soothingly. "We'll look after you, Joanna. We won't let any harm come to you, or . . ." he grinned suddenly . . . "to ourselves, if we can help it. Now, are you coming with us?"

I gave up. If he was determined not to take it seriously, there was not much more to be said. Taking my cue from him, I said lightly, "Well, of course, if you think it's okay, I'd love to come. I wonder if I could bring Penny? She's been a great help to me since I've been in Rome, and I don't want to go off and leave her at a loose end."

"That's the tall blonde in the silvery dress?" Frank asked.

"Yes, that's Penny."

"Charming," he said. "Quite charming. Yes, of course, bring her by all means."

"Well, thank you."

"And if you're driving up," said Gina, "you could drop in at the Villa Flora on the way. After all, we were there for nearly three weeks, you know. It might help."

"So it might," I said, but I wished she had not mentioned it.

Frank nodded, and said nothing would be easier. "And now," he added, "I really must go home." I saw, with compunction, that he really did look very tired. Roddy said he'd telephone for Frank's car.

When people say they are leaving and then have to wait for transport it creates an awkward hiatus in which nobody can find much to say. I made an excuse and slipped away from the group around Frank, with some idea of finding Penny and telling her of Frank's invitation. So it fell out that I was in the lobby when the doorbell rang. I picked up the house phone and heard a vaguely familiar voice announce that Signor Harmer's car had arrived.

"Isn't that Sandro?" I asked.

Yes, it was, he said. He was standing in for Signor Harmer's chauffeur, who had the evening off. When I heard his voice it came to me that he had driven me about several times and that I should really have given him a present of money. I was leaving Rome, and if I didn't do it now I should never do it at all.

"Why don't you come up, Sandro," I said, "and have a glass of wine while you're waiting? I'd like to have a word with you, anyway."

He got the message right away and said with alacrity, "That's very kind of you, signorina."

I spoke to Dino, and asked him to look after Sandro when he came. I went to my room to get some money to give him. As I was returning, I heard someone clapping their hands, followed by a sudden hush. Frank was on his feet, calling for a toast. I saw Dino wandering around filling glasses; it must have been pre-arranged.

The toast, it seemed, was to me "our hostess, our Joanna". He spoke in English, pausing every now and again so that Dona Perelli, by pre-arrangement too I suppose, could translate his words into Italian. He said nice things about me and said they all wished me a complete recovery and that 'all her memories may be happy ones'. He lifted his glass: "Joanna!" and everybody else lifted their glasses too and cried "Joanna, Joanna", and I felt the silly tears of easy emotion rising to my eyes. Then someone started calling for a speech.

Whoever it was got no further.

The blast of the explosion shook the room, its roar drowned every other sound, a burning light filled the night sky and eclipsed the moon and the stars.

Outside in the square the wreckage of Frank's beautiful car was blazing like a torch.

13

In the early morning two days later an elderly woman, dressed in the traditional rusty black with a black kerchief over her greying hair, emerged from the apartment house where I lived and made her way round the corner of the square. She was rather stout, carried a large plastic shopping bag, and waddled somewhat as she walked.

Round the corner a car was parked with the engine running. The old woman waddled on as if to pass it. At the very last moment as she came level with it, the rear door of the car opened, she stepped in, and was driven rapidly away.

"Brilliant," said Frank with satisfaction.

Roddy, who was driving, burst out laughing. "Brilliant's an understatement. I could hardly believe it was you. Were you scared?"

"A bit." That was an understatement, too.

"But where's Penny? Are we meeting her somewhere?"

"She isn't coming. She has to go home, to England . . ."

The telephone had woken us in what seemed to me like the middle of the night. Penny went to answer it. I heard her voice, sleepy at first, then sharp and frightened. I got up and went out to find her. "What is it?"

Penny was white-faced and her lips trembled. "It's my mother. She's had a heart attack." Grief and terror stared out of her eyes; tears gathered, ran down her white cheeks. "I've got to go, Joanna. I've got to be with Sue, she's only sixteen, God knows where the boys are, she's all alone and Mummy in hospital . . ."

"Of course," I said. "Of course." I put my arms round her and for a moment she clung to me like a child. I was desperately sorry for her, yet in an odd way I envied her her grief and anxiety. Who, after all, in all the world, did I care about like that?

I gave her a little shake. "Come on, love. Things to do. You've got to get dressed and pack some clothes. And phone the airport about a flight. I'll get some coffee."

"But what about you? Angelo said I wasn't to let you go anywhere without me, he made a big thing of it . . ."

"Angelo didn't know what was going to happen, did he? Now will you make this phone call, or shall I?"

But in the end she was still there in the flat when I left, as not a seat could be found on any flight to London that day until the late afternoon. So I had to leave her there when I set out alone to face the world in my elderly disguise.

That had been more of an ordeal than I had yet admitted. However effective Roddy might think my get-up was, I still felt exposed and vulnerable.

Frank was smiling at me sympathetically. "Are you all right?" he said.

"Oh yes, fine, thank you. Just rather uncomfortable in all this gear . . ." The padding round my body was becoming almost unbearably hot.

"Yes, I can imagine," Frank said. "Like playing Falstaff . . . all the same, I wouldn't shed it just yet. Let's get out of the city first."

And so, still wrapped in my disguise I sat and saw the last of Rome go by; then we were out on the autostrada, eating up the miles. Nothing had gone wrong, no one had recognized me, nobody was following us, so far as we could see. Roddy turned into the first service station we came to and stopped for me to alight before we had even reached the car-park. He then took the car away to park it while I made my way, still with my waddle, still with my shopping bag, to the door marked *Donne*.

I retired behind a locked door; off came the black dress, the foam rubber beneath it, the thick stockings, the clumsy shoes, the wig. Out of the shopping bag came a skimpy cotton dress with thin shoulder straps, a pair of high-heeled sandals, and the disguise was crammed into the bag in their place. A swish of cleansing cream, a wipe with cottonwool, disposed of the wrinkled make-up. Into the dress, the sandals, another wig (honey-blonde this time) and big, round sunglasses, and I was myself again . . . well not myself, exactly, that not being the idea; young again perhaps. I emerged from behind the locked door and found the powder room was empty; I could now safely and comfortably make up my face again without causing any remark, even if there were anyone to see. I thickened my eyebrows with a soft brown pencil, and with lipstick enlarged my lower lip into a pout. Lastly I extracted an elegant leather shoulder bag from the shopping bag. The shopping bag itself, plus its contents, I thrust into a rubbish bin.

Then I strolled out, unhurriedly, to join Frank and Roddy in the restaurant for some breakfast.

Seeing the two men sitting there, and few other people about, I felt suddenly mischievous. I subtly altered my walk, the pose of my head. With provocatively swinging hips, nose tilted arrogantly skywards, the pouting lips arranged in a sultry half-smile, I was a blonde bombshell strolling by on heels like stilts. Through my dark glasses I saw the instant attention, the glances, the appreciative grins . . . all of which faded comically to sheepish recognition as I walked over to join them.

"Impressive," Roddy said. "You nearly had me foxed again. Though I don't know quite why I'm so surprised; you've had enough practice."

"Not really," I said, pouring myself some coffee. "Up to now I couldn't go in for this sort of full-scale dressing up. I was going to see people who had to meet me as myself. I mean, I couldn't keep rushing off into loos and unsticking all that gear, could I? I had to make do with wigs and scarves, things like that, and hope for the best."

"I didn't mean that," said Roddy, "I meant that it's all just an extension of professional expertise . . . I must say, that hair suits you immensely."

"Thank you."

I drank my coffee, buttered a roll and ate it hungrily, felt more relaxed than I had for a long time. Whatever the dangers might still be . . . at least I hadn't to battle any longer against Frank and Roddy's disbelief that they existed. That had been disposed of the night Frank's car was blown up.

Thank God, no one had been blown up in it. Whoever wanted to kill Frank had timed it badly. When the sound of the explosion had died away I looked across the room and saw, in the doorway, Sandro the chauffeur, his olive skin turned an ashen grey; and knew then that by my invitation to come up for a drink and a tip, I had saved his life.

Nobody was seriously hurt, it turned out, though we learned later that some people in the street had been hit by flying glass. At the time I was most concerned for Frank, who took one look out into the square to where the car was blazing, reached for the arm of the chair he had been sitting in and lowered himself into it.

"Are you all right?" I asked. He was a bad colour, and I was frightened. There was a great deal of noise going on, both inside the room and outside in the street. Outside were shouts and running feet, the cries of people in a state of pain or shock, and the sirens of the emergency services, police, ambulance, fire-tender. The firemen whipped out their gear and began to spray foam all over the burning remains of Frank's Rolls.

"Pills," Frank said thickly. "Right-hand pocket."

I found them, fetched a glass of water; he took them and seemed more himself again.

"*Sandro,*" he said.

"It's all right. He wasn't in the car. He's here, he's fine."

"Thank God."

Howard Fortune came over to me; big, calm, authoritative.

"Joanna, I think someone should tell the cops that there was nobody in the car, and that the owner is up here . . . I'll see to that, if you like."

I nodded gratefully, "Oh, thank you . . . if you would."

"I'll send someone down then. We don't think Frank ought to be bothered with too many questions tonight. Roddy's phoning his doctor. If he comes along, he ought to be able to keep the questioning to a decent minimum. And what is there to tell, after all?"

"What, indeed?" I said. "Who could have wanted to do this?"

"God knows," said Howard. He looked at me keenly and added, "Poor Joanna. This is a rotten end to your party, isn't it?"

"I don't mind about that," I said. "I just feel I could do with some peace and quiet."

"That's what I thought . . . shall we try and tactfully get rid of this lot? I'll get Gina to give me a hand."

"Oh, please . . . that would be marvellous." And in a few minutes I saw him and Gina moving about the room, having a quiet word with one and another of my guests, who nodded and presently melted away. I turned to Frank, who smiled wryly at me. He said quietly, "I owe you an apology, Joanna."

"You do? Whatever for?"

"Because I didn't believe you when you said you were in danger. I thought you were fantasizing. It looks very much now as if we're in the same boat, doesn't it? And there's nothing very fantastic about it. Only too real . . . though God knows what it's all about."

"Never mind about that for now," I said gently. "Just rest."

"You take it all very calmly, don't you?"

"Used to it." I smiled.

Howard came back. "Well, that's it. The police inspector wants to see Frank, and the chauffeur too I suppose . . . and, by the way, a television film crew has arrived."

"Oh no," I said. "That's all we need."

"Quite. I don't think any of us feel like giving interviews, so if you don't mind, Joanna, Roddy and Gina and I will stick around for a bit."

"Of course," I said. "Glad to have you."

In the end, everything passed off easily and peacefully. Frank's doctor and the police inspector arrived almost simultaneously. The inspector was civil and not unduly pressing, especially when talking to Frank under the doctor's minatory eye; and, as Howard had said, what was there to tell? It looked as if he was going to be a bit more awkward with Sandro, whose story, however, was perfectly straightforward: he had collected the car from the underground garage of the hotel where Signor Harmer was staying. He had driven Signor Harmer to his evening engagement, taken the car back and garaged it. He had spent the evening playing cards with friends within reach of a telephone. When the call came for him to fetch Signor Harmer he walked back to the garage and took the car out again. No, he had not noticed anything unusual about the car. He had parked it where it remains now. He had only been out of it a few minutes when it exploded. As it seemed fairly clear that Sandro would hardly have planted a bomb in order to blow himself up, that seemed to be that; the rest of us had seen nothing at all until the moment of the explosion. The inspector went away, presumably to examine what remained of the car and question the garage attendant. He looked, I thought, as baffled as we all felt.

Penny had gone away quietly into the kitchen, made coffee, and presently returned with it. I think we were all slightly shocked; we sat about in silence, drinking the coffee, while Frank had a discussion with the doctor. Frank's natural resilience had come to his rescue; he was being amiable, humorous, brushing the whole thing off. The doctor's voice had a slight edge of acrimony. This was no way to spend one's convalescence, he said, as if it were Frank's fault the car blew up. Yes, he could leave Rome in two days' time, provided he spent the intervening day in bed, provided he did the journey in easy stages and didn't do any driving himself, provided there was someone to look after him on the journey. Penny and I said meekly that we were prepared to do that, and Roddy explained that he would drive the car; not the Porsche, of course, which was a two-seater, but a comfortable hire-drive car which, as Roddy said drily, he would personally see was vetted from stem to stern, and guarded until the moment of departure.

He had done more than that, it seemed, as he had found us a car almost as luxurious as the Rolls would have been, with a refrigerated drinks compartment tucked between the front and back seats. There was also, he told us over breakfast, a vacuum-packed picnic box in the boot, which meant that we did not have to stop for a lengthy lunch anywhere but could Get On — like all drivers on a long-distance run, Roddy was more interested in arriving than in travelling hopefully, and if he had his way, would prefer not to stop at all. From the security point of view, I had to admit this made some sense. However, I pointed out mildly that the doctor had said that Frank ought to travel by easy stages, and that I had told Steffy, when I telephoned her the day before, to expect us when she saw us.

However that might be, we didn't linger, and although I didn't really think that anyone was going to open up with a sub-machine gun on the forecourt of the restaurant, I was glad enough to be back in the car and on the move.

"How was Stephanie when you rang?" Frank asked, when we were on our way again. "Was she very worried?"

"About the bomb? She hadn't heard a thing about it, fortunately. I told her, of course, but once assured that we are all okay, she didn't seem to be bothered . . ."

"Ah," said Frank, grinning tenderly, "that's

Stephanie." I thought then, he's very fond of her, and wondered briefly why, if that were so, he chose to flaunt under her nose girls like Carole, young enough to be his daughter; surely Steffy couldn't like that so very much.

Roddy said idly, "It's a pity Penny couldn't come along. What happened?"

I explained. "It's such a shame all this should have happened — she was looking forward to coming with us, and after all the hoo-ha of the past week I feel I owed her some fun and relaxation —"

Roddy said in a puzzled tone, "I didn't realize you were so close to her."

I smiled. "I'm not, really, I suppose. Except the way one can get close to people very quickly in a crisis. I've only known her a couple of weeks. I met her through Angelo —"

"Angelo?" said Frank. "I thought you two didn't get on?"

"Oh well," I laughed, "that was all a lot of nonsense. A misunderstanding. We're the best of friends now."

It would have been fine, I reflected, if that had been strictly true; but in fact when Angelo telephoned the previous day he had disagreed sharply with my plans to leave Rome, and was also particularly irritating about the bomb episode, asking what seemed to me a lot of way-out technical questions which of course I couldn't answer. Eventually I had said crossly, "For heaven's sake, Angelo, what difference does it make whether it was a time-bomb, or attached to the ignition, or however? The car blew up. It could have killed Frank, or the chauffeur, or both, or half a dozen people in the street, but thank God it didn't. What it did do was convince Frank that there's a real problem and I'm not imagining things. I mean, there's got to be a connection, hasn't there?"

"Oh, I agree," said Angelo drily, "but what kind of connection, that's what I'd like to know."

"Wouldn't we all?" I said. "Anyway, Frank knows now that we're both at risk, so he and Roddy too are bound to take it all more seriously and be extra careful . . . so I'll be as safe with them as I'd be anywhere . . ."

"If you think," Angelo shouted, "that you're going to be safe buzzing round the roads in Italy in the company of a sexagenarian with a heart condition and a narcissistic film actor who never sees anything beyond the end of his beautiful nose, you're more of an idiot than I took you for."

I laughed. "Oh, don't be so ridiculous. Anyway, I'll have Penny with me . . ."

But I hadn't, of course.

"Didn't you ask him to the party?" Frank asked, still, apparently, talking about Angelo.

"Oh yes, I did, but he couldn't make it. Had to go away on business." I wasn't going to say what business. Without a lengthy explanation of the background, it wouldn't make much sense to the others anyway.

The long hot day wore on, and the journey with it. The heat shimmered on the roadway in front of us, but it was cool and fresh inside the car with the air-conditioning functioning efficiently. After a while conversation died. Frank let his seat down into the fully reclining position and went to sleep.

I would have liked to go to sleep as well, not having had much as a result of Penny's early telephone call. But there was no chance to do that. I took over the driving for a while to give Roddy a rest, but whichever of us was not driving had another job to do — to check the following traffic. Any car which seemed to remain in the same position, neither gaining on us nor falling back, was watched for a while. If it held its position too long, we found an opportunity to slip into the slow lane. Any car following us intentionally would have to get into the slow lane too, thus making its intentions obvious

—always supposing it could execute that manoeuvre at the right time anyway. On most occasions the volume of traffic would simply sweep it by. After some time it seemed pretty clear that nobody could be following us, or that, if they had, we had lost them.

Roddy had thought up this system and discussed it briefly with me after breakfast when Frank had left us for a few minutes. "Don't want to alarm the Old Man any more than we have to, do we?" I noticed, too, while we were in the restaurant, that the car was plainly visible from where he sat, and he rarely took his eyes off it. Angelo was wrong about Roddy, who was being alert and serious, and plainly knew what he was about; and it seemed to me odd that Angelo, normally so cool and objective, should be so prejudiced about him.

Around lunch-time the traffic thinned. A couple of juggernauts passed us, and then a large Mercedes, illegally doing the ton down the fast lane. He swept by and vanished in a cloud of dust, and after him, for a few precious moments, there was nothing. At that moment, with the road behind us empty, we reached the turn-off, slipped into and were down and through the underpass and on to a quiet country road before anyone could have seen us.

Frank woke up when we stopped and asked sleepily what was going on.

"Lunch," said Roddy, getting the picnic box out of the boot.

We were in a small valley; the road wound narrowly along it, a ribbon of white dust. On one side of us were narrow strips of maize and vegetables; on the other willows hung over an unseen stream, I suppose a small tributary of the Arno; and above, on both sides, the neat green terraces of vines mounted to where the first outcrops of rock began. There was not a soul about; only a fool works in the midday sun in Italy. The heat haze was such that everything seemed to be swimming in the blue air.

As a picnic, the lunch was far above picnic standards. We ate melon and parma ham, and followed that with *vitello tonato*, one of the nicest of Italian cold dishes — veal in aspic, stuffed with a savoury fish mousse. There were individual salads to go with that, and afterwards helpings of the tiny dark strawberries which grow on the hillsides around Rome, soaked in wine and sugar and topped with whipped cream; the whole feast washed down with frosty glasses of dry Orvieto. It was, all of it, perfectly delicious; the sunlit valley an oasis of tranquillity; the idea of danger seemed totally unreal and far away.

The threat was not here, for no one had seen us come. I had to remind myself that it is precisely at the moment when you relax that trouble is likely to start.

Frank, certainly, seemed completely relaxed. Lunch over, he lit a cigar. He looked at me quizzically through the smoke, having, I suppose, caught an expression of doubt on my face. "All right, all right," he said, and laughed.

"I'm sorry," I said hastily. "It's really not my business . . . I was only . . . well, I was thinking of you, that's all."

"Don't do that, sweet child. Think of yourself," he said. "Think of yourself." And there was a kind of sadness in his tone which brought reality crashing back into the forefront of my mind.

Roddy was placidly fixing our position and working out the remaining mileage. We were doing very well; we should reach Steffy's by late afternoon. "So if you want to go and have a look at the Villa Flora on the way, Joanna, you've bags of time to do that."

"Oh," I said. "Yes."

"Don't you want to?" Roddy asked.

"It isn't that," I said hastily. "I was just wondering . . . there's nobody there now, they say. Maybe we wouldn't be able to get in."

"That's all arranged for," said Frank.

"It is? But how . . ."

"I rang up the hotel in the village . . . they know us around there, don't forget; we were there some weeks . . . the old boy who looks after the house isn't on the telephone. I've fixed it so that he'll let the hotel have the keys and we can pick them up from there. What's the matter?"

"Oh . . . nothing, really. It's . . . it's very kind of you to fix things, Frank . . . I suppose it's just that I hadn't really made up my mind yet to go there, and now, well, I feel committed."

"Of course you're not committed," said Frank gently. "The fact that we've arranged about a key doesn't commit you to anything. But just think about it a minute, Joanna. Whatever this complex is about the lemon garden . . . and that may mean absolutely nothing . . . it would make sense, surely, to go and have a good look at a place which meant a great deal in your life. Where you did some pretty good work, for one thing. There are associations there, too."

I was silent.

Roddy said, "Frank's right, you know. It makes sense, love, it really does. It's not just the lemon garden, it's the whole place you ought to look at."

The peace had gone from the little valley;

404

the prison-house of fears closed around me again. But all I said was, "All right."

We packed up the lunch things and put them away, and Roddy found his way along the valley and out again to where we could rejoin the autostrada as it snaked away through the hills. Frank finished his cigar, let his seat down again, and once more went to sleep. Like that his head was almost in my lap. It struck me what a remarkable head it was. With some of the lines of age, of illness, of just living itself, smoothed out by sleep, he looked peaceful and noble, like a statue on some ancient tomb, a patrician of some sort, a Roman senator perhaps. I thought how dazzling he must have been when young, adored, no doubt, by many women. Where, I wondered, did that leave Steffy and the big thing they were supposed to have had going at one time? Of course, she had not married him but Angelo's father, and had retired into a quiet life; whereas he had gone on to ever new heights of fame and prestige. Yet the relationship had survived after a fashion, mellowed into friendship . . . all passion spent, an old people's thing. I didn't really understand it, but supposed vaguely that I might, one day. If I lived that long.

★ ★ ★

We made good time over the rest of the journey and arrived in Caravaglia, the village where the hotel was, as it was waking up from afternoon drowsiness; holiday-makers, just emerged, perhaps, from an afternoon's sleep, filled the tables on the verandah at the side of the hotel, drinking lemon tea or *caffè freddo* or eating huge creamy ices; clatter from the kitchens proclaimed that the first preparations for the evening meal were already on the go. Roddy said he'd get the key, then added doubtfully, "Maybe you'd better come too, Joanna. Don't think the manager here knows much English."

The manager seemed delighted to see us, remembered about my accident, asked if I were fully recovered. Were we back to stay? I explained that we were only passing through. He asked fondly after Gina; naturally, she would be the one to make the most impression on the local people, a great Italian star, loved and venerated by two generations. "And the *padrone?*" he added. "The old gentleman? He is well, I hope?"

The old gentleman. Frank wouldn't like that much, I thought.

"If you mean Signor Harmer, he's outside in the car," I said, and the man came hurrying out after us to shake hands with Frank and faze him with rapid expressions of goodwill which I had to interpret. We were invited to have drinks on the house, but refused politely: on our way back, perhaps?

"He seemed pleased enough to see us," I said to Roddy as we came away. "I thought you said the locals got fed up with us when we were here."

"So they did . . . the residents, retired people and such, folk with holiday homes, that sort of thing. But the real locals — people who run the hotel and the shops and so on — they thought it was all right. Brought them a lot of business. Filled up the hotel before the season started. And we all used to drink there in the evenings — nowhere else much to go, when you know you've got to have a night's sleep and be up at five-thirty next day. It was somewhere to escape to, for a breather." He gave Frank a sidelong glance and winked at me. "Well, here we are." A bend in the road, an abrupt turning, the gates which the old man had closed behind the funeral cortège. Roddy got out to open them. I sat silently looking at the front of the house, which meant no more to me than it had done before.

Roddy unlocked the big front door and we walked into the empty house. A square hall, pillars, the staircase, a door open on the right leading into a long room which seemed to run the length of one side of the house.

"Well," said Frank cheerfully, "this is the *salotto*. The room where the party was held."

I looked about me. I had never expected it to be empty like this: the floor a great sweep of polished marble, the panelled walls bare of pictures. Only the moulded ceiling, a riot of flamboyant cherubs and swatches of flowers and fruit, was left, and two large chandeliers. The room was shuttered, creating a greenish gloom. Roddy switched on the lights and the two men waited patiently while I walked up and down, trying to extract some meaning from the place. But for me it was simply a large, empty, anonymous room, unfurnished with objects, unpeopled by memory.

I said with a sigh, "It's no good, I'm afraid."

"Relax," said Frank. "You're trying too hard."

"I've always tried too hard," I said. "It's difficult not to. But there's nothing here for me to latch on to, anyway. Look, I think I'll go into the garden for a bit. No, don't come with me, please."

We got the various bolts of one of the french windows undone, and I opened it and went out into the open air.

The garden was sleepy and murmurous with

the heat of afternoon; a sweet place of wandering paths and gentle declivities, shady bowers where one could get relief from the sun, and small, gracious surprises — a fountain here, a little statue of a child there — and everywhere shrubs and climbers with a burden of blossom.

I seemed to know my way, or rather, I let my feet take me, without conscious decision, in the direction of the lake. Once, on the path, I faltered and looked down, expecting to see something, some object, lying there in front of me; but there was nothing there, and I walked on.

And so I came, at last, to the lemon garden.

It was better kept than Steffy's; the trees had been pruned and the lemons gleamed, greenish-gold, on every branch, giving off, in the heat of the sun, the inimitable scent of the ripening fruit.

I stood there, as I had stood in the other lemon garden. I breathed in once more the scent of the lemons. I looked out over the lake, so blue and kindly in the light of the sun, the lake which had given up its own kind of strange fruit, gathered in by a fisherman's net.

And then I knew how that fruit had been planted, and by whom.

I had never thought it would be like that. I

had thought of it as, perhaps, a flood of light, or a great trumpet blare of knowledge. At other times it had seemed to me that it could only come inch by inch, a long slow process, the way it had happened up to now: the small flashes of association, with objects and places and people, which would slowly and painfully make up the whole picture.

But it was not like that at all. It was simply *there,* my memory, whole, total, as if a window had been opened, or a curtain drawn back. It was as if the past had only been patiently waiting for me, saying casually, *I was there all the time, you see. But you weren't looking.*

And all of that would have been a matter for rejoicing, if it had not been that in the foreground lay the hideous truth.

A movement caught my eye. A man was walking down the garden towards me. I could see, as he came closer, that he was smiling.

I wanted to run, but there was nowhere to run to.

For a few short moments I stood there, paralysed with terror, watching him approach. There was no way, I knew, that I could pretend that I was still in ignorance, could ward off what was going to happen.

He knew me too well for that: he had watched me so often on the set. My very stance and my movements told him. He knew how I expressed terror, panic, distress. I might get myself together and put on the mantle of another part, but I had given myself away already.

So we stood there, looking at each other. He went on smiling, enjoying his power, knowing that I had reached the end of the line.

Now I knew him, my enemy, my destiny. I had come here to remember. I would remain to die.

14

There was a full moon that night. Even if there had not been, it would have been almost as bright as day, with lights streaming from every window in the Villa Flora. Lights everywhere, lights and music, bursts of laughter, the hubbub of talk, the champagne-bubbling razzmatazz of a show-business party.

I ran from it, crying, after the quarrel with Roddy, that dreadful, humiliating, public quarrel. I had made a scene, said things I wished unsaid, and other people besides Roddy had heard them. I could see them now, the covert glances, some amused and others malicious. It was the kind of incident which makes a field day for gossip columnists: the sexy young star who could pull any bird he wanted; the two girls, myself the one with whom his name was linked, and the other one. An extra, getting a break and a line to say because Frank had noticed her. She was far too beautiful not to notice. Far more beautiful than I . . .

How terrible it was at the time, the grief and jealousy, and how far away it all seemed now, as if it had happened to someone else. In memory I saw myself running away in my long white dress, fumbling in my evening bag for the car keys, sobbing and stumbling.

I started the car and for a moment or two sat there with the engine running. Surely Roddy would come out after me, to find me? Surely he would not let me go? But he didn't come. Nobody came. If I wanted to make a fool of myself, that was my business.

I drove back to Steffy's along the coast road. I drove fast and badly, often crashing the gears, but I got there safely enough. The villa was in darkness. I let the car gently into the drive, knowing that Steffy would have taken her pills and was probably asleep; though I hoped, vainly as it turned out, that she wouldn't be.

I left the car standing outside the house and went indoors. As I expected, everything was silent and still. I crept up to Steffy's room and opened the door gently, but she was deeply asleep and I was not quite selfish enough to wake her. I went into my own room and took my dress off. The zip stuck, and I tore at it impatiently, breaking a fingernail. I bundled the dress up and flung it into the wardrobe.

Then I threw myself face down on the bed and cried for a long time.

The order of things after that seems a bit vague to me now. I think I got up after a while and paced about the room. Then I went to have a shower, the falling water all mixed up with my tears which still kept falling. I towelled myself dry. Now my mood had shifted into another gear. It was no less obsessive, but now I wanted action. I knew I wouldn't sleep.

I looked at my watch, which was lying on the dressing table. It seemed to me that a long time had passed and I was surprised to find that it was still relatively early. I put on a shirt, jeans, sandals. I snatched up my evening bag which had the car keys in it.

I was going back to the Villa Flora.

I had no idea what I would find there. The worst, perhaps — that Roddy and the girl were still together and I had been totally supplanted. In the bewildered obsessive way I was thinking then, or rather not thinking, even that possibility drove me on. The party was probably still in progress, but I didn't care about that. I wasn't going to join in it again, just let myself into the house. Somehow I would find Roddy and whatever was going to happen then, would happen . . .

When I got back to the Villa Flora, I was puzzled to find the cars all gone and the front of the house in darkness, and for the first time it occurred to me that it was later than I thought. I put my wrist to my ear;

the watch had stopped. I thought I remembered seeing some reflected light on the garden as I drove up the drive, so I parked the car, killed the engine, got out and walked rather irresolutely around the side of the villa towards the terrace, where I knew the big french windows were unlikely to be locked. There was no staff living in the house; the extra help hired for the party would have cleared up and gone away. I doubted very much if Frank and Roddy would have locked up before they went to bed. If they had gone to bed.

I approached the terrace through a belt of ilex trees. They masked it from my view, though through the leaves I could see lights shining from the back of the house.

As I came out into the open I saw that the light outlined two figures on the terrace, a man and a woman. The scene was so extraordinary that it stopped me in my tracks. The man was smoking a cigar and his whole pose was one of studied indifference. The woman's back was towards me; she was tense, excited, her whole attitude one of attack. She was speaking softly and rapidly and I couldn't distinguish everything she was saying; something about having waited all her life for this.

He said in English, "I would be obliged

if you would go away. I don't know you, or what you want. I don't speak Italian."

And then she said, more loudly, *"Verstehen Sie besser Deutsch, mein Herr?"* And began to laugh, though without any amusement, as he turned towards her and said in the same language, "Shut up!"

"Oh yes," she said. She still spoke in German, they both did, and I had to strain to understand. "You don't want to hear what I have to say, do you? For now you are a great man, a famous artist. Nobody knows who you really are, except the handful of thugs in uniform who were with you that day, and they have reason to be silent. There is only me. Only I know how you killed the old ones for sport and took away my childhood and my honour and left me for dead . . ."

"It was war," he said. "A lifetime ago. I was eighteen, knowing nothing of life. Only war, and the army." It almost seemed as if he were pleading with her.

She answered softly, "And I, *mein Herr,* I was a child. Child though I was, I never forgot you. How could I not remember? So beautiful you were, as a young man. A face never to be forgotten, *nicht wahr?* The face that haunted my dreams, but not the way a young girl's dreams should be haunted . . .

beautiful and evil, full of cruelty and mockery and hate. So I remembered you, and the years went by and I saw your picture in the newspapers and I knew you had fooled them all somehow, the Americans and the English, a good actor even then. I have kept watch, all these years. I promised myself that one day I would expose you for what you are. I knew one day I would have my chance. If I hadn't been delayed, I would have had it tonight, in front of all the people —"

"And been arrested," he said drily, "and taken away, perhaps, to an asylum."

"Perhaps. Do you think I care what happens to me? I've seen you and I know you, and just to confront you is good enough, to face you with the buried past, remind you of how evil and corrupt you really are —"

She was close to him now. She spat in his face and cried out, *"Mörder! Mörderisch schwein!"* And then his control snapped. He grabbed hold of her. He had her by the throat.

I had never seen anyone killed. For a moment I couldn't grasp what was happening, that I was actually witnessing one human being deliberately doing another to death. Then suddenly I knew it was all too real. I didn't think what I was going to do, I rushed out foolishly from the shelter of the trees.

I cried out, "No! No!"

By that time it was too late. He was lowering the limp body to the ground; he looked up and saw me; then, terrified, I turned and ran.

I didn't get far. A tree stump tripped me up, I went down with a crash and lay there for a moment winded by the fall. Then he was upon me, dragging me to my feet, holding me in a bruising grip with those hands, the same hands which so lately, a few minutes ago, had choked a woman to death. He was breathing in gasps, as I was; I looked up into his face, a face I knew and trusted, the face of a man I admired, even revered: the face of a killer. I was overwhelmed with waves of sickness; my knees gave under me, and if he had not been holding me I would have fallen again.

"You little fool," he said. "Why did you have to come back?"

I croaked at last, "I came back to see Roddy."

"Roddy's in bed and asleep. Let's hope he stays there. Well, now you're here you'll have to help me, won't you?"

"Help you?"

"To get rid of her."

"I can't! I can't!"

He had stopped gasping now and was master of himself. He said very quietly and drily,

"Oh, but you're going to, Joanna. You're going to do exactly what I say."

It doesn't seem so surprising, looking back, that I blotted out the whole of that nightmare. I was too terrified of him not to do exactly what I was told. I tried not to look at the woman's face, blackened and terrible as I knew it would be. He made me help him carry her; she was no slip of a girl, but a woman in middle life, thickened and heavy. We took her into the lemon garden because we couldn't be seen there from the house; we laid her on her face in the grass . . . The night was still and beautiful; the moon still rode high in the blue-black sky, and the scent of the lemon blossom hung on the air.

It was then that one of her earrings fell off and lay, gleaming, in the ground. He was momentarily turned away from me; impelled by instinct I snatched it up and put it in the pocket of my jeans.

"Get her clothes off," he said.

"What for? What are you going to do?"

"Put her in the lake. What are you waiting for? Get on with it."

I looked at the inert body in the grass and cried out through hysterical sobs, "I can't touch her again, I can't."

And then he slapped me, hard, across the face.

"Do as I say," he said.

Without knowing it, he had done me a service. My hysteria stopped abruptly, my mind cleared and I saw the situation whole, in all its cold, menacing pattern. He had killed once and now I was a witness. To save himself he would kill again. To save myself, I had to keep my head and take part in this macabre exercise, no matter what it cost me.

I said quietly and neutrally, "I'm sorry I was hysterical, but this has all been a great shock to me. I mean, it's not the sort of situation one comes across every day."

And then, to my amazement, he smiled, and said gently, "Of course not. Poor Joanna, it isn't very nice for you, I know that. But . . . desperate times, desperate measures. I didn't mean to kill her, you know. She provoked me unbearably, that's all. But it's done now. There's nothing more we can do for her, poor thing. Except dispose of her. Don't worry. It will all be over soon, and then you can forget it ever happened."

I was not deaf to the menace in the last phrase, however dulcet his tone might be.

And then we set to work. The most hideous part, for me, was unfastening her bra and somehow getting the straps over her arms, the cups away from her flaccid breasts . . . When

420

it was done, at last, he bundled the clothes together, tied them up with the bra and weighted them with her handbag and some stones. And then we carried her down to the shore and put her in the boat that was moored there.

"Can you row?" he asked.

"Yes."

"Then you'd better do it. These strenuous sports don't agree with me, nowadays."

So I rowed the boat, with its terrible cargo, out into the lake. I could see the lights of fishermen, scanning the water, luring the lake trout. But they were too far away to see what we were doing.

After a while he nodded at me to stop rowing.

"This will do." He dropped the clothes overboard; weighted with the stones, they went circling down through the clear water. Tipping the body over after them was a hazardous business but it was done, at last; and then I was alone with him, my usefulness at an end. I rowed back to the shore in silence, my mind working overtime. The slope from the shore up to the garden was quite steep. He had said he couldn't row because it didn't agree with him; a heart condition perhaps? I remembered his heavy gasps when he caught up with me among the ilex trees.

When the boat was beached I leapt out and ran. Terror giving me strength, I went up the path from the beach like a mountain goat. I heard him lumbering after me, like a great bear on my tracks. I had one thought now: to reach the car. As I reached the shelter of the ilex trees, something, somebody, moved in front of me; I collided with whoever it was, I pushed him with my outstretched hands and flew past him down the drive to where the car was standing, and opened the door and flung myself into it. The engine started at a touch, thank God, and I was in gear and away and out on to the main road and driving up the Gardesana as a thing possessed . . .

I looked in the mirror continually, watching for the lights to appear. I knew he would follow me; it was the only thing left for him to do. I knew, too, that his car was a great deal more powerful than mine. I took the bends and the gradients with my foot on the floorboards. And then at last, along the curve of the lake, I saw the lights coming, gaining on me. I took the next bend too fast, I knew I was taking it too fast, I remember fighting the wheel frantically to keep myself on course . . .

And then, suddenly, I knew no more.

* * *

"So it worked," he said gently. "And you've remembered."

He made no attempt to approach nearer to me. He was smoking a cigar again. He stood there, big, relaxed, a genial figure, fatherly, kindly; a light breeze from the lake lifted tresses of that silver grey leonine thatch of his, and blew them about.

"Yes," I said.

"I thought you might."

My panic was receding. In the odd way this seems to happen to me, I was now quite calm. He was old and I was young. I was healthy and strong and he had a bad heart. Unless, of course, he had a gun and . . . but he wouldn't do that, couldn't do it, there was Roddy . . . I only had to keep him talking, and Roddy would come out to find us.

"So why bring me here?" I said. "If you'd had your way, you would have had me killed by this time."

"Ah, yes. You really have had quite a charmed life, my child, haven't you? Luck, and Angelo's interference, and inefficiency on the part of certain people . . . they've all been on your side. Plus, I must admit, a certain infirmity of purpose on my part, from time to time."

"So that's why you didn't see to it right away," I said, "as soon as I got out of hospital . . . or even before that; I suppose it could have been done. You took a big risk, didn't you? Any of the times we've met, I could have remembered and denounced you —"

"Yes," he said, "it was a gamble, certainly. And it was never intended to go on for so long. As it did . . . and as, fortunately, you continued not to remember . . . I used that time to erase any trails which might lead to me in the future. And then, at first . . . she hadn't even been found. If you had denounced me then, would anyone have believed you? Poor Joanna. Poor, sick Joanna, turning against her friends. It happens so often in such cases, doesn't it? And at that stage the doctors didn't believe you would ever recover your memory, anyway. All that was needed just then, it seemed to me, was a little insurance —"

"You mean, the Frightener?"

"Of course. The whole thing was set up to make you seem a prey to nightmare delusions. Yes, pretty effective, that. I really think that if you hadn't begun to get ideas, the odd scraps of illumination, and hadn't pursued them with such determination, you might have been safe. I'm really very fond of you, you see. You're a lovely girl and a gifted one and it's all a great shame. But I have to think of myself first. They don't have capital punishment in this country, but I don't intend to spend my declining years rotting in an Italian jail."

He seemed in no hurry, smoking his cigar, talking slowly and, as it were, comfortably. I couldn't think what he intended to do. Instinctively I knew my only hope was to be very still, as in the presence of a wild animal; to speak gently and evenly, make no sudden movements.

I said conversationally, "You're a clever man, Frank. It certainly was a very effective gamble. What about the flowers you sent in Rome, and the note inviting me to visit you? Window-dressing?"

"Of course," he nodded. "You weren't, actually, supposed to receive the flowers, or the note. A tragic irony. Flowers and a friendly message, sent unwittingly, when already it was all over. Only, of course, it wasn't all over." A slight edge crept into his voice.

"And the bomb in the car?" I asked. "More window-dressing? To make it seem that you too were threatened?"

"Ah, yes. A nice touch, don't you think? A pity about the car, though; I was fond of that Rolls. Still, it's insured."

"Sandro might have been blown up with it —"

"So he might." He smiled, and waved the cigar. "But he wasn't though, was he? A bit of luck, that."

For a moment, sickened, I couldn't speak. Then I managed to say, "And Dorello? Was that, too a bit of luck?"

"Dorello," he said. "Dorello . . . ah, yes, the little sneak thief. I think he believed that we had a big house party that night, good for a haul of valuables. Stupid as well as greedy, you see. I mean, these days nobody who has any money actually carries the stuff and genuine jewellery stays in the bank. I suppose we shall never know now whether he actually got inside the house and drew a blank . . . anyway it must have seemed like a piece of luck for him to be able to watch everything that happened, material for blackmail. I suppose he tried it on with you first, and then discovered that you genuinely did not remember. So then he came to Rome and turned his attentions to me and that, naturally, was his undoing."

"Naturally." Keep the dialogue going — that was the only defence I had. I said quietly, "You still haven't said why you brought me here. I mean, surely the one thing you've been afraid of is that I'd remember what happened. Now, you seem quite glad I have."

"Justification," he said, nodding.

"What?" I really didn't understand.

He explained with staggering simplicity, "If you'd been disposed of, still not knowing anything of what had happened, it would always have been on my conscience. There would always have been the nagging thought that the whole thing might not have been *necessary*. As I said before, I'm fond of you, Joanna. But, you see, you have remembered, now, haven't you, so you're still expendable, I'm afraid."

"Oh yes," I said, "I can see that. But if you do away with me here and now, you'll have a lot of explaining to do, won't you?"

He smiled. "Ah, what a bright girl you are. Brave, too. You're right, of course. I'd have far too much explaining to do. However, the contractors, shall we call them, haven't been as efficient as I hoped —"

"The contractors," I said quickly, "I wondered about them. People who kill for money. Who are they, and how did you find them?" *Keep him talking* — but where, oh where, was Roddy?

"No reason now why I shouldn't tell you, I suppose. You've heard of Guiseppe Lucione?"

"Who hasn't?"

Lucione. One of the top men in the international crime business. He had no police record; everybody knew about Lucione and

427

nobody could touch him. Many of the rich and famous who thought it was chic to know Lucione were entertained royally on his luxury yacht, while his operatives ran the vice-rings, the extortion rackets, the traffic in drugs, from which his vast wealth was amassed. The operatives did the killing, too, which went with all that. I wasn't surprised that Frank knew Lucione. In one respect at least — their disregard for human life — they were two of a kind. It did surprise me, though, that Frank's problem had been worth Lucione's attention. Having nothing to lose, I said so. "Small beer, surely, for his organization? Perhaps that's why it didn't work." I added coolly, "Perhaps you should ask for your money back."

"Why yes," he said, with a macabre twinkle, "I nearly did. Especially after the Milan fiasco — the wretched Mrs Pearson from where was it . . . Solihull? Her red hair was her undoing, poor little bitch."

I said thickly, "Don't talk about her like that."

"Ah, there speaks Joanna's tender heart. Steffy told me you were upset, when she telephoned me. Poor innocent Steffy, unwittingly telling me what I needed to know, so that the abduction scheme could be activated . . ."

"So it was Steffy told you? Not the old

man on the train?"

"What old man on the train?"

Signor Paraduca. An innocent lover of detective stories, after all . . .

Up to then, I had been playing for time, but it now seemed that Frank had time to spare. It struck me suddenly that he was waiting. For what?

It was better to know.

"So what are you going to do now?" I asked.

"Ah yes. I've dreamed up a little scenario of my own. You're going to be snatched, Joanna . . . kidnapped."

"You tried that before . . ."

"So we did. And Angelo got in the way. But there won't be any slip-up this time. You'll be snatched, and I shall be very brave and try to rescue you, and get shot in the leg . . . I'm not looking forward to that very much, but it's necessary . . . then away you'll go, and Steffy will get some menacing telephone calls, but you'll never be found alive. It's very simple and neat, really."

"And Roddy? What have you done with him?"

"He's been taken care of. Oh, don't look like that, not killed. Overpowered, and tied up in the house. I shall stagger in presently, genuinely wounded and bleeding, incoherent with distress about you of course, and will

429

have a terrible job freeing him. He'll never know what really happened."

My tongue was sticking to the roof of my mouth, but I managed to say thickly, "You mean someone will come and take me away and . . . and kill me later on?"

He wasn't smiling now. He looked at me sorrowfully. "I am sorry. I really am sorry. It breaks my heart but it just has to be this way. They should be along any minute now," he added, as if we were waiting for a train. "Don't be frightened, Joanna. It will be very quick, it won't hurt."

He looked towards the house and added placidly, "Here they come now, I think," and I looked where he was looking and saw a fleeting glimpse of them, these men who were coming to take me, and heard the sound of running feet; and then I saw the expression on Frank's face change to one of stark amazement and fear and the four of them were upon us, not the thugs I had been expecting, but Angelo with a gun in his hand, Roddy looking pale under his tan and somewhat the worse for wear, Nico the reporter, and to my utter astonishment, that highly respectable banker, Giorgio Castelani. Precisely at the moment when I knew I was safe all the spurious calm deserted me and I found myself shouting, "He did it, he killed her, don't let him get away!"

"He won't get far," said Angelo.

Roddy rushed over to me. "Jo, darling, thank God you're all right!" He put his arms round me and I was glad of them. Angelo, typically, showed no such tender concern. He could see I was alive and in one piece. He looked cold and concentrated, a man with a job to do. He took no further notice of us, but walked down the path through the lemon garden towards Frank. "Stay where you are, Frank. I've got you covered and the place is surrounded."

Frank took no notice. He turned and ran, the lumbering heavy run of an elderly man, towards the lake. We saw him falter after a few steps; he seemed to shrink and shudder, his hands clutching at his chest. Then, slowly, it seemed, as in a slow-motion film, he toppled over and fell, like a great tree falling, to the ground; and almost at the same moment the air was rent with the sound of sirens and squealing tyres, and suddenly the garden was full of uniforms. Giorgio looked over to me and nodded. "Here comes the law. We seem to have convinced them, after all."

"But Angelo said —"

"He was bluffing."

We watched while Angelo went over to Frank and bent down, feeling for his heart.

Two of the policemen joined him and one of them took his coat off, knelt down beside Frank and began to try to revive him. I wanted to cry out, *Don't do it, let him die, his life is over.*

I heard Roddy, as from a long way off "What's been going on? What do you mean, he killed her?"

"The woman in the lake. I was there, I saw him do it. We were lured here, Roddy. What happened to you, back there?"

"I went out to the car to get some beer and three guys jumped me —"

"Yes. That's what he said would happen."

"Three against one, I was getting the worst of it, then Angelo and his mob arrived in the nick of time . . . what? You mean it was *planned*? By Frank?"

"I'm afraid so. He meant to kill me . . ."

"But what about Angelo? How did he know?"

"You'd better ask him," I said.

I saw the policeman who had been trying to revive Frank stand up, shaking his head. He said something to Angelo, who shrugged his shoulders and began to walk back up the garden towards us. I knew what he was going to say before he said it. It may seem absurd but at that moment I was filled with a strange kind of grief. I didn't think about

432

the man who had had me hunted through the streets of Rome, who even a few minutes ago was telling me calmly how he planned my death. I remembered the other one: the fiery genius, the man who stood like a giant among his contemporaries: the big, kindly stormy figure, who had bullied and cajoled and taught me through weary weeks of filming, and by so doing had drawn from me the acting performance of my life. It could be that I would never work so well again without him: the man who had been two men, who had been, perhaps, a little mad. I suppose it was partly reaction as well, but it was only then that I began to cry and tremble. Roddy held me stroking my hair and murmuring endearments. Angelo stood in front of us, waiting patiently. After a bit he said quietly, "It's all over, Joanna. You're safe now."

"Yes, I know." There was something so dry in his tone that it pulled me together. I dashed the tears out of my eyes to look at him; there was no expression on his face at all.

"I've remembered," I said. "Everything."

"Good. Because these chaps will want a statement from you." He nodded at Giorgio. "She could do with some brandy, I think," and he walked away, back to the house.

"I've got some in the car," said Giorgio. "Let's go."

In the car, sipping the brandy, I said, "Giorgio, what on earth are *you* doing here?"

Giorgio grinned. He looked rather the worse for wear too, but happy and somehow boyish, as if he had been in a scrap and thoroughly enjoyed it. "Repaying a debt," he said: and I remembered about Lisa, his little girl, whom Angelo had rescued. I remembered too what Kate had said about Angelo; kind and concerned, yes, but nevertheless enjoying himself, finding the challenge irresistible. It was the same now, just the same. He had come in time once more to save my life, and I knew I should feel warmed and grateful. Why I should feel so chilled instead, I had no idea.

To me afterwards, there was always to be something dreamlike, not quite real, about the practical mopping-up operations which followed. We sat in the car in silence while I tried to adjust myself to relief from fear, to the knowledge that I was once more a perfectly normal human being with a past and now, thank God, a future as well. We saw the ambulance come, and the heavy stretcher carried into it. The three men who had attacked Roddy came out of the house, handcuffed, to be bundled into a police van.

They were followed by Mario, the 'doctor' from Denzano, who must, I suppose, have been holding them up with the gun which he now handed to a policeman: "One of theirs," I heard him say, and a joking exchange followed. Then he came over to the car and bent down to the window to speak to me: *"Come va, signorina?"*

"Benissimo, grazie." We grinned at each other, embarrassed, and he added, "I owe you an apology," and I answered, "Not at all, I owe you one, I think." I put my hand out of the window, and instead of shaking it he carried it to his lips. "You are a very brave lady," he said, and went away. Nico had disappeared, gone, Giorgio said presently, to telephone his paper. I said vaguely, "What's he doing here? I thought he had to go back to Rome —"

Giorgio laughed. "That's right. But he disobeyed instructions and stayed on. He's got the biggest scoop of his career so far as a result, so my guess is all will be forgiven."

"Oh. That means we're going to be all over the front page tomorrow?"

"I fear that's only too likely."

Later, at the Questura, telling my story to an inspector, a policewoman, and a tape machine, I felt some of my panic return, fearing a high-powered interrogation. But they were civil enough, and when the statement had been transcribed and I had signed it, I summoned up enough courage to ask, "Am I implicated in all this?"

"Implicated? How do you mean, signorina?"

"In England it's called being an accessory after the fact. I helped him put her in the lake."

"Under duress."

"Yes. But I did do it."

For the first time, the inspector smiled. "The three ruffians we picked up at the Villa Flora are all singing like canaries, each trying to implicate the others. I don't think you need have any anxiety on that score. But of course, we must ask you not to leave Italy at present; you are our principal prosecution witness."

"But he is dead."

"Quite so. But his accomplices are not."

15

"But how did you know?" I asked.

We were all gathered in Steffy's big room where I had sat that evening . . . weeks ago? years ago? . . . telling Frank my troubles and listening to his soothing reassurances.

I had told them my part of the story. I had done it as briefly as I could, knowing how painful it was to some of my listeners. Roddy sat on the sofa beside me with his arm around me. He was being very subdued, for Roddy, and very loving towards me. Angelo was there, of course, and Giorgio and Kate, and a quiet grey man I now knew to be Bernardo Menotti, Elena's husband. Nico Parisi had gone back to Rome, armed with enough material to keep his exclusive story going for the next twenty-four hours.

Steffy was there, too, sitting a little apart from us all. I was worried about her — she looked much older and somehow shrunken. I hadn't been present when she was told of Frank's death and of his guilt, so I don't know how she reacted at first. Now she was holding whatever she felt deep within herself.

Angelo was sitting at a table on which there were a lot of box files and folders; I wondered vaguely what they were. He had rather the air, Angelo, of a chairman about to open a meeting, dry and formal.

"How did we know," he repeated. "Well, of course, we didn't know. Things added up, that's all. Nico and I had both come up here looking for answers . . . which is not to say that we were asking the same questions. The facts are that in the course of doing this, Nico got a breakthrough last night; and so, almost too late, did Bernardo and I.

"But this is Bernardo's story. Only he can give you the background, and he has undertaken to do that. I am sure everyone here understands that this is all very distressing for him, and would like him to know that we appreciate him making the effort."

We all murmured.

Angelo nodded at me and added, "Joanna, perhaps you would translate for Roddy. Everyone else understands Italian, and Bernardo's English is rather limited."

"Yes, of course," I said meekly. Those brisk polite words were almost the first he had spoken to me since we had returned from the police station.

Bernardo said heavily, "Signore, Signori . . . I am afraid that this is rather a complicated history. My wife and I had been separated for some time, so that I was not close to her in her last years. But it is clear to me now that her mental, her psychic, health had not improved. That was, the reason for the destruction of our marriage in the first place, and now, when I look back, I cannot reproach myself enough for having failed her. If I had been more patient, more understanding, she . . . she might be alive today. I don't know how much you understand about the terrible effects that a very bad early experience can have on the human psyche; how lasting, how deadly, a wound can be inflicted . . ."

He took out a handkerchief and blew his nose.

"Forgive me," he said. Angelo said gently, "Bernardo, if you'd rather not . . ."

"No, no. I would prefer to go on. It is as well, I think, for me to speak of this. To bring it into the open . . . it is healthful, isn't it?

"It happened in the autumn of '44, when Elena was twelve years old. Her mother had died some years previously and Elena was living with her grandparents in a small villa in the hills above the Ligurian coast. Her father had deserted from the Italian army and joined the Resistance. Her grandfather had been a professor at Turin University who had lost his post during the Mussolini regime. The whole family was deeply anti-fascist and the old man entirely approved what his son had done. The old people not only looked after Elena and took charge of her education, the villa was also a centre for the partisans, a place of refuge for escaped Allied prisoners of war and a hiding place for arms and ammunition. At this period the Allies were advancing north through Italy, the Italian army and the German forces retreating before them and being harassed as they went by the partisans.

"Thus, to the villa one day that autumn there arrived a small group of German soldiers, who had been cut off from the main body of troops to which they belonged and had lost their bearings. They were all very young men, no more than boys I should imagine, who had spent all their youth under Hitler and were deeply indoctrinated with Nazism; one must suppose this, because of what happened. The NCO who had been with them had been killed, and they were leaderless except for one who was a natural leader and who must therefore be held responsible for all that took place. At first it seemed that they would merely demand food and a billet for the night, and go on their way. The old people acted calmly. Elena's grandmother cooked pasta for them and they were given some wine. Both grandparents spoke good German and this also helped create an atmosphere on their side which, if not friendly, was at least courteous. While they were doing all this the old people must have been intensely anxious about the existence of the arms cache in the cellar, but were careful not to betray themselves. Unfortunately the soldiers took too kindly to the wine and demanded more; they became drunk and uproarious. When, to quieten them, the grandfather said he would fetch some wine from the cellar the leader insisted on going with him; he alone, among the group, was not so drunk as the others. Not so drunk that when he followed the old man into the cellar, he did not think to search beyond the wine racks and find the cache of arms."

He was silent again, and in the silence somebody said, "Oh, my God."

"The moment they returned, the young man driving the old one before him with the butt of the sub-machine gun he still had at his hip, the grandmother knew at once what had happened; what also, perhaps, was going to happen. She signalled to Elena to leave the room. Thus for the time her life was saved; she said to me she often wished it had not been. She heard the shouting, the shots, the screams, the hideous laughter, while she crouched against the wall in the next room, too terrified to move. Then the firing and the shouting and the laughter stopped and there was silence. Then, into the silence, one of the men said, 'Where's the girl?'

"And it was then that she came to herself and dashed into the hall and tried to flee. But it was too late." He sighed. "Did I say my wife was a lovely girl, a lovely woman? She was a lovely child, too. I have seen a photograph of her that her father had. Taken before that happened. I don't know where it is now but I can still see it; the pure young page on which nothing has yet been written.

"There were eight of them. She told me she didn't remember the others at all, as individuals, that is. Only the leader. She always hated handsome men, and I thought this odd until she told me this story. He, this young man, had great personal beauty, a beauty that was hideous to her eyes but which she never forgot.

"I don't know why they didn't kill her too, when they had finished with her. There was, I understand, some activity in the area and they may have decided to get out right away; or, perhaps, there were some tiny glimmerings of human conscience? Who can

442

say? She remained there in the house, unconscious, with the bodies of her grandparents until the local partisans found her, and carried her to a neighbouring farm where she was nursed back to health. To physical health, that is.

"The war ended, her father survived and was restored to her. She continued her education, grew up to all appearances a normal girl, with all wounds healed, all horrors forgotten. But it was not so. Perhaps, after a greater lapse of time, with no reminders of the past . . . But that was not to be. About six years later, when she was eighteen, Elena found a picture in a magazine."

We all stared at him; it seemed like an anti-climax.

"The picture was of a rising young film actor, who had made his name in England and was now launched on Hollywood and stardom. So far as Elena was concerned, it was totally unmistakable. This was the same man. She told her father of her discovery, as, later, she told me. Neither of us took it seriously. The publicity surrounding the young man made no secret of the fact that he had come to England as a displaced person; but we could not believe that a young German conscript could so fool the Allied Commission that they accepted him as

443

a helpless victim of the war. Now, of course, we know better and that such things did happen now and then.

"So we both failed her, you see. And I knew no more of the obsession this man had become for her, until Angelo and his friend Nico persuaded me to go with them and open up her cottage, and in a chest hidden under a pile of junk in the cellar, we found . . . these."

He gestured towards the folders on the table. Angelo handed them round to us, one each. Mine was marked: *1951*. I opened it. It contained some press cuttings and a couple of glossy photographs, the kind that would have come straight from a Hollywood studio publicity department. One was even autographed with a flourish: *yours very sincerely* . . .

I'd thought, looking at the old man sleeping in the car, what a dazzler he must have been when young. An understatement. From what I could see of it, this was no smooth-featured matinée idol but a face of great power and magnetism.

From what I could see of it.

The photograph was defaced. A thick pen stroke each way, forming an X was slashed across the handsome face. Violent words of abuse were written across it. The anguish and hatred were almost palpable. I turned the folder over and some glossy scraps of photographic print fell out . . . another picture, of the same face, cut into tiny irregular pieces. Suddenly, almost telepathically, I seemed to see the hands which had held the scissors, thin, veined hands, trembling hands, cutting, cutting, cutting. I began to feel faintly sick.

I looked over Roddy's shoulder at his file. She hadn't defaced all the pictures. I saw once more the same handsome face, now with fine lines beginning to gather, and a sag under the chin. 1960, nearly ten years later. I thought, she watched him grow old.

"These files we have here," Bernardo went on, "are only part of what we found. The rest is with the police. All the material was carefully filed, docketed, and dated. She had subscribed to press-cutting agencies both here and abroad. There were notes of enquiries she had made personally, payments to enquiry agents she had employed and reports from them. There was a diary of a vacation she spent in Poland during which it seems she almost succeeded in establishing that Harmer had had a Polish mother, whose maiden name he temporarily adopted and used to deceive the Allied Authorities."

"None of this was conclusive. The files were Elena's museum of hate, you might say, and also a record of pursuit, but it is plain from the last entries in the record that she had come to a dead end. She must have realized that she was never going to establish enough firm evidence on which to act; and that even if she did, she might not get very far with it. The Second World War was so monstrous an event, so many millions of people were killed, tortured, gassed, incinerated. By the side of such crimes, the incident at Elena's home was but a small atrocity.

"So, we must assume, it was at this point that she had what must have seemed to her a stroke of luck. Harmer came to Italy. Of course he had been here before on private visits, but he had never worked here before. Even so, there would have been little chance for Elena to meet him or confront him. If it had not been for the party at the Villa Flora." Bernardo sighed, and drank from the glass of wine at his side.

"We think," he added heavily, "that Elena must have known about the party at the Villa before she went on holiday, that probably she purloined the invitation card. She was a journalist, after all, she worked on *Il Messaggio*. Parisi tells us that the paper's film critic is an irascible man who never goes to parties given by film companies: he would probably have thrown the invitation in the wastepaper basket. But all this is conjecture. And now, I think, I should ask Angelo to take up the story."

We all murmured again to thank him. He acknowledged this with a little formal bow, and sat back in the shadows.

Angelo said drily, "All right, then. We went up to Elena's cottage yesterday, Bernardo and I. We looked everywhere, as we thought, and found nothing. In the early hours we abandoned the search, for the time being, and slept. We were woken, this morning, by Nico; he had driven up from Verona to find us, there's no telephone there. He had decided to check back over the car-hire firms in Denzano, to see if any of them could remember Elena. He drew a blank from most, and then, last night, he found a very small outfit, father and son, a repair shop and two aged Lancias they used as taxis. The son had never seen Elena. When the police came, the father had been in hospital. Interviewed there, in some post-operative pain and partially sedated, he said he didn't recognize the woman and she had certainly never been a passenger in his taxi. By the time Nico came on the scene, father, recovered, was back in business."

As Angelo told the story, I could see it in my mind's eye: Nico's casual approach, the offer of a drink in a nearby bar; the touch of human appeal, *she was my friend, a lovely lady, I want to find her killer . . .* The long look again at the photograph, much racking of brains, and finally the double-take, the typical Italian slap on the forehead: *mamma mia,* how could I be such a fool, how could I forget, *of course . . .*

The point was, he *hadn't* taken her anywhere. He had had much to drink that day, good enough reason in itself to refuse. It was his daughter's wedding day, the celebrations were still going on. So he sent Elena away . . . but of course he remembered the date. It was indeed the day of the party. Had she said where she wanted to go, Nico asked? More brain racking provided the answer: near Caravaglia? The Villa Flora could it be?

"We think, now," Angelo went on, "she must have walked all the way, and thus arrived when the party was over. When we found the cache of papers about Frank Harmer, we knew, at least, why she had wanted to go there. But even all this wasn't conclusive. It told us that Frank Harmer, as a young man, could have been involved in monstrous acts, of child rape and murder; it didn't prove he *had* been. What we knew was that Elena believed he had been; that she had gone to the Villa Flora, almost certainly in the hope of confronting him there, and had never been seen again until her body was recovered from the lake.

"Not conclusive, as I say, but enough to make me drop everything and make tracks to the nearest public telephone, to try to reach Joanna and head her off before she and Penny left Rome on a journey with the man who might be a killer. As we know, I didn't reach Joanna in time; Penny was still there, but she did not know the number or even the make of the car they were travelling in, so interception, either by the police or ourselves, was not possible. We had no clue to what Frank's plans might be — always supposing him to be our man — or whereabouts, on that journey, he would put them into effect. Except for two small things. One was that I didn't believe he was any longer capable of killing Joanna himself — so it would have to be an ambush, carried out by others. And Kate had told me the previous day about her telephone call to Joanna, her idea about the Villa Flora and the other lemon garden. I asked Penny about this and she confirmed that possibly, even probably, Frank, Roddy and Joanna would call there on their way here.

"So we were playing a guessing game, gambling. The police certainly thought so, and to begin with they simply laughed at us. In the end we got a minor concession — one plain-clothes man with a radio. (As it turned out he didn't hesitate long before sending for reinforcements.) We went down to the Villa and waited, with the results you know."

When Angelo stopped speaking, there was silence. He looked around, inviting questions. Nobody seemed to want to ask any.

Angelo sighed. "Well," he said, "there it is. The whole story, so far as we'll ever know it. The curious thing is that Elena could have done Frank very little harm, really. She had no proof; she was known to be a neurotic lady, and neurotic ladies sometimes get strange ideas about eminent and distinguished men. In any kind of legal action, opposing counsel would have made mincemeat of her."

"That wasn't why he killed her," I said. "He said he was unbearably provoked, remember? That he didn't mean to do it? She reminded him of a past he wanted to forget, that he had ever been like that, done those things. He'd put it all behind him, he'd changed so much —"

Somebody said, "But not enough, it seems."

"No. Not enough."

We all fell silent again. Remembering. Not remembering . . . it struck me then how memory was the key to the whole of this story. The woman who could not forget, the man who wanted to forget: they had both gone beyond remembering. The one that was left — myself — had had no difficulty at all in forgetting, in putting shock and horror away, as it were for another time, when I would be stronger and more able to cope with it. Amnesia is a medical term, so it had seemed to me and everyone else like a sickness. Only now I recognized it, in myself at least, with thankfulness, as a sign of health.

People began to stir a little, as if they wanted to break up the gathering but did not know how. I said suddenly, "There is just one thing that still puzzles me — the earring, the one I had, was stolen. Who took it?"

There was a small sound, between a gasp and a sob, somewhere beside me. I looked round and saw Steffy staring at me and biting her lip.

"Oh, Steffy, darling," I said. "Why?"

Steffy stammered, "I didn't understand what was happening . . . it frightened me, the way you were then, and you said you thought there was something evil about it. These associations, whatever they were I was sure they were doing you harm — I said

451

to Frank —" She gave the little gasp again, and put her hand to her mouth.

I said gently, "So you told Frank about it, and he advised you to throw it in the lake. And that's what you did, isn't it?"

"Yes. I did it for the best. I'm sorry —"

"There's nothing to be sorry for," I said. I saw her eyes were full of tears. I thought, she loved him, she's always loved him, and now she can't even remember him with happiness. I went and put my arms round her. She patted me in acknowledgement, and put me gently aside.

The others began to say good-bye. Bernardo Menotti went first. He came to me, and kissed my hand as Mario had done, and I thanked him again for his help. "How could I do less?" he said. He looked at me carefully with his sad, shrewd eyes and added gently, "Put all this business behind you, signorina. You are young and healthy, and gifted, I believe. You have a rich life in front of you. Don't let it be spoiled by past horrors."

"No," I said, "I'll try not to. And thank you again."

Steffy said good-bye to him, and to Giorgio and Kate, and she thanked them too. She embraced Angelo, who held her tight for a moment and said something like, "Darling, it will pass." She shook her head and smiled, and then she excused herself and walked away, a small lonely figure, up the stairs to her room.

We watched her go. Angelo turned to me. "Look after her," he said abruptly.

I said, astonished, "Are you going?"

"I've left some stuff at Giorgio's. And after that I must get back to Rome. I've got work to do. And it's all over now, isn't it?"

I felt both chilled and confused. "Yes," I said, "I suppose it is."

"Let me know when you want to leave and I'll make some other arrangement. She ought not to be left here on her own."

"No, of course not. Well, this is good-bye then. And, Angelo — thank you for everything."

"You're very welcome," said Angelo.

The three of them drove away and Roddy and I were left, looking at each other.

"Why did you let him go?" said Roddy.

"What?"

He didn't repeat the question. He got up, wandered restlessly round the room. I didn't speak. I had nothing to say.

"It's late," he said at last.

"Yes."

"After a day like this one, I don't feel much inclined to drive back to Rome tonight."

"Of course not. You're very welcome to stay —"

He came and stood in front of me, picked up one of my hands and held it.

He said gently, "I'll stay tonight, if I may. But I shall be leaving in the morning, first thing."

"I see," I said; though I saw nothing, still sitting there in a bewildered calm.

"You're a lovely girl, Joanna. But you're not for me. And I'm not for you. Whatever it was we had together . . . it's gone, hasn't it? Anyway, you need some time to sort yourself out."

"Yes," I said. "I expect you're right."

Roddy left, as he said, first thing in the morning. Steffy did not get up for breakfast; I went in to find her while she was drinking her coffee; she looked, among her furbelows and ruffled pillows, a tiny, peaky creature, suddenly aged.

"Are you all right?" I asked.

She smiled faintly. "I will be. When you get to my age, it's like Angelo said — everything passes. And you're safe, and well, and yourself again, Joanna. That makes up for everything. Now I expect there are a lot of things you want to do. You mustn't think you have to stay with me. If you want to go off with Roddy —"

"Roddy's gone," I said. "He left early."

"Oh!"

"So now they've all gone." I tried to laugh. "Now it's all over, everybody seems to be running from me as if I had the plague."

"Do you mind?"

"About Roddy going? No. That was all just a big infatuation; I suppose I was never really in love. After I lost my memory, I could never get him back into focus again. I can't now. It's all right; he understands. He doesn't really want me either."

"I see," said Steffy. She frowned. "What about Angelo?"

"What about him?"

She hesitated, and seemed to make up her mind about something. "It's the money," she said. "It's always been the money. You've got too much —"

"Steffy," I said, *what are you talking about?*

She looked at me with a sort of exasperated affection.

"Darling Joanna," she said, "if you don't know, there's no point in my telling you, is there?"

16

The following afternoon I came off a plane at the Leonardo da Vinci airport, intending to take a taxi into the city.

Of course it wasn't, actually, quite as simple as that. Oblivious of the fact that I was now News, I'd been congratulating myself: no luggage, no Customs, of course, on an internal flight, and therefore a minimum of formalities — none of that tiresome hanging about which makes such a mockery of the speed of flying.

I could get away quickly and easily, or so I thought.

I saw them just a fraction of a second before they saw me, the eager knot of people, the cameras, the microphones. I turned and dived back through the press of people coming off the plane behind me. Coming up the ramp behind the passengers was a ground stewardess. She looked at me curiously. I was rushing in precisely the opposite direction to everybody else, a direction which led only back to the tarmac, and I expect I looked a bit distracted, as well.

"Can I help you, signora?"

"Yes," I said. "Yes, you can indeed." I

explained rapidly; her face cleared, and then she looked delighted. "Of course!" she exclaimed, "I thought I recognized you. Come with me."

She was capable and resourceful; she whisked me out into the open again, round the outside of the airport buildings until we reached the freight section. There she paused, looking at me a trifle doubtfully. "Would you be willing to travel into the city on a truck?"

"Why not?" I laughed.

"Good. Then I will ask the driver over there — he's just finished loading, he'll be leaving soon." I watched her while she talked to the man, gesturing back towards me, and saw him peering at me, and the grin splitting his swarthy face, as he said as I had said, "Why not?"

I shook hands with the girl and thanked her, and said something about, if there was anything I could do . . . to express my appreciation, I meant; I couldn't offer her money.

She smiled. "You can give me your autograph."

"But of course!"

A pen was found, a notebook. I scribbled a message of thanks, and my name.

Handing it back to her, I said, "That seems

very little in return for your kindness."

"Well . . . there is something else. Something I'd love to know."

"I'll tell you if I can. What is it?"

"Are you going to marry Roddy Marchant?

"No."

Her romantic disappointment was comical. "Oh! But I thought —"

"So did a lot of people," I said with a grin. "We haven't quarrelled. We're just good friends, as they say. Good-bye, and thank you again."

So it was that, riding in the cab of a lorry, I successfully dodged the press and the television cameras which had been waiting for me at the airport. At some time during that journey along the road which leads from the airport into the city of Rome, I thought of Elena: she, too, had hitched a ride on the way to a confrontation. A different kind . . .

The lorry driver was flirtatious but not offensively so, and anyway he had his lorry to drive and traffic was heavy. I daresay he got a lot of social mileage later out of giving me a lift, as for the moment the whole story was headline stuff. I asked him to put me down on the outskirts of the city, and walked along until I picked up a taxi.

It was coming up to the time of year in Italy when the beautiful season is no longer beautiful, at least in Rome, where, crossing the street, one runs for cover from the remorseless sun as if escaping from a downpour of rain; where everyone who can afford it runs for cover, to the mountains or the sea. It is then that Rome begins to have a shabby, dusty look. A scurf of litter lies in the gutters; the grass in the parks is scorched, tan colour, and even the leaves on the trees look as if they're tired of life. Shop windows burst into a rash of red streamers announcing sales; the city seems given over to the old, the poor, and the unwary foreigners lured to Rome by package tours, unwarned that once there it will be too hot to sightsee unless one starts at six in the morning. At such times the heart of Rome continues to beat, but it beats more slowly, and there is a kind of sadness in the weighted air.

I was one of the people who didn't need to be there. My signature was the open sesame to unlimited credit; I was free to go anywhere in the world I wanted to be; but where I wanted to be was here. I knew now, since I had woken up, as I put it to myself that I didn't want the kind of freedom that Nonno's money gave me. In a way, it was a mockery of the freedom I wanted. The rich make their own world, divided from the rest of humanity by a wall of glass. I

459

couldn't live like that. The money I earned by my own efforts was real and precious, the rest nothing but a burden to be thrown off. Only when that was done could I live the way I wanted to, as a person in my own right.

I sat on the edge of the seat, mentally pushing the taxi along. It seemed a long time before it drew up before the tall apartment block, where I sprang out and overpaid the driver, and ran into the building. Going up in the lift I felt sick with apprehension and eagerness.

I hadn't telephoned. For all I knew, when I knocked on that door, nobody would answer.

However, when I reached it I could just hear, inside, the clacking of a typewriter. I rang the bell. The typewriter stopped clacking, the door opened, and there he was. He stared at me. His back was to the light, and I couldn't see his expression.

"Joanna," he said slowly.

"Aren't you going to ask me in?"

"Of course."

He opened the door wider and I passed by him into the living-room. I looked at the clutter on the desk, the paper in the typewriter and said flatly, "If you're busy, I can go away again."

"Don't be silly. Can I get you a drink?"

"Please. Something long and cold. I've come straight from the airport. The city feels like a furnace. I don't know how you stand it."

"Air conditioning." He was busying himself with the drinks and ice, his back turned to me. "I shan't be standing it for long anyway. I'm leaving tomorrow. How is Steffy? She's not on her own, is she?"

Steffy. His concern for her. None now, it seemed, for me.

"Steffy's all right. You said not to leave her alone, so I've persuaded her to go and stay with Kate for a day or two."

"I see. Fine." He came over to me, carrying my drink.

"How is Roddy?" he asked.

"Roddy? All right as far as I know."

"You didn't travel with him, then."

"No." I added lightly, "Everybody asks me about Roddy. A stewardess at the airport asked if I were going to marry him."

"Did she now? That's a bit much, isn't it?"

"Too personal, you mean? She'd just done me a very good turn so I didn't mind." I explained about my escape from the TV cameras and my ride on the lorry.

"Poor Joanna. I'm afraid there's going to be quite a bit of that for a while. Your fame has gone before you."

"Hardly fame. Notoriety's more like it. You haven't asked me what I answered."

"So what did you answer?"

"No."

"What?"

His face didn't tell me anything. I thought in despair, I've never known how to talk to Angelo, we're always at cross-purposes, never on the same wave-length, why did I think it could ever be any different? I said loudly, "No. That's what I said, no. No, I wasn't going to marry him. I could have said as well, no, we're not lovers any more, and no, I'm not in love with him and don't think now I ever have been. But she didn't ask about all that." I stopped, took a deep breath, and said, "Why did you go off like that yesterday?"

"I thought," said Angelo, "you didn't want me to stay. Why didn't you ask me to?"

"Because I thought you didn't want me to . . ." Another silence.

"This is silly," I said feebly.

"It is, isn't it?"

It was now or never. "Steffy says it's always been the money —"

"Oh well," said Angelo. "If you're in love with a girl with a millionaire grandfather, your feelings are liable to be misinterpreted."

I wasn't taking it in. As always with Angelo, I was in pursuit of the surface argument. "Oh come on," I said, "when have *you* ever cared what other people thought?"

"Not what other people thought. You. What you thought."

"That's stupid, why ever would I . . ." I looked into his eyes, read there everything I wanted to see, couldn't believe it, did a sort of double-take and eventually stammered, "What was that you said just now?"

"My dear, dear love," said Angelo, "I think you heard me quite well the first time."

A little later, I got my breath back and muttered against his chest, "I loved you all the time, you know."

"Good. That's all right then."

"It nearly wasn't. Because I didn't understand what was happening, and you were no help."

"No. Well, we both know why that was."

"I'm going to get rid of the money. Nonno's money. Give it away. I suppose one can do that?"

"Why not?"

"Of course, I still have to work out who or what to give it to. You'll help me with all that, won't you?"

"What? Oh, sure, sure . . ."

"You're not listening," I said.

"Better things to think about," said Angelo cheerfully; and then, "Oh hell!" as the doorbell rang loudly. "Shall we let them go away again?"

"Yes, let's . . ."

The doorbell rang again, lengthily as if someone were leaning on it. There were sounds outside as if there were more than one person there, quite a lot of people in fact. They were shifting around and talking to each other. We remained quiet as mice, listening.

"Your friends from the airport," said Angelo at last. "Don't you think? The media in full cry and they've tracked you down. Shall we see them and get it over with?"

Talking to reporters was the last thing I wanted to do just then, and I said so.

"They'll only hang around, you know. Waylay you later. Come on. Say as little as possible and leave the rest to me."

"All right," I said reluctantly. "How do I look?"

"Beautiful," said Angelo briskly. "Comb your hair."

So I did that, and we opened the door.

There were a lot of them, filling the corridor just outside the flat; mostly men, but one or two women too. We stood in the open doorway, not asking them in. Flash bulbs flashed, microphones were thrust forward. The onslaught of questions burst over me.

"Ladies! Gentlemen!" Angelo held up his hand for silence and miraculously got it. Of course, most of them knew him . . . in no time at all the situation was under control. In the end, it was all simple enough: had I recovered from my ordeal, my several ordeals; how did it feel to have recovered my memory; what did I think now about Frank Harmer? I said truthfully that I was very happy to be alive and well; to be able to remember was marvellous even though there were some things I'd rather forget, naturally. Frank Harmer had been a great film director; in that field I owed him a lot. No, I was not glad he was dead, just glad he hadn't succeeded in killing me. I thought suddenly of Sandra Pearson, so I explained about her: looking straight into the camera I said, meaning it with all my heart, "I want her husband to know how terrible I feel, knowing that she died in mistake for me, and I send him my deepest sympathy." They liked that, the TV people especially.

Then a woman reporter pushed her way

to the front: was I going to marry Roddy? No, I wasn't, I said, we were just good friends, and added, looking her in the eye, "That is not a polite way of saying we're lovers, either." Someone at the back tittered. The lady came back for more. Why had I returned to Rome so soon and what were my future plans? At that, I couldn't think what to say.

Angelo said it for me.

"Miss Fleming came back to Rome to see me. I'm afraid we can't tell you anything very definite about our plans . . ."

You could almost see the ears pricking up and the eyes getting beadier.

"Your plans?" someone said.

"*Our* plans," Angelo agreed amiably — "Because they're not yet decided in detail. However, we do intend to be married. Very shortly."

"*Angelo,*" I muttered.

He had his arm round my waist and it tightened warningly.

Someone came back with, "Isn't this a very sudden decision?"

"Not really," said Angelo blandly, "we've been thinking about it for some time. But of course Joanna's accident and illness, and all the rest of this unhappy business, supervened. Now I hope you will all excuse us.

We aim to go out to celebrate this evening."

So, more than a bit taken aback, but loving it, they congratulated us and wished us well, and at last we were able to close the door behind them.

"*Well!*" I exploded, half angry, half laughing.

"What's the matter?" Angelo asked mildly.

"What's the *matter!* Look, even in Italy, this *is* the 1980s and . . . what were you trying to do, save my face or my reputation or something? We haven't said a word about being married. You haven't even *asked* me —"

"Ah," said Angelo complacently, "if that's all the fuss is about, that's soon remedied." He struck a romantic attitude, and said in languishing tones, "Joanna, my beloved, will you be my wife?"

"That's not the *point*. I didn't come here expecting you to marry me, and you needn't feel you've got to —"

"Of course not. I don't feel I've got to. And I haven't got to. But I'd sure like to. What about you?"

"Oh, do stop clowning," I said crossly. "I'm trying to be serious, and there you go, jumping the gun and making a joke of it —"

"Jumping the gun, yes," said Angelo. "I admit to that. Making a joke of it, no." He peered at me and added whimsically, "Joanna, don't look now, but I think we're fighting again."

"No," I said, caught his eye, and sighed. "Oh well, we always have, haven't we? It may be a bit of a problem, don't you think? We'll have to sort ourselves out a bit."

"Starting tomorrow," said Angelo. "In the meantime, for God's sake, hold your tongue and let me love, as your Shakespeare said."

"John Donne, actually."

"What?"

"It was John Donne said it. Not Shakespeare."

"Who the hell cares who said it?"

I started to giggle. "Angelo, don't look now, but I think we're . . ."

"Fighting again?"

"Sort of . . ."

"And like I said, we can sort all that out tomorrow. Or the day after. Dear love, don't you realize there's plenty of time, now, for everything? With any luck, we've got all our lives before us."

"Yes. I suppose . . ." I realized, suddenly, what he meant, how accustomed I had become to the urgency of every day, to the menace of tomorrow, or the thought that it might never come at all. Now there it was, tomorrow, as shining and certain as anyone's tomorrow, in this uncertain world, can ever be. I looked at Angelo and saw

468

that he understood, that he knew what I was thinking, that the closeness between us was already there.

Sorting things out a bit . . . perhaps we didn't need to.